D1809369

Destiny Of
The Sword

80003384903

First Published in Great Britain 2012 by Netherworld Books an imprint of Belvedere Publishing

Copyright © 2012 by J. Jones

All rights reserved. No part of this publication may be reproduced or transmitted, in any form or by any means, without permission of the publishers or author. Excepting brief quotes used in reviews.

First edition: 2012

Any reference to real names and places are purely fictional and are constructs of the author. Any offence the references produce is unintentional and in no way reflects the reality of any locations or people involved.

A copy of this work is available through the British Library.

ISBN : 978-1-909224-00-1

Netherworld Books
Mirador
Wearne Lane
Langport
Somerset
TA10 9HB

Northamptonshire Libraries & Information Services NC	
Askews & Holts	

DESTINY OF THE SWORD

THE CHRONICLES OF ARKADIA

J. JONES

Chapter 1

Kern Razak stroked his neatly trimmed beard as he stared intently at the slumbering village below, his piercing blue eyes searching for any sign of danger. Aside from a couple of disinterested looking sentries lolling about on a porch and the occasional bark from a restless dog, the place was quiet.

And why wouldn't it be? It's just another drab unassuming village in the middle of nowhere, he mused.

They were all beginning to look the same to him.

His horse whinnied and started to fidget beneath him, as if sensing the excitement to come. He patted the beast reassuringly on the neck and whispered some calming words in its ears. The horse snorted with frustration, but then obediently quietened down.

Kern sat up and looked again at the village nestled in the valley below. His men were few in number and their greatest chance of success therefore depended on achieving total surprise. If the villagers were to see them coming and were able to mount some sort of determined defence it could easily turn out to be very costly in terms of men lost. Whilst that would see a welcome increase in his share of the profits, it would also make the long return journey even more perilous. No, he needed to keep as many of his men alive as possible, at least until they got back to Narmidia. Once there a few of the newer recruits and outlanders might need to meet with unexpected accidents. It was a comforting thought and he found himself smiling at the notion.

Satisfied that their presence had not been detected and that no ambush awaited them, he reached over and drew his sword, the sun momentarily glinting off its blade. Behind him he could hear the sound of his men readying their own weapons in anticipation of the signal to attack.

One of the sentries below appeared to suddenly stare right back at him and Kern froze even though he knew that his black clothes made him virtually undetectable against the dark trees to his rear. After a minute or so the sentries returned to their original positions, clearly reassured that whatever they thought they saw, was not a threat.

How wrong can a man be?

Taking the reins in one hand and resting his sword over his right shoulder, Kern gently urged his horse forward out of the shadows and down the slope. From the confines of the woods behind him, his men slowly emerged, weapons at the ready.

After about thirty paces Kern raised his sword high in the air before pointing it down at the village. Almost as one his men steadily increased their speed until eventually they were galloping down the hill towards the unsuspecting village.

***

Another night's uneventful sentry duty was drawing to a close and Cray Murl's thoughts were steadily turning to his comfortable bed and the beautiful woman who waited there for him. He leant back precariously in the rickety wooden chair in which he had sat for most of the night and closed his tired eyes, momentarily enjoying the warmth of the early morning sun as it bathed his face. Somewhere in the village a dog barked, briefly disturbing the tranquillity, but otherwise everything was quiet. In his mind Cray could feel his wife's soft skin and smell her lightly perfumed golden hair. He smiled contentedly to himself.

"You're thinking about Helan again aren't you?" interrupted the deep and familiar voice.

Cray reluctantly opened his eyes and saw his friend Elam grinning down at him, as he leant against the porch railing a few feet in front of Cray. No matter what he was asked to do, the village blacksmith always did it with a smile. The big man's cheerfulness was infectious.

"Can you blame me, Elam?"

Elam forced himself upright, stretched his aching back and scratched the stubble on his chin, whilst he contemplated his friend's question. "No, you're one lucky man, Cray Murl and don't you forget it. There's a whole queue of men waiting to take your place if you ever hurt her and I'm at the front."

"I'd never do that," replied Cray earnestly, touched by Elam's fondness of his wife. He was disturbed, however, to

2

learn that Helan was the object of so many other men's desires, something that wasn't going to help his growing sense of insecurity where she was concerned. Not that he was surprised. Her beauty was unsurpassed by anyone in Lentor or the surrounding villages. The only real surprise had been when she had agreed to become his wife a few months earlier. Elam was right; he really was a lucky man.

"Good," said Elam. Satisfied that he had made his point, he expelled a huge yawn, the subject now apparently closed.

Something in the distance suddenly caught Cray's attention and he peered anxiously at the hill that rose up behind his friend to the east of the village. Shielding his eyes against the sun as it slowly climbed into the cloudless blue sky, he scanned the crest of the slope and the dark tree line behind. He hadn't been certain, but for the briefest of moments he would have sworn that he'd seen the glint of metal caught in the bright morning sunshine. It had gone as quickly as it had appeared.

Elam noticed the concerned expression that briefly crossed his friend's face and turned to follow his gaze. All he could see, however, were the lush green slopes of Piper's Hill as they slowly climbed towards Beggar's Wood.

"Did you see something, Cray? Should I sound the alarm?" asked Elam excitedly. Rumours had been rife about raiders roaming the countryside killing and pillaging, for some days now, though not everyone believed them true.

"No, it was probably nothing, Elam, relax. I thought for a moment that I saw something on the edge of the woods, but there's nothing there. I'm just tired." As if to reinforce his point, Cray once again leant back in the chair and closed his eyes. *If the old man catches me lazing around like this he'll go berserk. Stupid old fool still thinks he's in the army. What gives him the right to order people around all the time? Just because he was a hero in some battle a lifetime ago doesn't mean that we should all bow and scrape to him for the rest of our lives.*

Finally satisfied that Cray was right and that there wasn't anything out there after all, Elam started to relax once again. Turning to face Cray, he noticed that his friend's expression now appeared bitter and melancholy. "What's the matter,

Cray, worried you can't satisfy your young wife?" asked Elam laughing, trying to cheer his friend up.

"*No*, not that it's any of your damned business anyway," replied Cray feigning indignation. He didn't need to open his eyes to know that Elam was baiting him. "I'm just sick of this damned guard duty if you must know. We're out here tired and hungry whilst the old man and just about everyone else in the village is tucked up in bed. What's more have you noticed how we always seem to get lumbered with more duty than everyone else?"

"If you don't like it, why don't you speak to Jeral, I'm sure he'll be accommodating?"

"Oh, he'll be accommodating all right; at the point of a sword."

"You could always challenge him," said Elam smiling. He knew full well that his friend wouldn't be that stupid. Jeral Tae was a big man in every sense of the word, dwarfing even Elam. Despite his advanced years, he would still be a formidable opponent for anyone foolish enough to challenge him to single combat. For a simple carpenter like Cray to go up against him would have been nothing short of suicide they both knew.

"You could try talking to him, Elam, he likes you. After all, you volunteered for this stupid job whereas I was forced into it," suggested Cray. Elam didn't reply. "Elam?" Cray opened his eyes just as his friend's body jerked violently forward and for a moment Cray feared that Elam was about to vomit over him. They momentarily locked eyes before Elam slumped to his knees, his shocked expression made worse by the trickle of blood that escaped one corner of his mouth. Then without uttering a sound, he collapsed to the floor in front of Cray, two arrows protruding from deep between his shoulder blades.

Cray leapt to his feet, the wooden chair crashing noisily to the porch floor behind him. Thundering down Piper's Hill, as if Tanith the Lord of Kaden was after them, were a large number of heavily-armed riders, the sun at their backs giving them a dark and menacing look. Jeral had drilled them endlessly for such an eventuality, but now that it was actually happening, panic threatened to overwhelm Cray. Unsure whether to firstly retrieve his sword that lay teasingly out of arm's reach or to sound the alarm, he hesitated. It was a mistake that was to cost him his life when an arrow struck him fatally in the chest. He fell to the porch floor next to Elam's body and his last thoughts as he watched the horsemen fan out through the sleeping village were of his pretty wife waiting in bed.

Had it not been for the petrified scream of an old woman who had risen early to milk her cow, the raiders would have achieved total surprise. Nevertheless, by the time the men of the village had emerged bleary-eyed from their homes, the riders were seemingly everywhere, setting buildings alight and killing anyone who might pose a threat.

Kam Martel stood on his porch studying the scene in front of him with the trained eye of an experienced warrior. The village was under attack from a group of horsemen perhaps twenty to thirty strong. Judging by the clothes they wore and the weapons they carried, some of them were Narmidians. Much of the village was burning and the air was thick with smoke, as the tinder dry thatched and wooden roofs burned unchecked. Some of the raiders were riding around setting buildings alight, trying to panic the villagers and cause confusion. It was a diversionary tactic, Kam realised, as Narmidians usually raided villages for slaves and in particular, young girls.

Cries of pain and terror tore through the early morning air and Kam watched helplessly as a young girl of no more than fourteen or fifteen was scooped up by a burly looking raider as he rode by. He tried hard to recall the girl's name and cursed old age when he failed to do so.

The sound of hooves racing towards him from the left caught his attention and he casually stepped off his porch and into the street. Apparently unfazed by the imminent danger, he glanced nonchalantly in the direction of the approaching rider. No more than thirty paces away, one of the raiders was coming straight for him. His curved sword was raised high above his shoulder ready to arc down and remove Kam's head with one slice. He had either failed to see the heavy looking axe that Kam held in his right hand, or thought that he was just an old man and an easy kill. It was a mistake and not one that he would ever get the chance to repeat. In one rehearsed fluid movement, Kam stepped back and swung his axe at just the right moment, its blade lodging itself deep in the rider's unprotected midriff.

The force of the blow knocked the man clean off the horse, his lifeless body sending up a cloud of dust as it hit the ground with a thud. Kam walked to where the raider lay, put one foot on the dead man's chest and gripped his axe handle. Then with a satisfied grunt, he yanked his axe free, leaving a trail of blood and glistening entrails as it exited the man's body.

A scream from across the street made him look up just in time to see one of his neighbours run through with a sword before another raider beheaded him. The man's wife was screaming hysterically. She looked frantically from her husband's mutilated body to her eldest daughter called Leisha who was being dragged into their cabin by the two raiders. The girl's nightgown was torn and it wasn't hard for Kam to guess what they had planned for her. He adjusted his grip on the axe and started to cross the street.

From his concealed position behind the lumber wagon, Eryn had watched in awe as the man he considered to be his father, had downed the terrifying looking horseman with just one blow of his axe. He had always known that his uncle had once been a great warrior, the village elders often recounting tales of his bravery as they shared a jug of ale round the hearth. To Eryn's great disappointment, however, his uncle rarely spoke of it himself.

Eryn had been fast asleep and dreaming of his mother when the screaming had woken him. As with previous dreams, his mother's image had not been clear, her face blurred and undefined. He knew that she was beautiful, because everyone he'd ever spoken to about her had said so, but to his continuing despair her face was always tantalisingly out of his reach. A memory he couldn't grasp.

Eryn had lain there for a while with his eyes closed, no longer asleep, but not yet fully awake either. Had the screams been fragments of a long-suppressed memory that had finally managed to manifest themselves in his most cherished dream?

He couldn't remember much about the night his mother had been cruelly stolen from him by the horsemen, but he did remember the screams and his feeling of helplessness. He also remembered that despite his tears and shouts his father never came and rescued her. His father had always promised that he'd be there to protect them, but when they'd needed him the most, he'd let them down. He'd lied. One day he would find his so-called father and make him pay for his broken promises.

When a terrified scream from just outside his window had startled him back to the present, Eryn had leapt out of bed and grabbed his bow, ready to face whatever was happening by his uncle's side. Instead his uncle had told him that the village was under attack by raiders and had ordered him to hide behind the lumber wagon once he had made sure that his sisters were safely hidden. He had pleaded with his uncle to let him help, but to no avail. He would get his chance to fight his uncle had assured him, but not today.

Ever since his father had turned his back on the world and left Eryn and his sisters to be raised by his brother, Eryn had considered Kam to be his father. He loved and respected the man above all else and would do anything to please him; anything but this. His tender age had prevented him from being able to save his mother all those years ago, but he'd be damned if he was going to let the same thing happen all over again. If something happened to his sisters or Tayla, the girl he planned to marry, whilst he skulked behind a wagon, he'd never be able to live with himself. Worse still, he'd be no better than his father. His uncle would be furious that he had disobeyed him, but he'd worry about that later.

Confident that his sisters were as safe as they could be, Eryn was just preparing to make a run for Tayla's home, when a scream from the other side of the street distracted him. He looked up and saw that his neighbours were under attack.

Eryn watched as his uncle slowly walked across the street towards two men who were excitedly tearing at Leisha's nightgown, as they dragged her towards the cabin. Her distraught mother had tried to help her, but had been viciously punched by one of the raiders and now lay crying on the ground, her nose broken and bloody.

There was no urgency or panic in his uncle's walk, Eryn noticed, just a certainty of purpose. Leisha was Eryn's friend and he wanted nothing more than to help his uncle rescue her, but he had Tayla to worry about. Besides, something told him that it wasn't his uncle who was in mortal danger.

Eryn knew that whilst the raiders were distracted by his uncle, he should make his move and run to Tayla's, but he was unable to drag himself away from the scene unfolding before him. He had never seen his uncle fight and was totally transfixed.

One of the two raiders finally noticed Kam approaching and after warning his comrade, he released his grip on Leisha and turned to face Kam.

"Hurry old man, come and embrace your death, for I will make it swift; I have far greater pleasures awaiting me," he said in the common tongue. He glanced longingly at where his friend stood restraining the virtually naked Leisha and licked his lips with anticipation. He would quickly despatch the old man and then take his turn with the girl.

Kam did not reply and instead continued walking towards the raider slowly hefting his axe over his right shoulder as he neared him.

The old man's demeanour was not one of fear, the raider noted and when he saw the cold look in Kam's eyes, he wondered if perhaps there was more to this old man than he had anticipated. He glanced nervously over at his comrade for reassurance, but he was too busy trying to restrain Leisha, as she kicked and clawed at him, to offer any. When he looked back at Kam, he noticed for the first time, the streaks of fresh blood running from the blade of the fearsome looking axe that he carried. The raider fidgeted, shifting his weight from one leg to the other, frequently swallowing with nerves. Volunteering for this raid suddenly didn't feel like such a good idea after all.

The speed with which Kam charged at him, took the raider by complete surprise and he stumbled backwards to avoid the attack, raising his sword as he did so. Kam's razor sharp axe head smashed through the blade and continued its downward journey severing the man's arm at the shoulder with a sickening crunch. Dark red blood spurted out from the wound like a fountain. The raider screamed in agony, but fear gave him the strength to continue backing away from Kam, his eyes never leaving the axe which was now covered in his own blood. In his panic to evade the next blow, the raider stumbled over the headless body of Leisha's father and hit the ground hard ending up flat on his back, his feet resting on the corpse as if it were a foot rest.

Kam stepped round his friend's body and stared down at the stricken raider, his axe poised to strike. The raider's eyes were wide with fear and he was babbling and pleading for his life in what sounded to Kam like Narmidian, though he wasn't sure. Nor did he care. There was no mercy or pity in his eyes, just a cold resolve. The raider's last thought before his head was hued cleanly from his body, was that it had indeed been a bad idea to volunteer for this raiding party.

Cursing out loud, the other raider reluctantly released his hold on Leisha, his lust for the young girl only narrowly outweighed by his desire to avenge his friend. He gave an angry shout and rushed at Kam who turned to face him axe at the ready. The raider was no more than five strides away from Kam when an arrow suddenly lodged itself in the raider's chest, quickly followed by another. He staggered around briefly, a surprised look upon his face, before a single blow from Kam's axe sent him on his way to the afterlife.

Kam turned to see who had come to his aid and was annoyed to find Eryn approaching from his place of concealment on the other side of the street, a bow in his hands and a proud smile upon his face.

"Eryn, I told you to stay hidden behind the wagon. Why...?" The frightened look that suddenly crossed Eryn's face cut him short.

"Behind you, Uncle!" Eryn shouted as he pointed beyond where Kam was standing.

Kam spun round quickly, but was still too late to react and the raider, who had emerged from a nearby cabin, ran him through with his lance. Almost immediately blood began to ooze from the corners of Kam's mouth and trickle into his greying beard. The raider gave the lance a spiteful twist, revelling in the old man's agony, though Kam denied him the satisfaction of hearing him cry out. He collapsed to his knees in front of his attacker, his mighty axe dropping harmlessly from his hands. The raider looked at his two fallen comrades and drew his sword, eventually lowering it to hover just by Kam's neck.

"Make it clean, you son of a whore," snarled Kam between gurgles of blood.

"As you wish," hissed the attacker, as he stepped behind Kam and slowly raised his sword.

Despite the agonising pain, Kam forced himself to kneel upright and to look straight ahead. If he had to die in front of Eryn and the others then he would die with dignity if not honour. But the raider, whom Kam had decided was Cardellan judging by his accent and the sword he carried, was taking his time in delivering the killing blow, no doubt savouring the moment.

A typical Cardellan, thought Kam. *They are without honour.*

What sounded like a grunt of pain from the man behind him, momentarily distracted Kam and he twisted his body as best he could to see what had happened. The Cardellan had also turned to look behind and as he did so, Kam was able to see the knife protruding from the man's back.

"That's for my husband, you murdering pig," said the woman as she spat blood from her broken nose into the raider's shocked face before stepping back.

There was a sudden hiss of air and then a gentle thud, as an arrow whistled past the Cardellan's face before burying itself in the front wall of the woman's cabin. The Cardellan glanced nervously towards Eryn, unsure whether to deal with him before he could fire another arrow or to slay the woman who had just stabbed him. Judging that he had enough time to kill the woman and then charge the bowman before he could shoot again, the Cardellan raised his sword ready to strike. The woman screamed and instinctively covered her face, as she waited for the blow that would send her to join her husband in the afterlife.

The Cardellan had judged wrong, however, and Eryn's second arrow flew quick and true, hitting the man in the neck and killing him instantly. His lifeless body collapsed to the ground behind a grinning Kam Martel.

Torn between concern for the girl he loved and his uncle, Eryn dropped his bow and raced across the street to where Kam knelt dying. He fell to his knees in front of him horrified by the sight of the lance sticking out from both sides of his uncle's body. Tears threatened to spill down his cheeks at any moment, though he knew that his uncle would disapprove of such an open display of weakness. He swallowed hard and tried to compose himself determined not to let him down. Silently praying that Tayla was safely hidden somewhere, he gently placed a hand on his uncle's shoulder.

"Hold on, Uncle, I'll get help," said Eryn as he went to stand, but Kam weakly grasped his left sleeve and urged him back down so that they faced one other.

"It's too late, Eryn."

"No, it can't be," replied Eryn, as the first tear meandered slowly down his cheek. Kam looked away, giving the young boy the chance to wipe it off without shame.

"It's too late I tell you. Accept it, I have."

Eryn did not want to believe that the man he considered to be his father since his real one had left was dying right in front of him. He had always thought that the hero of Slinden Plateau and Kato's Reach would live forever. The reality, however, was that Eryn could see the life-force draining from his uncle's once bright eyes. He reached down and grasped the lance ready to pull it free, a gasp of surprise escaping him when he saw the pool of dark blood in the dirt between his uncle's knees.

"Leave it, boy you cannot save me."

Eryn nodded and let go.

"Why did you not do as I instructed, Eryn, and remain behind the wagon? Are you determined to disobey me at every opportunity?" The irony of Kam's last comment was not lost on Eryn.

"I'm sorry for disobeying you, Uncle, but I was worried about Tayla and wanted to make sure she was safe. Then when I saw you were outnumbered I thought that you could use my help. I only wanted to fight by your side and make you proud."

11

"I admire your courage lad, but you know that I'm already proud of you. You're only a boy and not yet ready to fight." A chesty cough wracked Kam's body and more dark red blood issued from his mouth. He had seen enough death in his time to know that the end was close.

"I have seventeen summers, Uncle; that makes me a man."

Kam managed a smile despite his pain. "Listen to me and listen well, Eryn, because I can hear my ancestors calling to me as I speak. There are more things to being a man than mere age, such as honour, loyalty and common decency; this you would have learned in the fullness of time. Now, however, you are going to have to learn these things earlier than other boys your age. Promise me that you'll look after your sisters and see that they marry good men. Promise me also that you'll find it in your heart to forgive your father."

A brief look of anger flashed across Eryn's face at the mention of his real father, but it was gone as quickly as it appeared. "The first part of what you ask is easy. I will find them the strongest and bravest men to marry."

"No, you must find them good, honest, hard-working farmers or millers, men who will be there for them when they need them most, not off gallivanting around the countryside playing at soldiers." Another huge cough and specks of dark arterial blood splattered Eryn's face and clothes.

Eryn winced at his uncle's suffering yet his pride in the dignified way he bore his pain, was boundless.

"As you wish, Uncle," replied Eryn though in truth he couldn't imagine why his uncle would say such a thing when he had been such a great soldier himself.

Behind Eryn, the woman with the broken nose clamped a hand over her mouth to stifle her sobs as she knelt by her husband's headless body. Leisha, who had fetched a blanket from the cabin with which to cover her nakedness, looked on silently, her body trembling with shock.

"And what of my other wish?" prompted Kam.

"Forgive me, Uncle, but you ask too much. How can I forgive a man who abandoned us when we needed him the most?"

"You mustn't be so hard on my brother, Eryn. He loved

you all more than you will ever know. He was heartbroken that day he came back to find your mother missing. Five long years he spent trying to track her down, during which his only companion was grief. When he finally came home without her, his guilt had all but consumed him and he couldn't face the world, much less the children who reminded him of his beloved wife. He did what he thought was right," said Kam, every word a struggle now.

"Maybe, but he still should have been there for us. All I can promise is that I will try to forgive him, though I can only offer small hope of success. Each passing day sees my hatred of the man grow for the way he abandoned us."

"Still you must try," pleaded Kam, grasping the boy's arm as tightly as he could manage. "Promise me."

Eryn nodded slowly. "Very well, Uncle, I promise that I will try."

"That is all that I can ask." He tried to focus on his nephew, but his vision had clouded over, his time nearly done. "The Chariot of Souls approaches, Eryn. Listen, under my bunk...a gift ...from your father. He wanted you to have it when... you became a man ...perhaps today is that day after all. Use it wisely."

Eryn wanted to tell his uncle that he didn't want anything to do with a gift from his father, but to do so would only have served to upset his uncle during his last moments on Chell. Instead he kept a still tongue and grasped his uncle's arm.

The sounds of battle and women screaming had died down, though thick, dark smoke still hung in the air as a pungent reminder of the tragedy which had befallen the remote country village. Eryn glanced round, suddenly aware of the quiet and of the small crowd which had gathered near them. When he looked back at his uncle, Kam's body had slumped forward and his head lolled lifelessly on his chest. Free from his uncle's disapproving gaze, Eryn began to sob openly. Leisha's mother crouched down beside him and put a comforting arm around his shoulders.

"Make way, make way I say," said a burly man, with a shaved head and heavy drooping moustache as he pushed his way to the front of the crowd. "The old dog's gone has he?" asked the man as he knelt down next to his dead friend and

Eryn. Then in a quieter voice that only Eryn and Leisha's mother could hear. "Stop that snivelling, son, your uncle wouldn't want it. Besides there're people watching."

Leisha's mother quietly tutted at Jeral's refusal to let the boy openly grieve, drawing a withering look from him that demanded her silence.

Eryn wiped his eyes with a grimy sleeve and tried to pull himself together. He was the head of the household now and needed to act like it.

"Is it over?"

"It is," replied Jeral.

"Will they be back?"

"I shouldn't think so. What with the three dead here and the other bodies I've seen lying about I'd say we gave them a bloody nose they weren't expecting." He winced at his choice of words when he caught sight of Leisha's mother again.

"Eryn! Eryn!"

Eryn recognised the frightened voice of his youngest sister Marta and he stood to block her view of their dead uncle, as she pushed her way through the crowd. She would have to be told of course, but not like this he decided.

"I'm here, Marta, what is it? Why didn't you stay in the hiding place like I told you?"

"You didn't," she replied indignantly, as she strained her neck to see what everybody was looking at behind her brother. Marta was seven years old and had no recollection of either parent. She wrapped her small arms around her brother's waist, hugged him tight and then started to sob.

"It's all right, Marta, they've gone now, you're safe," said Eryn as he hugged her back. A terrible feeling of foreboding suddenly washed over him and his eyes started to scan the huddled crowd. When he couldn't find who he was looking for, he grasped his sister by the shoulders and pushed her back slightly so that he could look directly into her face. "Marta, where's Keira? Why isn't she with you?" The little girl just stared back at Eryn, tears rolling down her cheeks. "Marta, I asked you where your sister is."

"They took her, Eryn, I'm sorry." The answer had come not from his sister, but from a disembodied voice somewhere in the gathered crowd.

"What?" asked Eryn incredulously, as he looked to where the voice had appeared to have originated. The shock of what he had just been told threatened to make his legs buckle at any moment.

"The raiders, they took her," said a stocky middle-aged man who had moved to the front of the crowd. He was covered in blood, but from what Eryn could tell it wasn't his.

"Yes, and a number of others as well," added a woman from somewhere to the rear of the crowd.

"Which way did they go?" asked Eryn.

The middle-aged man glanced towards Jeral, unsure whether he should impart the information and preferring to defer to the village elder's guidance. Jeral gently shook his head and the man looked down to the ground rather than meet Eryn's angry gaze.

"I asked you which way they went?" repeated Eryn, his anger starting to rise.

"North," said someone anonymously deep in the throng, drawing an angry stare from Jeral.

"Will you look after Marta for a while please, Mrs Morn?" Eryn asked turning to face Leisha's mother as she dabbed gently at her broken nose. Her face was swelling up by the minute and a livid bruise now adorned her left cheek. He felt guilty asking her, but they had been neighbours for years and she had been like a surrogate mother to him and his sisters.

"Of course I will, Eryn, you know that," she replied. "But please don't do what I think you're about to do."

"I have to. You heard my uncle's dying wish that I look after my sisters. Am I to let him down within minutes of his heart ceasing to beat?"

The woman nodded her understanding if not her approval.

Eryn smiled his thanks and turned to once again face his youngest sister. "Marta, you're going to stay with Mrs Morn for a while okay?"

"But I don't want to, I want to stay with you, Keira and Uncle Kam," she replied through a torrent of tears.

"I know you do, Marta, but the bad men have taken Keira and I need to go after them right now so that I can bring her back. I need you to be a brave girl and stay with Aunty Myra. Can you do that for me?"

Marta wiped at her tears with the back of her grubby hand and nodded dutifully.

"Good girl," said Eryn as he kissed her on the forehead and hugged her once again. It was then that she caught a glimpse of her dead uncle's body slumped a few feet away and began to scream for all she was worth.

"Uncle Kam!"

"No, Marta, uncle wouldn't want you to see him like this. Go with Aunty Myra, there's a good girl," pleaded Eryn as the girl struggled to get through to where her uncle's body was slumped.

"I don't want to; I want to see Uncle Kam," screamed Marta as she fought hard to escape Eryn's grasp.

Eryn looked to Myra and nodded, indicating that she should take Marta away and with Leisha's help, she managed to bundle the little girl away from the grisly scene. Eryn watched Marta being led away and swallowed hard to prevent his own tears from reappearing. In the space of a few short minutes his world had come crashing down around him. His uncle, whom he had worshipped like a father, was dead, one sister had been abducted and the other was heartbroken and may never recover. Hardening his resolve before self-pity could get too firm a hold, he silently vowed to avenge his uncle and to rescue Keira. Watched by the small crowd, he turned and started to cross the street to what was now his cabin.

"And where do you think you're going, young Master Eryn?" asked Jeral.

"To saddle my uncle's ...*my* horse and pursue the raiders of course; they've got Keira," replied Eryn bitterly.

Jeral bridled at Eryn's disrespectful tone, but decided to let it pass – this time. "I know they have, lad, but you're not going anywhere, not yet anyway. Now is the time for cool heads, not rash action. Besides, there are people to be buried and wounded to be tended. Show your uncle some respect."

"My uncle is dead and if I delay any longer, the trail those raiders are leaving will go cold. The best way I can honour my uncle is to get my sister back and fulfil my promise."

Jeral stared at the young man for a few seconds, but it wasn't Eryn that he saw. Instead he found himself staring at a young Jeral Tae, determined and with a belly full of fire ready to take on the world.

"I was a young man once, Eryn and understand your desire to go after these men and rescue Keira, truly I do. But the passing years have demonstrated many times that this is not always the best way to handle such things. Your uncle, Sulat rest his soul, would have been proud of your courage. He would not, however, have been proud of your recklessness. You have no plan, no notion where they're going and no idea how to rescue her, let alone how you're going to deal with the armed men who hold her prisoner. Any rescue mission has to be planned and thought out."

"I cannot wait whilst all of the things you say are done. By the time that they are and by the time the village elders have talked the matter to death, Keira could be halfway across the known world and I would never find her again."

"Perhaps, but I still advise caution," urged Jeral.

"I'm sorry, Jeral, I know that you mean well, but I simply can't wait whilst men who have seen too many summers plan and debate, but do nothing. If I was to lose Keira because of my indecision or cautiousness, I could never live with myself; I hope that you understand that."

"Your mind is set then?"

"It is," said Eryn as he locked eyes with his uncle's friend. Jeral nodded slowly and believing his point made, Eryn turned once more to cross the street to his cabin, the crowd parting before him.

"Oh, Eryn, one last thing," Jeral called after him.

Irritated at the further delay, Eryn spun round to face the old general and as he did so, a pile driver of a punch caught him square on the cheek and Eryn crumpled to the ground unconscious.

Jeral winced with pain and caressed his knuckles as he stared at the young man's body lying on the ground before him. Twenty years ago he could have done that without a second thought, but now he wasn't sure who it hurt more, him or the person he punched.

He hated the thought of getting old. The victor of so many

battles it looked like the one enemy that he wouldn't be able to defeat, was old age. It wasn't a comforting thought. Suddenly feeling surly and bitter, he glared at the gathered crowd.

"Anyone else planning on doing something foolish?" Most shook their heads whilst others visibly cowered away from the grizzled old warrior. "Well what are you all gawping at? Somebody get some rope and tie him up, whilst the rest of you see to the wounded and the fires." Nobody moved. "Now!" he bellowed. "And somebody cover those bodies up," he added, nodding towards Kam and Jak Morn. This time everybody fled in different directions.

Whilst the men fought the fires and dug graves the women split up into groups to tend the wounded and look after the children.

Jeral stared longingly down the street in the direction the raiders had fled. Eryn was right, they should be pursuing them. What's more a man of his experience should be leading the rescue party instead of giving orders to pot-bellied men and old women. He'd dared to believe that he led a contented life as a village elder since the king had dismissed him, but now that he had again briefly enjoyed the sweet taste of battle, he knew that it was a lie.

He would never be able to settle to village life like his friend Kam, nor did he particularly want to. He had enjoyed the skirmish with the raiders, brief that it had been and longed for the thrill of a proper battle. Deep down though he knew those days were over for him and that it was time to pass that mantle onto somebody else. He had a feeling that somebody might just turn out to be Eryn. With a heavy heart, Jeral turned away from the road that led north to adventure and glory and began to make his way into the village centre to oversee the burial parties. It was going to be a long, hot and tiring day.

Chapter 2

Teren Rad wiped the sweat from his brow with the back of his hand and glanced at the huge pile of wood he had chopped that morning. He had only meant to cut enough wood for the next couple of nights, but already he had chopped enough for at least the next two weeks. He gently flexed his fingers trying to relieve the shooting pain he tended to get in both hands whenever he'd been doing something physical. There was no disguising it, he was getting old. The first sign that the relentless march of time was finally catching up with him was when he had noticed the grey flecks of hair appearing at his temples. Then he'd started to feel the cold of an evening which was why he was chopping firewood and now finally he was getting pains in his joints.

He sighed as he once again hefted his axe over his shoulder. He didn't like getting old and it was not something that he'd planned for. He was born a soldier and he had expected to die as one; a young one. Many had tried to grant him his wish and one or two had even come close, but in the end none had been strong or lucky enough. It was beginning to look like his final battle was to be against time itself. He knew that it was a battle that he could not win, but it was one he intended to prolong. If he was not to be permitted a warrior's death, then he would make time wait for his demise and the best way he could do that was by keeping himself fit and active.

Smiling at his renewed sense of defiance, he raised the axe high above his head and was about to bring it crashing down onto another block of wood, when something out of the corner of his eye caught his attention. He gently lowered the axe and stared into the distance trying to ascertain what had distracted him.

At first he couldn't see anything and he cursed his failing eyesight for playing tricks on him. He had been sure that there had been something there a second ago. He rubbed his eyes with grubby fingers before once again peering off into the distance. Far to the west he could just about see that there were several grey pillars of smoke swirling in the clear morning sky. He watched as they climbed ever higher, their density lessening until they were no more than a wisp. He tried to place where the smoke was coming from, though in truth he had known instantly; he just didn't want to believe it. The village of Lentor was burning.

Has the blacksmith's or baker's caught fire and spread throughout the village? he wondered.

It was possible, especially as most of the homes and businesses were built of wood and thatch. He tried to convince himself that was the cause of the smoke, but deep down he knew that it was unlikely. His warrior's instinct, forged on numerous battlefields, told him that something was wrong, very wrong. Lentor was under attack.

He thought about his children, his former neighbours and his old war comrades, Kam Martel and Jeral Tae and his grip on the axe handle tightened. If they were under attack, his two old friends would no doubt be in the thick of the fight and exacting a high price from their attackers.

I should be there standing shoulder to shoulder with them not hiding up here in the mountains.

Lentor was many miles away and even if he left immediately, as fast as his aging body could take him, he'd get there long after it had all ended he realised. He thought again of his family and the life that he had left behind and the memories came flooding back. They swamped him quicker than he could deal with them and his emotions momentarily threatened to overwhelm him. No, he had made the right decision; there was no going back now. What was done was done. There was no point dredging up long-forgotten memories that could only hurt him. Even so he couldn't help but worry about those who had once meant something to him.

Still mean something to me, he corrected himself.

He leant on the axe handle watching as his former home of Lentor burned far in the distance.

Who had attacked them?

Common sense told him that it was probably bandits of

some sort, but he also found himself wondering whether the impending war with the Delarites had begun whilst he stood chopping wood.

Although he lived high in the Lonely Mountains pretty much as a hermit, he was not completely cut-off from the outside world and the occasional traveller or shepherd would willingly trade news for a tankard of homemade ale or a lump of bread and cheese. Teren had heard about the almost anarchical state Remada now found itself in under the new king. He had lay awake many nights weeping for the thousands of her sons who had died protecting its sovereignty only to see it squandered by this fool who had ascended the throne.

The latest traveller to have passed by and spoken to Teren some two weeks ago had told him that it was an open secret that the Delarites were massing for war.

Teren stared at the burning village far to the west silently debating what to do. If the war had started, what was he going to do about it? *Nothing* was the answer he realised. His days of fighting had ended when he had chosen that life for himself.

The chance for a warrior's death still appealed greatly though and Teren could feel his blood pumping with renewed vigour just at the thought. Anything was preferable to wasting away through the ravages of time, until eventually one night he would go to bed and never wake up again. There he would remain until some traveller, some stranger, found his rotting corpse and buried him – if he was lucky. It was a horrible thought and one more reason why he should answer the call of his blood and hurry to the smoke and battle.

The rational part of his mind reminded him that he had chosen to turn his back on that life when he had moved to the mountains, although admittedly the circumstances had not been of his choosing. No, it was someone else's war now; he was content with his peaceful and secluded life. It was a lie he knew, but it was a convenient lie at that moment in time. With a mighty roar borne of frustration, Teren hefted the axe up and brought it down with a thunderous blow that split the block of wood in two and left the blade buried deep in the trunk below. Teren grunted with satisfaction for in his mind that had been the head of a Delarite soldier, not a lump of wood.

He wriggled the blade free and bent to pick up another block of wood to split, when his instincts suddenly told him he was no longer alone. He hadn't seen or heard anything, but he just knew that someone was close by. He quietly sniffed the air and was sure that he could detect the faint smell of stale sweat, a smell he had grown accustomed to in the army. He was positive somebody was approaching him from behind and from their stealth it was unlikely they had come in peace. He placed a fresh block of wood on the chopping top and slowly straightened, resting the axe shaft over his right shoulder as he did so.

"You know it's both dangerous and rude to come onto another man's property uninvited and worse still to then not announce yourself."

Teren waited a few seconds, long enough he figured for a genuine traveller to speak up and atone for their rudeness. When no apology or sound of any kind was forthcoming, he decided that they were in all likelihood contemplating whether or not to attack him, now that their presence had been detected. He decided to take the initiative and with a speed that belied his age, Teren swung the axe round in an arc, silently praying that his instincts were right and he wasn't about to decapitate a woman or child.

It was over in a few seconds. As the blade made contact Teren was able to make out that the person behind him had been a warrior of some sort. The axe blade had cut the man's head off in a spray of blood before continuing its journey and removing his right arm, which had evidently been raised high above his head. The arm simply dropped, but the man's head, a look of shock etched on his face, bounced once on the ground before slowly coming to a halt at Teren's feet. A couple of seconds later the man's body toppled over landing crumpled between his head and arm.

Teren scratched his straggly beard and looked down at the dismembered body. It had been a good call on his part and he was pleased to see that his instincts were as sharp as ever. He nonchalantly slung the bloody axe over his left shoulder and almost fell over with surprise when something hit the axe blade making a loud clanging noise. Instinctively he dropped to a crouched position, making himself a smaller target though at that moment in time he wasn't even sure what threatened him. A few paces away he spotted a knife lying in the grass, which somebody had evidently just thrown at him. Had it not been for the fact that he had slung his axe over his shoulder at exactly the right second to deflect the blade, he would now be riding on the Chariot of Souls he realised. Fate had other plans for him it seemed.

Teren glanced left and saw another man dressed in similar clothes to those of the man he had just killed, approaching fast. He was about ten paces away and was reaching for his sword. Teren knew that he had to react quickly and he launched himself into a sprint carrying the axe in his right hand. It was going to be close. With a bellowing roar the likes of which had frightened many enemies over the years, Teren managed to cover the last few paces just in time. He barged into the other man shoulder first sending them both tumbling to the ground.

Although clearly winded the other man was on his feet in seconds and was soon bending down to pick up his fallen sword. Teren had managed to hold onto his axe but would never be able to stand in time to meet the first stroke of the attacker's blade. Reaching out he grabbed a handful of dirt from the ground and hurled it into the man's face just as he was closing on Teren. The man stopped and bent forward to rub his eyes, momentarily blinded. Seizing his opportunity, Teren pushed himself to his feet and lumbered towards the man, hefting his axe into position for the kill. The other man had recovered quicker than he had anticipated though and just as Teren raised his axe to deliver the killing blow, the attacker suddenly raised his sword high and brought it straight down in an attempt to split Teren's head open.

Teren reacted just in time and held his axe above his head in a blocking manoeuvre. Had his axe merely been an ordinary woodsman's axe, the attacker's blade would have surely sliced through the wooden handle and on into Teren's head, but it wasn't. The axe he had been using was a Carliri war axe. A fierce killing weapon, it had a long wooden handle which was reinforced on either side by thin strips of iron, that protected it. Teren's arms jarred from the blow, but he was otherwise unharmed.

If his attacker was surprised by the sturdiness of his axe, he didn't show it and rained another two huge blows down onto the axe handle, obviously hoping that it would eventually give way. The attacker's third swing was countered by a huge sideways swing of Teren's axe, but the man managed to nimbly sway out of its path and Teren was lucky to get his guard back up again in time. Another two blows clanged against the axe shaft before the attacker suddenly changed tact and swung low in an effort to hamstring him. Teren had somehow anticipated the move and had leapt above the swing landing just in time to parry another two blows from the attacker's sword.

They circled each other warily, the attacker grinning confidently whilst Teren was just grateful for a breather, however short the respite.

"You move well for a big man," the other man said, "but you are tiring. How much longer do you think you can keep this up?"

"As long as I have to," Teren replied, though he'd been wondering the same thing himself. "Besides, I'm just getting started."

The other man twirled his sword around in a number of fancy moves, clearly trying to unnerve his opponent, but Teren had seen it all before and wasn't easily impressed. Then he made a couple of feints which Teren responded to, whilst always retaining his guard.

"Why don't you make it easy on yourself, old man? Lay down your axe and I will make yours a quick death. Prolong this charade and you will die slowly and in much pain. What say you?"

Teren locked eyes with his assailant and smiled. "You talk too much. It's a sign of weakness and fear." The other man was about to reply when Teren suddenly launched a ferocious assault of his own, swinging his deadly axe first one way then another seeking an opening in the other man's defences. His opponent was momentarily startled and was pushed onto the back foot, but his quick reflexes enabled him to parry every blow until finally one enormous swing of

Teren's axe shattered the sword blade.

The attacker looked at his blade in disbelief and realising that it was now useless for offence or defence, hurled it at Teren, who simply batted it away as if he was swatting a fly.

"Still glad you came, sonny?" asked Teren as he slowly advanced on the other man.

The attacker glanced round desperately searching for something to use as a weapon or to fend off the old man's axe, but there was nothing to hand. He turned back to face Teren, but as he did so he felt a terrible pain in the side of his head; then it all went dark.

***

The man had no idea how long he'd been unconscious, but when he finally came to, the sun was high in the sky. Something was wrong though and for a few seconds he couldn't place what it was until the old man with the axe started walking towards him upside down. He started to wriggle furiously, but that merely aggravated the headache he was just becoming aware of.

"I wouldn't do that if I were you. It's likely to make your pain that much worse, especially with all the blood rushing to your head."

The man groaned and looked up, finally working out that he was hanging upside down from a sturdy looking tree branch, approximately half a man's height above the ground. He was bare-chested and his hands were bound behind his back. He twisted his body just enough so that the rope turned slightly enabling him to face the axe man.

"What do you want, old man?"

Teren stood a couple of paces away from the dangling man, chewing on a piece of meat, the meat's juices squirming out of his mouth and trickling down into his unkempt beard. He finished his meat and threw the bone onto the fire, the fat causing the flames to briefly flare and crackle. He wiped his mouth with the back of his hand, took a pace forward and punched his captive as hard as he could in the stomach. The man had been unprepared for the sudden blow and yelled with pain as he took its full force.

"A bit of respect to start with," said Teren as he watched the man's suspended body swing gently back and forth on the rope. "Oh, and by the way, I ask the questions, not you."

"You can rot in Kaden, old man, because I will tell you nothing," said the other man, before he spat at Teren, the spittle landing near Teren's boots.

Teren sighed and punched the man twice more, putting every ounce of effort into the second blow. "I don't think you understand the gravity of your situation, sonny, so it looks like I'm going to have to educate you." He stepped directly in front of the man's slowly twisting body and made a great show of displaying the knife he was holding. It was the knife the man had thrown at him before Teren had even been aware of his presence and which had clattered harmlessly against his axe blade.

"A nice blade this, very sharp. The last I heard it was only the assassins of Tula who carried these. Is that what you are, little man; an assassin?"

"I'm not telling you anything you whoreson," the man snarled back.

Quick as lightening, Teren slashed the man twice across his bare chest, causing him to scream out in pain.

"The first one was for an incorrect answer to my question and the second one was for my mother, Sulat rest her soul. Now let's try that again. I'm going to ask you questions and you're going to answer them honestly. If you do, I won't kill you, but if you don't then I will and I'm going to take my time over it. Do I make myself clear?"

The man just stared at him blankly, as the sensation of blood trickling down his chest and onto his neck momentarily distracted him. Teren reached out and sliced him again, causing the man to scream out and curse Teren once again.

"I said do you understand?" asked Teren.

"Yes, I understand, damn you to Kaden," replied the man, his eyes never leaving the knife which Teren continued to toy with.

"Good. So you are an assassin of Tula, yes?"

"Yes," replied the man reluctantly.

"Now why would a couple of assassins from Tula, because I assume your comrade was one also, want to kill me?"

"We weren't sent to kill you," replied the assassin.

"Then why did you attack me?"

"We were looking for food and wine when we stumbled across your hovel."

Teren tensed at the insult, but in the end decided to let it go unpunished, for a while anyway.

"And you thought that you'd just kill me and help yourself, eh? Why didn't you just ask me for some food? You wouldn't have been the first travellers I've fed?"

"Tulans don't ask, they take," sneered the assassin. "Besides, would you have welcomed us into your home?"

Teren thought about that for a moment. "No, I would have killed you at the first opportunity. Assassins are the lowest of the low in my opinion. You're nothing but murderers in the night, too afraid to fight real warriors man to man." Teren turned his back for a moment and then suddenly spun round and slashed the man across his chest again.

The man cried out in pain, his chest now a tapestry of cuts which ran red from his blood. "What was that for; I answered your questions?" he shouted at Teren.

"For calling my home a hovel and for thinking you could just come here and take what you like. Now before you bleed to death, tell me what two assassins of Tula are really doing in the Lonely Mountains. Have a care though, because if I don't like your answer, the next cut will open your throat. Speak."

The assassin was getting alarmed at the amount of blood he could feel running down his body. "We were sent to find and kill somebody."

"I could work that much out for myself; you're assassins after all. Now don't try and stall, sonny, you haven't got the luxury of time. Who were you sent to kill?" Teren had moved closer to the assassin and now held the tip of the knife perilously close to his throat.

The man licked his lips with nerves unsure how little he could get away with telling his captor whilst preserving his life. The look in the older man's eyes was cold and as hard as steel. He decided that he would tell him as much as he had to. "We were sent to track down and kill Ro Aryk."

"Ro Aryk! The captain of the Royal Bodyguard. Why?"

"Because somebody important wants him dead. Anyway, he is no longer the captain of the Royal Bodyguard; the king released him."

"Now why would the king do that I wonder?"

"I do not know. We are not always told why somebody must die just that they must. Now I have told you what you wanted to know, old man. Cut me down whilst I still breathe," snarled the assassin.

"Not just yet. I still have more questions," replied Teren as he pondered the news of Aryk's fall from grace. He had heard that the young king was a fool, but to dismiss the captain of his bodyguard and more importantly, a trusted and wise adviser when war was looming, was madness. "So who has ordered his assassination?"

"I can't tell you that. A Tulan never reveals his patron."

"Wrong answer," said Teren. He looked at the man's bloody chest. "Looks like I've run out of room. I'll have to start carving other parts of you." He moved the knife point down holding it dangerously close to the Tulan's groin. "Are you sure there's nothing you want to tell me?"

"All right, all right, I'll tell you. It was the king's personal adviser, Livic Pendar."

"I do not know him," said Teren more to himself than the assassin. In the distance a wolf howled and a few seconds later it was joined by several more. "Why would this Pendar fellow want Aryk dead?"

"What? I told you I don't know," replied the assassin who was now beginning to feel increasingly faint.

"Wrong again," shouted Teren as he once more raked the knife across the man's chest. "What do you know; there was room for another one after all."

"I don't know," the man screamed, "I don't know. Perhaps he just wants Aryk out of the way or sees him as a potential threat. Now cut me down like you promised."

Teren looked at his prisoner hanging upside down and smiled before wiping the knife blade clean on the man's trousers and then sticking it through his belt. "A nice knife that – you don't mind if I keep it do you? No! I didn't think so."

The wolves howled again, much closer this time.

Teren doused the fire and packed a few things into a leather bag which had been leaning against a nearby tree. Then he strapped on a long sword and tied a cloak around his neck. Lastly he picked up his axe, the blade of which was stained with dry blood.

"Oh, just one more thing, assassin. Are there more of you out looking for Aryk?"

"No, we always work in pairs; there is more profit that way," he replied through sobs of pain.

"So I see," said Teren as he reached into his bag and pulled out a small brown pouch which was full of silver. He had removed it from the Tulan whilst he was unconscious.

"Give that back, it is mine," snarled the assassin.

"Yes, it was and now it's mine," laughed Teren. A wolf howled from very nearby startling both men. "Time to be going, I think."

"Hey, where are you going, old man, cut me down?" shouted the assassin, a touch of desperation creeping into his voice.

"I said I wouldn't kill you if you answered my questions honestly and I haven't," replied Teren turning round to face him. "But I never said anything about them not killing you." Teren nodded to his left and the Tulan twisted on the rope to follow his gaze. On the edge of the clearing stood half a dozen large wolves which had converged on the area after picking up the scent of fresh blood. They watched Teren warily as he laughed and walked off into the trees in the opposite direction and finally out of sight.

Teren had not gone far when the agonised screams of a dying man reverberated through the trees. He smiled and walked on. He wasn't sure yet where he was going, but he knew now that fate didn't plan on letting him live out his life in peace on the mountains after all. His destiny apparently lay elsewhere and with a new if yet undefined sense of purpose, Teren headed down and out of the Lonely Mountains.

Chapter 3

It wasn't until mid evening that all of the fires had been extinguished and the bodies buried according to their sacred rituals and by then most of the villagers were tired and hungry. Jeral Tae had driven them hard throughout the day, keeping them busy so that no one had time to dwell on the morning's events. Nor did he want any more of the villagers trying to race off after the raiders seeking vengeance, though he doubted any would be that foolish. Still it was better to be safe than sorry.

Those villagers who didn't have small children to look after or seriously injured loved ones at home, gathered in the village hall for a meeting called by the surviving village elders. By luck or design, the raiders had left the village hall untouched, a welcome relief for those who had lost their homes and had nowhere else to stay. In truth it was no more than a large wooden barn, with a thatched roof that tended to leak when the heavy rains came, but to many it would now be home until the rebuilding process could begin.

"Friends, I know that you're all tired and need to grieve in the privacy of your own homes, those that are fortunate enough to still have one that is, so I won't keep you long," said Stil Lordik the chief village elder. He was a frail and tired looking man with a shock of white hair but his voice was steady and assertive and cut across the subdued conversations taking place throughout the hall. "However, the village elders thought that you'd want to hear the damage caused by this morning's raid at the earliest opportunity."

The conversations stopped and everybody's attention focussed on the man standing on the dais. The rumour mill had been working overtime during the day and people were now clamouring for the truth. Stil stared out across the sea of faces before him and wished there was somebody else to deliver the news. Despite his apparent confidence, he truly hated public speaking and tended to get very nervous, but as chief village elder, it was his responsibility.

"Neighbours... it is with a heavy heart that I must impart this information." He shifted his body weight from the left leg to the right and tugged nervously at the sleeve of his tunic, the first beads of sweat already appearing on his forehead. "The raid this morning has cost us dearly, both in terms of good friends and property." His eyes suddenly fell on Eryn, who was sporting a decent bruise on the side of his face. He had been released from his bonds earlier that evening, once he had given Jeral his word that he would not try to pursue the raiders until after the meeting. "Some of us have been affected worse than others." Stil managed to tear his gaze away from Eryn, the cold and determined expression the young man wore unsettling him. He shifted the weight back onto his left leg and scanned the crowd, which waited anxiously for the news below him. He looked down at the list resting on the table and a tear rolled down his cheek as he once again saw the names of some old friends who had been killed that morning. The crowd waited impatiently, but still he didn't speak.

Realising that this was a task too far for the old man and that the crowd's patience would only last so long, Jeral stood and walked over to his fellow elder, clasping him on the shoulder.

"It's all right, Stil, I'll do it."

"Thank you, my friend," replied Stil choking back the tears. He briefly covered his friend's hand with his own before shuffling back to his seat at the rear of the dais.

"This is not an easy thing to tell, so I'll get straight to it," began Jeral. "Twenty-seven neighbours lost their lives in this morning's raid and another twenty-one are injured, four of them, grievously." Murmurs of conversation broke out all over the hall and after a few seconds Jeral raised his hand for silence. "A list of those killed and wounded is available and will be posted on the hall door on my way out. That unfortunately, isn't the end of the bad news." More murmurings, louder this time. "Another seven of our people were taken away by the raiders." This time the murmurings became an explosion of sound as dozens of outraged and frightened people spoke at the same time, all demanding information and news.

Jeral Tae looked down at the crowd before him and not for the first time, wished that he was just an ordinary citizen rather than a leader of men and someone the people looked to in their time of need. But he wasn't and their need had never been greater than now.

"Friends." The noise continued. "Friends," he shouted a little louder this time, a few people near the front seemed to notice and ceased their conversations, but there was still too much noise. "Silence!" he finally bellowed and like a ripple in a pond, the message to stop talking and listen spread to the farthest reaches of the hall. "Thank you."

"Who's been taken?" shouted a woman at the back of the hall.

"Seven of our young women have been abducted, all aged between fourteen and twenty-one," replied Jeral.

"But why?" asked an old man sitting to the left of the hall.

"Sulat help us! I know you're an old man, Vikal, but has it been so long that you've forgotten what a young girl is for?" replied a middle-aged man with thinning hair and a short wispy beard. Several in the crowd, particularly those closest to him, laughed.

"Watch your mouth, Bratak," shouted a man in the crowd. "Some of us have lost daughters this day."

Pular Bratak did not recognise the voice and strained his neck to see who had spoken, but was unable to identify them in the throng behind him.

"The good news is that unless they give their captors too much trouble, I think they're probably safe for the time being," said Jeral, trying to regain control of the situation. Pular Bratak was an obnoxious man at the best of times and Jeral didn't need his careless remarks igniting an already charged atmosphere.

"Why do you say that?" asked Livan, the village baker, as he stood at the front of the crowd comforting his wife. Livan's sixteen year old daughter, Tayla, was one of the seven girls abducted, but judging by the blood on her father's clothes, they had not taken her easily.

Jeral studied his neighbour for a few seconds noting the wound to the shoulder he had received during the raid. Livan was a quiet family man who liked to keep himself to himself.

Always polite and friendly, he would have been the last person in the village Jeral would have expected to have put up a fierce fight, but according to a number of witnesses he had done just that. Being the village baker, Livan had been one of the few people up and dressed when the raiders struck and his premises had been amongst the first to be attacked. The way the raiders had sought out places like the bakery made it seem as if they knew exactly where the young girls lived. It was more than mere good luck or coincidence, he was sure of it. That thought continued to gnaw away at Jeral and he decided that he would give it more consideration when he was alone.

He suddenly became aware of the overpowering silence around him. He looked down and his gaze was met by a mass of expectant looking faces staring back up at him. Clearly they were waiting for him to speak and he silently berated himself for becoming distracted.

"I'm sorry, Livan, what did you say?"

"I asked what made you so certain that the girls wouldn't be hurt."

"Because I believe that they've been taken as slaves to sell."

The hall exploded in uproar, as everybody surged forward at the same time, shouting and asking questions. Jeral waited for the noise to die down of its own accord this time and it was several minutes before he spoke again.

"As potential slaves they are worth something to the raiders and that will keep them alive. There is no profit in a dead slave."

"Where will they take them?" shouted somebody in the crowd, though Jeral couldn't make out who had asked the question.

"East, probably to Salandor or perhaps Narmidia."

"But they rode north," protested another villager.

"That could be for any number of reasons," replied Jeral. "They could be going to rejoin their main party, they could be off to launch another raid or they could just be trying to throw any rescue party off their scent."

"Or you could be wrong about everything." This comment brought the hall to an abrupt silence as everyone waited to see how Jeral would react to the insult Pular had brazenly thrown at him. Only a very brave or very foolish man would dare to insult Jeral Tae in such a manner and Pular Bratak was not known for his courage.

Jeral's right hand moved tantalisingly close to his sword hilt, but changed direction at the last moment ending up inside his tunic where he feigned an itch. He would have liked nothing better than to end the life of that worthless piece of scum Bratak, right there and then, but unfortunately there were more important matters to attend to. He did not doubt, however, that the day would eventually come when there would be no such distractions. Then Bratak would get what was coming to him. He just prayed that he would not have to wait too long for that day to arrive.

"So were they Narmidians then? What were they doing so far west?" asked Rom Tagral, the village mason as he sought to break the awkward silence.

Jeral forced his gaze away from Pular and looked at Rom; not to do so would have been disrespectful to the man. "Some of them were Narmidians, but there were also Cardellans and others with them."

"So mercenaries then?" asked Livan.

"No, not mercenaries, bandits. They're not fighting for anyone but themselves, but they have been hired by someone to grab slaves. They've been raiding other villages in the area, for some weeks now."

"So who will have hired them?" asked Stil who had apparently regained his composure and had now come back to stand beside his friend in a show of support.

Nodding his acknowledgment of the old man's gesture, Jeral turned back to face the crowd. "They could have been hired by a wealthy Narmidian merchant or by anyone else from a dozen lands for that matter. We may abhor the notion of slavery, but there are plenty who don't, particularly in the east. If we're ever to see our women folk again, you'd better hope that they've got a paymaster lined up, otherwise their chances of surviving unmolested are greatly reduced."

Livan's wife began to wail and the baker buried her head into his chest. Jeral instantly wished he'd been more sensitive in his answers, but then that was not his way.

"So how come you know so much about them, old man?" shouted Pular.

Jeral bristled at the lack of respect in the man's tone and found himself clenching and unclenching his fists in an effort to control his rising anger. The urge to jump down from the dais and teach Pular some manners, was almost overpowering. It was well-known that the two men did not see eye-to-eye, but the challenge in his voice at a time when the whole village should be pulling together, surprised even Jeral.

"Because I have asked some of my old army contacts to keep me informed, that is how," replied Jeral in a tone that did nothing to disguise his loathing of the man.

"If you knew that other villages in the area were being attacked, why didn't you warn us, we might have been able to do something to prevent this?" A few sparse mutterings of agreement emanated from around the hall. The disdain in his voice was plain for all to see and Jeral wondered if this was going to develop into an open challenge to his authority. He was fast beginning to wish that it would, if only so he could vent some of the anger he felt inside after that morning's raid. If Pular was planning on launching a challenge, he would find Jeral more than willing to accommodate him.

"Do something? What exactly did you do, Pular Bratak, when the raiders come, except hide under your bed that is?" The majority of villagers laughed openly, though some clearly sensing the onset of trouble began to back away from around Pular and his small group of friends.

"I was in the thick of the fighting, doing my civic duty," Pular snarled back.

"In the thick of it were you? Yet not a drop of blood from either you or the enemy do I see on your clothes," replied Jeral. More murmurs from around the hall, this time in support of Jeral.

"How dare you accuse me of cowardice, old man? All of these men will verify what I have said," Pular snapped back indicating the men around him.

Nodding, Jeral looked at the assortment of village ruffians and drunks standing around Pular, all of whom were equally devoid of any signs of battle. "And a fine upstanding bunch of citizen witnesses they are too, the cream of our community no less," replied Jeral, much to the amusement of many in the crowd. He raised his hands to curtail the laughing when one or two of Pular's associates cursed and made to approach him. "Please, if you have something to say, gentlemen, join me on the dais." Jeral's right hand wandered slowly, but menacingly towards his sword hilt, an action which didn't go unnoticed by his would-be attackers who seemed to have had second thoughts. "No, nothing to say? Very wise. Perhaps you're not as stupid as you look, after all."

"Gentlemen, please, this isn't helping anyone, least of all those poor girls taken hostage," said Stil trying to calm the situation. "Please go on, Jeral."

It took Jeral a few seconds to compose himself and recall what he'd been saying. "I was asked whether we could have done something to prevent this and the answer is probably no. We had sentries posted, but they evidently didn't have time to raise the alarm. I did suggest some months ago that perhaps we should consider forming our own village militia with a view to guard duties and patrols, but as you all know the opposition to the idea was strongly championed by our good friend Pular over there. Instead, sentry duty had to be shared by a small band of volunteers who agreed with me and one or two on punishment duty. Ultimately, it wasn't enough."

A glint of metal off to his left, caught Jeral's trained eye and he knew instantly that one of Pular's associates had drawn a knife and was getting ready to hurl it his way.

"You'd better either put that knife away or throw it true, neighbour, because if you don't I'm going to come down there, cut you open from throat to navel and feed you your own entrails. Decide quickly, whilst the choice is still yours," said Jeral without looking in the man's direction.

The tension in the air was almost palpable, as the crowd backed away from between Jeral and Pular's group, leaving both parties in clear sight of one another.

After one of the longest minutes Stil Lordik had ever known, he watched his friend release the tight grip he had on his sword hilt and his shoulders start to relax. The danger had passed for now, the man having seen sense and put the knife back in his tunic. The events of that evening would not easily be forgotten, Stil realised and at some point in the future there would be a reckoning for Pular and his cronies for the disrespect they had shown Jeral. He did not envy them.

"Another wise choice," said Jeral, again without looking in his adversary's direction.

"Enough of this."

The words had been spoken from somewhere over to Jeral's right. The constant interruptions were getting to be a source of irritation and Jeral glanced over to see who was responsible this time. Standing up and glowering at him, with a sizeable and angry looking bruise on his left cheek, was Eryn.

"Do you wish to address the crowd, Eryn?" asked Jeral.

"No, I do not wish to speak; all I've heard all night is talk. Instead of standing around here arguing amongst ourselves, we should be out chasing the raiders." Ripples of conversation spread throughout the crowd, whilst a few nodded in silent agreement. "Every minute that we waste standing around here makes the task of catching up with them that much harder."

"And what will you do if and when you catch up with them, Eryn?" asked Raul Janus, a local farmer whose property had been burned and eldest daughter, Rosa, abducted.

"Kill them of course. It is no less than they deserve."

"And just how do you plan to do that, when we couldn't do it here in our own village?" asked one of Pular's men. "There were at least thirty of them and they're armed to the teeth. We're just farmers, blacksmiths and...boys." The last word was said in a derisory tone, much to the amusement of his companions.

"They die just as easily as anyone else; why don't you take a look at the bodies of the eight raiders who did not leave the village this morning?" he shot back.

"Perhaps, but they were killed by men, not a boy." Again his friends laughed their support.

"Maybe if you'd clambered out from under the table you hid beneath, you would have seen that this *boy* accounted for two of the raiders lying dead outside," replied Eryn, the challenge in his voice plain for all to hear.

"You insolent pup, I'm going to slit your throat," snarled Pular's man as he strode towards Eryn, his right hand reaching inside his tunic for what Jeral assumed to be a knife. The man had covered half the distance between them, when he suddenly crashed to the floor having tripped over Rom's deliberately outstretched leg.

He came up spitting with fury, but undaunted the big mason stood his ground. The smaller man reached inside his tunic once again, a look of alarm suddenly crossing his face.

"Looking for this, friend?" asked Jeral holding a vicious looking knife in his left hand. He had jumped down from the dais and picked up the knife when it had fallen out of the man's tunic during his tumble. The man suddenly looked worried. "By all means, please feel free to continue your conversation with Rom." Jeral was smiling, but it was a smile laced with menace.

Pular's friend turned back to face the mason who somehow now looked even taller. He was glaring down at him, a look of amusement on his face. Swallowing hard, the man glanced nervously towards his friends for signs of support, but none were forthcoming. Mustering what little resolve he had left, he stared back up at Rom. "This isn't over, Tagral; they'll be another day when your guardian isn't around."

Rom held his stare and didn't flinch, apparently not in the least bit perturbed. "I would be disappointed if it was. You know where to find me. I don't need any help to squash a bug like you," and with the minimum of effort, he shoved him back a couple of strides, the man just managing to keep his footing, but not his dignity.

"And if you ever want your knife back, you come and see me, maggot, though you might not like the way I return it," added Jeral.

Pular's friend spat on the floor in front of Rom and stormed through the crowd towards the exit, barging people out of the way as he went, closely followed by Pular and the others.

"That's a shame, I was just starting to like those lads,"

said Jeral to no one in particular, drawing an exasperated look from Stil.

"Thanks, Rom," said Eryn, "but I could have handled him."

"I'm sure you could have, son, but why should you have all the fun, eh?"

Jeral smiled to himself; the boy was going to do just fine without old Kam. "The boy...sorry, Master Eryn, says that we should go after the bandits: what do you think?" he asked turning to face the remaining crowd.

"With one or two exceptions, we're no match for those men. We'll just end up with more widows. Let's send for the army and let them hunt them down," said a man, whose name Jeral couldn't immediately recall. He did remember, however, that he lived in one of the homesteads just outside the village.

"The nearest army garrison is over two day's ride away and by the time they get organised and return here, five days will have elapsed. We'd be lucky to pick up their trail again let alone catch them. I don't really think that's an option, do you? Besides, if the rumours about the Delarites are true, chasing a band of raiders isn't going to be their top priority," replied Jeral.

"Let's hire some men to go after them for us then," suggested Livan. Many in the crowd muttered their approval and nodded but Jeral was slowly shaking his head.

"It would take too long to find and recruit enough men to go after them and by then, the raiders will be long gone. Secondly, such men don't come cheap and are not to be trusted. We might simply be swapping one problem for another."

"Then what do you suggest, Jeral?" asked Lyuria, an attractive and much sought after woman in her late thirties, who had been recently widowed.

Jeral stroked his long moustache and thought for a moment, his eyes never leaving the woman. She held his gaze and smiled back. *A confidence borne of beauty no doubt.* "It seems to me that if we want our women folk back, we're going to have to go and get them ourselves, there's no other choice," he eventually answered.

"Finally," said Eryn drawing one of Jeral's trademark withering looks.

"But we've already said that with the exception of you, all of the men capable of successfully undertaking such a task were killed in this morning's attack. The rest of us would be lambs to the slaughter. Besides, many of us have other commitments to look after in the village, families and businesses," protested a man in his mid-fifties, with grey hair and terrible eyesight.

"I know, my friend and it will be for every man here to search his soul as to the right thing to do, but I must say that I think some of you do not give yourselves enough credit. I will lead this mission, as I have neither a family nor a business to worry about. Who here will join with me?"

Eryn immediately stepped forward. Jeral went to say something in protest, but Eryn's defiant look told him that this was one battle that he wasn't going to win. Instead he just nodded at the boy. Others began to step forward, notably most of the fathers and brothers of the girls who had been abducted.

Stil Lordik sidled alongside Jeral and placed a hand on his friend's shoulder. "Your bravery and dedication to duty are above reproach, my friend, but I'm afraid that you cannot go, your place is here."

The small group of volunteers, who heard what Stil had said to Jeral, began to whisper amongst themselves.

"What do you mean I can't go, Stil, of course I can? I'm the ideal man to lead the party, you know it and they know it."

"Be that as it may, Jeral, you cannot go. When you joined the Council of Elders you swore to protect and serve the village till your dying breath."

"I don't need reminding of my oaths, Stil," snapped Jeral, instantly regretting his tone. "Besides, isn't that what I would be doing, protecting the village, if I help track down and kill these raiders?"

"Don't bandy words with me, Jeral Tae, you will only lose. Oratory is my battlefield. You are needed here and here is where you must stay. If we have learned anything from this morning's raid, it is that we have become too complacent about our safety. We should have listened to you all those months ago and formed some sort of militia. Who knows, we might have been able to prevent some of the killing and saved some of those poor young girls. No, here is where you are needed most."

"But what about the girls? Who will lead the rescue party?" protested Jeral.

The other village elders had come to stand next to them and they all turned to face the small group of volunteers standing before them. Jeral silently cursed, as one by one, the volunteers melted back into the crowd leaving Eryn stood alone. They'd obviously overheard Stil telling Jeral that he couldn't go and no one it seemed was willing to join the rescue party if Jeral was not going to be there to lead it.

"What is the matter with you?" screamed Eryn. "Why do you change your minds?"

"I'm sorry, Eryn," said Livan. "It was a fool's errand with Jeral leading us, without him it's a suicide mission. We'd all be killed in the first encounter." The other volunteers who had rejoined their families muttered their agreement.

"We can't just give up on the girls, they're depending on us. What about Tayla?"

Livan swallowed hard and refused to meet the young man's accusing gaze.

"We have no choice now, but to leave it to the army, Eryn. I'll send a rider out on the fastest horse we've got first thing tomorrow morning. I'm sorry, there is nothing else to be done," said Stil.

"Well I'm still going after them. I'm not giving up on my sister and fiancée just like that," said Eryn turning to leave.

"Your what?" asked Jeral incredulously.

Eryn felt his face flush and silently cursed his loose tongue. As he turned back to face Jeral he hoped that his reddened face wasn't noticeable in the shadowy light provided by the flickering torches dotted around the hall. "My fiancée... Tayla."

"What?" roared Livan.

Jeral smiled wryly to himself at the anger displayed by the normally docile baker. Apparently finding out second-hand that your young daughter was betrothed was liable to do that to a man, however placid he might normally be.

"I'm sorry, Livan, we were planning on telling you, but it just never seemed to be the right time," said Eryn.

"There would never be a right time to tell me such a thing," the man shouted back, looking to his wife for support. His wife, however, seemed quite unperturbed by the news. "Did you not hear what the lad just said, woman? Our daughter is betrothed."

"Oh, calm yourself, Livan, or you'll bring on your chest pains, it's no big deal. We were married when we were not much older than them. Besides, Eryn's a nice lad."

"That was different."

"How?" asked his wife.

"It just was and what do you mean, it's no big deal? Wait a minute, you knew didn't you?" the question was rhetorical.

"Yes, I knew, so what?"

"Why didn't you tell me, woman?" Livan's face was crimson with rage.

"Because like the lad said, there never seemed to be a right moment."

"And this is?"

"No, but at least it's out in the open now," his wife replied smiling.

Livan was about to launch another verbal onslaught when Jeral decided to interject before things took a turn for the worse. If it got ugly between Livan and his wife there was only going to be one winner and it wouldn't be Livan. The baker had enough wounds for one day he decided.

"I don't mean to interrupt, neighbours," he lied, "but the point will be moot if we are unable to get the girls back." Both parents cast their eyes to the ground in shame.

"Sorry, Jeral, you're right of course. My apologies," said Livan, casting one last angry look Eryn's way.

"No apology is needed, old friend," replied Jeral. "Now, is there no one else willing to go with Eryn, no one at all?"

"I'll go with you, Eryn," said Tav Rhem.

All eyes turned to the young man sat quietly to the left of the dais.

"Tav, I appreciate your support, really I do, but I don't

think it's a good idea," said Eryn somewhat embarrassed. Tav Rhem was regarded as the village simpleton. He was a harmless young man of about twenty-one, although no one knew his age for certain, but he had a mental age of someone much younger. He earned his keep by cheerfully doing the jobs nobody else wanted to do and although he was a likeable enough sort of boy, he could only really count Eryn as a friend. Eryn was the only one who truly spoke to Tav as an equal, whilst most of the others just seemed to tolerate him.

"Actually, Eryn, I think it's a very good idea," said Jeral.

Tav beamed with pride.

"You're not serious, Jeral, it will be way too dangerous for him?" protested Eryn.

"It is going to be way too dangerous for both of you, but if your mind is set on doing this thing, then I think that it's a good idea for Tav to go along. At least with someone else with you, you'll be able to take it in turns to sleep and stand watch."

"I suppose so."

"There's no suppose about it. Now is there nobody else willing to join them?" Jeral's eyes scanned the crowd and most of the men could not meet his gaze and those that did felt as if their very soul was being scrutinised. It wasn't a nice feeling. "Then the boy and the..." Jeral glanced towards Tav who appeared busy in a world of his own as he often was, "and Tav, put you all to shame."

"This is ridiculous, Jeral. What chance does a boy barely old enough to shave and the village simpleton have against a cut-throat group of bandits? None, that's how much. We can't let them go, it will be tantamount to signing their death warrant," said Stil.

"Maybe, maybe not. What they can't achieve by force of arms, they may be able to achieve by guile." Stil looked unconvinced. "Besides which, I don't think we'd be able to stop him this time."

"No, you wouldn't," said Eryn striding towards them. "My mind's made up."

"Then may Sulat watch over you," said Stil patting Eryn on the shoulder before joining the throng of people leaving the hall.

Jeral waited until it was just him, Eryn, and Tav left in the hall. "So what's your plan, Eryn?"

"Head north, try and pick up their trail and see if I can muster some help along the way."

"That won't be easy. Men will want paying and you have no coin," replied Jeral.

"I know, but there has to be some men out there who are still willing to fight for honour or a cause. Maybe I'll pick up some help on the way through some of the other villages that they've attacked. Their men might not be such cowards."

Jeral winced at Eryn's brazen condemnation of his neighbours. "Don't be too hard on the men of Lentor, Eryn. They're frightened and many have suffered a loss this day. Some of them aren't thinking straight. Maybe some will join you in the morning after all."

"Not Bratak and his friends though I doubt," said Eryn.

"No, not Bratak and believe me when I say you're better off without them. Better to have your enemy in front of you than behind."

"Then I shall just have to hope that I can find some decent men along the way."

Jeral nodded his agreement, though in all honesty whilst he admired the boy's spirit, he doubted his chances of success. He thought long and hard before uttering his next words, but decided that it was worth the risk of upsetting Eryn. "You could always seek out Teren Rad; I'm sure that he would help you."

Jeral watched as the boy struggled to contain his anger at the mention of his father's name. "Why would I ask for help from a man who chose to abandon us all those years ago?"

"Because he's your father, Eryn," replied Jeral holding the boy's angry gaze.

"He gave up the right to call himself my father when he walked out on us seven years ago. The only father I ever cared about died fighting the raiders this morning."

"Well if you cannot find it in your heart to ask him for his help for yourself, do it for Keira, as he is her father as well. I know that if I had a daughter and she was abducted I would want to go after her captors. I wouldn't let anyone or anything stop me, so please think again I implore you."

"I'm sorry, Jeral, I respect you more than you will ever know, but please don't ask this of me. My uncle asked much the same thing with his dying breath and that is burden enough. Besides, as far as I'm aware nobody has seen or heard of him for many months, he could be dead for all I know, or care."

Jeral studied the boy's face wondering how much truth was contained in his words. "That is true, but if you don't look, you may never know for sure. All I can tell you is that if I were to undertake a quest such as yours, I would want someone like your father watching my back. However, I am not the one going so the decision must of course be yours."

The look that crossed Eryn's face suggested that Jeral's words might have struck a chord. "My uncle used to say that my father was the greatest warrior that ever lived before he went into exile. Is that true?"

Jeral inhaled deeply, before blowing out his cheeks. "Maybe. He and Kam Martel were two of the most courageous men I have ever known. The mere fact that they were standing in our front line used to cause ripples of fear throughout the enemy ranks and stiffen the spines of our own men. I will say no more on the subject, but if you do decide to seek out your father, if only for Keira's sake, you might want to start your search near the top of Stap Mountain. That is the last place he was seen alive, although that was some time ago."

Eryn nodded, but Jeral had the feeling that he had not done enough to convince the lad to seek his father's help. "Regardless of whether my father is the greatest warrior or not, I still wish that you were coming, Jeral."

"As do I, lad, as do I. I wish you both good fortune," he said smiling over at Tav, "and a safe journey home. We shall send for the troopers, but do not put too much store by them, as war is coming and they will be needed elsewhere. Cunning and guile must be your closest allies." He clasped Eryn's forearm in the warriors' embrace and patted Tav on the shoulder as he walked out, shaking his head and muttering Teren Rad's name to himself.

Eryn watched the old man limp out and suddenly felt very weary, the events of the day finally catching up with him.

Tav smiled at Eryn and held up a small figure of a man he had made out of a rope end. Tav was easily distracted and would have no concept of the dangerous mission for which he had so eagerly volunteered and Eryn felt another wave of guilt wash over him.

"That's good, Tav, really good. Now come, we must both go and get some rest, for tomorrow we start a great adventure."

"An adventure, great! Tav likes adventures, especially when it's with his friend, Eryn."

Together the two young men left the hall and headed out into the surprisingly chilly night air. Eryn stopped and stared up at the clear night sky, marvelling at a million pinpricks of light that glinted down from their dark velvet background.

Where will I be tomorrow when I look up at these same stars? he wondered.

Doubt began to suddenly gnaw away at his resolve until he forced himself to think about Keira and Tayla, frightened and alone. Doubt was a sign of weakness his uncle used to say, so there would be no more of it. Tomorrow he began the search for his sister and fiancée and the fulfilment of a promise. He would either succeed in his quest and return to the village a hero, or he wouldn't return at all. After wishing Tav a good night, Eryn strode over to his empty cabin to prepare for the journey ahead.

Chapter 4

Hidden behind a large oak tree, Ro Aryk had silently watched as three men ransacked his camp. After failing to find anything they considered worth stealing they had helped themselves to some of the meat that he had left slowly roasting on a spit whilst he gathered more firewood.

They are either very confident or very stupid, thought Ro as they hunkered down around his fire, clearly not worried by the prospect of the camp's owner returning at any moment. *But then why should they? There are three of them and they know by the set up of the camp that I am alone. Unless it's a trap.* He scanned the tree line for any sign of men lying in wait, but found none.

Ro had been tracking a large Narmidian raiding party for some days and the three he now watched were its scouts, sent on ahead to look for targets and possible threats. He knew from past experience that Narmidian scouting parties usually consisted of four men and the obvious lack of a fourth member of this particular party, troubled him. Still they did seem blissfully unaware of his presence. *Unless it's a trap.* The thought continued to gnaw away at him.

After satisfying himself that more men were not concealed in the undergrowth around his camp, Ro reached into the small pouch he wore about his waist and pulled out a *Jemtak.* A weapon favoured by the Lotari, a *Jemtak* was a small metal star with five razor sharp points that you hurled at your enemy. In the right hands it was a silent and lethal weapon. The Lotari were a strange and almost reclusive people who lived far to the north. Several years ago whilst on a mission near the Lotari lands, Ro had been given a number of *Jemtak* as a gift after he had come to the aid of a small Lotari convoy that had been attacked by bandits. Since then Ro had made every effort to perfect his technique in their use and whilst he didn't profess to be an expert, he could use them to great effect, especially over short distances.

He gripped the *Jemtak* lightly in his right hand trying to

conceal its existence and slowly emerged from the tree line and into the camp.

"Has no one ever told you that it's rude to enter another man's camp uninvited?"

The three men appeared genuinely startled by the sudden appearance of the tall stranger and staggered to their feet reaching for their swords as they did so.

"There was no one here so we helped ourselves; I hope you don't mind," said one of the men laughing. He had olive coloured skin, jet black hair and a drooping moustache all suggesting that he was a Narmidian or from the lands to the east. He also had a recent and painful looking scar running the length of his left cheek.

"So I see," replied Ro pointedly looking at his few possessions lying scattered around the ground. The tall blond haired man on the left of the three raiders was slowly easing his right hand towards his sword hilt, an action that didn't go unnoticed by Ro. "Now, if you all turn around get on your horses and leave I am willing to overlook this error of judgement - this time."

"And if we choose not to?" asked scar face.

"Then it will end badly for all of you I'm afraid, starting with him," said Ro nodding in the direction of the blond man who had been surreptitiously reaching for his sword. "You choose."

The three men looked at one another, clearly worried about this stranger's self-confidence when confronted by odds of three to one. Still, a challenge had been issued and it had to be answered.

"I weary of this, prepare to die, Remadan," said the third man who'd been standing on the right. He tossed the lump of meat he had been gnawing on into the dwindling camp fire and drew his sword.

Before anyone else could react, Ro hurled the *Jemtak* at the blond man on the left, two of its spikes burying themselves deep in his forehead before his sword even cleared its scabbard. He was dead long before his body hit the ground.

The other two looked at their fallen comrade in surprise, shocked at the speed with which the stranger had despatched him. Immediately after throwing the *Jemtak,* Ro had reached over his shoulder, swiftly drawn his two-handed sword and charged. Unsure whether to fight or run, the two men hesitated for a split second and in that instant Ro brought his huge sword down in a powerful arc that cleaved scar face's head clean off its shoulders.

The remaining raider charged at Ro with his sword held high above his head. He brought the blade down swiftly, clearly intent on slicing Ro's head in two like a melon, but Ro had already raised his own sword to parry the blow. The sound of metal on metal reverberated through the forest, startling some roosting crows in the nearby trees to a panicked flight.

What the raider lacked in skill, he more than made up for in speed and power. He relentlessly swung his sword at Ro probing his defences, though for his part Ro never appeared unduly concerned, meeting every blow and thrust with a block or a counter-strike.

After a couple of minutes, the raider began to tire, the ferocity of his onslaught diminishing with every swing. Then he suddenly delivered a huge horizontal swipe which Ro had to duck to avoid losing his head. The power of the swing caused the raider to stumble slightly as the momentum carried him forward. It was the opening Ro had been patiently waiting for and as the raider staggered in front of him, Ro kicked out with his left leg catching the raider behind the right knee. The raider howled with pain as he collapsed to the ground in an undignified heap. He struggled furiously to get up again, terrified that a killing blow from Ro's huge sword was mere moments away, but Ro surprised him. Instead of burying his sword deep into the man's body, Ro smashed the heavy sword hilt into the side of his head rendering him instantly unconscious.

Ro sheathed his sword and stared down at the man at his feet, whom he had decided, was probably Cardellan. Satisfied that he was out cold Ro had just bent down to haul the unconscious man up, when the sound of running feet approaching from behind startled him. Even as he turned he was reaching for his sword, but all of Ro's warrior instincts told him that he was going to be too late. Racing towards him with his sword poised to strike and a triumphant look upon his face, was the missing fourth scout.

I should have made sure they were alone before revealing myself.

Even as Ro made a futile effort to raise his sword and block the impending blow, the man's body shuddered, not once but twice. Ro watched as the look on his face turned from one of triumph to one of surprise and then pain. The sword dropped from the raider's hands and then he collapsed to his knees. He stared wide-eyed at Ro as if he still didn't comprehend what had happened to him and gave a wracking cough. Dark red blood trickled from his mouth as his lungs began to fill and then he slumped face first into the forest floor, two crossbow bolts protruding from his back.

Twenty or so paces behind the dead raider, someone in a hooded robe was in the process of slinging a small crossbow over their shoulder. Ro couldn't make out their face and was unsure whether they approached as friend or foe. Their actions certainly suggested that they were friendly but Ro was unsure whether he could take that risk and decided that he wouldn't yet sheath his sword. He would let them make the first move.

"It seems I owe you my life, friend," said Ro by way of greeting.

The figure approached slowly, but didn't reply and Ro's apprehension grew with each passing second. His grip on his sword's hilt tightened accordingly. The man wore the garb of a priest, but Ro realised that counted for nothing. Many a wolf had worn a sheep's clothing, so he would remain vigilant.

When they were only a few paces apart the figure stopped and pulled back their hood to reveal a man in his forties with thinning brown hair, wide grey eyes and a cordial expression.

"You can let go of that now, you're in no danger from me," said the newcomer nodding at Ro's sword. "Nor do you owe me anything. As for being your friend, only time will tell. Friendship has to be earned."

"Wise words spoken earnestly. If not friend then what should I call you?" asked Ro returning the smile and sheathing his sword.

"My name is Arlen Meric of Vahira," replied the stranger.

"Then whether you accept it or not, I am indebted to you, Arlen Meric of Vahira, a debt I shall not forget lightly. I am Ro Aryk, formerly adviser to King Taylen and captain of the Royal Bodyguard." He bowed slightly, an action copied by Arlen.

"You're a long way from the royal palace, Captain Aryk."

"Not far enough to escape the king's assassins I fear," replied Ro ruefully.

"These fellows? They don't look like assassins to me," said Arlen indicating the four bodies lying around the camp.

"No, not them. They were pathfinders for a Narmidian raiding party."

"Pathfinders?"

"That's the Narmidian word for scouts," explained Ro.

"Narmidians you say? They don't look like Narmidians to me," said Arlen, "not all of them anyway."

"Two of them are. The other two are a Cardellan and a Vahiran. I'm surprised you didn't recognise him as one of your own countrymen," said Ro giving Arlen a searching stare.

Arlen chose to ignore the question although Ro noticed the look of embarrassment that fleetingly crossed the man's face. "What are Narmidians doing in Remada?"

"Plundering, raping and taking slaves."

Arlen shook his head in disgust. "But why here, why Remada? Are there not territories nearer their home that would provide the same evil gains for less effort?"

"Of course, but they sense our weakness and seek to take advantage. Like a pack of wolves the Narmidians, Cardellans and others are all circling and nipping at Remada's ankles. Meanwhile the Delarites muster their troops on our northern border for an invasion. And what does our brave new king do? He buries his head in the sand and surrounds himself with weaklings and sycophants."

"I take it that is why you are a *former* adviser and not by the new king's side right now then?" asked Arlen. "No offence intended by the way."

"None taken. I have spent many weeks warning King Viktus that the Delarites were preparing for war and that our borders were being violated on a regular basis. At first he accused me of overreacting and exaggerating. Then as the irrefutable evidence about these incursions began to mount he started to go into denial, accused me of living in the past and eventually banished me from the palace. Now I have learned that his new personal adviser, Livic Pendar, has sent assassins to silence me."

"So has the king done nothing about these threats?"

Ro laughed derisively. "He's gone hunting, thrown balls and sent envoys to the Delarites, none of whom have come back. Not alive anyway. I served his father for many years, a great man who loved his country. Wherever he is now, I fear he weeps at his son's disregard for his nation's safety."

"Yes, he was a good king as I recall. He would not have let Narmidians and other vermin infest his lands."

"Believe me, Arlen, if King Taylen still lived, he would have ridden out at the head of his army to confront the threat a long time ago and I would have been by his side. The Delarites would have been smashed the moment they dared to cross our frontier," replied Ro passionately.

"Instead you find yourself a fugitive in your own country and on the run from assassins no less. Not a happy state of affairs I wager?" said Arlen.

"No, but it is not one that will last forever. When war eventually breaks out the king will finally realise that he needs men like me and will send word. Then there will be a day of reckoning for snakes like Pendar."

"And in the meantime all you have to do is avoid his assassins and any number of enemies wandering the countryside. Sounds easy," said Arlen smiling teasingly.

"When you put it like that, no," said Ro returning the smile, "but my spies tell me that the Delarites could invade any day now. As for Pendar's assassins, they had better hope that they find me before I find them."

"Yes, I can see that you don't suffer fools lightly," said Arlen as he glanced around at the four dead men. "And what about the rest of these fellows?"

"By now they're probably wondering where their scouts are though I doubt they'll come looking for them. If they've not already done so, they'll soon head back to deliver their slaves to whoever hired them. If things were different I would happily hunt them down and show them what happens to men who raid our country and violate our women. Unfortunately, there are bigger things to worry about. When the Delarites invade, the king will need me even if he doesn't know it yet, so I can't afford to go chasing bandits halfway across the known world."

"Did you just have the good fortune to run into these men or is there more to it?" asked Arlen.

"I've been tracking them for a while now, hoping to run into a cavalry patrol to help me confront them, but I haven't seen one. I lost track of them a couple of days ago and these pathfinders were the first contact I've had with them since. It was foolish of me to confront them the way I did; I knew full well that their pathfinders always work in groups of four, yet still I went charging in," said Ro.

"It is as well that I was passing by then," said Arlen smiling.

Ro nodded returning the smile. "That it was. But tell me, Arlen, what is a priest of the Golden Tree doing 'just passing by' so far from Silevia?" Ro enjoyed the brief look of surprise that flickered across Arlen's face.

"How did you know?" asked Arlen grinning.

"Lucky guess."

Arlen stared back and raised an eyebrow in a silent quest for the truth.

"It is rare that one comes across a priest who is proficient with a crossbow and who also carries a sword," replied Ro nodding towards the sword hilt which was protruding out from under Arlen's cape. "These are not the normal tools of a priest's trade, not even in these troubled times, unless of course he is a member of the fabled Order of Goresh, warrior priests from the land of Silevia."

Arlen gave a small chuckle. "Forgive me I am guilty as charged. I think that we might well become friends after all. Arlen Meric from the House of Lindar, Second Priest of the Golden Tree and a general pain in the backside to the whole Order of Goresh, at your service." Arlen gave a small bow.

"Something tells me, Second Priest of the Golden Tree, that your own journey here is not without incident and I look forward to hearing about it. However, as the rest of this raiding party may already be on their way here, I suggest that we move on."

Nearby a lone wolf howled its pitiful cry and was soon answered by more than a dozen others. Ro stared in the direction from which the howls had originated, but was unable to see the wolves in the dense forest which surrounded them.

"The sooner the better I think."

"Couldn't we stay and eat first; I'm starving and what's left of your roast looks most appetising?" asked Arlen.

Ro pointedly looked at Arlen's ample girth. "I suspect that you are many things, Arlen, but starving isn't one of them. By all means help yourself to whatever these men left, but eat it on the move. If you don't I fear you might soon be sharing it with our Narmidian friends unless the wolves get here first."

"I thought you said that they wouldn't come looking for their missing scouts?"

"No, I said they probably wouldn't; there's a difference. Do you really want to take that risk just to calm your rumbling stomach?"

"Perhaps I'll eat on the move as you suggest," replied Arlen grinning.

"Very wise. Narmidian raiding parties are usually about fifty strong and even allowing for the fact that they've almost certainly lost men during the various raids they've carried out, I would guess there would still be about thirty or so left."

"Then I definitely agree we should be on our way. Neither the Narmidians nor the wolves strike me as good dining companions," said Arlen. He strode over and helped himself to a large strip of what was now overdone meat from the spit, before dousing the fire with water.

Ro walked over to the body of the first man he had slain and tugged the *Jemtak* free of the dead man's head before wiping its points clean on the man's cloak. A groaning from his right startled him and he spun round swiftly drawing his sword as he did so. Arlen was quickly by his side, his own sword free of its scabbard. Laying a few paces away and slowly coming to, was the man Ro had knocked unconscious with his sword hilt.

"Mmm, I'd forgotten about him in all the excitement," said Ro matter-of-factly.

"Do you want me to send him on his way to the afterlife?" asked Arlen resting his sword on his right shoulder.

Ro looked at Arlen, surprised that a priest, even a priest of the Golden Tree, was willing to kill someone in cold blood. "No, I want to question him."

"As you wish," replied Arlen. "But make it quick."

Ro knelt down and grabbed the now conscious but still badly dazed man by the scruff of his tunic, pulling his face towards his own.

"Where are your friends taking the women you have abducted?" The man just stared blankly back at him. Ro gave him a violent shake, the movement causing the man to wince from the sharp pain that shot through his head from the earlier blow. "I asked you where your friends were taking the women – now tell me."

"Why should I?" the man spat back. "You're going to kill me anyway."

"Maybe, maybe not," replied Ro.

"I wouldn't be too worried about that if I were you," said Arlen leaning over the man. "If I were you I'd be more worried about the method of my passing to the Underworld." He smiled menacingly as he toyed with a small but vicious looking knife he had taken out from under his cloak. The raider looked worried for the first time.

"I'd listen to him if I were you, friend. He's a priest of the Golden Tree and all the stories you've ever heard about their cruelty and expertise at inflicting pain, are true," said Ro taking his cue from Arlen and disguising his own surprise.

The Cardellan swallowed hard, glancing from Ro, to the knife and back again. The Silevians were despised by his people, yet also feared. He was indeed aware of the many tales of Silevian cruelty and it was the main reason that Silevia had never been invaded. No one wanted to risk being captured and skinned alive by the Silevian priests. What his people didn't know was that the tales were perpetuated by the Silevians themselves to deter their larger and more powerful neighbours from thoughts of invasion. Silevia was a beautiful country, rich in raw materials and many nations cast envious eyes in her direction.

"It's time to talk," said Ro. The Cardellan stared back at him, trying to gauge whether he was bluffing. "He's all yours, Arlen," said Ro getting up and walking slowly away.

"Excellent," replied Arlen smiling. "We are running short of so many body parts to experiment upon. The High Priest will be very pleased and I shall be well rewarded for what I do here." He knelt down beside the Cardellan and grabbed his left ear, the serrated knife perilously close behind it.

The Cardellan visibly paled. "No, wait, please, I'll tell you."

Ro stopped and turned around. "How do I know that what you tell me is the truth and not just what you think I want to hear in an effort to save your pathetic life?"

"I swear that what I tell you will be the truth," the Cardellan replied wincing as Arlen twisted his ear painfully.

"I don't believe you, sorry. Cut away, Arlen," said Ro.

The Cardellan screamed as he felt the cold steel touch the sensitive back of his ear. "They're taking the women to Martak in Narmidia to sell them as slaves, I swear it."

Ro held his hand up as if instructing Arlen to wait. "Martak, are you sure?"

"Positive," replied the Cardellan, his eyes wide with terror. "A rich merchant with a taste for your skinny western women hired us to obtain some for his amusement."

"How do you get your slaves through Salandor?" asked Arlen.

"We pay the local tribal leader a toll and he lets us pass through his territory. If we don't touch their villages, they turn a blind eye to what we're doing."

"Salandori dogs! I've never cared for them very much," said Arlen.

"They're a divided nation, Arlen and probably don't feel strong enough to stand up to the Narmidians and Cardellans. If they were to invade they'd pick them off one tribe at a time," said Ro.

"You understand the situation well, my friend," said the Cardellan regaining some of his composure.

"I'm not your friend and if I ever find out that you're lying, I will come after you and let my friend here harvest whatever parts he wants from your worthless body," said Ro icily. "Let him go, Arlen."

"Are you sure? I was getting rather attached to this ear." He gave it a vicious yank to prove his point, before letting the man up.

The Cardellan made for his horse, but Ro stepped in his way. "Uh, uh, you're walking."

"Have mercy. It will take me months to walk back to Cardella," pleaded the man.

"Better get started then," smiled Arlen.

"Cardella's that way," said Ro pointing. "I'd be grateful I still had legs upon which to walk if I were you."

The man turned from Ro and stared at the Silevian for as long as he dared and then after spitting on the ground, stormed off into the forest, the laughter of the two men mocking him as he went.

"Was it wise to let him leave, Ro? What if he finds the others and brings them back looking for us?"

"I don't think that there's much chance of that, Arlen. Even if he does manage to run into them, they're unlikely to want to risk running into a rescue party just for the sake of avenging one man's pride. Narmidians are too selfish."

"Do you think there are some then, rescue parties I mean?" asked Arlen.

"I'd like to think there are still men of honour in this land. I know that if my wife or daughter was taken I'd want to go after them."

Arlen nodded his agreement. "To where do we head then?"

"I'm heading north, but there is no need for you to accompany me; the assassins are not after you."

"True. But as I don't fancy running into thirty angry Narmidians on my own, I think that I'll come along if it's all the same to you. Besides, how will you be able to repay your debt if you're nowhere near me when I do need help?" asked Arlen.

"I thought you weren't bothered about me repaying that debt?" replied Ro.

"Ah, well, let's just say I'm getting used to the idea of having a personal bodyguard. You never know when that might come in handy." Arlen was beaming and Ro couldn't help but like the jovial priest from the land of Silevia.

"Very well then let's make haste. Do you ride?" asked Ro.

"Yes, badly and infrequently. It is not something for which I have great affection."

"I think that you'd better try and overcome your prejudice, my friend, because if we do run into trouble, it will be the quickest way for us to escape."

"As you wish," replied Arlen reluctantly.

After finding where the raiders had hidden their horses, Ro selected three and set the fourth one loose.

"Why do you take three horses?" asked Arlen.

"One for you and two spares. If one or more of our horses tires or goes lame, we can simply swap over." Ro took the extra horses by the reins and headed north.

After a last look round, Arlen grabbed the reins to the remaining horse and followed Ro out, unable to shake the feeling that he was being watched.

Behind them the bravest of the wolf pack began to tentatively scurry into the camp, the smell of recently killed meat enticing them beyond their timidity. Ro and Arlen were barely out of sight when the first wolf sank its teeth into the leg of one of the dead raiders.

Chapter 5

"They should have been back by now, Kern, what do you want to do?" asked Beren glancing nervously between his leader and the track leading westwards from which their pathfinders should have emerged hours ago.

Kern's gaze focussed on a point several hundred paces down the narrow dirt track as if willing the missing men to reappear on his command. It was a hot day and a bead of sweat meandered down his cheek before eventually dropping from his face onto the ground below. "We'll give them five more minutes and then we go."

Beren looked at his leader incredulously. "Go? Have you taken leave of your senses in this accursed heat? One of the pathfinders is Arif, nephew of the Sultan of the Eastern peoples. It will not sit well with him if we return without his beloved nephew. It is bad enough that we let him scar his face during a fight, but to leave him behind will be unforgiveable to the Sultan."

"What does it matter, if he's dead?"

"You don't know that, Kern. They could just be down the track for all you know."

"No, I don't know that for certain, but what would you have me do; wait here until we're found by a passing Remadan cavalry patrol or worse still a whole column of Remadan soldiers? If we remain here much longer that is what is going to happen and I for one don't fancy explaining why we have a score of their womenfolk tied to our horses and are heading east."

"But the Sultan?"

"The Sultan will be told that his nephew died a hero killing many of the enemy in the process," said Kern.

"And if he turns up later looking fit and well after we've told the Sultan that he's dead, then what?"

"Then we'll proclaim it as a miracle," said Kern smiling.

Beren shook his head in dismay at his leader's lack of concern for the Sultan's reaction and then decided to try a different tact. "What if one of the men should say something when they've had too much wine?"

"Then they would face the same fate as us. The Sultan will not trouble himself with trifling details like who was responsible and who just happened to be there; we will all die the same agonising death no doubt, the men know that. Besides, there will be more than enough coin for everyone to guarantee their silence. Now go and get them on their feet and ready to move; your constant fretting starts to weary me."

With a last wishful glance down the empty dirt track, Beren turned and made his way over to the small group of men who sat watching their female prisoners, some out of duty and some with more lustful intent. After barking out a few orders, the men were soon mounted on their horses, the Remadan women tied together by rope forming a long line between the front and rear riders.

Kern mounted his horse and turning from the dirt track, dismissed all thoughts of the Sultan's nephew from memory. He rode slowly up the line of prisoners staring intently at each one as he passed. Most looked down rather than meet his gaze, but one had enough backbone to meet his gaze head-on. Kern stopped his horse and glared down at the girl who he estimated to be no more than fifteen or sixteen summers old. Her counter stare never wavered under his scrutiny and he secretly admired her courage. He liked women with spirit and this one looked like she would provide a challenge. Maybe he'd keep her for himself. She would make a worthy addition to the House of Razak.

"What is your name, girl?" he asked his eyes never leaving hers.

"Keira," the girl replied.

"Keira. That is a pretty name. A pretty name for a pretty girl."

"Enjoy it, because it's all you're going to get off me, you Narmidian pig."

Beren who had been sat just a few paces away awaiting his leader's instructions to move out, jumped off his horse and raced over to where Keira stood, his whip raised to strike her.

"Hold," shouted Kern.

Beren glanced at his leader and then back at Keira clearly fighting the urge to disobey his leader and give the insolent Remadan girl a couple of lashes.

"Do as I say, Beren and leave her. Besides, how many times have I got to tell you not to use the whip on the pretty ones as it lowers their worth? Use it on the old and ugly by all means as they are already damaged, but not the young and pretty. Especially this one. I have plans for her."

"As you wish, Kern," replied Beren with one last venomous look at Keira. He started to back away towards his horse and Keira blew him a kiss. Beren stopped desperate to go over and teach the girl some manners Narmidian style, but decided that he'd wait. Kern wouldn't always be around and then she'd get what was coming to her.

"Let's move out, my brothers. I want to be out of this decaying country as soon as possible and into Salandor. The sooner we are home the sooner you will be able to spend your coin in your favourite whorehouse, or if you are really unlucky, the sooner you'll be home with your wives." His men laughed heartily, pleased to be on their way again. Each was acutely aware of just how precarious their position was, so far from home and so few in number.

The temperature steadily rose throughout the day and with no wind to cool them, the girls had become increasingly weary and thirsty as the day wore on. They had only stopped once during the journey when the afternoon sun had been at its zenith, but after that they had pushed on until the order had finally been given to make evening camp. Released from their guide rope so that just their hands were bound, the girls had collapsed almost too tired to eat the scraps of meat and stale bread their guards threw to them.

Believing the girls to be too exhausted and too frightened to contemplate escape, Kern had posted just three guards that night. He was more concerned about being taken unawares by Remadan soldiers than he was of the girls escaping and the sentries had therefore been instructed to listen out for the sound of approaching horses.

It was a little after midnight when Keira woke. She wasn't sure what had woken her, but her keen senses told her that something wasn't right. She lay still, silently listening to the sounds of the night around her. A horse whinnied quietly in its sleep and somewhere in the distance an owl hooted as it watched the ground for prey. Something definitely wasn't right, she could feel it. Every one of the girls was constantly in fear of being raped and Keira braced herself ready to lash out should she feel the rough hands of a Narmidian suddenly clamp her mouth. Tayla and the others kept warning her to stop provoking the guards and to be a little more submissive, but she could never be that way. That wasn't how her father or Kam Martel had raised her to be.

A movement to her left caught her eye as one of the girls, she couldn't see who, slowly rose to a crouched position. Nearby, another girl who Keira recognised as Esther, followed suit. After quickly checking that none of the sentries were looking their way, their attention focussed elsewhere, both girls stood and silently ran for the nearby trees. A few seconds later they were followed by a third girl. In front of Keira, Tayla began to rise, but Keira rolled over and dragged her back down to the ground.

"Let me go, Keira," hissed Tayla.

"No, Tayla, stay where you are."

Tayla began to struggle against the other girl's grasp, but she was too strong for her. "Please, Keira, let me go, I can't take it anymore; I'm so frightened."

Despite the poor light afforded by the moon, Keira could see that Tayla was near to tears. She reached over and did the best she could to hug her. "I know you are, Tayla, we all are."

"You're not," whispered Tayla defiantly.

"What you think because I stand up to them that I'm not scared? I'm petrified, but it's the only way I know how to deal with this."

"Then come with me, now, let's run," implored Tayla, as she longingly looked in the direction the three other girls had run.

Keira shook her head slowly. "They'll never make it. They don't know where they are, how to get home or who's a friend and who's a foe. They'll be other opportunities for escape, better ones."

Even as she tried to convince Tayla a shout went up from one of the perimeter guards as he caught a fleeting glimpse of the third girl just ducking into the cover of the trees.

"See they're already missed," said Keira.

"But surely now that they've made it to the trees they are safe?" asked Tayla.

"I wish it were so, but it isn't. With no light and such a short head start, unless they're very lucky they'll be caught within minutes."

"Merith wasn't meant to go. It was just supposed to be Naomi and Esther. She must have overheard them planning their escape."

"You knew that they were going to try and run tonight?" asked Keira.

"Yes, I asked if I could go, but they said that it would be too many and that I had to plan my own escape. When they ran I just thought that I'd take my chance and go after them. There wouldn't have been much they could do about it then."

"If Merith hadn't had the same thought as you, they might have made it, but by following them a few seconds later she's put all their lives in danger," said Keira.

Around the girls, the camp was a flurry of activity as Kern ordered some of his men to stand guard over the remaining captives whilst he sent the others out in pursuit of the runners. He stalked up and down in front of the girls who remained and Keira very wisely chose not to meet his gaze this time.

It was not long before Merith was dragged unceremoniously back into the camp, kicking and screaming, before being dumped at Kern's feet where she curled up into a ball sobbing.

"Any sign of the others?" Kern snarled at one of the men who had dragged the girl back.

"We've got one of them and Talik's on his way back with her and we know where the other one is headed. It's only a matter of time," replied the raider.

"It had better be," replied Kern staring menacingly at the man who had been one of the three he had left on sentry duty. His expression and tone suggested that the matter was not closed. Swallowing nervously, the guard hurried back out into the woods to help his comrades in the hunt for the remaining girl. It was not wise to displease Kern.

Merith was crying for all she was worth now, huge wracking sobs that reverberated around the silent camp.

"Silence, girl, or I swear I will cut off your head."

Merith looked up at the Narmidian leader with bloodshot eyes and tried to stifle her sobs, but such was the level of her despair that she was unable to cut them off completely.

"I said silence," shouted Kern as he cuffed the girl with the back of his hand sending her sprawling to the ground. He was just considering administering a quick kick for good measure when the sound of people approaching from the woods caught his attention. He looked up to see his men dragging one girl back to camp, whilst Bolic, a mountain of a man, carried the other one under his arm. The girl wriggled and kicked furiously, but was never going to be able to free herself from Bolic's grip. The girls were dropped to the ground next to Merith.

Kern stood studying them for a minute. There was always someone who tried to escape but if he'd been a gambling man he would have wagered his money on the defiant one, the one called Keira, being the one to run. Surprisingly she had shown good sense and remained in the camp. She was evidently intelligent as well as attractive and feisty. His desire for her was increasing.

"What shall we do with them, Kern?" asked Beren.

It was a good question. He couldn't let their actions go unanswered yet any punishment visited upon them would surely leave a mark and consequently devalue them. Still he had to make an example to dissuade any of the others from trying something similar.

"I have tried to be reasonable with you and have restrained my men and you reward me by running away in the middle of the night. This is unacceptable. What do I have to do, build cages to keep you in?" The question had been rhetorical. "Whose idea was it?" No one answered. "I said whose idea was it?" Again nobody answered. Kern grabbed Merith by the hair and yanked her head back exposing her throat. Slowly and deliberately he withdrew a small dagger and held the blade to her throat menacingly.

"Mine, it was my idea," said Naomi looking up and meeting Kern's stare with tear-stained eyes.

"Then watch and remember the cost of your foolishness," said Kern as he quickly sliced his knife across Merith's throat killing her instantly.

Some of the watching girls started to wail and scream in terror until Kern roared at them to shut up lest they wanted to meet the same fate. For all he knew there could be a Remadan or Delarite army camp nearby and he didn't want to attract any unwanted attention.

"Now I didn't want to do that, but you forced me. Her death has cost me a lot of money so I warn you now against any more foolish escape attempts because the next one to try it will not die so painlessly I assure you. Now get some sleep, we leave at the break of dawn," said Kern as he bent down to wipe his dagger clean on the folds of Merith's dress.

***

Those who managed to get some sleep were woken at first light and after allowing them a few minutes to eat some bread and cheese, they were soon heading east again towards the lands of the Salandori. The guards had made no attempt to bury Merith's body and instead merely tipped it into a nearby ditch where it would soon fall foul of any passing wolves and scavengers.

It was not until mid-morning that Kern gave the order to stop for a few minutes and the girls collapsed to the ground as a jug of water was passed down the line under the watchful eyes of the guards.

"If the guards see you do that, they're going to kill you for sure," Keira said to Tayla as she passed her the jug.

Tayla drank greedily before passing it on to the next girl in the line. "If they see me do what?" replied Tayla suspiciously.

"You know what, leaving little bits of your dress on the trail; I've been watching you and if I've noticed, it won't be too long before one of them does. Why are you doing it?"

"So that the rescue party knows which way to go of course," replied Tayla as if the answer was obvious.

"They don't need your little bits of rag for that; they can just follow the trail of bodies."

"That's not funny, Keira." Tayla quickly looked away and closed her eyes as a guard walked by and eyed the two girls suspiciously. When he moved on Keira spoke again.

"It wasn't meant to be, Tayla. I'm not joking. If they see what you're doing they'll kill you – or someone else. Besides, who do you think is going to come after us?"

"The men of the village of course."

"Maybe, but I heard the men talking about a war with Delarite coming. If that's true all the men will have to join the king's army. He won't spare any men to go after a handful of women. We're on our own I'm afraid," said Keira.

Tayla looked crestfallen. "Maybe that's true, but my fiancée will come after me."

"Your what?" asked Keira incredulously.

"My fiancée."

"I didn't know you were betrothed, Tayla. Who's the boy?"

Tayla seemed to blush and couldn't meet Keira's eyes for a few seconds. "Eryn, your brother."

"I know who Eryn is, Tayla, but what's he have to do with all of this?"

"Eryn is my fiancée," replied Tayla.

"On your feet, it's time to move on," shouted Kern as the girls were manhandled to their feet.

Keira, however, continued to stare at Tayla open-mouthed.

When Tayla turned briefly to face her, Keira mouthed the word "Eryn" and her friend nodded smiling at Keira's surprised expression.

Before Keira could say any more, however, the column was once again on the move.

The journey was long and slow, the column only able to move at the speed of the slowest girl and Kern constantly fretted about running into a Remadan patrol. Whilst he had no qualms about his men being able to deal with such an eventuality, there would inevitably be casualties and he could ill-afford to lose any more men. He was more concerned that any patrol they destroyed would soon be missed and that a larger force would be sent out to investigate. Then if the rumours were true about an impending Delarite invasion, there were their patrols to consider. He had no idea how the Delarites would react if they ran into his column; they might just wave them on or they might slaughter everyone, there was no way of knowing. No their best chance was to try and avoid everyone, which meant taking country routes and bypassing all towns and villages. It was going to put more time on their journey, but would be the safer option, he hoped.

Twice during the afternoon they had to take cover at the sound of approaching hooves. The first time had been a Remadan messenger racing past for all he was worth whilst the second had been a small patrol of Remadan cavalry being pursued by a much larger force of Delarites. The war it seemed had begun. Kern had no idea what happened to the men that were being chased nor did he care. All that mattered was that they hadn't noticed him or his party.

It was inevitable that as they travelled farther east towards the Salandori border, that they would run into more patrols. Any invading army from the north was sure to come that way as it was the quickest route to the Remadan capital and bypassed the huge Forest of Palithir. As a consequence, his men would have to be increasingly vigilant and the distance they could cover each day would surely dwindle. With a growing sense of unease he urged his men on.

Chapter 6

Radek Templar stared out of the guest room window at the rolling meadow, the Forest of Garn and far beyond that, the Mountains of Kontaka, over which some dark clouds were now gathering.

There's a storm coming, thought Radek, though he couldn't shake the feeling that the clouds were an ill omen for something far worse than a summer storm.

Far beyond the Kontaka Mountains, lay the open plains that ran the length of the border between Remada and Delarite. Radek closed his eyes for a moment and wished he was crossing the plains back to Remada. It was a vast stretch of land that had been fought over many times, ownership often passing to the victors. It was a land filled with a plentiful supply of game and also contained the life-bringing, River Tilus, though the Delarites called it by another name which he didn't care to recall.

Radek shivered and pulled his heavy cloak tight about his shoulders. It was a warm summer's day outside as it had been for some days now, but Radek had not been able to keep himself warm since the day he arrived at the Grand Palace. It was as if the whole place was covered in a cold malice that pervaded your bones and perhaps even your very soul.

Grand Palace, that's a joke, thought Radek as he lowered his gaze to look at his immediate surroundings. Once the Grand Palace had been just that; grand and majestic, but now it was largely neglected and deteriorating. Yes its battlements and fortifications were still formidable perhaps even impenetrable, but everything inside was going to ruin, or at least the bits he had been permitted to see. It was a grey and drab place full of grey and drab people and Radek Templar could not wait to leave, though that could not be until the conclusion of his business there.

As King Taylen's chief envoy, he had been involved in many negotiations over the years, several of them in that very palace, but none had ever been as difficult and protracted as

68

this one. First the Delarite king had kept him waiting for the better part of two days before he even deigned to see him, blaming the delay on unavoidable urgent matters of state. Then when he did eventually agree to see him, instead of listening to what Radek had to say, he had immediately launched into a tirade of lies and false accusations against Remada. He had then stormed out of the chambers leaving Radek red-faced and confused.

Radek knew that King Herat was not an idiot and realised that he had done these things as a political insult to Remada's chief envoy and therefore by association, to her king. Later that day the Delarite king had again summoned Radek, this time welcoming him like an old friend and didn't even mention let alone apologise for his behaviour at their earlier meeting. More mind games, Radek realised.

The king had politely listened to Radek's greetings on behalf of his king and then sat patiently as Radek made an impassioned plea for peace to prevail between their two great nations. King Herat had then thanked Radek for the gold and silver that he had brought with him as gifts, but which were ostensibly bribes to dissuade Herat from waging war on Remada. He had then dismissed Radek and said that he would consider everything he had heard and would summon him back to court when he had completed his deliberations. Radek now stood shivering in his chamber awaiting that summons.

He watched some of Herat's soldiers drilling in the courtyard below and replayed the conversations with the king over and over in his head. Had he done enough to avert war? He certainly hoped that he had. Remada was in no fit state to fight a war, nor would she be in all likelihood for many years to come.

The new monarch, King Viktus had turned out to be a huge disappointment and had let his country go to wrack and ruin. The only difference between what Viktus had done and what the tyrant upon whose summons Radek now waited had done was that Herat had deliberately neglected his country whilst building up his armies. By contrast, King Viktus had let his country deteriorate through sheer disinterest and detachment preferring instead to spend his country's treasury on lavish balls, hunts and now bribes. The inevitable result of this folly was that Remada was now weak and at the potential mercy of some of her stronger neighbours. Remada was like a sheep surrounded by wolves and the wolves were closing in. So weak was she now that she couldn't prevent Narmidian raiders from carrying out almost daily incursions across her borders, killing, raping and abducting her people.

Radek shuddered at the indignity and shame of it all. This would never have happened if King Taylen had still been on the throne. No, if that had been the case he would have been delivering an entirely different message to this madman. Sadly, King Taylen was never coming back and nor were Radek's old friends Kam Martel and Teren Rad. When the three of them had been together supporting King Taylen, Remada had been strong, fair and just. But the king was dead, Martel had been forcefully retired and as for Rad, nobody knew where he was for certain or whether he was even alive. His guilt and personal grief had broken the man and now he was either dead or living out his life in isolation.

Now the young king was advised by mere pups with no experience of war or peace, wet behind the ear fops who said whatever the king wanted to hear. Radek had only held onto his post because the former king's will had insisted that his son retained his services for five years upon succession to the throne, of which this was the first. It was like going through the motions though. The king would pretend to listen to his advice and then dismiss it, usually accepting the ill advice of one of his sycophants in its stead.

When the head of the second emissary sent to Herat's court by King Viktus came back absent a body, Radek noticed that none of the king's advisers volunteered to be the next to try. Instead, encouraged by the king's chief snake, Livic Pendar, they suddenly decided that this was a job for a man with a wealth of diplomatic experience and had all suggested Radek represent Remada. King Viktus had readily agreed, seeing this as a situation in which he could not lose. If the old fool succeeded in preventing war between Remada and Delarite, the king would be hailed as a hero by his people. If he failed and the Delarites killed him, he would finally be free of the dinosaur his father had saddled him with. As for the Delarites, he would just continue sending gold and silver to try and buy peace. Radek had seen the cunning in the king's plan but was powerless to do anything about it. King Viktus was still his king and regardless of his dislike of the man, Radek was determined to do his duty as he had for over thirty years.

At first King Viktus had chosen to pretend that there was no threat from Delarite and had done nothing. It had been Ro Aryk, captain of the Royal Bodyguard who had finally persuaded the king to send someone to the Delarites, but Viktus had not heeded his advice. Instead of sending a message to Herat that would convey Remada's strength and willingness to fight, he had decided to try and appease the tyrant. Radek and Aryk had protested saying that the message would only serve to demonstrate Remada's weakness and invite aggression. For their troubles Aryk had been dismissed from service and now had Tulan assassins hunting him, whilst Radek had been sent on a fool's errand.

Oh, well, thought Radek, *perhaps they will not kill me. After all, I am the king's chief envoy and I'm well respected throughout the lands of the west. My friend's are many and my death would not be well received in some quarters.* It was a forlorn hope he knew, but it gave him something to cling to whilst he waited.

A sharp rap on the thick wooden door disturbed Radek's thoughts and he absent-mindedly invited the knocker to enter. "Come."

A huge man wearing the uniform of King Herat's bodyguards stepped through the door and smiled at him. It was not a smile that Radek found very warm or sincere.

"King Herat requests your presence immediately."

Radek issued a short nod and after quickly glancing around his chamber, walked out past the guard and started down the corridor which he knew led to the king's court room. The sullen guard followed him out and down the corridor never more than a few feet behind the envoy.

As he walked, Radek tried to yet again consider all of the king's possible answers and what response would be appropriate in each circumstance. Eventually he decided to just let it play out. There was no point trying to second guess Herat's next move as the man was an enigma, completely unpredictable and quite irrational. No, he would have to think on his feet. He had plenty of experience of this and had faith in his own ability. What he didn't have faith in was Herat's ability to see reason and commonsense when it was staring him in the face.

Maybe I can enlist Princess Cala's assistance if things don't go well, thought Radek.

The great double doors that led to the courtroom were in sight now and either side of them stood two equally large and brutish looking guards. Standing nervously and somewhat conspicuously to the right of the doors, were the two Remadan soldiers who had been sent as an escort for Radek.

Radek's mind returned back to Princess Cala. He had yet to fathom out her role in all of this. He knew of course that Herat wished to marry the princess, but he doubted it was just for her stunning beauty though that would have been more than enough for most mortal men. No, Herat clearly had another reason; an alliance probably, but what was in it for her country? He was still contemplating that point when the guards swung open the huge doors revealing the bright and crowded courtroom beyond.

Radek stole a quick glance at the two Remadan soldiers that had been sent to accompany him to Delarite and noticed that they both looked pale and anxious. He smiled at the soldiers in what was probably a futile attempt to reassure them, then after taking a deep breath, he walked assuredly into the king's courtroom with his head held high, his two escorts falling in behind him.

The courtroom was crowded and Radek could feel dozens of pairs of eyes boring into him as he made his way at a respectful pace towards King Herat. It was eerily silent in the courtroom except for the footfalls of the Remadan soldiers behind him and the four Delarite guards who now marched just behind them. Radek stopped half a dozen paces in front of the throne, bowed to an acceptable level and then waited silently to be addressed.

Herat stared at the envoy for a few seconds, clearly trying to intimidate the older man, but Radek had seen it all before and was well above such simple and futile mind games. Instead he just stood there patiently waiting until finally the king spoke.

"I have considered everything you said earlier today, envoy and I have also consulted the auguries," he began. "Whilst Delarite is keen to maintain the peace that currently exists between our two nations, I cannot allow this slight to go unpunished. To avoid conflict between us and to maintain honour, Delarite demands that Remada cedes the area between the existing border and the White River with immediate effect."

Radek tried to disguise his shock at the demands the king had just made without any prior discussion of the matter.

"To what slight do you refer, majesty, because if Remada has caused any offence to the House of Herat, I can assure you that it was unintentional and that I will do everything in my power to redress the matter?" asked Radek.

"I refer to the constant incursions over our borders by Remadan soldiers, who are attacking and destroying our villages in the area. This is a clear provocation which cannot and will not go unanswered," replied the king.

"I know of no such raids, your majesty and certainly none authorised by my king. However, we are also being raided on an almost daily basis by bands of Narmidian slavers and perhaps your nation is suffering the same blight but from the Datians to your north masquerading as Remadans."

Herat smashed his fist into the arm of his throne and leant forward gritting his teeth.

"Are you calling me a liar, envoy?" Around the hall, Radek heard the hiss of swords being withdrawn from their scabbards as men loyal to Herat prepared to protect their king's honour. Herat had sprung his trap. Radek did not turn but sensed that his two escorts also had their hands on their sword hilts. He prayed that they would have the good sense to leave their swords in their scabbards. To do otherwise in a king's court, particularly this king's, was to invite certain death. Radek had to play this one carefully, as their lives may very well depend on his next words.

"I meant no offence, majesty," he said bowing slightly. "I was more concerned that perhaps those advising you had not investigated the matter properly. If you say that these men are Remadan, then I am of course willing to accept your good word on the matter and when I return to King Viktus's court, I will arrange for these brigands to be hunted down and punished accordingly. I am sure that my king would be more than happy to compensate you for the losses your people have suffered."

"Yes, he will, by ceding to me the territory between our border and the White River."

"As I said, your majesty, I am sure that King Viktus will be happy to compensate you for any losses incurred, but that land is the bread basket of Remada as I'm sure you are aware and without it, a large portion of our people will go hungry. Remada cannot afford to lose such land, as I'm sure your majesty understands."

"Can Remada afford to make an enemy of Delarite?" asked Herat.

"Remada has no desire to make an enemy of anyone, your majesty but neither can we let our people starve. Perhaps there is something else you desire from Remada? I am authorised to sanction almost anything on behalf of my king."

"Then sign this," said Herat as one of his aides rushed forward and handed Radek a scroll and quill.

A premeditated trap indeed thought Templar as he took the scroll and began reading. Sighing he rolled the scroll up and looked at Herat. "I am sorry, your majesty, but whilst I am authorised to make concessions on behalf of my king in the interests of continuing peace, I cannot sign a document that will in effect condemn up to a quarter of our people to starvation. There must be something else which your majesty desires?"

The king was smiling but it wasn't a pleasant smile. It was the smile of a man who had his prey well and truly cornered and knew it. Radek found himself wondering if this was how a sheep felt when surrounded by a pack of wolves.

The king was about to speak when the large doors at the back of the court swung noisily open. Trying to maintain his poise yet grateful for the brief distraction, Radek turned slowly to see who had joined their audience. A large and truly fearsome looking soldier wearing the blue cloak of the Gremlin Corps, Delarite's most feared army, marched urgently through the hall towards where the king sat. After giving the three Remadans a disdainful sideways glance, he briefly knelt in front of King Herat before rising to whisper something in his king's ear. Radek, who had been watching the hushed discussion closely, noticed dried blood splattered up the soldier's cloak. He was also holding something in a cloth sack by his left side.

The king nodded, his gaze returning to the Remadan envoy standing in front of him. The Delarite soldier took up a position to the right of his king, his expression unreadable.

"Friends," said King Herat standing and addressing the audience at large.

For the first time since he had been summoned back to the court, Radek caught a glimpse of Princess Cala standing in the throng to his left. She looked worried he noticed an expression which did not sit well on such a pretty face. She caught the envoy looking towards her and smiled sweetly back at him, though it did nothing to hide the concerned look in her eyes.

"General Malik brings us great news," continued Herat. His gaze swept those in his hall, intent on making sure he had everyone's full attention. "The Remadan city of Pirus has fallen to our Third Army; the war has begun."

A great cheer resounded off the stone walls of the court whilst Radek stared at the king in horror. As the cheers died down, he took a step forward and addressed the king.

"Whilst I stood here talking peace with you, your army has started a war with your full knowledge?" The question had been rhetorical but Herat chose to answer anyway.

"For too long Remada has seen fit to dictate terms to the nations of the west, but now you are weak and vulnerable. The time has finally come to free ourselves of the Remadan yoke once and for all." He turned and nodded to General Malik who reached into the cloth sack he had been carrying and tossed its contents onto the floor in front of Radek.

Radek looked down at the thing that had come to rest on the floor just in front of him and had to swallow hard to prevent the meagre contents of his stomach from resurfacing.

Staring up at him from wide lifeless eyes was the severed head of a man he knew very well.

"I'm sure, Remadan, that you recognise the face of Governor Hala. I understand he used to be in charge of Pirus. It seems he no longer deserves that title." Herat laughed an evil malevolent laugh that was copied by many within the court.

Radek's eyes were fixed on the head of the former Governor of Pirus and his ears barely registered the muffled sound of his two bodyguards being slaughtered behind him. By the time he had gathered his wits and looked round, both men were already laying dead on the cold courtroom floor.

His eyes wide with an indignant rage and acutely aware that his own life expectancy could probably now be measured in seconds, Radek spun round to face the king and was momentarily shocked to find him standing right in front of him.

"This is outrageous. How dare you murder men who accept your hospitality and visit you on a mission of peace? The whole of the southern continent will hear about this and the name Herat will become a byword for treachery," said Radek with more conviction than he actually felt.

"Yes, they probably will, but not from you I fear." Concealed within his right hand Herat held a small dagger, which he then proceeded to thrust in and out of Radek's abdomen several times before the envoy finally stumbled forward grabbing the king's cloak for support. Herat reached round and grabbed the hair at the back of Radek's head and yanked it hard, exposing the man's throat. In one expert movement he sliced his throat open, the gaping wound releasing a torrent of blood which poured down Radek's lifeless body. After wiping his dagger clean on the envoy's shoulder he shoved the man's body backwards with a look of disgust. "General Malik."

"Your majesty?" replied Malik coming smartly to attention by his king's side.

"Send word to all our armies. Let the invasion of Remada begin in earnest."

"Immediately, your majesty," said Malik as he turned to go.

"Oh, and General Malik, one more thing."

"Sire?"

"Well done."

"Thank you, sire. It was a great victory in your name and may we have many more."

"Indeed. Now go. Let's be at these Remadan dogs as soon as possible," said Herat.

Malik nodded curtly and marched off at a brisk pace to find messengers. War had come to the lands of the west and Malik was keen to be at the forefront of it. There was much glory to be had.

The king's closest adviser, Voltar, shuffled alongside Herat. Voltar was an old man, though nobody knew for sure quite how old he was, perhaps not even Voltar. He had served the House of Herat for many generations, as adviser and then seer, often predicting events many years before they came to fruition. Despite the old man's eccentric ways and his apparent abstinence from personal hygiene, the king often sought his counsel and advice. It had been Voltar who had alerted the king to Remada's weakness and encouraged him to wage war against them, but only after Herat had corroborated Voltar's claims through the use of spies. Still he was useful and the common people of Delarite feared him and his magical abilities. So too did Herat's remaining enemies within his realm. Although they were now few, they did still exist much to Herat's annoyance and it therefore made sense to Herat to keep Voltar around, at least for a little while longer.

Herat had smelled Voltar's approach long before he saw him.

"Speak," said Herat in a tone barely concealing his annoyance at the distraction.

"What about him, lord, will his murder not be looked on sourly by some of our neighbours?" said Voltar nodding towards the dead Remadan envoy.

"Why should it?" replied Herat.

"Radek Templar was a popular and well respected man, my lord, a man whose quick mind and way for words has averted many wars and saved many thousands of lives. Many feel that they owe their life to him."

"Enough to wage war against us?" asked Herat suddenly concerned. Delarite was strong enough to challenge Remada, but was not yet strong enough to wage a war on several fronts should some of the nearby nations side with Remada.

"Probably not, my lord, but there may be some who will do everything else in their power to thwart your plans short of declaring war on you."

"On us, Voltar. Whatever fate befalls me will most assuredly take you as well. You are hated even more than me," said Herat.

Voltar smiled revealing broken and rotten teeth, bowing slightly as he did so. The sight revolted Herat even more. "As you say your majesty."

"Do not concern yourself, Voltar. Our campaign in Remada will be swift and decisive; as foreseen in your vision was it not?"

"Indeed it was, your majesty, but there are always variables which can affect the final outcome one way or another. Even a seer cannot predict all of those."

"If I thought that was truly the case, Voltar, that your visions were half-baked and ill-conceived, I would have no further use for you, so take a care in what you say. Anyway, by the time any of the other states do decide to come to Remada's assistance, it will be too late. We will shock them with the speed of our victory and terrorise them into compliance with the ferocity of our rule. None will dare speak out against us much less take up arms out of fear of being the next to feel our wrath. Now go, your stench turns my stomach," said Herat turning his back on the seer.

Voltar bowed as low as his aged and bent spine would allow him and shuffled off into the shadows. Herat turned back and watched him go. The old man was fast becoming a source of great irritation to him and he would have to give some serious thought as to whether the old man's occasional correct prediction was enough to justify him staying alive. Herat hoped not and judging by the whispers and disgusted looks thrown Voltar's way by those who still remained in the courtroom, his passing would not be mourned. It was something he would have to think on.

Chapter 7

As he'd watched Voltar skulk away, Herat had caught sight of Princess Cala trying to surreptitiously sidle into the corridor.

"You are leaving us so soon, Princess Cala?"

Princess Cala froze as she felt all eyes look her way. As she slowly turned, she forced her most charming smile.

"I thought it best I now head back to Lydia to prepare our army, your majesty. Lydia will not want to miss out on her chance for glory."

"Indeed. Surely though there is no need for you to go yourself? Anyone is capable of bearing such a message. Your bodyguard, Letiri, for example," said Herat.

"Ordinarily, sire that would be true, but as you know Letiri is a mute and would be unable to answer any questions my men have. Besides, sire, as well as a princess I am also an officer in my father's army and as such my place is with my soldiers."

"That is a pity, Cala. I had hoped that we could be married within the week and could then take a tour of my new province of Remada as part of our honeymoon."

"That is truly appealing, sire, but there will be plenty of time for such indulgencies once the war is over. For now, my priority is to return home and mobilise our forces. Delarite cannot have all the glory." Cala smiled and her whole face seemed to light up.

Herat gazed on her beauty and wished that the words exchanged between them were sincere and not just a charade being played out. Herat had known for some time now that the princess had been sent to his court not as a prospective wife as he had hoped and initially believed, but as a spy. Lydia did not intend to join with Delarite in its conquest of Remada and was instead gathering intelligence whilst buying time to strengthen its own defences. However, Herat's spies had infiltrated the Lydian court and had sent word back to Herat warning him of their treachery. Far from being strong,

Lydia was in fact weak like Remada. Lydia had hoped to conceal her weakness from Delarite by pretending to be her ally, thereby dispelling any notions of invasion Herat might have been harbouring.

Herat smiled back at her. *Well now they were going to pay for their treachery.*

A few days previously and under the cover of darkness, Delarite's Fourth Army had crossed the border and entered Lydian territory. By now the conquest of their country was well and truly under way. Princess Cala was totally unaware of her country's fate and a close watch had been kept on her to ensure that no messengers reached her. Lydia and its princess would pay for their duplicity.

"Very well, Cala, ride back to your father and tell him to prepare for war. Delarite looks forward to having Lydia as a strong right arm." *An arm I shall sever most painfully.*

Cala bowed slightly and after allowing Herat to kiss her right hand, she turned and made for her chamber, closely followed by Letiri. Behind her, Herat beckoned a soldier over to him.

***

A little over an hour later, Cala and Letiri left Herat's palace and were riding as fast as their mounts would take them, towards Lydia and home. It was mid-morning and Cala hoped that with a couple of horse changes along the way, to arrive in Lydian territory sometime during the night. They had been riding for less than an hour when Letiri rode alongside Cala and signalled for her to stop.

"What is it, Letiri, we must keep going if we are to reach Lydia tonight?" said Cala, as much with her hands as with her mouth. Letiri was a deaf mute whom she had bought from a slave trader several years before after taking pity on his plight. She had immediately granted him his freedom and in gratitude he had intimated that he wished to serve Cala. Since then she and General Tain had trained him to be a warrior to such an extent that he was now a very capable fighter and Cala's trusted bodyguard.

Letiri pointed behind them and made a gesture with his hand that Cala knew meant riders. *So we're being followed?*

"How many, Letiri?" she asked with her hands.

The bodyguard held up four fingers.

"Herat's men?" her hands asked.

Letiri nodded.

Herat must have seen through our deception. I take it the wedding's off then? she mused to herself. "Then we shall stop here and prepare them a trap," said Cala already looking around for suitable hiding positions. When she turned to face Letiri it was clear that he hadn't understood everything she had said. She spoke slower the second time making more hand gestures to elaborate her instructions.

Letiri shook his head violently and signalled that he would take care of them alone and that she must ride on.

"No, Letiri, it is too dangerous, we must both face them."

The mute became very agitated and demonstrated with his hands that he insisted that she went on and that he would be okay. He gave her a flash of his enormous smile, his immaculately white teeth a deep contrast to his dark skin. Then as if to strengthen his point, he withdrew his huge curved sword.

Cala wasn't happy but it was evident that Letiri had made up his mind. He was not a slave she could command and although she could ignore him and stay anyway, to do so would antagonise him and could endanger them both. He was a fearsome warrior and she didn't doubt that with the element of surprise he could dispatch all four pursuers, but she still didn't like it.

"You be careful, Letiri and don't take any unnecessary risks, you understand? I shall be waiting for you further up the road."

Letiri signalled that he had understood but then intimated that she was not to wait for him, but to keep going. When he had killed their pursuers he would ride and catch up with her, but she was not to wait. Cala nodded, but had no intention of riding far ahead without him. She smiled, leant out of her saddle and planted a light kiss on the big man's forehead. Letiri rewarded her with another of his trademark grins making Cala giggle, as she always did when he flashed that winning smile. She watched him turn and gallop off back down the track towards the enemy and after uttering a small prayer to Sulat, turned and headed once more towards Lydia.

It was early afternoon by the time Cala had found herself a small ledge in some rocks to hide in and she was starting to get anxious. Had Letiri been successful against their pursuers then surely he would have been along by now as she hadn't ridden hard since leaving him.

Unless he took another route in case there were other eyes watching them?

It would not have surprised Cala in the slightest if Herat had sent two tracking parties after them; the man was as cautious as he was repulsive. She was still considering that thought when the sound of a horse galloping towards her caught her attention.

Just one. Letiri had been successful after all.

She was about to stand and call his name when she heard the sound of a second set of hooves converging on her position.

She toyed with the small bow she carried and quietly withdrew several arrows from the quiver slung over her back, just as two riders came into sight. They were Delarites and wore the blue cloak of Herat's beloved Gremlin Corps. Cala closed her eyes and prayed to Sulat that Letiri was still alive somewhere, perhaps only wounded, but her heart knew different. Still there were only two of them left now and one of those had a nasty looking leg wound which had been hastily bandaged.

Letiri did not die cheaply it would seem. I will avenge you my friend.

The two riders sat conversing for a while, clearly unsure what route Cala had taken. The wounded soldier was all for turning back but his comrade had warned him that to do so meant certain death. King Herat did not suffer failure well.

The wounded soldier nodded in reluctant acknowledgment and leant forward to tug his bandage tighter to try and stem the flow of blood. A gentle thudding noise caught his attention and he looked up just in time to see the arrow pierce his comrade's chest, before his body toppled from his horse. The riderless horse bolted and the wounded man's horse made to follow after briefly rearing up and it was all he could do to keep his balance. This had given Cala the time she needed to change positions. After jumping down from the ledge, she had run around to the opposite side of the rider, who by now had got his horse under control and had drawn his sword.

The soldier glanced at the ledge where he'd fleetingly caught sight of Cala and was alarmed to find that she had disappeared. He glanced round and found her standing a few paces off to his left with an arrow notched and pointing directly at his head. He locked eyes with the princess trying to gauge her resolve; his options he realised, were not limitless. Gritting his teeth he was preparing to charge at her when Cala spoke.

"Don't do it or you'll never see your family again."

"I wouldn't be so sure of that, princess," he replied, looking for any sign of hesitation in her face, anything that would give him an edge.

"Oh, I've never been so certain of anything in my life, trooper. Now you can either throw down your sword and ride back to Herat alive, or you can be really stupid and attack me. That way won't end so well for you. It's your call."

"Do you know what King Herat does to failures? He ties them spread-eagled to stakes and slices open their stomachs to entice the wolves and crows. It is an agonising and prolonged death and not one I wish to endure. For me, therefore, there is no choice. Unless you are prepared to throw down your bow and accompany me back to King Herat that is?"

"I'm afraid not. Do you believe in Sulat, trooper?" asked Cala.

"Of course." He automatically touched an amulet hanging around his neck.

"Good, because you're about to meet him."

The arrow pierced the man's exposed throat and he was dead long before his body hit the ground.

Cala looked at the fallen body and shook her head. Such a needless death and yet another one attributed to Herat's arrogance. She slung her bow over her back and ran to her horse which had been tethered out of sight around the corner. She wished that she could ride back up the track, find Letiri's body and give it an honourable burial, but to do so would expose her to unnecessary danger and delay her return. Letiri would have been the first to scold her for such a risky venture. Besides, time was against her and every hour spent searching for his body, was one less for the journey to Lydia.

Forgive me, my friend.

She nimbly climbed onto her horse and was about to head for home again when a rhythmic thumping noise drifted through the early afternoon air. She looked back down the track the way the soldiers had come and for a moment she worried that Herat had sent other riders after her. After listening for a few seconds longer she finally decided that it wasn't the sound of riders she could hear, but something else. She turned and slowly started to climb the small hill behind her upon which she had hidden to fire her first arrow. If there was anything to see she would surely be able to see it from the top of that hill.

The incline was steeper towards the top than she had realised and fifty or so paces from the summit she had climbed off and gently led her horse up by the reins. By the time she neared the summit, she was puffing hard from the exertion, but the noise was much louder and whatever was causing it wasn't far away. She tethered her horse to a small bush and wriggled the last few paces on her stomach. What she saw when she got there made her gasp with shock. Stretched out for what seemed like leagues, were columns of Delarite soldiers marching solemnly down a narrow track, flanked on either side by cavalry. Cala had never been very good at estimating numbers but she knew there had to be thousands of men on the track below and they could only be heading one way; Lydia.

So that dog Herat has betrayed us before we could betray him.

The realisation that Herat must have planned this days if not weeks ago, which meant that he had merely been toying with Cala, incensed her.

She made to worm her way back down to her horse when a Delarite cavalry scout suddenly appeared to her right. She flattened herself against the ground and prayed that her horse would remain silent and unseen. The rider stopped a few paces in front of her down the other side of the hill and watched the columns of soldiers marching below him. The slightest movement or sound from Cala and he would spot her. Eventually he nudged his horse forward and Cala thought that she was in the clear until something close by made a cracking noise. The rider stopped instantly and whirled round in his saddle whilst Cala instinctively reached for the dagger in her belt and held her breath.

"What kept you, Rahid?" said the rider relaxing.

"That new officer wanted to see me about something," replied a second rider who had ridden up from Cala's left.

Cala let out a quiet sigh of relief though she was far from in the clear. She had thought that she was about to be discovered but it had just been the sudden approach of the other rider that had startled the man in front of her. Unfortunately there were now two of them mere paces away from her and if discovered she doubted she could take them both down with just a dagger and remain unnoticed. She considered readying her bow but realised to do so might make a noise and decided to wait it out.

"What news?"asked one of the men.

"How would I know? Officers don't confide in mere soldiers like you and me," replied his friend.

"So you don't know where we're heading?"

"We're heading for Lydia, but whereabouts I don't know. I did overhear a couple of officers talking about the invasion. Apparently the Fourth Army's nearly overrun the country already; we're just going there to help clean up. Then it's probably on to Remada."

The first rider grunted his agreement and then after taking a swig of water from his flask, nudged his horse forward and away from Cala, closely followed by his comrade.

Cala lay there for a couple of minutes digesting what she had just heard. Not only was Lydia under attack but had been for a couple of days at least. Whilst she had stood around in Herat's castle spying and pretending to be his ally, Lydians had been dying. The thought made her feel both sick and guilty. All she could do now was head back to the capital and hope that the situation wasn't as bad as the Delarite soldier had said. If the capital had fallen, then Lydia was lost. So too, she realised, were her father and sisters.

Biting back her anger, Cala waited a couple of minutes to

make sure the Delarite scouts didn't suddenly double back and then slithered down to her horse, careful to mount it below the hill line.

All that mattered now was getting back to her father's palace in Tahara and saving as many of her people as she could. Maybe things weren't as bad as she feared, she tried to tell herself. Although Lydia was in no shape to fight a long war against a stronger enemy, she was not completely toothless.

Perhaps my father and General Tain are repelling the invaders right now.

If things were as bad as the Delarite soldier had described, then she needed to extricate as many of her father's soldiers as possible, withdraw to the west or even into Remada, regroup and then strike back. It was probably wishful thinking, she knew that, but it was all she had. With a heavy heart and a long ride ahead of her, Cala galloped off into the afternoon sun.

Chapter 8

"What do you think, Eryn, is it safe to go down there?"

"I don't know, Tav, it looks okay."

"I hope so, Tav's real hungry."

Eryn slapped his friend on the shoulder. "I know you are, Tav, so am I, but don't you ever think about something other than food?"

Eryn had to stifle a laugh at the quizzical look that had settled on Tav's face as he earnestly considered what he thought to be an important question. "No, not really. Tav likes food. Oh, and Sali. Tav likes Sali." Tav started to flush bright red at his own admission.

"Really? Sali Kalf. I never knew you felt that way about her, Tav," said Eryn who was starting to look at his friend in a new light.

"Tav's liked Sali for years, but she thinks he's a dummy and laughs at him." Tav's shoulders sunk as he recalled all the times Sali had called him names or ridiculed him whenever she caught him spying on her, which was quite often.

Eryn felt his friend's pain. "Don't worry about it, Tav, she's not the only girl in the village. Besides, you never know you might come back from this journey a hero and have to fight the girls off."

"Do you really think so, Eryn? Tav would like that."

"Anything's possible, Tav, anything."

"That's great, Eryn, Tav would like that. Fight the girls off and be a hero."

"That's right, Tav."

"But first we eat, right?"

Eryn laughed quietly. "Yes, first we eat. How are you going to fight the girls off if you don't have any energy?"

It was a flippant remark, but Tav lay there quietly smiling to himself and considering his friend's question. Eryn meanwhile continued to study the village below as dusk slowly started to draw in around them. There was no sign of any raiders nor was there any indication that there had ever been a struggle there, but Eryn was determined to be as cautious as possible on this journey. Most of the people back at his village were expecting him to fail. Others like Bratak no doubt even hoped for it, either out of spite or shame at having not accompanied him. The only one, who had shown any real support, was Jeral Tae, though he had initially been against him even going. Eryn wanted to repay Jeral's faith in him and prove the others wrong. Most of all he just wanted his sister and fiancée back so that he could keep his promise to his uncle. It would not look good, Eryn decided if he were to get captured or killed by raiders in the very next village.

The village upon which he now gazed was called Porta and Eryn had been there a few times with his uncle to trade or to buy goods. The people were usually friendly and some were even relatives of people he knew back in Lentor. There was no apparent reason to fear the place yet something about it just didn't seem right.

"I'm starving," said Tav suddenly, apparently oblivious to the fact that they had just discussed the need for food only a few minutes before.

"Come on then, Tav, let's see if we can't get something to eat down in Porta," said Eryn finally deciding to risk visiting the village.

"Really?" Tav didn't need to be asked a second time and was soon on his feet and walking down the slope towards the village entrance, Eryn running behind him in an effort to catch up.

They were approximately half way down the slope which led to Porta when Eryn finally realised what was different about the village; it had armed sentries on its gates. Every village usually posted a night watchman or two, but none could usually afford to post several armed men on the gates especially during the day when their services were sorely needed gathering crops and the like.

Their approach had been noticed and after shouting a warning, the two sentries on the gate were soon joined by a dozen or so other men. Some were armed with bows whilst others carried axes, scythes and swords, all of which had clearly seen better days.

"That's close enough," shouted one of the men whom Eryn didn't recognise. "State your business in Porta."

"My friend and I are on a quest and we seek food and shelter for the night. We would welcome any brave enough to join us on our mission if there are any minded to do so," replied Eryn.

"And what is this quest that you speak of?" asked another.

"We are from the village of Lentor beyond those hills and in the next valley," began Eryn.

"I know where Lentor is sonny, not that I recognise you. I asked you what this great quest is that the good people of Lentor see fit to send two boys barely old enough to shave out to do." Several of the man's companions laughed.

Upset by the man's tone, Eryn's hand slowly reached for the hilt of the sword his father had left him and which Kam had kept hidden under his bunk for all these years.

"Careful, son, think what you're doing. There are a lot of nervous people in this village and many of them are standing in front and behind you," said the man whose comments had upset Eryn.

Eryn glanced round and was surprised to see two men standing silently behind them with arrows poised to fire. Clearly somewhere down the hill these men had been concealed behind an outcrop of rocks or bush and acted as forward lookouts. Eryn cursed his naivety and let go of his sword hilt.

"Now, I'm going to ask you one last time and I suggest you tell us the truth. What are you doing in Porta?"

Eryn's mind was racing. Did he tell them the truth like he planned or just tell them the bare minimum? It certainly wasn't the sort of welcome he had expected and all his carefully laid plans and speeches were now in tatters courtesy of the villagers' belligerent attitude. He opened his mouth to speak but was cut short by the sound of someone pushing through the throng of people which had now gathered to hear what the two boys had to say.

"Out of the way, let me through," said a gruff voice as the people in front of him reluctantly parted. Eventually the man made it through to the front and stood staring at the two lads in surprise. "Eryn! What in Sulat's name are you doing here?"

"You know these boys, Alek?" asked the man who had done most of the talking.

"Of course I do, you idiot and so do you if you took the time to look properly. That's Eryn, Kam Martel's nephew and his friend Tav," admonished Alek.

"Kam Martel's nephew?" The colour seemed to drain away from the man's face. "Sorry, lad, no offence, but we can't be too careful around here anymore. There's talk of raiders in the vicinity," said the bearded man apologetically.

It pleased Eryn to see that the mere mention of his uncle's name caused fear and respect in equal proportion and decided that it might be something he could use to his advantage at some point in the future. There was nothing to be gained, however, by telling the crowd that Kam Martel had been killed, Eryn decided and he hoped that Tav would follow his lead. If he did tell them, their new found respect might quickly dissipate.

"None taken and as for raiders, it is of them that I wish to speak," replied Eryn.

"First you'll come and eat supper at my place won't you?" asked Alek.

"We'd be glad to, sir. Tav is starving," replied Eryn.

Alek laughed heartily. "As I recall, you're always starving, Tav." The boy beamed back at him. "Come then and let's see what we can do about that. Nerys will be glad to see you and I'm keen to hear the news of Lentor." Alek turned to the bearded man and his companions. "Double the guard tonight, Durl. I fear what the boy has to tell us won't be good news and then pass the word that we'll be holding a meeting in Arun's barn shortly after dark."

Durl nodded his acknowledgment and began organising the sentry shifts whilst Alek and the two boys made their way to Alek's cabin.

After the initial shock of seeing Eryn and Tav so late in the day, Nerys had rustled them all up a hot stew with chunks of homemade bread and it was a satiated Eryn who settled into a chair by the fire whilst Tav went for a lie down.

"So tell me, Eryn, what news of Lentor and your uncle," asked Alek as he settled into a chair opposite Eryn and stoked the fire. Just as interested in the news as her husband,

Nerys came and stood behind Alek's chair, wiping her hands on her apron a she did so. The sad look and the way Eryn firstly cast his gaze down into the flames confirmed Alek's suspicions that it wasn't good news he was about to hear. "Eryn?"

Eryn looked up to meet Alek's concerned gaze and for a minute it looked like he was going to cry, but then he seemed to regain his composure. Forcing himself to sit up straight Eryn glanced firstly at Nerys and then at Alek before finally speaking. "Yesterday morning, just after dawn, a large band of raiders attacked our village. They killed our sentries before they could raise the alarm and then were among us killing and burning. They killed many people, good people and they escaped with several of our women folk."

Nerys covered her mouth with her right hand to stifle the cry she felt rising.

"Who were they?" asked Alek.

"My uncle said they were mostly Narmidians, although there were other nationalities with them."

"Bandits then."

"Probably, but their aim seemed to have been the capture of girls and women."

"Narmidians and Cardellans often raid for girls, whom they then sell as slaves in the lands to the north and east," said Alek.

Nerys's hand moved from her mouth to her husband's shoulder where her grip seemed to tighten with every morsel of bad news Eryn imparted.

"Your uncle and some of the others put up a fight no doubt and made some of these Narmidian dogs pay a price I trust?"

Eryn nodded. "We killed several of them, but we were unable to stop the others escaping with the girls."

"We?" asked Alek with raised eyebrows.

"I killed one with an arrow," replied Eryn proudly.

Alek nodded approvingly. "And what does your uncle plan on doing? Come to that, why has Lentor sent you boys to warn us? Why didn't they send a rider?"

Alek watched as Eryn's gaze once again momentarily fell away and he suddenly dreaded the answer.

"My uncle was killed fighting the raiders."

Nerys's grip on her husband's shoulder became too painful and he glared up at his wife and then at her hand. She removed it without speaking.

"I am truly sorry to hear that, Eryn. You know how much your uncle meant to me. We were as brothers."

Eryn nodded but was suddenly unable to speak for fear that his emotions would betray him and he'd give in to tears. There would be time for mourning later. Now was a time for revenge. He had to remain strong if only for his sister's sake.

"You poor boy," said Nerys walking over to Eryn and throwing an arm around his shoulders and giving him a quick hug. "What of your sisters?"

"Keira was taken by the raiders, but Marta is at home being cared for by some of our neighbours," replied Eryn.

"Oh, no!" cried Nerys. This time the hand over the mouth wasn't enough to stifle the tears that had been threatening.

Alek leant forward, picked up the fire poker and turned the logs in the hearth again, causing the flames to briefly flare up. He allowed the renewed warmth to penetrate his aging bones, bones that somehow felt older than they did just an hour ago. Grief could do that to a man he'd heard and now he knew it to be true.

"So what brings you and young Tav out here to Porta? Surely you should be at home comforting your sister and rebuilding your village?" asked Nerys.

"He's going after Keira," Alek answered for the boy. "The real question is where the other men of Lentor are?"

"Is that true, Eryn? Please, dear Sulat, tell me it isn't true," said Nerys before Eryn could reply to Alek's question.

"I have to. I can't let them just take Keira, Tayla and the others," replied Eryn.

"Who is Tayla?" asked Alek.

"She is my fiancée. We were to marry in the autumn."

If he was surprised at the news, Alek didn't show it although Nerys seemed to briefly cheer up.

"In which direction did the raiders ride off?" asked Alek.

"North."

"They didn't pass through this village thank Sulat, so they probably turned north east towards Delarite once they were

92

out of sight. They'll probably keep changing direction in order to throw any pursuers off their scent."

"That is why we must get after them as quickly as possible. Neither Tav or I can track, so without help we could lose their trail very easily," said Eryn.

Alek nodded his understanding. "So why are there only two of you? Other families in Lentor were affected by this raid, not just yours?"

"Most of the brave ones died fighting. Some want to stay and protect what's left of their families in case the raiders come back and others want to leave the pursuit to the army. The rest are just cowards. I plan on picking up help along the way."

"That is what you are doing in Porta then," said Alek.

"That and we were looking forward to some of Mrs. Tabel's stew," replied Eryn turning to smile at Nerys.

Nerys smiled back at the young boy before turning to face her husband. "Will the men of our village go with them, Alek?"

Alek thought about it for a moment and then replied. "We will ask them to, but I seriously doubt it for all the same reasons that the men of Lentor gave. If Lentor's men won't mount a pursuit for their own people why should ours?"

Both Eryn and Nerys went to respond but Alek held up his hands to stay their protests. "Hold your tongues. I did not say they shouldn't go with him, I merely stated what I thought they will probably say. I sincerely hope that I am wrong, but we will see. Now come, the people will be gathering in Arun's barn to hear what you have to say. Tell them everything for many have friends and family in Lentor, but do not expect them to volunteer help as their priority must be their own families."

***

Virtually the whole village waited in Arun's small barn to hear what Eryn had to say and Alek had offered to speak on Eryn's behalf in case the lad felt intimidated by such a large number of people. Eryn had declined the offer saying that the news might have more impact being told by someone who was actually there and that if he faltered at all in his recounting of the facts, so be it. Besides why should men

93

follow him if he couldn't even stand up and talk in front of a couple of hundred people?

The villagers had listened intently to Eryn, only the occasional sob from one of the women or a hushed curse by one of the men, punctuating his tale. When he'd finished, the place had erupted in uproar as a hundred different conversations sought prominence over one another. Alek let them curse and argue among themselves for a few minutes before eventually bellowing for silence. The silence was immediate and complete, the people of Porta knowing better than to upset Alek Tabel.

Alek had then spoken to his friends and neighbours inviting certain individuals to air their opinion and thoughts on the matter. All had demonstrated their anger and dismay at what had befallen their neighbouring village, but when Alek had told them of Eryn's plan to go after the raiders and his need for volunteers, all had fallen silent. Alek cast his eyes around the barn allowing his gaze to linger on those who would be best suited to going with Eryn, but most refused to meet his eyes.

Eryn had shouted out in dismay that it could be their village that was attacked next, but that was countered with the argument that it was therefore even more important that the village men remain near their homes ready to defend them. One by one the families had then begun to file out of the barn some offering their condolences and excuses as they went, others hurrying out to hide their shame or embarrassment.

Eventually all that remained in the barn was Eryn, Alek and several of the older men, men who had seen service in the king's army and fought in the northern wars. They shook their heads in disgust as their neighbours hurried out.

"If I was but ten years younger, Master Eryn, I would gladly join you, if only to get away from the wife," said one of the old men.

"Wouldn't we all? Our neighbours shame us, Alek. Our friends from Lentor call for assistance and we turn our backs; what does that say of us?" said another.

"Do not be too hard on them, friends and please, Eryn, do not think badly of us either. People are scared. Scared for them and scared for their families. If someone could guarantee that the raiders would not return whilst we were away leaving the village defenceless, then many would travel with you. Unfortunately, no one can give us that guarantee, although I agree that it is highly unlikely that they would return. Consequently all that are able to offer to come with you are old men like us. Men who have seen too many winters yet still feel the fire in our blood," said Alek.

"And who are keen to escape their nagging wives," added another smiling at his friend's earlier comment.

"Yes, that too," smiled Alek. "The truth of the matter is though, Eryn, that whilst we have experience, we are too old and would slow you down. If you are to have any chance at all of catching these animals before they sell their captives, then you must move swiftly."

"But even if they do that, Alek, what will two boys be able to do when they catch up with them? The Narmidians will string them up and torture them for fun," said one of the other old men. He watched as Eryn paled at the thought. "Sorry, lad, but it is the truth."

"Eryn may have better luck in the next village or the one after that. Somewhere along the line he will find men willing to help them, though that help will no doubt be at a price rather than out of the milk of human kindness," said Alek.

"Jeral Tae says I should try to find Teren Rad," Eryn suddenly blurted out. "He thinks that he will help me."

The group looked at Eryn in surprise. "Firstly, Eryn, nobody knows where Teren is for sure or whether he's even alive. All we know is that he was last known to be living up in the high mountains somewhere, but that was years ago. Secondly, he is a broken man who chose to hide himself away from people. He has no reason to change and come and help you. I think you would be better off looking elsewhere for your help," said one of the old men.

"I agree with you and have no inclination to find him. From the stories I have heard, though, he is just the sort of man we need to help us."

"He certainly used to be, Eryn, but even if he still lives, he may no longer be the man you have heard about," said another of the men.

"I still think it would be a good idea to seek him out, Eryn," said Alek. "He has a right to know what's happened to Keira."

"He lost that right when he walked out on us all those years ago," Eryn bit back.

"Maybe, but it is not my place to judge. All I'm saying is that if my daughter had been taken by raiders, I'd want to know regardless of what's gone on before. Some things transcend pride, Eryn," said Alek.

"I know, but like I said, it was Jeral's advice and it's a piece of advice I'm choosing not to follow. Besides, Teren Rad was last seen in the Lonely Mountains to the east. My way is north after the raiders." Eryn noticed the disappointment in Alek's eyes. "I know that this must seem like a fool's errand to you, Alek, but I must try. Even if we can't persuade anybody else to help us, I must try. Honour and my own pride demand no less. Besides, how will I ever be able to face my uncle in the afterlife if I do not try out of fear?"

Alek inwardly sighed at the lad's persistent refusal to acknowledge Teren Rad as his father. "You could not. Come, the hour is late. You will both sleep at my place tonight and then eat one of my wife's legendary breakfasts before you set off in the morning. Who knows, maybe some of the villagers will have changed their minds by then and will be ready to join you."

***

Like the people of Lentor the day before, however, the villagers of Porta did not change their minds. Instead, after eating a hearty breakfast, Eryn and Tav walked out of the village watched only by Alek, Nerys and two weary sentries. The rest of the village it seemed had chosen to remain indoors until they had departed lest they see their shame reflected in the boys' faces.

"May Sulat watch over them," said Nerys to her husband as she watched the boys stride off into the distance, wiping a tear with the back of her hand.

"Indeed," was all Alek could bring himself to answer.

"Do you think that Teren would help them, Alek?"

Alek turned to look at his wife and then turned his gaze to

the distant Lonely Mountains. "If he still lives and if someone tells him what has befallen Lentor and his daughter, I'm sure he'd be after those raiders like a bolt from a crossbow and Sulat help them then. But the boy is stubborn like his father and won't seek his help. We must hope then that Teren hears the news from someone else and goes after them of his own volition. If not I fear we'll never see those boys again if they catch up with the raiders."

Nerys sighed, nonchalantly smoothed the creases out of her apron and headed back to their cabin leaving her husband watching the boys. As he watched them disappear into the distance, Alek found his thoughts turning to the old days. Days when men like him, Teren, Kam Martel and Jeral Tae were away fighting in the northern wars all those years ago. Those had been good days. Days of honour, loyalty and glory. They were gone now, only recalled by old men who told stories round camp fires or for drinks in the tavern. Now Kam Martel was dead and quite possibly Teren Rad as well and with every passing day he was beginning to sense that his own time was coming to an end. Maybe he should have gone with the boys and enjoyed one last adventure before it was too late if it wasn't already. That wouldn't have been fair on Nerys though he decided and the truth of the matter was that he knew he'd miss the comforts of home too much. A warm bed, good cooking and a soft body to curl up next to on these cold nights took some beating at his age.

Alek shook his head in self-pity and turned to walk back to his cabin. As he did so a terrible shooting pain caught him in the lower back and he cried out with surprise. No, he'd been right; he was too damned old to be considering such things. Quests and adventures were for young men. Flexing his back gently to relieve the pain he now felt, he was rewarded with a loud crack as one of his joints freed itself. Grunting with satisfaction, he shuffled his way back home.

Chapter 9

Something was wrong, very wrong; there wasn't a single villager in sight either in the village itself or in the nearby fields. Teren scratched his straggly beard whilst he contemplated what might have befallen the village of Tarle. Were they all in the village hall having a meeting? He doubted it for they would surely have posted guards as the smoke from Lentor was clearly visible from the village. Perhaps they had all evacuated the village fearful that whoever had attacked Lentor was now on their way to them. That was possible he decided, but then surely they would have taken some of their livestock with them to sustain them on their journey. Judging by the number of animals wandering aimlessly and untended around the village, they clearly hadn't done so.

He was still considering all of the possibilities when a flicker of movement at the far tree line a hundred paces or so the other side of the village caught his eye. Teren flattened himself against the grass and hoped that whoever it was hadn't seen him. Slowly, in ones and twos, people began to emerge from the trees and wander warily towards the village. Teren estimated that there were no more than fifty people in all and most of those appeared to be young children and old people. If these were the villagers as he suspected, then what had happened to all the others he wondered?

His thoughts briefly turned to his old friends in Lentor and he prayed to Sulat that they were all safe. The scene before him told him that this was most unlikely. His heart urged him to make all haste to Lentor but the bedraggled look of the few people who had emerged from the trees persuaded him otherwise. First he would go down there and find out what had happened. He pushed himself to his feet and after a cursory glance around he began to slowly pick his way down the last bit of mountain slope towards the village.

The handful of remaining villagers had gathered in the central square and Teren was almost among them before a young girl finally noticed his approach. She screamed for all she was worth before burying her head in her mother's skirt. The frightened villagers turned as one to look at the fearsome looking man walking towards them and began to bunch tightly together. The children all started to wail and cry whilst three of the old men took a step forward brandishing rusty looking scythes and spades.

Teren stopped and spread his arms in what was supposed to be a gesture of peace, but their expressions suggested that they were not convinced. He realised that with his unkempt hair and matted beard, he probably looked every bit as fierce and dangerous as whoever these people had evidently been attacked by. One of the old men had his eyes fixed firmly on the axe Teren was carrying as if he expected Teren to use it to cut them down at any moment. Teren caught his gaze.

"Don't worry old timer, I'm not here to hurt you."

The old man licked his lips and swallowed before nervously glancing at his two companions for support. Both seemed unable or unwilling to say anything.

"Then why are you here stranger?" the axe watcher eventually managed to say with more assurance than he actually felt. He tightened his grip on the scythe as much as he could with his arthritic hands, the pain almost intolerable. If this newcomer was going to attack them, better he do it now whilst he could still hold his weapon, such that it was.

"I was on my way to Lentor and thought I'd stop here for ale and a lump of cheese, but as I came down the mountain I noticed something wasn't right here."

"Where are you from, stranger?"

Teren pointed back over his shoulder with his right thumb. "From there."

"The Lonely Mountains? Nobody lives there," said the old man incredulously.

"I do," replied Teren. The three old men exchanged nervous glances again, clearly unsure what to do with this wild looking mountain man. "So what happened here?"

"Raiders," said another of the old men before spitting on the ground in apparent disgust.

Teren looked at the man waiting for him to continue but he apparently felt that there was no need to elaborate.

"Raiders?" prompted Teren looking back at the other two men, hoping for better luck from them.

"Narmidians and scum like that," said the first old man. "Showed up mid-morning and took us completely by surprise."

Teren glanced round. "I can't see any bodies; did your young men not put up a fight?"

"What's left of our young men was working in the fields over that hillock, but as that is the direction from which the raiders came, I assume they've all been killed or maybe fled."

A howl of anguish went up from one of the women standing behind the three old men, as a mother or wife heard what she already feared to be the truth.

"You said 'what's left' of your young men; what did you mean?" asked Teren.

"A couple of weeks ago some of the king's soldiers came to our village and took many of our young men as recruits for the army. We told them that we didn't have enough men to work the fields let alone defend ourselves and that if they took some of our men, we'd be defenceless, but they didn't care. They had a quota to fill and didn't care about some backwater village like this. Besides, many of the young men were only too happy to go. Life in a village like this doesn't offer much in the way of adventure and glory, but the king's army, well that's another thing. If I'd been twenty years younger I'd have gone with them," said the first old man.

"If you'd been twenty years younger, Chal, you'd still have been too ancient," said the other old man finally finding his tongue. "You can barely hold that rusty old scythe as it is."

Chal chuckled. "You're probably right, Ged. You're not going to kill us if I put this damn scythe down are you, stranger?"

"Like I said, Chal, I'm only passing through; you're in no danger from me so put your weapons down, all of you. While you're at it, ask that old man to put down his bow and arrow before he does himself a mischief," said Teren nodding towards another old man who had taken up a position behind a building to Teren's right.

"You noticed him then?" asked Chal sounding disappointed.

"A long time ago. You sure he even has the strength to pull back the string?"

Chal laughed again, warming to the stranger. "Probably not, but Pim's one of the strongest around here right now." He signalled to the other man to come out of hiding and join them.

"Then you are in trouble indeed. Now tell me more about these raiders. How many of them were there and what direction did they go?" asked Teren.

"We're not sure, but about twenty, I'd guess. They came from the direction of Lentor and rode off north. They'll be some distance away by now," said Ged.

"Maybe not," said Chal. "They've got captives with them and they're on foot so that should slow them down somewhat."

"They took captives from your village?" asked Teren.

Chal cast his gaze down at the ground momentarily as if the shame was too much to bear. "Girls and young women mostly. I imagine they plan on making slaves out of them."

Teren nodded.

"They already had some captives with them, so it looks like we weren't the only village to be hit by these barbarians," added Ged.

"Others? How do you know?" asked Teren.

"As we... ran for the trees, we could see a small group of women being guarded just outside the village by two or three of the raiders. They weren't from this village. My guess is that they're from Lentor since that's the direction from which they came. The place seems to have been set alight from what I can see," said Chal.

The shame these old men felt in fleeing to the woods with the women and children was obviously proving to be a heavy burden to them. "You did the right thing, Chal, all of you. You managed to save some of your people. If you'd try to fight, you would almost certainly have all perished."

"Thank you, stranger, your words are a comfort. Will you still go to Lentor even though that is the direction from which the raiders appeared? I fear you will find no comfort there," asked Chal.

"I suspect you may be right, my friend. I do not yet know

and will have to think on it. Maybe I'll head to Lentor and see what fate has befallen it, though I think we already know, or maybe I'll head north and see if they show up in Porta. My guess is that they'll head for home now. There are only so many slaves they can handle and they have a long journey ahead of them."

"Will you go after them?" asked Ged.

"If I find that these raiders did indeed attack Lentor and the smoke I have seen on the horizon would suggest that they have, then yes, I will probably go after them," replied Teren.

Chal's eyebrows shot up in surprise and he stared at the stranger wide-eyed and surprised. "You plan on going after them alone?"

"If I have to."

"Then the least we can do is to provide you with something to eat and drink on your journey," said Chal gesturing for Teren to follow him.

Chal led him to a small but well maintained log cabin pretty much in the centre of the village. Three stairs led up to a small porch upon which a table and two old wooden chairs stood. It reminded Teren of his old home back in Lentor and for a moment or two he could see his wife Valla sitting in one of the chairs cuddling their baby whilst their other two children played out front.

"You all right, stranger?" asked Chal as his wife, Claryssa pushed past him to fetch some food and water for Teren.

"What? Yes, I'm fine, thanks, just remembering something that's been a long time forgotten."

"Memories are like that aren't they? Especially the painful ones. Always seem to sneak up on you and take you by surprise when you least expect or need it."

Claryssa reappeared carrying a small knapsack which she handed to Teren. "There's not much in there I'm afraid, those men took nearly everything." She began to cry and Chal put his arm around her shoulder and hugged her close.

"I'm grateful for whatever you've given me," said Teren slipping the knapsack into the larger bag he carried over his left shoulder. "Did you lose anyone in the raid?"

Claryssa began to sob harder and Teren could see that the old man was fighting hard to keep his own emotions in check. "Our daughter, Petra was killed trying to protect our granddaughter, Shala."

"What happened to... Shala?" asked Teren though he already feared he knew the answer.

"They took her. She's just twelve years old." The plight of his granddaughter was too much to bear and Chal's own tears began to flow freely. Teren averted his eyes to protect the man's dignity.

"I'm sorry," was all Teren could utter. Hollow empty words which were no comfort at all he knew. "What will you do now? Leave?"

"And go where? No, we will stay here in the hope that some other stragglers will return and some of the girls might escape. First, however, we must go and see what has happened to the men who were working in the fields when these Narmidians came," replied Chal.

Teren nodded. "You said the army came and took many of your young men away. Why?"

"You really do live in the mountains don't you? Do you never get any news?" asked Chal incredulously.

"Rarely. That's why they're called the Lonely Mountains and why I like them. So tell me, why is the army taking men away?"

"You truly haven't heard?"

"I've heard that the Delarites are mustering for war, but is there more? Have they already invaded?"asked Teren.

"War is upon us my friend. News reached us the other day that the Delarite's have invaded Lydia and are preparing to attack us. Just yesterday we heard that the Cardellans were also gathering on our border and preparing to ally themselves with the Delarites. For all I know now they may already have invaded. Every able man is being called up."

"Cardellans! Those dogs are always looking for a fight," said Teren spitting on the ground.

"Well they won't get much of one this time will they, our young king has seen to that? He's more interested in strutting around in all his finery than protecting his people and our army's become little more than a joke. I've heard men are deserting quicker than they can conscript them. This would never have happened in King Taylen's time, but then you'd know that wouldn't you, Teren?"

Teren looked at Chal in surprise. "You know who I am?"

"Everyone's heard of the great Teren Rad, hero of Slinden Plateau and Kato's Reach. Some of your enemies called you Teren the Terrible as I recall."

"Some of my friends too," laughed Teren, "but for a different reason."

"With good cause I'm sure, my friend," said Chal clasping Teren's forearm in the warrior's embrace. "I wish you good fortune in your travels, Teren Rad, wherever fate takes you."

"Thank you, Chal. I wish you and your people good fortune too. Dark days are ahead for all of us it seems," replied Teren. He turned to face Claryssa. "In case I run into the raiders is there anything you could give me that I could show to Shala, to prove that I am your friend? If I find them I'm likely to have to move quickly and a simple token might be enough to persuade her to trust me."

"You're going to try and rescue them?" asked Claryssa, her face brightening.

"If I run into them and the opportunity arises, I will do my best, but I can promise nothing," said Teren suddenly feeling as if he'd been backed into a corner.

"You believe that they are still alive then, that there is still hope?" asked Claryssa.

"So long as they've not provoked their guards in any way, then yes, they'll still be alive; you can't sell a dead person. The trick will be finding them before they're sold on. So yes, there is always hope, Claryssa," replied Teren.

Claryssa removed a brooch from her shawl and handed it to Teren. "Here, show this to Shala if you find her. She's always coveted it and I've promised to give it to her when she reaches her eighteenth summer."

Teren briefly studied the brooch. It wasn't made of any precious material he recognised and didn't appear to be worth much; its value he decided must be purely sentimental. He nodded at the old man and his wife and turned to leave. Behind him the rest of the villagers had gathered.

"Is it true that you're going after the raiders, mister?"

asked one young boy as Teren made his way through the throng. Teren didn't answer.

"That's Teren the Terrible," he heard an old man's voice say. "Those Narmidians don't stand a chance."

Teren was soon heading north out of the village towards Porta, his heart torn in two. One half urged him to hurry west to Lentor to check on his children and friends, whilst the other part told him to go after the raiders. If he didn't, no one else would it seemed and young girls like Shala would be sold on to some fat, decadent tribal chief in Narmidia, never to be seen again.

Just like Valla, his conscience taunted him.

He buried the thought deep in the back of his mind as he'd done so many times before. It troubled him how he had suddenly been cornered into going after the raiders, the hopes of the villagers of Tarle resting on his shoulders, yet here he was following the raiders' trail.

As he left the village boundary to a crescendo of cheers and good wishes from the remaining villagers, Teren realised that he probably had little choice. Remada was in trouble and needed help. Ravaged by marauding Narmidians and beset by attacking Delarites and Cardellans, the country he loved but had ultimately turned his back on, needed his help. It needed men like Teren, and Kam Martel. He took out the knapsack of food Claryssa had given him and with a growing sense of purpose, he strode out for Porta.

***

Picking his way across the rough country between Tarle and Porta had been hard work and it was not until late afternoon two days later that the small village of Porta came into sight. Teren stopped briefly to rest his aching feet and gazed down at the small cluster of wooden cabins below him. Somewhere down there was a cosy little tavern he had frequented on numerous occasions when he was younger and he smiled at some of the memories as they drifted back.

The village looked intact and there was no visible sign of any damage or fighting; Porta had been lucky it seemed. Wishing that the village was nearer than it actually was, Teren sighed and began the descent focussing on the thought of a tankard of ale whenever the ache in his feet became too painful.

Mountain life had kept Teren reasonably fit and strong, but the walk had nevertheless tired him and it was a somewhat irritable Teren who on his arrival at the gate was confronted by two nervous looking guards. They had challenged the fierce looking man from some distance away, but he had just ignored them and kept walking. Shouting out your name and business was somewhat undignified and he had no intention of letting that happen to him because of two weak-kneed sentinels.

"I asked you who you were and what you wanted," said one of the guards. "Did you not hear me, old man?"

"Oh, I heard you, sonny," replied Teren.

"Then why didn't you respond?"

Teren fixed him to the spot with a withering glare. "Because I was waiting for you to show some respect and ask me politely." The menace in his voice was clear for all to hear.

"Maybe we shouldn't have bothered at all. Maybe we should run you through right now where you stand," said the other guard, much to his friend's amusement. "Nobody's going to miss a vagrant like you."

"I'll tell you what, sonny. I'm hot, tired and thirsty, so I'm prepared to let that insult go unpunished this time if you let me through right now. Otherwise things around here are going to turn a might ugly. Decide quickly, because I'm not a patient man."

Their self-assurance and arrogance was waning, Teren could see it in their eyes. One of them had also just noticed the fearsome looking weapons Teren was carrying, but apparently one more act of bravado was necessary on their part. Other armed men were approaching the gate from inside the village.

"You'd be dead with two arrows in your back before you even moved," said the first guard, but even as he spoke, he suddenly realised that the two guards with bows stationed further up the hill, had not followed the stranger down.

"Oh, you mean the two fellas hiding behind those rocks up yonder?" said Teren smiling. "They won't be joining us

106

quite yet I'm afraid, they're taking a little nap." The guards and the men gathered behind them looked at Teren quizzically. "They didn't show me any respect either. Time's up, gentlemen." Teren didn't move but his eyes took in the subtle change in posture as the two guards took a firmer grip on their sword hilts.

"Enough!" the word was spoken with enough authority to gain everybody's attention, though Teren remained alert to any danger. "You two get back on guard duty, I'll handle this. The rest of you go back to whatever you were doing. There's no danger here unless you create it." The crowd slowly started to dissipate. "I'm sorry about that, old friend, but these are dangerous times, we cannot be too careful." He grasped Teren's forearm in the warrior's welcome.

"That being so, Alek, I suggest you put some men on guard duty and not these fools," said Teren derisively and loud enough for the guards to hear. They mumbled a response but were shrewd enough to keep it out of Teren's earshot.

"Don't be too hard on them, Teren. They are just farmers and the like, playing at soldiers and they're all we've got since the army came and took the cream of our men folk."

"I heard the same at Tarle," said Teren.

"You've been to Tarle? How fares it?" asked Alek.

"It was raided earlier today. The young men were working in the fields when they came and were slaughtered where they stood so I'm told. Then they fell on the village. Some of the old folk and young children managed to escape to the woods, but everyone else was taken as a hostage." Alek spat on the ground in disgust. "I've come to ask what you know of Lentor. From the mountains I could see pillars of smoke. Have you heard anything?"

Alek cast his gaze down at the ground briefly, clearly trying to gather the strength to utter the words his friend did not want to hear, yet nonetheless expected. "I'm sorry, Teren, Lentor was attacked by raiders. The villagers put up quite a fight apparently, but to no avail. Many were killed and several girls and young women were abducted. Keira was taken, Teren, I'm sorry." Alek watched the full range of emotions flit across his friend's face.

"Has Kam or Jeral gone after them?" asked Teren.

Alek took a deep breath before speaking. "Kam's dead, Teren. He died in the fight, but not before he took several of those heathens with him. Jeral's been ordered to stay behind by the village elders. Besides, like the rest of us the general's too old for such escapades."

"Then who leads the rescue mission, Alek?" asked Teren. His friend hesitated. "Alek?"

"There is no rescue party as such, Teren. Only two have gone after the raiders, the rest believing that they should stay and guard what's left of the village. A wise decision perhaps as now we learn that the Delarites are headed this way."

"To Kaden with the Delarites. I never had the men of Lentor down as cowards. Who are the two men who have at least shown a backbone?"

" Eryn and Tav," replied Alek.

Teren's eyes widened in shock. "They've let two boys go after a band of Narmidian raiders whilst they cower and cry at home?"

"Not boys, Teren, men, they're men now," said Alek though he knew the information would not assuage his friend's anger.

Had that much time really passed? thought Teren.

"Not only was Eryn's sister taken, but also his fiancée. He's sworn to get them back no matter how long it takes," added Alek.

"His fiancée?" said Teren incredulous.

Alek smiled broadly and nodded. "You've been gone a long time my friend, much has changed."

"Too much it would seem," replied Teren. "How do you know all this, Alek?"

"Eryn and Tav turned up here last night and left again early this morning. What are you going to do now?"

"And you let them go?" asked Teren angrily, ignoring his friend's question.

"I had no choice, Teren. They are free men after all." Teren nodded his reluctant agreement. "What will you do now?"

"Go after them I suppose."

"Is that wise, given your... history?"

"I have no choice, besides on their own they won't stand much of a chance," said Teren.

"Nor will the three of you. I'm sorry old friend, but you're not the man you used to be. Can you really hope to defeat so many?"

"I would have preferred a few more swords behind me, but if I have to do it alone, then so be it. I would feel much better with the axe of Kam Martel standing beside me," said Teren.

Alek nodded and smiled. "I wish I could come with you, Teren, truly I do. I owe you that much and more. But Remada is in great peril and her king is a fool. I have thought about it and if they'll have me I intend to try and get a commission in the cavalry, so I can help beat these Delarites once and for all. They could use another wily old head like you, particularly as Kam is no longer with us."

"The Remadan Army had the best years of my life and what did it get me? A broken family, that's what. Besides, the new king doesn't sound like the kind of man I could fight for. This time I'm putting personal matters first."

"I understand, my friend, but I still had to ask. I too would feel better with the mighty sword of Teren the Terrible swinging into the enemy next to me."

"More like Teren the Tired at the moment, but thank you anyway. Maybe my reputation will precede me and persuade these Narmidians to let their captives go," said Teren.

"Maybe. That being so, I reckon you've got time for a quick ale and something to eat at the tavern before you go, or are you planning to stay the night and make an early start tomorrow?"

"No, I can't afford to let either party get too far ahead of me, so I'll be leaving a little later. As for the ale, I thought that you were never going to ask," said Teren smiling.

His friend laughed and slapped Teren on the shoulder. "Follow me, old timer and whilst we're walking you can tell me just how badly you hurt my men hiding up the hill." Together they strolled to the village tavern watched by the two sentries.

Chapter 10

They'd made good time since leaving Porta early that morning, but now both boys were dead on their feet. Eryn's initial excitement at undertaking the quest to rescue his sister and fiancée had started to wear off long before they came across the bodies lying in the meadow. Now despair and despondency were threatening to overwhelm him. Eryn was no expert, but it appeared to him that the soldiers had been caught out in the open and taken by surprise, probably by some cavalry.

They had tried to flee for the safety of the trees from which Eryn and Tav had just emerged, but never made it. Most had been cut down from behind and only one or two had died facing the enemy. Eryn had seen Remadan soldiers before when they'd passed through Lentor and immediately recognised their uniforms. He'd looked around for anyone wearing a different uniform, but hadn't found any. Either the attackers had hauled their dead away, which seemed unlikely, or they'd taken the Remadans so completely by surprise that they'd not suffered a single casualty.

But who had attacked them? Jeral Tae had talked of the Delarites to the north preparing for war with Remada and that seemed most likely. If that was the case and the Remadan Army was already retreating as indicated by the bodies they'd found, then the war clearly wasn't going well. It was another danger he and Tav would have to be alert to.

He'd briefly considered the possibility that the raiders had attacked the soldiers but that made no sense. The soldiers had been fleeing south, presumably from an enemy that appeared from the north, a completely different direction to the one the raiders were last thought to be heading.

Suddenly fearing for their own lives, the boys had fled north trying to put as much distance as possible between themselves and the grisly scene in the meadow.

With each passing hour Eryn began to wish he'd swallowed his pride and gone looking for Teren Rad after all.

Despite their differences and history, Eryn would have felt a whole lot better with his father by his side.

He is no longer your father, his mind chastised him. *He gave that right up seven years ago when he walked out and left you and your sisters. You don't need him. You can do this.*

The battlefield had been a gruesome sight, the likes of which neither boy had ever seen before and although Tav didn't fully understand what was going on, it nevertheless seemed to trouble him greatly. Neither boy spoke for some time afterwards, each lost in their own thoughts and worries.

As the afternoon had worn on though and the distance between them and the scene of the battle had widened, their mood had lightened. By the time that they reached the outskirts of Ederik shortly after dusk, they were both tired and hungry, but considerably more cheerful, thoughts of the morning almost erased.

"Where's that, Eryn?" asked Tav.

"I believe it's the town of Ederik, Tav," replied Eryn scanning the scene before him from their concealed position behind some shrubbery.

"Will we be able to get something to eat there?" asked Tav.

Eryn smiled to himself. As always, Tav's first thoughts were of food, though Eryn was just as hungry, his stomach growling sporadically in protest at the lack of food.

"Hopefully, Tav. First we've got to make sure that it's safe down there."

"Looks okay to Tav."

"Yes, I know it does, Tav, but looks can be deceiving. My father once warned me about this place and said that I should always try and avoid it. Because of its location it is a staging point for travellers, merchants and all sorts of people, many of them bad. If we go down there we must be careful and try to draw as little attention to ourselves as possible, you understand?"

Tav nodded vigorously, his need for food far outweighing any thoughts of danger.

Eryn smiled at his friend and after one last glance at the scene in front of him, he patted Tav on the back, stood up and slowly began to make his way down the slope towards the town perimeter, closely followed by Tav.

The first thing that Eryn noticed about Ederik as they drew nearer, was that it was considerably larger than he had first thought and was in fact a bustling town. The second was that unlike Lentor or Porta, it did not have any sentries, or at least none that he could see. It made Eryn wonder why they didn't fear the raiders or Delarites until an unsettling thought crossed his mind.

What if far from fearing the raiders here they actually welcomed them?

From what his father had told him about the place it was not impossible. He had said that every type of lowlife infested the town and whatever you wanted or needed, there was always someone there who could get it for you – for a price.

Could that include slaves? he wondered.

For the briefest of moments Eryn dared to hope, but the rational part of his mind screamed back at him that it was very unlikely. It had only been a couple of days and whilst he and Tav were on foot, the raiders were on horses and would surely be far away by now. *Yet the slaves aren't on horses.*

Eryn began to walk quicker as his hopes began to rise, leaving Tav momentarily trailing behind.

They were just entering the town when it suddenly dawned on Eryn that he didn't have the slightest notion what to do if he did run into the raiders and their hostages, there, or anywhere else for that matter. As usual he'd rushed head first into something without thinking it through. If the raiders were here and he didn't handle the situation just right, both he and Tav could both be dead within a matter of minutes. It was a sobering thought. Eryn stopped, his mind a mass of conflicting emotions.

"What's the matter, Eryn?" asked Tav, a look of concern on his face.

Eryn looked at Tav. *Poor gentle, kind Tav.* He was a loyal friend who hadn't hesitated to volunteer to come with Eryn, the only one in the village who had. *What were you thinking letting him come along?*

"Eryn?"

"Sorry, Tav, I was miles away."

"That's okay; Tav often does that, especially when he's thinking about food."

"Let's see if we can't find you some then, Tav, shall we?" said Eryn dredging up a new resolve and confining his doubts to the dark recesses of his mind.

The boys walked slowly into the town and Eryn remained constantly alert for danger, his hand never straying far from the hilt of his sword. The roads through the town were dusty and rutted from old cart tracks. The streets were quite busy, but no one showed much interest in the two strangers, most ignoring them completely or giving them cursory looks at best. They were just two more strangers in a town full of them.

They turned left into what appeared to be the main thoroughfare of the town and stopped. The road ahead looked pretty much like the others they'd just walked down, except on either side of this one were taverns, shops and a stable. The few houses that were dotted between the various businesses were ramshackle and unwelcoming. Eryn assumed that was the reason why most of their owners were standing around in groups outside. He thought it strange, however, that they were all women and was shocked that many of them were so scantily dressed, that it was almost indecent. Eryn tried to avert his eyes as he walked along. Tav didn't even seem to notice.

As they walked past them a few of the women and girls had called out to Eryn and Tav to come over and join them in their house. Eryn had thanked them for their kind offers of hospitality and then apologised saying they had business to attend to. Eryn smiled to himself as he walked along. His father had been wrong about this town, that or perhaps it had changed since he was last here. Everyone was so welcoming and friendly. The first order of business, Eryn had decided, was to find somewhere to eat. Eryn had no idea where they should go, so when the next woman called over to him, Eryn obliged.

"Now what can we offer you two handsome boys?" asked the woman as a number of other equally scantily dressed women came and stood by her, smiling at the boys as they did so.

Eryn looked down at the ground wondering if all the women in the town were shameless. "I was just wondering if you could tell me where my friend and I could get a meal and somewhere to sleep for the night. We can pay," said Eryn glancing up momentarily and finding himself being appraised by the eldest of the women.

"That's just as well, because none of my girls come for free," said the woman.

"Oh, I don't know, this one's kind of cute," said a young ginger haired girl who had all but draped herself over Tav.

"Cute don't pay the bills though does it?" the older woman snapped back.

"So can you help us or not?" asked Eryn starting to feel slightly uncomfortable as a young blond girl ran her fingers through his hair whilst yet another girl held onto his left arm.

"Well I can certainly offer you a bed for the night, but I don't think you'll be getting much sleep."

"What about food?" asked Tav.

"What do you think I run here, a tavern?" snapped the woman.

Both boys looked blankly back at her.

"Idiots! Run along to your mothers whilst we wait for some real men. Girls."

The last word had been a command and two of the girls had instantly ceased their attentions and walked back behind the older woman, but the blond haired girl lingered a few seconds longer.

"Try the *Wild Boar*. They offer food and a bed of sorts. It's not the nicest of places if you know what I mean, but it's probably the best this place has to offer. Just watch your backs," said the girl.

"Lilly!"

The young girl looked briefly over her shoulder at the older woman before looking back at Eryn. "Be careful."

"We will and thank you, Lilly," smiled Eryn.

Lilly returned the smile before turning and hurrying back to the woman's side.

"Well go on then, move along," said the woman. "If you don't want any of my girls go and get lost, you're bad for business."

Eryn raised his eyebrows in contemplation. He had absolutely no idea what business the woman ran nor why he and Tav were bad for it. Nevertheless it was clear that the woman didn't want them around. Following his own advice of not wanting to attract unnecessary attention, he nodded to Tav and together they strode off.

Eryn tried to think about Tayla as he wearily trudged up the street, but instead all he could think of was Lilly. He glanced over his shoulder and saw that the girls were fawning over two men in much the same way they had him and Tav, but Lilly's eyes were on Eryn he noticed. He smiled and waved to her before continuing up the street, his mind troubled.

About a hundred paces further on and on the opposite side of the street, stood the *Wild boar* tavern. Lilly had been right in her description, Eryn realised as he looked at the dilapidated looking building, with small windows and crumbling walls. It was only for one night Eryn reminded himself and once they were in their room they could shut the door to the outside world and get some much needed sleep. He just hoped that the doors had locks. Eryn glanced over at Tav and saw that he too appeared anxious at the thought of entering such a rough looking establishment.

"It's only for one night, Tav and I think we're both so tired we'd sleep anywhere. Besides, we can get something to eat here according to Lilly."

Tav's face seemed to brighten up at the mention of food.

Eryn reached out and put his hand on the old looking wooden door and pushed just as someone opened it from the inside. Eryn stumbled forward crashing into the man who had just opened the door. For the briefest of moments they locked eyes before the man put a hand on Eryn's chest and shoved him so hard that he staggered back out of the tavern and into Tav, sending them both crashing to the ground in an unceremonious heap.

The man and his two companions laughed at the two boys as they tried to untangle themselves and stand.

"Next time you'd better look where you're going, boy, if you know what's good for you," said the man who'd done the shoving.

Just as Tav managed to haul himself up, one of the man's

two companions shoved him back onto the ground with his foot, much to his friend's amusement.

"Stay on the ground where you belong, worm," laughed the third man, before slapping his friends on the shoulder and guiding them off down the street to their next port of call.

Eryn watched them go and quietly prayed that they would run into some trouble of their own.

"Tav doesn't like it here very much, Eryn. Perhaps we should move on," said Tav as he lay flat on his back in the dirt.

Eryn reached down and extended his hand to his friend who gratefully accepted the tug to his feet. "I know what you mean, Tav, but it's too late to move on. Come on, you'll feel differently when you've some grub in you."

"Tav's not very hungry now."

Eryn looked at his friend in feigned shock. "Not hungry? That will be the day. Oh well, I guess I'll have to eat yours as well then," he said as he pushed open the tavern door and walked in, closely followed by a nervous Tav.

If the other occupants of the tavern had noticed the earlier altercation, they didn't show it, the boys' arrival drawing nothing more than a few disinterested glances from some of the other patrons. The tavern was crowded and the smell of tobacco and stale sweat hung in the dry atmosphere. Situated all around the edge of the room were a number of little nooks and crevices containing a table and a few chairs. Based on what his father had told him of this town, Eryn could only guess at what dark deeds and bargains were struck in such places. Most of these hideaway spots were occupied by small groups of men in deep discussion. As Eryn surveyed the room he began to draw the odd suspicious glance if his gaze lingered too long in any one place.

There was just one such table where Eryn could not make out its occupants though he could see that there were only two men sat there. Set in the deepest darkest recess of the tavern, their faces were shrouded in shadow and Eryn found himself wondering what nefarious deed they were plotting. One of the two men seemed to move his head as if he was looking directly at Eryn and although Eryn could not make out the other man's face, he felt sure that he was being scrutinised.

"Doesn't do to make eye contact with most of the people in here, young sir," said the voice from behind Eryn.

Eryn turned to see the tavern keeper looking down at his bar as he dried a tankard with a cloth that Eryn doubted had ever been washed.

"I'm sorry what did you say?" asked Eryn.

The tavern keeper looked up briefly before resuming his downward gaze. "I was just giving you a piece of friendly advice and suggesting that you try not to make eye contact with any of the people in this bar; they don't like it and it can lead to a shortening of one's life expectancy."

Eryn looked at Tav and gently twisted his head round so that he was looking straight ahead at the bar and away from trouble. "Thanks for the warning."

"Don't mention it. You new in town?"

"Yes, we're just passing through," said Eryn.

"Son, everybody's just passing through this town."

"We just need something to eat and somewhere to sleep for the night. A young lady recommended here. Do you have a room?"

"A young lady recommended us did she?" a small smile developing on the tavern keeper's face. "You did well finding one of those in this town."

"Yes, her name was Lilly," replied Eryn not really understanding what the tavern keeper meant.

The tavern keeper's smile grew tenfold. "Lilly! I've never heard her called a lady before. Many other things, but never a lady."

Again Eryn didn't know what the man meant, but he was sure that it wasn't flattering. He desperately wanted to challenge the man over his implied insult, but decided against it. At the end of the day, apart from Lilly, the tavern keeper was the only person to have shown them anything resembling genuine kindness since they'd arrived.

The tavern keeper looked up when Eryn didn't reply and sensing that he may have offended the youngster broke the awkward silence that was developing. He wasn't the first young man to fall for Lilly and he probably wouldn't be the last.

"Find yourselves a table and I'll have some food brought

over to you, though it won't be much I'm afraid, just some bread and cheese and perhaps some soup. Whilst you're eating I'll have my wife prepare one of the rooms for you."

"Thanks," said Eryn already looking round for a table. He found an empty one on the far side of the tavern, virtually opposite the two men hidden by the shadows. Even as they made their way across the floor, Eryn could feel their eyes watching their every move.

The food had gone down well, hot soup washed down with as much bread and cheese as they could manage, which after their physical exertions during the day, was considerable. Eryn took another sip of his ale and surveyed the room, careful not to look directly opposite him at the two men hidden in the recess.

"How was your food, young sirs?" asked the tavern keeper after suddenly appearing out of nowhere to collect their plates and dishes.

"Really good, thanks," said Eryn genuinely. "I've never seen Tav smile so much."

The tavern keeper looked at Tav who was indeed smiling like a Delarite cat.

"Well I'm glad you liked it. Your room is ready whenever you want it. Just give me or Maryke a shout and we'll show you up there."

"Maryke?" asked Eryn.

"My wife." The tavern keeper stepped back so that they could see the fearsome looking woman standing behind the bar who just happened to look up at the exact moment Eryn was looking her way. She smiled perhaps misreading Eryn's look. He tore his eyes away.

"You're a lucky man," said Eryn hoping those were the appropriate words.

"No I'm not, I'm bloody cursed and you know it, though she used to be really pretty when she was younger."

"Really?" asked Eryn sounding doubtful.

"No, I just like to say that because it makes me feel better. Now listen, you boys should drink up and get up to your room and lock the door. There's nearly always trouble here lately just before I lock up and it would be best if you weren't around when it came. Some of these men are real nasty and would kill you just as easily as look at you."

"Okay we will, thanks, but first there's something I've got to do," replied Eryn. The tavern keeper made to leave, but Eryn grabbed his sleeve. "Has anyone said anything to you about some dead soldiers?"

"Dead soldiers? No, but they'll be plenty of them to talk about soon, won't there?" replied the tavern keeper. "Why do you ask anyway?"

"A few leagues back, south of the village, we came across a meadow, there were... dead soldiers. Remadans. Are the Delarites here already?"

"Well the war has begun so I'm told and I keep hearing rumours of sightings all around the countryside from people popping in here, but we haven't seen any in Ederik so far. Wouldn't surprise me if there were some Delarite spies around though, so you boys make sure you are careful who you talk to."

"We will thanks," replied Eryn. "But aren't you afraid that they'll come here and start killing people?"

"Come here! I doubt they'd do that, no reason to, we're not a military town. Anyway, even if they do, they can't be any worse than most of the people who frequent my tavern normally. Who knows, they might even bring some order to the place, because Sulat knows, we need it."

Eryn nodded his thanks, his mind racing through all the possibilities.

The tavern keeper nodded and wandered off to chat with some of his other patrons.

"Follow me, Tav," said Eryn.

Tav swallowed the dregs of his ale and stood to follow his friend. "Where are we going, Eryn?"

"To get some help I hope," replied Eryn without turning round.

Eryn made his way up to the bar and turned to face its occupants, one or two had watched his progress across the floor, but most seemed disinterested and assumed he was just ordering more ale.

"Men of Ederik," Eryn called out loudly. No one appeared to notice. "Men of Ederik," he called out again, louder this time. One or two of the men on the tables nearby seemed to

119

notice and glanced his way, weighing up whether he was worthy of their time or not.

"What are you doing?" asked the tavern keeper a worried expression on his face.

"Don't worry I'm not going to cause any trouble," Eryn replied.

"I hope not," said the tavern keeper, "or you'll see why they call her Mad Maryke."

"Men of Ederik!" Eryn had shouted this time and his raised voice had the desired effect as every set of eyes that he could make out, turned his way, as the room fell into a hushed silence. "Forgive the intrusion, but I knew no other way to grab your attention."

"What do you want, boy, some of us are busy," called a middle-aged man with a moustache. He was greedily fondling a young girl who was sitting on his lap, a fake smile on her face.

"Yeah, give him a couple of minutes and he'll be done," called another, drawing much laughter from just about everyone else in the room.

Behind the bar, the tavern keeper's hand tightened on the wooden club he kept hidden there, but the man enjoying the attention of the whore didn't react as he'd expected. Instead he was clearly anticipating greater pleasures than cracking the head of the man who had insulted him. Besides, there was always tomorrow.

"So what is it, son, spit it out," said another man sitting close by.

"My name is Eryn Martel and this is Tav Rhem, we're from the village of Lentor."

"We didn't ask for your life's story – get to the point," said a man sitting next to the whore. He slowly began to slide his hand up her thigh drawing giggles from the girl and a withering look from the man whose lap she was sat upon.

Eryn knew that he was already losing the scant attention of the room's occupants. He had to hurry. "A couple of days ago our village was attacked by a band of raiders." He hesitated as the tavern door swung open and the three men they had tangled with earlier made their way back in, excited looks upon their faces when they noticed the two boys.

"Seven of our women were taken captive and it is thought that they're being taken east to be sold as slaves." Eryn looked around the room trying to gauge their mood, but whilst one or two shook their heads at the news, most appeared totally unmoved by the revelation. It was only then that it dawned on Eryn that one or more of the raiders might be in the town told to stay behind and check that no one was following. They could even be in that very tavern, in which case he had just put Tav and himself in great danger. It was too late now for a faint heart, so he decided to push on.

"So what's this got to do with us?" asked the man who had pushed Tav down with his foot earlier, giving voice to what most men in the tavern were thinking.

"Tav and I are going after them and we're looking to recruit men to help us in our quest."

For a moment the room fell silent and then it exploded with noise, the raucous laughter bouncing off the walls and ceiling of the tavern.

An old and ugly whore, who only the most desperate or the very drunk ever went to, was suddenly shoved forward into Eryn, the boy catching her fall at the last moment.

"You can keep that old hag, son, as a replacement for the women you lost. No charge. Besides, she probably reminds you of your mother," said the man who had shoved her his way.

The tavern keeper's grip on his club, tightened still further. This was definitely going to end badly. He glanced over at Maryke and saw that she too anticipated trouble, her right hand hovering perilously close to where he knew she kept a small knife secreted in her dress. Well at least when trouble came, they'd be ready this time.

"You don't ever speak of my mother, you hear me? Ever," screamed Eryn his hand reaching for his sword hilt.

"Why not, we all knew her and any one of us could be your father?" laughed the man who had barged Eryn into the street earlier. The man noticed Eryn's hand gripping his sword hilt. "You so much as try unsheathing that tooth pick and I'm going to use it to gut you and your friend real slow."

Eryn was red in the face with anger, his grip on the sword almost painful. His desire to run over and stick the man with

121

his sword was overwhelming, but he and Tav were hopelessly outnumbered and he had given the tavern keeper his word. He slowly released the grip on the sword hilt.

"You are not worth it. I was told this was a town of scum and vagrants, but I didn't want to believe it. I thought there had to be some good men here, some with a shred of honour and decency. Turns out I was wrong and looks like I can add the word 'cowards' to the list," spat Eryn making for the door.

Behind him the tavern keeper winced. The lad might have got away with scum and vagrants, because for the most part it was true and they knew it. Nobody, however, liked to be called a coward.

As one the three newcomers launched themselves at Eryn and Tav, all five of them ending up wrestling in a heap on the floor. Around the room women began to scream and chairs began to crash noisily to the floor as the men eyed each other warily. Unprovoked attacks broke out all over the tavern as men sought to settle old scores.

Eryn was trading punches with the leader of the group whilst the other two took turns to punch Tav in the stomach. Two more men, who had clearly felt insulted by Eryn's words, pinned Tav's arms to his sides. Three other men made their way over to where Eryn was surprising his opponent with the strength of his punches and he was soon over-powered and taking a similar beating to Tav.

The man who had barged Eryn out of the way earlier, wiped his mouth with the back of his hand, the sight of his own blood incensing him still further.

"I'm going to carve you like a lump of meat, boy," he said as he pulled a vicious looking knife from under his tunic. He was just stepping forward to make good on his threat when two men whom Eryn couldn't remember seeing in the tavern, came sprinting across to join the melee. They took the man's friends completely by surprise and sent them all sprawling to the floor. One of the two men was wielding a small bar stool like a club with devastating effect and the two men holding onto Eryn were unconscious before they even knew what hit them. If he didn't know better, the man with the knife would have sworn that one of the men looked like a monk or priest.

He was still contemplating that fact as he raised his knife and prepared to join the fight.

A sudden sharp pain at the back of his head made him feel nauseous before he collapsed to the floor, the knife dropping harmlessly from his hand. Behind him, the tavern keeper gave a respectful nod at the club he held in his right hand.

With three of their number laying sprawled out on the floor and taking no further part in the proceedings, two of the remaining attackers fled from the tavern keen to put as much distance between themselves and the mad priest as possible. Others who had been considering joining the fight whether out of a sense of hurt pride or merely for the fun of it, melted anonymously back into the crowd leaving just two attackers to deal with. The tall man who accompanied the stool wielding priest quickly despatched one with a series of considered and precision blows that sent the man crashing to the floor, whilst Eryn and Tav dealt with the remaining one.

The four stood in the middle of the tavern surveying the carnage around them. Broken furniture and bodies littered the floor, including one with a nasty looking gash at the back of his head which was bleeding profusely. Eryn looked up and saw the tavern keeper holding a short wooden club standing just behind the crumpled body. Eryn nodded his thanks.

"Far be it from me to ever turn custom away, but I think you gentlemen have outstayed your welcome and I'd thank you to be on your way." The tavern keeper's tone suggested that the point wasn't up for discussion.

Eryn walked over to the tavern keeper and extended his hand and after a few seconds deliberation he clasped Eryn's hand and shook it.

"Thank you for your hospitality," said Eryn genuinely.

The tavern keeper laughed, unsure whether the young lad was being sarcastic or not. "You're lucky, young man. Normally they're quite hostile towards strangers."

Eryn smiled. "Well thank you anyway," he said glancing at the prone body of the man the tavern keeper had slugged over the head.

"You're very welcome. My sister Danah, lives in Lentor, with her husband Rac and son Jash. Do you know them?"

"I know them, they are well-respected," replied Eryn.

The tavern keeper beamed, but then his face darkened as a thought crossed his mind.

"They're fine," said Eryn as if reading the man's mind. "I saw them just before we left."

Relief seemed to wash across the tavern keeper's face. "Thank you for those few words of comfort. I hope that you find the women from your village."

"Thanks."

"Now, without wishing to appear ungracious, I really think it would be a good idea if you and your friends left."

"What about you? He's not going to be too happy when he wakes up," said Eryn nodding towards the body at his feet.

"*If*, he wakes up. Don't worry about me, I'll be fine. You forget I've got Maryke," replied the tavern keeper smiling.

The man who looked like a priest turned and left first followed by Eryn and then Tav, the remaining man lingering a few seconds longer. He waited until the others had safely left the tavern before walking slowly over to the bar and placing a couple of coins on the bar top.

"For any damage and inconvenience."

The tavern keeper looked at the coins and nodded his thanks. "The best way you can thank me, stranger, is to get on your horse, ride out of town and never come back."

"Consider it done, though if you had any sense you'd follow us. There's a storm coming, a Delarite storm and it's headed this way." The words had been spoken to the tavern keeper but were meant for everyone.

"We've got no quarrel with the Delarites, or anyone else for that matter. Some of my customers are Delarites. We're just a small town in the middle of nowhere. I can't see them bothering with us," said the tavern keeper.

"Somehow I don't think that's how they will see it, but it is for every man to choose his destiny. I wish you luck with yours." With a last look round at the tavern's customers, most of whom glared at the stranger with open, yet restrained hostility, he turned and left, the bar erupting into a cauldron of angry debate as soon as he walked through the door.

His companion and the two young lads were waiting outside in the street prepared for trouble, but relieved when none materialised.

124

"We owe you our thanks and probably more," said Eryn looking at the two men.

"You are most welcome, Eryn of Lentor, but I suggest that we leave further pleasantries and introductions until we are far from this den of devils."

"I'll second that," said the man who looked to Eryn an awful lot like a priest, though he dismissed the notion as ridiculous. Who'd ever heard of a fighting priest, especially one who could wield a bar stool so proficiently in a brawl?

"Do you have horses, Eryn?" asked the tall man.

"No, we arrived on foot," replied Eryn almost embarrassed.

"Then it is as well that we have two spare horses we can give you."

"Really? You brought spare horses with you?"

"Not as such, we acquired them yesterday, their previous owners having no further use for them. Now, please, follow me," said the tall stranger.

Chapter 11

Despite all of his best intentions, Teren did not leave Porta to the next morning. After eating a hearty meal at the tavern, the likes of which Teren hadn't tasted for more years than he cared to remember, the two men had started to drink. As the ale flowed and the stories of past adventures were recounted to an ever growing audience, Teren completely lost track of time. By the time he finally noticed that it had turned dark outside he was too drunk to walk out of the tavern let alone chase after anybody. Unperturbed he had gamely tried, his efforts at standing and his subsequent collapse to the floor, drawing much good-natured laughter from the crowd. Eventually he had fallen asleep at the table, snoring loudly despite the noisy chatter of those around him. It had taken Alek and five other men to carry him back to Alek's house where he was laid on the spare bed to sleep it off.

The morning sun had already climbed high in the sky by the time a bleary-eyed and somewhat grouchy Teren stumbled out of the spare bedroom and onto the front porch of Alek's house. Alek and his wife were deep in conversation but ceased immediately when Teren appeared, causing a few seconds awkwardness.

"What hour is it?" asked Teren, his voice thick and his throat dry.

"A little after mid-morning. Did you sleep well?" replied Alek.

Teren put a hand to his left temple as a pounding headache welcomed him to the new day. "Yes, I did...thanks. Why didn't you wake me, you knew I had to get straight after them?"

"You weren't in a fit state to go after anybody."

"Maybe not last night, I grant you, but you should have woken me early this morning," protested Teren, his addled mind already trying to wrestle with the dilemma of how he was going to make up the distance between himself, the boys and the raiders.

"Your body obviously needed the sleep, Teren, otherwise you would have woken yourself," said Nerys handing Teren a mug of cold water from the well.

Teren stared at the woman for a moment considering the truth of her words before taking the proffered mug and downing the water in three huge gulps, the cold water soothing his parched throat.

"Maybe, but I still think you ought to have woken me." He was determined to have the last word on the subject it seemed and after exchanging a brief look of frustration, Alek and his wife dropped the subject.

***

After stocking up with provisions and bidding his friend farewell, Teren was soon on his way heading north-east. If Alek was right about the boys' intentions then they would be heading north in the general direction the raiders were last known to be travelling. Sooner or later the raiders would have to turn north-eastwards towards their homelands and Teren figured if he headed that way straightaway, he'd eventually run into one or other group. It was a long shot though and any number of things could go wrong he knew, not least of which could involve either party stumbling into the invading Delarite Army. Still, it was all he had to go on.

It was a hot day, perhaps the hottest of the year so far and by the time Teren slumped in the shade beneath a large yew tree to eat and take a much needed drink on board, he had easily sweated the last vestiges of ale from his bloodstream. He took another swig from his water flagon and glanced around at his surroundings. He was in a small lush green valley, which was populated by a few sparse trees and the odd bank of shrubbery. Somewhere nearby was a small brook or stream as he could just about make out the sound of water gently meandering down the valley from its source high in the Lonely Mountains no doubt. The air was still and quiet, save for the occasional scampering of a rabbit as it tried desperately to evade the attentions of a large bird of prey circling high above. Having lived in the mountains for so long he really should have known the name of every animal and bird he realised and it was something he vowed to correct when he returned from this mission. *If you return,* his mind taunted him.

Teren's thoughts were dragged back to the present by the squeal of the rabbit as it realised it was in great peril. Out of nowhere and like a lightning bolt from the sky, the eagle or whatever it was, had swooped down and made a grab for the rabbit. Teren watched in fascination as the rabbit zigzagged across the ground, desperately trying to shake off its pursuer. Just when Teren thought the rabbit's time was up, it shot into a bolt hole, leaving the bird crying in frustration as it pulled out of its dive and once again climbed into the azure cloudless sky. After circling for a brief time, the bird climbed still higher before eventually flying off in the direction of the Lonely Mountains, seeking more compliant prey.

Teren glanced at the bolt hole into which the rabbit had fled and was surprised when the rabbit tentatively stuck his head out, its nose and whiskers twitching furiously as it tried to sense whether the danger had passed. Evidently satisfied that the coast was now clear, the rabbit hopped out and resumed its own never ending quest for food. Teren marvelled at nature's resilience and silently applauded the rabbit for evading its foe.

You're one lucky and very smart rabbit, my friend. May fortune continue to smile favourably on you. I only hope that Eryn and Tav are as fortunate.

It was a beautiful spot and if he hadn't loved the solitude and rugged beauty of the Lonely Mountains so much, Teren would have been pleased to settle down and see out the remainder of his days, right there. In his mind he could visualise a small wooden cabin with a veranda and...He stopped himself right there. He needed to focus. He was on a mission, a mission upon whose success a lot of lives depended. Fate had set him upon this path and he could not afford to be distracted by thoughts of settling down, family, children or any of the other trappings of a normal life. These things were not for him, not anymore. He was a taker of lives and he was good at it, damned good. He could hide away in the mountains for a while, but eventually his true skills and nature would be called on once again; he'd always known that in truth.

Before he could become any more morose or despondent, Teren quickly put the cork back into his flagon and gathered his stuff, sliding his sword back through his belt. He glanced around one last time, determined to burn the memory of this spot clearly into his mind. The rabbit sat a few paces away, still gamely foraging for food and after bidding him a silent farewell, Teren turned and resumed his journey north-east out of the pretty valley and towards the town of Briden. He had only gone a few paces when a terrible squeal from behind caused him to drop his pack and turn. In one fluid movement he had spun round, drawn his sword and now stood ready to confront whatever was approaching.

A few paces in front of him, the eagle was once again climbing back into the sky, the rabbit dangling in a vice-like grip in its talons. The eagle had only pretended to leave. Knowing that the rabbit had to come out once again to search for its own food, the eagle had merely bided its time and when the rabbit had shown itself, he had swooped down from high above.

You were smart, mused Teren, *but he was smarter. The strong and the smart will always prevail over the weak and the careless.* With that thought firmly to the forefront of his mind, Teren re-sheathed his sword and resumed his journey. Behind him the eagle flew towards the Lonely Mountains and home.

Despite the oppressive heat, Teren made good time during the afternoon and estimated that if he maintained the same pace, he should arrive in Briden by dusk the following day. By his estimation, given that the boys were a lot younger than him and assuming that they managed to avoid the Delarite Army and any other number of unsavoury characters lurking around, they shouldn't be too far from the town of Ederik by now. It was a lot of ifs and Teren felt his pace increase accordingly.

Half a league further on, Teren emerged from a copse into a small clearing. A couple of hundred paces in front of him stood what clearly used to be a very attractive stone farmhouse with a thatched roof. In front of it were various small pens where a handful of goats, pigs and chickens were cooped up. To the side and behind it stretched a number of small fields which obviously belonged to the farm but which appeared to currently be serving no purpose, their crops looking weary and on the verge of ruin. The whole farm seemed to be in a state of deep neglect and he began to wonder whether it had been abandoned, perhaps because of the imminent arrival of the Delarites. He quickly discarded that theory as the Delarite threat was recent and the state of disrepair of the farm would suggest that it had been slowly deteriorating over a much longer period than a few weeks. It was then that he saw the four horses tethered to a rail to the right of the farmhouse. Teren's instincts told him something was amiss and after drawing his sword, he slowly started to approach the farmhouse.

There was scant cover between the trees and the farmhouse and once he left the relative safety of the copse, Teren knew that if one of the riders was to suddenly come out, they'd spot him in an instant. Fighting the urge to sprint across the open land, an act which would render him breathless in the late afternoon heat and less able to defend himself should the need arise, he steadily began to walk towards the farmhouse. Every fibre of his being warned him that he was in great danger and to be vigilant. When the woman's scream rang out from the building, causing some of the livestock to become skittish, he realised, however, that the time for caution was already past.

Teren broke into a jog, steadily increasing his speed as he neared the farmhouse. He realised that unless something changed in the next few seconds, he was in all likelihood going to have to confront the riders within the confines of the farmhouse, where his large two-handed sword would be cumbersome and practically useless. Without breaking his stride, Teren dropped his large sword and quickly withdrew his smaller one. Although most men were terrified when they set eyes on the larger weapon, fearing the damage such a blade could do, it was in fact less deadly than the smaller sword which he now carried. Up close in a melee or a shield wall, the shorter, lighter sword was much more versatile and consequently in the right hands, more lethal.

Blowing hard he took one last deep breath as he raced up the porch steps before kicking open the wooden front door.

The door flew off its old and rusty hinges to land with a bang on the floor. In the space of a few seconds whilst surprise was still on his side, Teren assessed the situation. There were four people in the room. Three soldiers wearing a uniform he didn't recognise, probably Delarite and a woman who was lying on the kitchen table. The woman was naked, her torn dress and undergarments lying discarded on the floor nearby. Two of the soldiers were holding her down by the arms and shoulders, whilst the third, whose breeches were down, stood poised between her thighs, his hands holding them apart as the woman struggled frantically.

In the blink of an eye and before any of them had time to react, Teren swung the short sword at the man nearest him opening up his throat. The man instantly released his grip on the woman's arm, his hands darting to the gaping wound at his throat in a vain attempt to stop the fountain of blood which was now spraying everywhere through his fingers. The man next to him also released his grip on the woman, hastily fumbling for his long cavalry sword, but before he could withdraw it, Teren had rounded the table and shoulder charged him, sending the Delarite sprawling to the floor. Teren plunged his sword deep into the man's chest, ignoring the man's frightened expression and his hands which had been raised in a last minute plea for mercy.

The third soldier was by now desperately trying to tug up his tight cavalry breeches before the madman with the sword could turn on him. Teren pulled his sword out of the dead man's chest and turned to face the remaining soldier hoping that he would not yet be prepared to face Teren, but he was. What he was not prepared for, however, was what happened next. As quick as a flash and with an anger borne out of shame and indignity, the woman who he had just moments before been preparing to violate, pulled back her right leg and kicked him hard in the groin. The Delarite soldier instinctively bent forward and clasped his wounded genitals with both hands, but still managed to hold onto his sword. The woman was not yet finished with him though. Quickly sitting herself up, she reached forward and poked the rigid fingers of both hands straight into his eyes, causing him to drop his sword and scream loudly with the pain.

The man stumbled backwards staring blindly out of bloody and ruined eyes. The woman dispassionately watched from her perch on the table, as the man tripped over the broken door, collapsing onto his back. Teren walked past the woman and with one powerful downward thrust of his sword, ended the man's life and with it, his suffering.

The woman stared down at the bloody mess on the floor that had until a few seconds ago been a living, breathing man and screamed as the first tendrils of shock began to take hold. Teren had seen it all before. He quickly walked over to the woman and slapped her face until she stopped screaming at which point he pulled her close to him, his own body beginning to stir in response to the feel of her nakedness. She clung tightly to Teren her body convulsing with the powerful sobs that wracked her body. Feeling increasingly uncomfortable, Teren was just trying to gauge when it would be safe to try and disengage from her embrace, when he suddenly became aware of another soldier standing in the doorway. There had been four horses outside he reminded himself angrily. This one must have been round the back using the latrine or something.

He let go of the woman and quickly turned to retrieve his sword, turning back around just as the soldier started to tentatively approach him. The Delarite soldier was a young lad and one look in his eyes told Teren that he didn't fancy the fight and would give anything to be somewhere else right about then. Teren made a couple of half-hearted thrusts, which the boy struggled to parry and Teren could see that he was already contemplating how to extricate himself from the fight.

"Are you planning on sticking me with that thing, boy or just tickling me, 'cos I'm kind of in a hurry?" said Teren mocking the young soldier.

Feeling slightly humiliated, the young soldier suddenly lunged at Teren, who simply rolled his wrist deflecting the thrust safely to one side. The momentum of the hard thrust sent the soldier stumbling forward and after stepping to his right, Teren helped him on his way to the floor with a firm kick up the backside, laughing as he did so.

The soldier hauled himself to his feet, his sword hand

visibly shaking, but his outraged sense of honour demanding he try again. He was just about to launch a very basic sequence of strokes against his large adversary, when the woman screamed at them.

"Stop it both of you, please."

Teren's eyes never left the young soldier. "I think you're forgetting, lady, that this lad's mates were on the verge of raping you. I wouldn't be showing any pity if I were you."

"Yes, I know, but he didn't – he tried to stop them."

Teren watched the young soldier glance in her direction, his eyes widening and his jaw dropping in surprise when he noticed for the first time that she was completely naked.

"Well he didn't do a very good job of stopping them if you don't mind me saying," said Teren.

"He protested but they ordered him outside to watch the horses. They said he wasn't man enough. Please don't hurt him," pleaded the woman.

"Is that true, sonny?" asked Teren. The boy didn't answer, his eyes seemingly transfixed on the woman's naked body. Teren suddenly thrust with his sword, slipping the blade under his adversary's before flicking upwards, sending the boy's sword flying safely across the room. The sudden arrival of Teren's sword point at his throat managed to draw his attention away from the woman's nakedness. "Me and the lad here are going to have a chat outside. I suggest that whilst we're gone, you make yourself decent, for all our sakes."

For the first time since the whole horrible affair started, the woman suddenly found herself blushing at her predicament and hurried through to her bedroom to get dressed.

Teren ushered the young soldier out onto the porch to question him and to give the woman time to get dressed and presentable. Teren considered that he was a good judge of people and decided very quickly that the lad wasn't in any way a threat to either himself or the woman. He was probably a conscript who didn't want to be there either. Normal procedure would have been to tie him up and interrogate him as harshly as necessary, but the young man needed no encouragement with regard to providing information.

He told Teren that the invasion of Remada had begun the previous day following the successful conquest of Lydia. The cities of Pirus and Torogora had already fallen and were now occupied, whilst at least two Delarite Armies thrust into the Remadan heartland. He was part of a small cavalry force sent ahead to scout and to spread panic amongst the local populace. Their commanders had given them permission to carry out any atrocity or outrage they considered appropriate and according to the young soldier, there had already been many.

Teren shook his head and spat on the porch in disgust, just as the woman, now fully dressed, came out from where her front door used to be. She gave Teren a withering look.

"That's a disgusting habit and I'll thank you not to do it again whilst you're on my property," she said.

Teren looked at the woman dumbfounded. Hadn't he just saved this woman from the savage attentions of three men? Her gratitude was overwhelming. He couldn't quite find the right words to reply and settled instead for a grunt. He turned to face the soldier just in time to see the last traces of a smirk disappearing from his face.

"And you should take a care; I haven't decided what to do about you yet," he snapped, causing the young soldier to immediately straighten his face, though in reality he knew that if this man was going to kill him, he would in all probability have done it already. "I want a word with the lady in private, sonny, so I want you to take a quick stroll over there where I can see you, but don't even think of running. I'm having a really bad day so don't try my patience."

The young soldier nodded and slowly walked to where Teren had indicated, far enough to be out of earshot, but close enough for Teren to stand a chance of catching him if he decided to make a bolt for it.

"He says that he's part of an advance force of Delarites sent on ahead to terrorise and brutalise the population. It's a full-scale invasion and the countryside is crawling with thousands of soldiers. Pirus and Torogora have already fallen. The lad here didn't want any part of it, but like thousands of others he's been conscripted into the army. Says he was sickened by what the others were doing to you."

The woman briefly cast her eyes to the ground in shame, before finding a new resolve from deep within. "Like I said, he tried to stop them, but a young boy wasn't going to be any match for three men with just one thing on their mind."

"Maybe, but I'm still not sure about trusting him. I learned a long time ago never to trust a soldier, especially a Delarite soldier," said Teren.

"What about a Remadan soldier then?"

"Any soldier."

"Then why should I trust you?"

Teren looked a little abashed at his own trustworthiness being questioned. "Because I'm me and I know you can trust me. Anyway, I'm not a soldier."

"No, but you used to be," said the woman.

"What makes you so sure?"

"The way you killed those three animals in there, for one thing. Oh, and the tattoo on your arm. My husband, rest his soul, had one just like it."

Teren glanced at the faded and worn tattoo on his left forearm, a tattoo worn proudly by every member of the Ninth Ligara. "That was a long time ago." Teren seemed to momentarily drift off into a world of his own before suddenly snapping back to the present. "So what do you want me to do with him?" He nodded towards the young soldier who stood nervously a few paces away, occasionally glancing towards the woods as if contemplating making a run for it.

"Oh, just let him go; he's harmless enough."

"Let him go," said Teren incredulously. "What if he decides not to keep his base desires under control at the next farmhouse he stumbles across?"

"No, I don't think so. He's frightened – look at him," insisted the woman.

"Looks can be deceiving."

"Not this time." It appeared to be her last word on the subject.

"As you wish," said Teren as he straightened and walked to where the young soldier stood waiting. "You're free to go."

"What! You're letting me go?" said the soldier surprised.

"Isn't that what I just said, or would you prefer I ran you

through with your own sword, because if it was down to me, that's what would happen for what your mates were about to do?" asked Teren.

"But where will I go?"

"I don't know and I don't care either," said Teren honestly. He was sparing the kid's life yet he wanted more?

"I mean, I can't go deeper into Remada or your people will kill me and I can't go back to the army or I risk them executing me for cowardice or desertion," said the young soldier.

"You've got a problem then, haven't you, sonny, but it's your problem not mine. My alternative is still on the table regardless of what the lady says."

The soldier looked into Teren's cold hard eyes and could tell instantly that the man would cut him down there and then without a second thought or remorse.

"May I at least have my sword back so I can defend myself?"

Teren looked from the soldier to his cavalry sword and back again, as if he were weighing up any risk. Then with a grunt of derision, he stuck the sword into the ground point first in front of the soldier, his hand then surreptitiously travelling to the hilt of his own short sword. "Take your blade and be gone."

"And our horses?" The boy's negotiating skills were fast becoming a source of irritation to Teren.

"You can take one horse, but the other three stay," said Teren.

The soldier nodded and almost as a second thought, held his hand out for Teren to shake. Teren merely glanced at it and then stared into the young soldier's face, his look saying more than words ever could.

If the soldier was offended, he didn't show it and after sheathing his sword, he marched off to collect his horse. Teren watched as he mounted the smallest of the four horses and after nodding at the woman who was stood on the porch, he slowly trotted out of the farm yard in a northerly direction.

The risk of running into his own men was apparently more acceptable than running into a bunch of vengeful Remadans, mused Teren.

The woman walked over to Teren's side and watched silently as the soldier disappeared into the distance.

"What will his own men do to him if they catch him?" she asked.

Teren stroked his beard ponderously. "That depends on how good a liar he is. If he can convince them that they were ambushed and that he managed to escape, probably nothing. If they suspect that he ran, then that's another matter." Teren turned to face the woman, noticing for the first time just how strikingly attractive she was, the realisation rendering him momentarily speechless. The small smile on her face seemed to suggest that she was enjoying his attention and perhaps discomfort. Teren cleared his throat nervously. "Anyway, you shouldn't be worrying about him, you should be packing, but only lightly mind, I know what you women are like."

"Packing! Packing what and why?" asked the woman in surprise.

"I would have thought that was obvious. You can't possibly stay here with the whole Delarite Army nearby. I would have thought that today's little incident would have demonstrated that. Now please go and pack some clothes and a bit of food if you have it."

"I'm not going anywhere," the woman said indignantly. "This is where I live and this is where I'm staying."

"Look, lady, I ..."

"Tanya, my name is Tanya."

"Look, Tanya, I admire your guts, really I do, but there's courage and there's reckless folly and you staying here with thousands of Delarites swarming the countryside around you, definitely falls into the latter category," said Teren.

"Maybe, but this is my home and I don't see why I should be driven out. No one is asking you to stay. All I ask of you is that you see to the burial of those three men in my house."

"You want me to put our lives at risk by spending what precious time we have left, burying the men who were about to rape you?" asked Teren incredulously.

"They still deserve a decent burial. It is not for us to judge them," replied Tanya earnestly.

"All lowlife filth like that deserve, is to be tossed into a ditch somewhere where the maggots can feed on them," replied Teren just as earnestly.

"Bury them over there. I don't want them near my husband. Even I draw the line at that."

The woman was as stubborn as any he'd ever met and Teren realised this wasn't an argument he was going to win. With a nervous glance towards the far side of the clearing from which he would expect any Delarites to approach, he stomped off to the house to collect the first body.

Chapter 12

Burying the three dead soldiers had been hard work in the late afternoon sun, the ground rock hard from several weeks without rain. When Tanya appeared at his side bearing a tankard of cold water, she found him looking tired, hot and irritable.

"Happy now?" he said snatching the tankard from her and spilling some of its contents in the process.

"In a manner of speaking, yes. I couldn't in all good conscience have left this place with their bodies still above ground."

Teren sipped the cool water enjoying its feel as it soothed his parched throat, slowly reviving him. He was just about to take another sip when it suddenly dawned on him what she had just said.

"You've decided to leave then?"

"Yes, I have. I really don't want to, but I can see that to stay here would be to put myself in harm's way. I am extremely vulnerable on my own."

"Finally, some common sense," said Teren, expressing in words a sentiment he meant to keep to himself.

"There is just one small problem, before you go congratulating yourself too much."

"Oh, and what's that?" asked Teren as he greedily consumed the remnants of his drink.

"I have nowhere to go," said Tanya.

"You must have family you can go and stay with?"

"No, my husband was all the family I had. Apart from Alun."

"Alun? Who's Alun?" asked Teren.

Tanya glanced to her right and made a beckoning motion with her hand. From behind a large yew tree, a young boy of perhaps nine or ten warily began to emerge, glancing nervously to his mother for encouragement.

"It's okay, Alun, you can come out now, it's quite safe for the moment," said Tanya holding out her arm.

Safe wouldn't have been Teren's choice of words given that the whole Delarite Army was close by.

The boy ran to his mother's embrace, clutching her tightly whilst staring at Teren with a wide-eyed expression.

"It's all right, Alun, there's no need to be afraid, this is..." Tanya suddenly realised that she didn't even know the name of the man who had saved her. She turned to face Teren. "Please forgive my rudeness. After everything you've done I haven't even asked your name."

Teren smiled. "My name is Teren, Teren Rad." He watched Tanya's face for any sign of recognition, but if she did recognise the name, her expression didn't betray the fact.

Teren extended his hand for the young boy to shake, but instead of accepting the invitation, Alun buried his head deeper into his mother's skirt.

"I'm sorry. Ever since his father was killed, he's become very nervous, especially around men."

"There's no need to apologise on my account," replied Teren as he smiled at the boy. "I'm sure that over time we'll become good friends you and me, Alun, what do you say?"

Alun just stared back without answering. When it became clear that he wasn't going to get a response, Teren looked to Tanya.

"He hasn't spoken a word since his father's death," said Tanya apologetically.

"Not even to you?" asked Teren.

"Not even to me."

Teren's eyebrows rose in surprise, but he decided not to push the point. Something in the far tree line caught his attention and he appeared momentarily distracted, a fact noticed by a suddenly alarmed Tanya.

"What is it, Teren?" she asked following his gaze but not seeing anything that could cause his consternation.

"*Quiet,*" Teren snapped in a hushed tone, cocking his head slightly as if he were trying to listen more attentively.

Tanya turned to face Teren, noticing the concern etched across his face and the slow movement of his right hand as it reached for his large sword standing against a tree a couple of paces away.

"What do you see?" asked Tanya quietly whilst hugging her son even closer.

"I don't suppose you've packed some things for you and the boy have you?" asked Teren completely ignoring her question.

"I've packed a small bag with essentials and another with some bread and cheese, but I've not had chance to load the wagon yet."

"Good, we're not taking it. We've got to travel light and quickly. Go and get your bags now." His eyes had never left the tree line to the east.

Tanya was halfway across to her farmhouse, when a horseman burst from the tree line to the east heading at full pelt towards Teren. Tanya grabbed Alun by the hand and dragged him as quickly as possible to the house only turning to look back when she reached the relative safety of her porch. Teren had stepped out into the open facing the oncoming rider, his large two-handed sword held high above his head ready to chop down at the rider.

The rider pulled up a few paces away from Teren, the horse's hooves sending up a cloud of dust as it was brought to an abrupt stop. The rider held out his arms in a gesture of peace and it was only then that Tanya saw that it was the young soldier from earlier that day. She sent Alun into the house to retrieve their two bags and when he returned, they quickly made their way over to where Teren was now warily talking to the Delarite soldier. He had discarded his uniform and now wore some plain Remadan clothes she noticed. Tanya hoped that she had been right about the boy and that he'd at worse stolen the clothes or better still bought them. The thought that he might have killed someone for them was too much to bear, as it would be her fault for persuading Teren to spare his life in the first place.

"How many?" asked Teren.

"I don't know for sure," replied the soldier, "at least a couple of thousand."

"What is it?" asked Tanya as she joined the men.

The young soldier nodded at Tanya his face registering surprise when he saw Alun for the first time.

"The lad here says there's a troop of Delarite soldiers

converging on us. Tell her what you just told me," Teren instructed the lad. It was a ploy by Teren to make sure that the young soldier wasn't exaggerating. Any discrepancy between this version and the one he had just recounted to Teren would be vigorously challenged.

"After I left you I headed north. Twice I nearly ran into our cavalry and had to hide up. Before I got rid of my uniform I managed to speak with another scout I ran into. The invasion is going better than our officers even dared to hope and Remada's armies are falling back or disintegrating all over the country. Much of the north is already under Delarite control. I had to head east and then double back just to get here. The cavalry are everywhere and there's a troop not far behind me who could arrive here at any moment. They're probably looking for me and the men I was with this morning. You need to go."

"You forgot to mention that small detail to me, sonny," said Teren snarling.

"Well you know now," he shot back meeting Teren's angry stare with one of his own.

"What does it all mean, Teren?" asked Tanya.

"It means that we're pretty much surrounded and that whatever way we go we risk running into their damned cavalry."

"Surely that means we must head south away from the Delarites?" asked Tanya.

"Normally you'd be right, but unfortunately we can't go south for two reasons," replied Teren.

"And what would they be?"

"Firstly it's open country south of here until you get to the Lonely Mountains and we'd be easy targets for their cavalry."

"And the second reason?"

"I've got to head north."

"North! That's madness. Why?" asked the young soldier.

"That's my business."

"But surely the north is where they've come from? The Delarite border is only a hundred leagues or so to the north," said Tanya.

"I know that," snapped Teren much more aggressively

than he intended. "But right now I can't think what else to do unless you want to stay here and wait for their cavalry boys to come along and take turns humping you."

He regretted his words instantly and wasn't surprised by the ferocity of the slap that hit him squarely on his right cheek. The young soldier wisely looked away for a few seconds, whilst Teren and Tanya locked eyes. Eventually, swallowing his hurt pride, Teren apologised.

"What about Vangor; has that fallen yet?" Teren asked as he turned to face the young soldier again.

"It's still holding out I think."

"You think! Think harder. Did the trooper you spoke to mention it or not?" pressed Teren.

The young soldier seethed at the way the scruffy old man spoke to him, but wisely bit back the retort he would rather have uttered. "Yes, yes he definitely did. He said that it was all that remained in the north, but that it wouldn't last long as General Malik was leading an army towards it." The soldier noticed the brief flicker of recognition that crossed the old man's face at the mention of General Malik's name. "You know of General Malik?"

"Our paths have crossed once or twice," was all Teren would say in reply.

Tanya looked at the young soldier and was about to ask him a question when she noticed for the first time that he was holding his left side. She reached up and gently prised his hand away revealing a nasty looking wound that was bleeding badly.

"You're hurt! Why didn't you say? Quick, Teren, help me get him down and into the house."

"I'll be fine, honestly. We need to get going," said the soldier.

"What happened?" asked Teren.

"The trooper I was talking to became suspicious. I think he worked out that I was a deserter and tried to follow me. It wasn't his wisest decision today, but it was his last," said the soldier.

Teren grunted an acknowledgment, slowly warming to the young soldier. "Climb down and let Tanya have a look at you then we must get going. Any place is preferable to here.

143

You'd better come with us for the time being." Teren had just started to reach up to help the soldier down, when the rider's body suddenly jerked before slumping forward and eventually dropping to the ground, an arrow protruding from between his shoulders.

"Get the boy and run to the trees behind me – now," Teren bellowed at Tanya. Then he took a couple of paces forward and raised his sword above his head again and prepared to meet the two riders who were charging towards him with their own swords drawn.

After quickly glancing to her right and seeing the two riders, Tanya grabbed Alun by the hand and ran for all she was worth towards the beckoning trees, not looking back once.

The riders were approaching fast, their swords pointing down ready to skewer Teren, one from each side. He was going to have to time this just right he realised. He waited to almost the last second before surprising the riders by quickly leaping to his right and bringing his sword down in a powerful arc. The blade struck the nearest rider on the right shoulder and across the span of his back, slicing through his inadequate leather body armour and finding easy purchase in his flesh. The rider fell to the ground in a spray of blood.

Frustrated at being denied a target at the last moment, the other rider reined in his horse before it reached the tree line and turned around. Teren stood watching him, sword poised above his head. Cursing when he saw his friend's dead body lying on the ground a few paces from where Teren stood, the Delarite dug his heels into the horse's flanks and charged.

From the relative safety of the tree line, Tanya watched in awe as the Delarite cavalryman raced towards Teren. To Tanya it was a terrifying sight and one she knew that she would not be able to stand if she was in Teren's shoes right then.

But then you're not Teren Rad, one of the greatest soldiers Remada has ever known, she reminded herself.

When Teren had told her his name, the breath had almost caught in her throat with fear, though rationally she knew she had no reason to be frightened of him. Yet his name was synonymous with war, glory and death, especially death and although she didn't have any reason to fear him, neither did she have any real reason to trust him. That is why she hadn't made any attempt to acknowledge him when he had told her, despite the disappointed look on his face. Big man, big ego she guessed. Now as she watched him face danger once again to protect her and Alun, she knew that she could trust him. He was everything her husband had said and perhaps more.

The sound of metal striking metal reverberated through the clearing when the two swords clashed as the rider raced by Teren. The Delarite turned his horse and once again galloped towards Teren, his sword raised slightly above his shoulder. Again the swords clashed as both men parried the other's stroke, neither gaining an advantage.

The rider once again turned his horse, but this time instead of immediately charging at Teren, he paused briefly, as if weighing up his options. After a few seconds he came at Teren as fast as he could coaxing every ounce of effort from his horse. This time though, at the very last moment he altered the horse's direction sending it careering into Teren and barging him to the ground.

Teren was winded, but unhurt. Before he could drag himself to his feet though, the Delarite was on him, rearing his horse up onto its hind legs in an effort to crush Teren with its front legs. Teren rolled left then right, desperately trying to avoid the crushing blow the horse's hooves would deliver to his chest. Drawing on all his strength and praying that his timing was right, Teren rolled to his right and stood, sword at the ready.

His roll had taken the rider by surprise and as he struggled to calm his mount down, Teren saw that his moment had come. He reached up and grabbed the rider by his tunic and pulled with all his might. For a moment it looked like he hadn't done enough, but then suddenly the horse began to tilt towards Teren as the rider struggled to maintain his balance. Teren stepped quickly out of the way as both the horse and its rider came crashing to the ground in a cloud of dust. The man screamed with pain as the horse struggled back to its feet, relieving the pressure on his broken left leg.

Teren walked over to the stricken soldier and glared down

at him, a look of satisfaction on his face. The soldier feebly reached for his sword but Teren simply kicked it out of his reach.

"The war is over for you I think, sonny," said Teren. "Your life too if you don't tell me what I need to know." The Delarite's eyes were fixed on Teren's large sword which was sloped over his right shoulder. "Where are the rest of your mates?"

Teren watched as the man wrestled with his conscience. If he told the Remadan what he wanted to know and his commander found out he would probably be put to death, but if he didn't tell the Remadan what he wanted to hear, he suspected it was certain death.

"We are everywhere, Remadan, you cannot stop us."

Teren put his left foot on the man's broken leg and pressed down, instantly regretting it when the man screamed, a scream loud enough to wake the dead. Teren removed his foot and placed the tip of his sword at the man's throat, the action having the desired effect as the man instantly stopped screaming.

"Now I'll ask you again, where are the rest of your horsemen?" said Teren increasing the pressure of his sword just enough to pierce the skin and bring forth a drop of blood. The rider got the message.

"To the east of the forest between here and those mountains," said the rider nodding his head slightly towards the Lonely Mountains. "They're harassing the Remadan Army as it runs with its tail between its legs." He felt the sword point dig into his skin a fraction more.

"What about you and your mate over there? Why are you in the forest?"

"A few of us were sent in to make sure you Remadans weren't cowering in here. We were also looking for a few of our men that have gone missing," said the soldier wincing from the pain in his shattered leg.

"I've some good news for you then, you've found them," said Teren nodding towards the three freshly dug graves. "And your armies, where are they?"

"To the north and the east consolidating our gains here and in Lydia. Only the city of Vangor stands untouched in the north, but that won't stand for long once our army besieges it."

The young soldier had been right. "So you've invaded Lydia?"

"Lydia and Remada have the honour of being our first conquests, but there will be others I promise you. Why don't you face it, Remadan, you are trapped? It's only a matter of time before you and your woman are found. Treat my wound and I will speak well of you when my comrades come. Do nothing and I will have nothing but bad things to say. Then we will take turns with your woman whilst you watch before killing you both slowly. It is up to you." The Delarite smiled malevolently at Teren. It was the smile of a man who thought he held all the cards.

"You won't be able to say anything if you're dead, Delarite."

"True, but I think we both know that it is in your best interests to spare me. Self-preservation is a powerful motivator is it not?"

Teren nodded and slowly turned away just as the Delarite began to laugh. Quick as a flash, Teren spun back around and lashed out, his right boot connecting with the man's jaw with a sickening crunch, blood and teeth spraying out of his mouth.

Teren looked down at the unconscious man and smiled. "Not laughing now are you, sonny?"

Teren hurried over to where Tanya crouched over the young soldier's motionless body. She looked up as Teren approached.

"He's dead."

Teren nodded; he'd anticipated as much. "Then we'd best be going. His mates aren't far behind apparently," he said inclining his head towards the unconscious Delarite with the broken leg.

"We didn't even know his name," said Tanya sadly.

Teren looked dumbfounded. "He and his mate just tried to kill me and you're moaning because we didn't ask his name?"

Tanya looked up at Teren with a surprised expression of her own.

"You meant him, didn't you?" said Teren rather sheepishly and glancing down at the body lying next to Tanya.

Tanya decided that it was probably best not to embarrass Teren further. "He came back to warn us when he didn't have to. He probably saved our lives."

"Maybe and I'm grateful to the lad, but now we've got to look out for ourselves by moving, right now, or his death will have been for nothing."

"But what about...?"

"Forget it. There's no time for more burials, besides he was a soldier, he'd understand. Now we've got to go unless you want the Delarites to use your lad for target practice when they come?"

Tanya glanced over at Alun who was staring at the young soldier's body with a frightened expression and made up her mind. "No, of course not."

"Good, in that case, let's get going," said Teren, clearly relieved that he wasn't going to have to endure another round of arguments on the subject.

"Where are we going?" asked Tanya.

"Vangor."

"Vangor, why Vangor?"

"Because that's the only place within travelling distance that's still in Remadan hands, at least for the time being," said Teren.

"And it also happens to be to the north."

"That too."

"You never did tell us why it was so important for you to travel north," said Tanya probing for information.

"No, I didn't and maybe I'll tell you sometime, but not right now. At this moment in time the most important thing is to find somewhere safe for you and the boy."

Tanya smiled for what felt like the first time in years. Beneath the gruff exterior of this rugged looking man, there was a caring, sensitive side. "We'll be safe at Vangor?"

"Truthfully, I don't know. The lad said that a Delarite army was heading there right now, but Vangor has always been a strong garrison town with solid defences and should be able to hold out until a relief force arrives. So long as we get there before the Delarites and so long as the army hasn't been withdrawn or run, you should be okay there," replied Teren honestly.

"That's a lot of ifs and maybes."

"I know, but it's the best I can offer at the moment. To go south would be suicide I think. If our armies are running, the roads will be clogged with refugees, easy targets for their cavalry. Who knows, maybe they'll decide Vangor isn't worth the trouble and leave it alone," said Teren.

He didn't sound very convinced Tanya thought, but in the absence of a better suggestion, she was happy to go along with it.

"What about him, is he ...?"

"Dead? No, but he's going to feel a little sore when he wakes up later," replied Teren after following her gaze to the Delarite soldier who lay unconscious a few paces away.

She clearly didn't feel comfortable leaving an injured man, even an enemy soldier, lying out in the open, but to her credit, Teren noted, she didn't push the point.

After a last glance round and after kneeling and saying a few words over her husband's grave, a delay Teren didn't complain about, the three set off on foot heading north-east. There was still a couple of hours' daylight left and Teren was keen to put as much distance between the farmhouse and themselves whilst they could. The forest could be a dangerous place at night, but not as dangerous as remaining where they were.

Chapter 13

By the end of the fourth day, Kern's men were within spitting distance of the border, but the land around them was teeming with Delarite soldiers. The only Remadans Kern had seen were refugees hurrying south with whatever possessions they could safely carry.

Mindful of the earlier escape attempt and the proximity of the Delarites, every night Kern doubled the guard both on the girls and the camp's perimeter. This meant that a third of his men were on duty at any one time, something which didn't endear him to his already weary men. As he settled under his coarse blanket for the night, Kern decided he didn't much care what the men thought, so long as they continued to do what he commanded. Just to be certain though, he slept with his dagger under the blanket.

He wasn't sure whether the man had shaken him or it was some sixth sense warning him of danger, but Kern had woken in an instant, the blade of his dagger soon resting against the man's throat.

"You would kill me in my sleep, you dog?" Kern snarled into the man's face. Challenges to his authority were not uncommon but Kern would never have expected it from Varil, one of his oldest and most trusted men. Still greed was liable to do that to even the most loyal of men it seemed.

"No, Kern, I am not trying to kill you. I'm here to warn you," replied Varil his eyes wide with fear. One wrong word and he knew that his life was forfeit.

"Warn me, warn me about what?"

"Beren and some of the others have taken a couple of the girls into the woods."

"What! I gave specific orders for the girls not to be touched. Soiled goods do not fetch so high a price," spat Kern incensed.

"I know, Kern, but I don't think Beren cares. His brains have always been in his breeches you know that."

Kern removed the dagger from Varil's throat. "Sorry, old friend, but I can never be too careful."

"A wise precaution, Kern and one I follow myself," said Varil breathing a sigh of relief.

"How many of the men are with Beren?"

"There are five men with him in the woods, but I know some of the others in the camp have a mind to follow him if he makes a move. I would say that two thirds of the men are with him."

"Treacherous dogs! I'll see them all killed for this. What of the perimeter guards?"

"Those that are not with him have been killed," replied Varil.

"So no one watches for the soldiers?"

"No."

"No matter, there is nothing I can do about that now. First I must deal with Beren and his scum. Wake Galen and the others you know still follow me for certain and we will make our move. With you and Galen by my side, it doesn't matter how many of them there are they will still fail," said Kern.

Varil's expression changed and for a brief second he could not meet his leader's gaze.

"What is it, old friend?"

"It is Galen, Kern. He is with Beren," replied Varil.

The news that his good friend and toughest warrior had betrayed him and thrown his lot in with Beren, cut him like the sharpest knife.

"So be it, he will die like the others. Quietly wake those that you know are with us. Slit the throats of those you know that aren't."

"What of those I don't know? There are some new men who I do not yet know enough to trust," asked Varil.

"If there is any doubt, kill them, but do it silently. If they wake before we have levelled the odds, we will surely die."

Varil nodded and crawled off silently to wake the others whom he knew loyal and to carry out Kern's bidding.

Less than five minutes later, Varil walked over and crouched next to Kern and whispered that the camp was theirs. Kern wiped his knife clean on the tunic of the man he had just killed.

"How many?" asked Kern.

"Sixteen dead."

Kern nodded thoughtfully. "So many?"

"You told me to only spare those I knew were loyal."

Kern noted the hint of recrimination in his friend's tone. Sixteen dead sounded like a great deal many more than was necessary and he couldn't help but wonder whether one or two scores had been settled under the guise of his orders. No matter, it was done now. He looked at the men crouched behind Varil and nodded. There were only seven of them including Varil, but they were loyal and tough men. Only Galen and Beren were missing from the group of what he used to consider his most loyal men.

"So be it. Where are Beren and his dogs?" Before Varil could reply the sounds of a girl crying and the coarse laughter of at least two men drifted through the still night air. Kern stared in the direction from which the sounds had come. "Let's get it done, but I want Beren taken alive, understood? He more than the others, must pay for his treachery."

The small group of men huddled around him nodded in unison.

"What about them?" asked Varil nodding towards the girls who had not been taken.

"Leave two men behind to watch over them."

"That will make it pretty much even odds, Kern except that they have Galen," warned Varil.

"I know, but we will have the element of surprise. I will take care of Galen, don't worry."

The look in Varil's eyes suggested that he wasn't convinced, but he had the good sense not to say anything further. He quickly gave orders for two of the men to remain behind and watch the girls before the remaining men began to quietly make their way towards the trees.

No more than twenty paces inside the woods, Kern's party came across a small clearing. Signalling for his men to fan out, but keep quiet, Kern studied the scene before him. There were six men including Beren and two of the girl prisoners. One of the girls was bent forward over a fallen log whilst Beren raped her, two of his cronies holding her outstretched arms to prevent her struggling. Two more men stood holding another of the girls and watching the scene before them with lustful expressions. Galen stood with his back to Razak watching Beren and awaiting his turn.

Kern glanced round to where he knew his men were concealed and checked that they were ready. When everyone signalled back to him Kern quickly stepped into the clearing and mustering every ounce of strength he could, hurled the javelin he'd been carrying, at Galen's back. It hit home with a gentle thud, the point travelling through his body and protruding out the other side.

Whether it was the shock or surprise, Galen did not cry out in pain and it was only when he looked down and saw the point sticking out of his stomach, that he finally made any noise. It was not a cry of anguish though, but a roar of anger the likes of which Kern knew had petrified many an enemy.

The two men holding onto the other girl were the first to react, releasing their grip and reaching for their swords. One managed to draw his weapon before he was run through from behind but his companion was cut down before his hand even reached his sword's handle.

The two men who had been sat holding the girl's arms also released their grip frantically scrabbling backwards whilst trying to stand. One had his throat cut before he managed to get up and Varil beheaded the other.

By now Beren had struggled to his feet and was hastily pulling up his breeches. Galen, after recovering from the initial shock, had somehow pulled the lance out of his body and had turned to face Kern who was approaching him with his sword drawn. Galen drew his own weapon and swung wildly at Kern who ducked safely below his blade, before thrusting his own sword deep into Galen's side.

Galen howled with rage and although he momentarily staggered, still he did not succumb to his wounds. He came at Kern once again, swinging wildly and quickly. They were desperate strokes from a man who knew he was dying but who was determined to take his killer with him.

It would not be long Kern realised before loss of blood would tire Galen to such an extent that he would eventually collapse. Unless another opportunity to strike presented itself, all he had to do until then, was to avoid the man's erratic sword swings. How the man even remained on his feet was a mystery to Kern. He had always known that his former friend was as strong as a bear, but this was beyond comparison.

He swayed backwards as another powerful swing of Galen's sword arced through the air aiming to slice Kern's head off. He took another pace or two back encouraging Galen to come onto him, every pace sapping the man's strength and expediting his death. As if reading Kern's mind, Galen launched himself into one last powerful assault, the ferocity of which caught Kern completely by surprise as he believed the man's strength nearly spent.

Three times he managed to block bone jarring blows from Galen's sword and Kern was just beginning to wonder whether his strategy was working when Galen stumbled slightly and almost lost his footing. Kern seized his opportunity and sliced his sword into the back of Galen's left thigh, cutting him deeply and bringing him crashing to the ground. The big man howled with pain again but was powerless to stop what was coming. He was still spitting his hate when a powerful swipe from Kern's sword sliced off his head sending it flying through the air. It landed and rolled to within inches of where Beren was kneeling with two sword points at his throat.

Kern pushed the still kneeling body of Galen over with his foot and strolled over to where Beren stared at him with open hatred.

"Such is the fate of all traitors, Beren."

"Better to die a warrior's death than to continue to follow a spineless lamb," said Beren.

"Who said anything about you receiving a warrior's death?"

Beren's expression slowly turned from one of defiance to one of terror as the possibilities turned over in his mind. He knew what cruelty Kern was capable of if the need arose.

"You, Elanir and Nebu, remain here and deal with him," Kern said to Varil. "You know what I want done?"

Varil smiled knowingly. "It will be a pleasure, Kern."

"Good, I and the others will take the girls back to the camp and prepare them to move out."

"As you wish, Kern," said Varil placing his own sword point at Beren's throat. "You know what to do so get on with it," he then said to Nebu.

Nebu nodded and after indicating for his friend to follow him, they began to dig a pit.

The first thing Kern noticed when he got back to the camp was that the two guards were nowhere in sight and neither were their horses. The girls were all on their feet and talking animatedly though their voices started to trail off when they saw Kern and two of his men reappear with the two girls.

The torn dress and shattered look on one of the girl's faces suggested that Kern and his two companions had raped their friends and one or two of the braver ones started to hurl abuse at the men as they approached.

"Silence or I will have my men kill you all. You are all becoming more trouble than you are worth so heed my words." Kern was about to say something further when he saw the body of one of his men lying on the floor. He hurried over to him and crouched down, gently raising the man's head and shoulders with his left arm as support. "Akila, what happened?" The man was covered in blood and probably only had seconds to live.

The man opened his eyes slightly and managed a small smile. "Kern... I'm sorry, I failed you."

"Don't be a fool, my friend, you did not fail me. I cannot lie to you though, Akila, the Chariot of Souls is coming for you, so tell me what happened so that I might avenge your passing."

"Zalis, he was really one of Beren's men...he attacked me, freed the horses and then rode off with one of the slaves. I'm sorry, Kern."

Kern felt the man's body shudder as it issued one last rasping breath and then it was still. He closed the man's eyes and laid his body gently down on the ground.

Despite the risk of attracting unwanted attention, Kern issued a mighty roar of anger that made the girls cower and emptied the trees of the waking birds. Nebu and Elanir raced out of the trees, swords at the ready and were mystified when they could find no one attacking the camp.

"Kern, what has happened?" asked Nebu.

"That dog, Zalis was with Beren. He has taken one of the girls and freed our horses."

"What do we do now?"

"I don't know yet," snapped Kern.

"But we cannot walk all the way back to Narmidia especially with slaves; we'll be dead inside a day."

The desperation in the man's voice sickened Kern. "Some of us earlier if they continue to whine." Nebu clamped his mouth shut resisting the urge to say more. "You have dealt with Beren as ordered?"

"Yes."

"Good," replied Kern just as Varil emerged from the trees. Kern filled his friend in on what had happened.

"This is not good, Kern. What do you want us to do?"

"We will continue on, my friend. It will be slow and hard going at first, but sooner or later we'll run into a patrol and we'll relieve them of their horses. Give the prisoners some food and water and then we'll be on our way."

Varil nodded and hurried away to carry out his leader's orders.

It was always going to be a difficult journey, thought Kern as he watched his friend walk away, but now it was likely to be impossible, not that he'd tell the men that. They were loyal to a degree, but not to the extent that they'd jeopardise their own necks unnecessarily. They still had to travel hundreds of miles across potentially hostile country initially on foot and with slaves. Although they were now close to the border between Remada and Salandor, it did not fill him with hope. The Salandori, whilst not openly hostile to Narmidians, merely tolerated them because of their own fractured state. If they sensed weakness in the travellers they would cut them down without a thought and steal their slaves; the Salandori were not to be trusted.

***

A short while later as the first rays of sun began to lighten the sky, the small party of raiders and slaves were ready to move out.

After tightening his sword belt and slinging a small sack over his back which contained a few days' food and water provisions, Kern strolled into the trees where Beren and his

156

accomplices had been raping the girls. As he entered the small clearing and saw Beren, Kern smiled.

"Ah, so you are still alive. Excellent, I was hoping you would be," said Kern as he stopped alongside his former comrade.

Beren's hands and ankles were tied to four small stakes buried in the ground. Beneath his arched back and buried with the blade pointing up a mere couple of inches away from his skin, was a vicious looking knife. Kern marvelled at how the man had managed to survive this long without his muscles giving way forcing his back down onto the blade. Still, it wouldn't be much longer he realised with a small smile of satisfaction.

Beren was sweating profusely from the effort of keeping his back arched and away from the blade, but even as Kern watched, Beren's body dropped another inch until it was perilously close to the blade tip.

"Any last words, Beren, you traitorous scum?"

"Yes," began Beren, his voice cracked with pain and desperation. His arms had started to tremble violently from the exertion and would give out any second. "I curse you to Kaden, Kern."

"Oh, I am undoubtedly going there, but it warms my heart to know that you will be there long before me."

"And I shall be waiting for my revenge," Beren spat back before letting out a scream that made Kern flinch with surprise.

He tilted his head and smiled. The tip of the blade had pierced Beren's skin drawing the first drops of blood. Kern sat upright again and leant forward so that his face was only a few inches from Beren's. "It looks like your time has come, Beren. All you have to decide now is whether you continue to resist it and die the coward's way a little by little, as the blade slowly slices through your vital organs, or whether to die quickly like the warrior you once were. Which is it to be?"

The agony the man was in both from the blade and the effort of keeping his back arched, was etched on his face and Kern couldn't help but admire his former friend's strength.

"Go to Kaden," Beren snarled defiantly before spitting in Kern's face.

Kern wiped the spittle away with his sleeve and stood upright glaring down at the man whose death was imminent. "Wrong choice," said Kern as he placed his boot on Beren's chest and slowly pushed down.

Beren screamed with agony as the blade slowly punched through his back and then out the other side of his abdomen, where it was soon surrounded by an ever widening circle of blood.

With a grunt of satisfaction, Kern turned and started back to the camp where his men were patiently waiting for the order to move out.

"Are you all right, Kern?" asked Varil as his leader approached. "We heard screaming."

"Not mine, my friend, Beren's."

"Ah, then it is over?"

"I made my point."

Varil glanced at his leader unsure whether he had just made a joke and was supposed to laugh. Kern's face was deadpan, so he decided against it.

After sending a scout on ahead of them, Kern gave the order to move out and slowly the column resumed its journey to the east. It was going to be a long hot day.

Chapter 14

After spending the night in a secluded spot a short distance from Tanya's farmhouse, they had risen early and started their journey to the city of Vangor. As they cautiously made their way through the Forest of Palithir, Teren quietly muttered to himself about how life had suddenly got so complicated.

"How much farther?"

Teren heard the words but was so lost in his own thoughts that he failed to realise that the question was aimed at him.

"Teren?"

"Um! What?" replied Teren eventually.

"I asked you how far it was to Vangor," said Tanya, no hint of irritation in her voice.

"Not far." Teren appeared distracted.

"Care to hazard a guess at just how far or how long it will take?"

"It'll take as long as it takes, woman and no amount of bellyaching about it will alter that fact."

"I wasn't bellyaching, I was just asking," she replied slightly indignant.

"Sounded like you were bellyaching to me," said Teren glancing at Alun and winking. The boy offered a small smile in response and Teren considered that progress.

"Actually, I was just trying to make conversation. You're not the most engaging of company if you don't mind me saying," said Tanya.

"No, I don't mind you saying. In fact, I consider it a compliment."

"Then I'm guessing you don't get very many compliments."

Tanya waited for his retort but instead he suddenly stopped, raised his right hand and pressed a finger to his lips signalling for her to be silent.

"What is it?" she asked quietly ignoring his instruction. He didn't reply. "Teren, what is it, what can you see?"

Teren wondered what part of keep quiet she struggled to understand. *No wonder the boy doesn't talk,* he thought, *he'd never get a word in edgeways. It's a pity she isn't mute.*

"Quickly, off the road and into the bushes," said Teren quietly, already leading Tanya to some shrubs a few paces to the left of the track.

Tanya grabbed Alun's hand and together the three of them crouched down behind the bush silently waiting for whatever Teren had seen or heard.

Tanya was about to ask Teren yet again what it was that had caught his attention, when she suddenly recognised the sound of many feet walking towards them. Tanya raised her head slightly for a better view and grabbed the briefest of glimpses before she was quickly dragged back down by an irate looking Teren. There were soldiers coming up the road, many soldiers.

"Stay down," snarled Teren, "or you'll get us all killed."

Tanya nodded her understanding and contented herself by clutching a frightened looking Alun to her breast.

Teren briefly raised his own head for a better view before dropping down to face Tanya once again.

"Are they Delarites?" asked Tanya quietly.

"No, they're ours," replied Teren worriedly.

"Surely that's a good thing? We can go with them."

"Maybe."

The front soldiers were now no more than fifty or so paces away from their position, but showed no sign of having seen the three of them.

"Why are you so worried about our own men, Teren?" asked Tanya confused by Teren's reluctance to reveal their whereabouts.

Teren scratched his beard absentmindedly. "Well for one thing they're going in the wrong direction and for another they're not marching."

"I'm sorry, I don't understand what you're getting at," said Tanya.

"They're either retreating or deserting. The enemy apparently to the north yet they're heading south. If their morale and discipline was high, they'd be marching, not wandering aimlessly down the road like a rabble."

Tanya could understand his point but couldn't understand his reluctance to join them. Retreating or not they were still Remadans.

"Stay here while I go and speak with them and I do mean stay here," said Teren in a voice that he hoped brooked no argument.

Tanya went to protest, but one look at his face told her it probably wasn't a good idea. She nodded her understanding instead.

Teren drew his large sword and slowly walked towards the track. So lax was the soldiers' vigilance that they didn't notice his appearance until he virtually appeared in front of them. Teren placed his sword point down into the track and leant on the hilt watching the approaching soldiers. As the ragged column neared, Teren could see that they had indeed been in a fight and that it hadn't gone well. Many of the men carried wounds of various descriptions and further down the column he could see several wagons full of the more seriously wounded, being drawn by oxen. Without the need for a command, the front of the column drew to a halt several paces in front of Teren.

Teren stared at the dishevelled looking soldiers in front of him and shook his head slowly. The uniforms were for the most part dirty, bloody and ripped but he could still recognise the uniform of the Ninth Ligara, a regiment he had once been pleased to call home. What had happened to the brave men who had once been proud to serve? Teren's eyes scanned the gaggle of men in front of him who were staring back at him. Some looked in awe at the big warrior with the fearsome looking sword, whilst others looked frightened or disinterested. Some even appeared angry at the delay. He heard his name whispered and waited a moment for it to drift down the column.

"Now then, lads, where are you all off to?" asked Teren.

For a moment no one replied, and then a soldier with a nasty looking scar running down the left side of his face spoke up.

"South and away from those bloody Delarites."

"But the war's that way, lads," said Teren nodding in the direction they had just come.

161

"Maybe it is, but it's no longer our war," said another soldier. His tunic was covered in blood, but it didn't appear to be his Teren noted with satisfaction.

"Yeah, we're going home," said another soldier further back in the column.

"Ah, well I can't blame you for wanting to do that now can I, but just how long do you think it'll be before the Delarites reach your home? How safe will your families be then?" Teren let the question hang like an unanswered accusation. "Where have you come from?"

"Torogora," said the soldier with the facial scar. "The city's fallen."

"Aye, but it wasn't our fault," said another soldier next to him. "We were poorly led, poorly supplied and poorly used."

Teren watched as just about everyone within earshot nodded their agreement.

"What's going on? Why have we stopped?" said a voice some way back in the column.

Teren watched as three men barged their way forward, the soldiers in front of them reluctantly parting to let them through. Two were officers and the third, a man that Teren recognised, was a non-commissioned officer of approximately Teren's age. He gave a wry smile when he recognised Teren leaning on his sword before him.

"You," said one of the officers pointing at a soldier at the head of the column. "Why have you stopped?"

The soldier looked at his officer with a barely disguised look of disgust and instead of replying, he merely nodded in Teren's direction.

The officer's face turned crimson at the man's flagrant lack of respect for a senior officer. "Sergeant."

"Yes, sir," replied the man with the officers who had recognised Teren.

"Take this man's name for field punishment when we reach a suitable location."

"Yes, sir," replied the sergeant making no attempt to do any such thing.

"Your men might show you a little more respect, Colonel, if you developed a backbone and acted like an officer worthy of wearing that uniform," said Teren still leaning nonchalantly on his sword.

The officer spun round, as if noticing Teren for the first time. He looked Teren up and down weighing him up.

"What do we have here, a deserter, a Delarite spy?"

Behind him the sergeant raised his eyes to the heavens. Was there no end to the man's stupidity?

"Guess again," replied Teren.

"I don't know who or what you are, though my best guess would be a vagrant who's stolen a sword from a dead man, but if you don't get off the king's highway and out of our way, I'll have you run through," replied the officer.

Teren smiled, straightened and hefted the sword over his right shoulder. "Is that right? And just who are you going to get to do that, your men? They look as if they'd rather kill you than me given half a chance."

"Sergeant," barked the officer his eyes never leaving Teren.

"Sir."

"This man has insulted an officer of the realm and is obstructing the king's highway. I believe the punishment is death, is it not?"

"To go up against that man is certainly to invite death, sir," replied the sergeant barely able to contain his smile.

"What?" said the officer.

"I said to go up against that man is certain death. That's Teren Rad, sir." Unseen by the officer, the sergeant winked at Teren.

Teren watched as a flicker of recognition briefly crossed the man's face, whilst the other officer who had so far not spoken, seemed to pale considerably at the mention of his name.

"Teren Rad?" asked the first officer.

"Yes, sir, the man who led the counterattack at Slinden Plateau and the man who single-handedly held the line at Kato's Reach whilst reinforcements were fetched. Killed over forty men that day he did. I know because I was there. He's one tough son of a whore, begging your pardon, sir."

Teren recognised the look of a man who had got himself

into a situation he no longer desired, but one that he couldn't back down from.

"Sergeant, take six men and remove that vagrant from the king's highway."

"I've never disobeyed an order in my life, sir, not even the bad ones and believe me there's been more than a few of those, especially lately," said the sergeant.

The look that crossed the officer's face suggested that the implied criticism of his ability as an officer was not lost on him. "Good, well get it done then."

"Until now that is. You want him removed then with the greatest of respect, sir, you move him," and with that the sergeant moved to the side of the road and sat down. Slowly, but surely his action was mimicked by all the soldiers in the column until only the two officers and Teren were left standing.

"Captain Baradir, arrest that man," said the colonel to the other officer.

It was a job the younger officer clearly didn't fancy, but to his credit Teren noted, he didn't hesitate to obey the command, his face though betrayed his true emotions. Drawing his sword and sloping it over his right shoulder, the younger officer walked briskly towards Teren. "In the name of the king I am placing you, Teren Rad, under arrest for wilfully insulting and disobeying the lawful orders of one of his majesty's officers. Please surrender your sword and follow me."

"You know what, if it's all the same to you I don't think I will thanks," said Teren dismissively. "But thanks for asking."

A murmur of laughter rippled down the column of sitting soldiers as they openly enjoyed their officers' humiliation.

"This is your final warning, sir, surrender your sword now," said the young captain as he brought his own sword down and took guard.

Teren yawned, stretched and brought his sword down so swiftly and with so much power that he knocked the other man's sword clean out of his hands.

All Baradir could do was watch helplessly as his sword flew through the air landing some paces away to his right. He was just contemplating what to do next when Teren kicked his feet out from under him, sending the officer crashing to the ground in a heap, much to the amusement of the soldiers nearby. Teren brought his sword point to the officer's throat.

"Do you yield?"

The young officer's eyes moved from side to side, desperately searching for an alternative or something to strike back with. There were none. Teren understood that the man's honour dictated that he tried something, but it was futile and would only result in his death.

"Do you yield, Captain? There is no shame," said Teren.

Teren watched as the man silently wrestled with his conscience before finally accepting that his position was hopeless. If he refused, he was dead.

"I do, sir, you have my word," replied the captain with as much dignity as he could muster.

"Then on your honour as an officer, I'm letting you stand and retrieve your weapon. Let me down and it will end badly for you, understand?"

The captain nodded but looked hurt at the implication that his word wasn't good. Deciding that the man was probably honourable, Teren helped him up.

Enraged at the audacity of a man who had convinced his soldiers to disobey him and who had humiliated his captain in front of the men, the colonel drew his sword and charged at Teren swinging wildly as he went. Teren side stepped the first swing, swayed away from the next and ducked under the third.

"Put that thing away before you hurt yourself," said Teren.

His patronising tone did nothing but enrage the colonel still further and he lunged at Teren again with a series of strokes which Teren easily parried and deflected. Still the colonel came at him, but Teren contented himself with self-defence, hoping that the man would eventually tire and run out of steam. After one unexpected swipe of the colonel's sword almost caught Teren unawares, he decided enough was enough. With a simple three stroke combination Teren disarmed the colonel his sword point coming to rest on the other man's chest.

"Well go on then, kill me or aren't you man enough?" said the colonel staring straight into Teren's eyes.

So the man has a backbone after all.

For the briefest of seconds Teren considered granting him his wish, but with a great show of restraint he managed to content himself with just nicking the man's chest as he removed his sword. "You're not worth the effort. This sword is for killing men, not fops. Sergeant!" The sergeant got to his feet and hurried over to where Teren was waiting. "Please arrange for this man to be tied to a horse and sent on his way south will you?"

"It'll be a pleasure," said the sergeant smiling at Teren. "Come along please, Colonel."

"I'll see you hang for this, both of you," spat the colonel as he was led away by the sergeant and two men who had come to help without being asked.

"And you might want to gag him as well, Sergeant, now that I think of it," added Teren.

The sergeant didn't turn round or answer but simply waved a rag in his right hand, clearly having already decided to do just that himself.

Two minutes later the colonel was tied to his horse and gagged, scar face holding the reins of his horse as Teren approached.

"Keep heading south, Colonel and you'll be fine. If you make it back to the Royal Palace tell the king that the Delarites are roaming the north of the country at will and in force."

The colonel just silently glared at Teren, burning his face into his memory. Teren slapped the horse's rear and it sped off down the track the laughter and cheers of the men echoing through the trees behind it.

Teren turned to face the cheering soldiers, the sergeant standing just a couple of paces away from him, the captain to his side.

"It is good to see you, old friend," said Teren extending his hand. The sergeant stepped forward and grasped his friend's arm in the warrior's embrace.

"As it is for me to see you too," he replied.

"What ill has befallen the Ninth that its men wander

through the forest out of formation and with no scouts or skirmishers?"

"You just sent the reason for all of that, packing on that horse. Never in all my many years serving the crown have I ever known a worse officer. He had us retreat from Torogora when we should have stood, he sacrificed dozens of men to make good his own escape and he has spread defeatism and low morale throughout the ranks. These are still good men, Teren, who have been badly led and badly let down. No offence to you, Captain," said the sergeant turning to face Captain Baradir briefly before returning to Teren. "We bloodied the enemy at Torogora and could have done more if that coward's nerve didn't break. Who knows, we might even have managed to hang on to the city. Instead he ordered a hurried and ill-prepared retreat that left us strung out over leagues. Their cavalry have harried us the whole way to the forest and we have lost many good men. Men like Jarle Lit."

The sergeant watched as the news of a death of a mutual friend sunk in.

"Will they fight again?" asked Teren.

"Aye, with the right leadership they'll fight. They're desperate to avenge their comrades, but the colonel has them believing that everything is lost and that the war is practically over even though it's just begun. What are you thinking?"

"What news of Vangor?" asked Teren thoughtfully.

"Last I heard it still stood and the prefect was going to make a stand though they have little chance against the hordes of Delarites bearing down on them," replied the sergeant.

"They'd stand a better chance if we stood with them though?"

"Aye, that they would," smiled the sergeant. "We'd still be outnumbered by maybe as much as five or six to one I reckon."

"We've faced worse odds, old friend and survived."

"Yes, we have, but that might not always be the case," said the sergeant.

"We've got to do something to check their advance, Renus, or the whole damned country will be overrun within weeks. We've got to give whoever's commanding our forces the time to rally our men and mount a defence." Teren noticed the look that flit across his friend's face. "What is it, Renus?"

"A lot has happened since...since you went away. Neither Tae nor Aryk have the king's ear any longer. Tae has been put out to pasture and Aryk's an enemy of the state."

"Yes, I heard, but the king will eventually come to his senses and send for them and even if he doesn't, I can't see men like Tae and Aryk watching from the sidelines, can you?" asked Teren.

"No more than you I suspect," replied the sergeant smiling. "There is much to talk about, old friend, but first I suggest you address the men and tell them what you've got planned. With the right words, I'm sure they'll follow you."

Nodding his agreement, Teren turned to face the men as the sergeant signalled for them to stand and gather round. Only the orderlies who were tending the badly wounded remained out of earshot together with a couple of lookouts Renus had sent to watch the trail behind the column.

"Men of the Ninth Ligara, my name is Teren Rad." He surveyed the sea of faces before him trying to gauge their mood and was pleased to see that he had their undivided attention. "Some of you know me and the rest of you probably know of me. I once proudly wore the uniform that now adorns your sorry hides and it breaks my heart to see the men of the Ninth so downhearted and dispirited. What happened to the regiment that covered itself in glory at Malpala, Slinden Plateau, Kato's Reach and countless others? The men who fought in those battles were brave and proud. What I see before me now is a crowd of men full of self-pity. Defeatism is written across most of your faces. But I know that you are still brave men.

"Do you think that the men I served with all those years ago never faced defeat or tasted the bitterness of fear, because I can assure you that we did? What we didn't do was run away with our tail between our legs blaming our officers and say that we were beaten. We dusted ourselves down, regrouped and then fought back to avenge our fallen comrades. That is the way of the Ninth and always will be. First into the field and last to leave." Teren looked over the faces and saw that most were nodding their agreement a new sense of pride and resolve sweeping slowly over them. Now he would see if they would follow him.

"A few leagues in that direction is the garrison city of Vangor. From what we hear, the prefect intends to make a stand there and try and buy our army some time. The prefect is not a fighting man and has never served in the military, but he is a brave man and so are those men that stand with him. Without help and maybe even with it, they are as good as dead, yet still they stand because it is the right thing to do. Now I'm not your officer and I'm not even in the army anymore, but I'm going to Vangor to join the fight and to make those Delarite whoresons pay a heavy price for every damned step they take on our soil. I'll make them wish they'd never heard of Remada."

A huge spontaneous cheer went up as most of the men waved their swords and spears in the air. Sergeant Renus looked on and smiled; Teren Rad was working his magic again.

"So what say you men of the Ninth, will you march with me?" asked Teren. This time everyone cheered and then started chanting Teren's name.

"Nicely done as always, Teren," smiled Renus, as he sidled alongside his friend.

"Mister Rad." Teren turned to see who had addressed him so formally. Behind him and standing to attention with as much dignity as he could muster after his earlier humiliation, stood Captain Baradir. "What do you plan on doing with me, sir?"

"I don't plan on doing anything with you, Captain. These are your men to lead," replied Teren.

"I think we both know that there's no hope of them following me any time soon. However, with your permission I would be grateful if I could remain with the Ligara and fight with you at Vangor. Who knows, maybe I'll be able to redeem myself in your eyes and theirs," said the captain.

"You don't need to worry about what I think of you, son, it's what they think of you and more importantly still, what you think of yourself. Your colonel was a fop and a fool and you could never hope to learn anything from him, other than how to turn your back. We're going straight back into battle, a battle any of us will do well to survive, so there won't be any time to teach you stuff, you'll have to pick it up as you go along. Stick by my side and do what I tell you when I tell you and you'll be fine. If anything happens to me, then stick with the sergeant here. He's a miserable old sod, but he didn't get that old by not knowing how to handle himself. As far as the men are concerned you are still their captain and you must conduct yourself thus."

"Thank you ...sir," said the captain saluting.

"Don't thank me, son, I just got you killed."

The captain nodded. "What are your orders, sir?"

"How many men able to fight have we?"

"Last roll call, 279 including 26 walking wounded. There are another 16 seriously wounded on the wagons cared for by 5 orderlies," replied the captain.

"So few?" asked Teren. "What is the regiment's usual strength?"

"Eight hundred enlisted men and thirty-six officers and non-commissioned officers. We took a beating at Torogora and the rest we lost on the retreat."

"Desertions?" It was a dirty word and stuck in Teren's craw.

"Every night," replied the captain ashamed.

"Did you say that there were only sixteen seriously wounded? That strikes me as very low."

"They were left behind," said the captain suddenly unable to meet Teren's fierce and angry gaze.

"You left your own men behind to the Delarites? Don't you know what the Delarites do to their prisoners, wounded or not?" Teren's face was scarlet with anger drawing the unwanted attention of some of the soldiers close by. Teren was suddenly regretting his leniency towards both the colonel and the captain.

"The captain did protest most vigorously, Teren," said Renus. "He and the colonel had a proper falling out over it – I witnessed it." Renus watched as his friend tried to control his rising anger, a battle he eventually won.

"Well that's not the way we're going to do things now. Good Sulat! They were men of the Ninth. Captain, pick twelve men and a good sergeant as an escort for the wagons and order them south and out of harm's way. Sergeant Renus, you get some skirmishers out on both our flanks as we march. These Delarites could be anywhere by now and I don't want us being surprised on route. I've already had the pleasure of meeting some of their cavalry."

The sergeant nodded and marched off to carry out Teren's orders.

"Err, sir?" said the captain.

"What is it, Captain?"

"What do you want me to do about them?" the captain asked as he nodded towards a woman and a young boy who were walking towards them having just appeared from behind a bush.

Teren followed the captain's gaze and recognised Tanya and Alun. With everything going on he had clean forgotten about them.

"They'll also be going with the wagon party."

"Very good, sir," replied Captain Baradir.

"They were friendly after all then, Teren?" said Tanya as she and Alun arrived at his side.

"Friendly enough, yes, once I cut the head off the snake."

Tanya didn't understand the analogy and looked to Teren for an explanation but none was forthcoming.

"Tanya, I've arranged for you and the boy to be taken south with the wounded on the wagons. They'll look after you and get you both as far away as possible from danger."

"I thought we were going to Vangor?" asked Tanya.

"Slight change of plans. I'm going to lead these men and we're going to join the garrison at Vangor and try and hold off the Delarites in the hope that the king will come to his senses and organise a proper resistance."

"Then we'll come with you. I mended my husband enough times to make me a useful person to have around when the wounded start rolling in."

"I'm sure you are and I can't deny your logic, but you just can't," said Teren.

"Why not?" protested Tanya.

"Well there's the lad for one thing and I..."

"And you what, Teren?"

171

Teren looked uncomfortable with whatever he had to say.

"I won't be able to concentrate on the fight if I'm worrying about you."

An awkward silence hung in the air for a few seconds before Tanya broke into a huge smile, stood on tip-toes and planted a light kiss on Teren's right cheek.

Teren cleared his throat in a noisy attempt to conceal his embarrassment, much to the amusement of some of the men standing around watching.

"We'll be all right, Teren, let us come," pleaded Tanya.

"Haven't you got something to be doing?" Teren barked at the soldiers who had laughed at his embarrassment a few seconds ago and as he watched them hurriedly scuttle away, he turned to face Tanya.

"You're not making this easy for me, Tanya. I don't want any harm to come to you or the lad and to be honest, our chances of survival at Vangor are poor regardless of what I said to these boys. There are just too many Delarites and too few of us. I will fight a lot better if I know that you're both safe and far away."

"If it's going to be that bad, why go, Teren? You're not even in the army."

"I know, but sometimes a man has to make a stand and fate has decreed that my stand will be at Vangor. Besides, without firm leadership these boys will soon break and run," replied Teren.

Tanya nodded thoughtfully. Teren Rad was a warrior, always had been and probably always would be; if she wanted him to be part of her life and she was certainly thinking that way at the moment, then she was just going to have to accept him for what he was. She leant forward and hugged him, an embrace he reciprocated a few seconds later.

"You take care of yourself, Teren Rad, you hear me and when this is over you come looking for us."

His embrace tightened. "I will, I promise." His promises and quests were beginning to mount up.

Teren knelt down and gently held the young boy by his arms. "You look after your mother now, you hear?" The boy looked blankly back at Teren, but Teren smiled anyway. "Good lad."

A grizzled old sergeant whom Teren didn't recognise came over and stood to attention. "We're ready to leave, sir, if the young lady is ready."

"Very good, carry on, Sergeant," replied Teren, his eyes never leaving Tanya. "I'll see you both soon."

Tanya smiled and after clutching her son's hand, she followed the sergeant over to where their small wagon train was lined up ready to go.

Teren watched them leave and prayed to everything that he believed in, which wasn't much, that they'd be safe and that he would see them again.

"She's a fine woman."

Teren glanced to his right where Sergeant Renus was now standing watching the wagon train slowly make its way south.

"That she is, but with a stubborn streak like you wouldn't believe," replied Teren.

"None of my business of course, but is she your woman?"

Like you said, none of your business," replied Teren smiling. "Are the men ready?" he added apparently bringing the subject to a close.

"They are and the skirmishers are out."

"Then let's be on our way. We'll head north-east through the forest and then approach Vangor from the south east, hopefully before the Delarites arrive in any numbers. Tell the men to remain alert. Whilst the forest is too dense for any large scale attack, we could be harried by small flank attacks," warned Teren.

The sergeant nodded and marched off to pass the warning on.

"Captain Baradir?"

"Sir."

"Move the men out, Captain," said Teren as he gave one final glance to the south where the soldiers stationed at the rear of the wagon train were just disappearing out of sight round a corner.

"Yes, sir," replied Baradir and they were soon on their way.

Chapter 15

The road leading to the city's front gate was absolutely teeming with people and from Cala's vantage point on the ridge high to the right, it looked as if the whole of Lydia was heading towards the city. And they were in a hurry. Some were weighed down with heavy looking bags whilst others dragged carts behind them laden with their worldly possessions. Others seemed to bring nothing but the clothes they wore. All were in a rush to seek the safety of the city's walls.

Cala nudged her tired horse in the flanks and he reluctantly began to pick his way down the slope towards the field that bordered the road. Someone in the column of refugees screamed when they saw the rider suddenly appear to their right and a ripple of panic threatened to cause havoc. When they realised that it was only one rider and that that rider was Princess Cala, the screams turned to cheers and people stopped to wave or punch the air as she hurried by on her way to the city.

Princess Cala had a special affinity with the people and always had. Normally, she would have stopped and spoken to some of the cheering crowd, but today she rode on without so much as a cheery wave. She did not want her people to see the tears in her eyes and the desperation on her face. She had to be strong.

The crowd had parted as she approached the city gates and she was soon inside. A soldier she didn't recognise wearing the uniform of the Gate Guardians approached and took her reins whilst she dismounted.

"Where is Captain Felix, soldier, he should be here supervising at a time like this?" Cala asked the Guardian.

"I believe he's indisposed, your highness," replied the soldier unable to meet her gaze.

"Indisposed! You mean drunk?" asked Cala incredulously.

"I wouldn't know, your highness, I was just told that he was indisposed."

"Very well, I'll look into it myself." Captain Felix was a diligent officer and in all the years Cala had known him he had never once let her down or been negligent in his duties. He had most certainly never been drunk when he was supposed to be on duty. It was troubling and she would have to look into his absence later. Right now there were far more important matters to be attended to. "What is going on, soldier? Where have all these people come from?" As she spoke she noticed that the inside of the city was bristling with people.

"It's the Delarites, your highness. They've invaded Lydia and have quickly overrun several of our outlying towns and cities. There are rumours going round of atrocities. They say whole villages have been put to the sword, men, women and even babies. The people flock to us for safety," replied the soldier.

So Herat was going to avenge Lydia's perceived betrayal by killing hundreds of innocent people. "Thank you, soldier. Is the king still in his palace?"

"No, your highness. The last time I saw him he was on the city battlements organising the city's defence." The soldier turned and pointed when he saw the king standing on the battlements nearby.

Yes, that sounds like my father, amongst his men, spreading encouragement and cheer, whilst overseeing the city's defences. He won't want to leave anything to chance. Cala nodded her thanks to the soldier and hurried off to climb the steps to where her father was deep in conference with several of his senior commanders.

"Father."

"Cala," said the king with a huge smile. You made it back safely, thank Sulat."

"Did you ever doubt it, Father?"

"No, not really," replied the king, his grin widening.

"Welcome back, Princess Cala," said one of the officers with the king. He was a tall man, near her father's age, with a well-trimmed grey beard. His greeting was quickly echoed by the other officers standing there. All seemed genuinely pleased to see her again, although one or two looked somewhat surprised Cala noticed.

"Thank you, General Larit, gentlemen. Father we have been betrayed. It looks like Herat has known for some time that we had no intention of supporting him in his war. He's just been stringing us along as much as we have him."

"Yes, I know. It seems Herat has spies even at the Royal Palace," replied the king ruefully.

"How bad is it, Father?" The king looked tired as if he hadn't slept for several days.

"At least one Delarite Army has crossed our border, though we suspect that it's more. All of our northern towns have fallen and now we hear that a large body of men is heading due south whilst another sizeable force is headed our way. Our forces are in disarray and retreating on all fronts," replied the king with a catch to his voice.

"Father, one of the Guardians at the gate told me the Delarites are massacring our people, even children. Tell me it isn't true?"

"I wish that I could, but one of our cavalry patrols came across a village where everyone had been killed. Everyone. And the way some of them were killed." The king visibly blanched as he recalled the report from one of his officers who had told him that some of the villagers had been tortured and mutilated.

"Why would they do that?" asked Cala, her anger rising.

"Fear, your highness. Herat wishes to quickly subjugate Lydia so he can turn his full attention to Remada, so he will use every weapon at his disposal and fear is a powerful weapon," replied General Larit.

"How soon do you expect to be attacked?" asked Cala.

"We don't know for sure, as none of our scouts have made it back to report, but if I had to guess, I'd say that the main body of their force will arrive late tonight, but their cavalry could arrive anytime. It's only a guess though. We have no credible intelligence as to where exactly they are," said General Larit almost apologetically.

"Where is General Tain?" asked Cala, suddenly noticing that her father's most trusted officer wasn't there.

"He's gone to buy us some time, Cala," replied her father.

"What do you mean?"

"He's taken every man we could spare and headed

towards the enemy's last known position. We're barely ready for them now but if the enemy had shown up a couple of days ago or even yesterday, we wouldn't have been able to mount much of a defence. As it is we're not going to be able to do much more than delay their advance, but Tain has bought us those days."

"He's gone on a suicide mission?" said Cala accusingly.

The king briefly glanced down at the throng of people below him before answering. "In all likelihood, yes it is, but General Tain knew what he was doing. It was his idea. He said to tell you that his only regret was that he wouldn't be standing by your side when the enemy came. I think he had a soft spot for you, my dear."

Cala smiled despite the tears running down her cheeks. She had loved General Tain like an uncle and held him in the highest regard.

"What is the plan then, Father?" asked Cala pulling herself together.

"I have all the archers at my disposal, a legion of infantry and my personal guard. We will make our stand here and try and exact a hefty price for every moment they are on Lydian soil, firstly from a hail of arrows and then from cold steel."

"Did General Tain take all of my cavalry?" asked Cala.

"No, he took only enough to be able to harry the enemy without engaging them head on; the rest are waiting for you on the edge of the Forest of Anwin," replied the king.

"Good, then as soon as the Delarite cavalry arrive, the first and last thing they will see will be the Sikari Horse charging at them."

The king and his officers exchanged a look that Cala couldn't read, but she had a feeling she wasn't going to like its meaning.

"No, Cala, as soon as you've rested and had something to eat, you must take your men and ride south. My advice would be to cross the border into Remada and try and join forces there. Then side by side with our ally you will have your chance to avenge our people," said the king.

"No, I won't do it. I'll not run and leave our people behind in their time of need. My place is here by your side.

177

Besides, you're going to need every man you can get to help in the defence."

"It is not up for discussion, Cala, it's all been agreed."

"Not by me it hasn't," snapped Cala.

"Enough! It is decided. Commander Haylen has prepared the men and they are all saddled and ready to go as soon as you're ready."

"Father..."

"Cala, please, for once in your life, please do as I say. I have to stay for the sake of our people, but you can escape and live to fight another day."

"But you'll be killed, Father, where's the sense in that?"

"If that is my destiny, so be it. Even if I wanted to run, Cala, how could we save everybody? You've seen the people pouring into the city. They've come here to be safe. They expect their king to protect them, so how would it look if I fled and left them to their fate? I won't do it."

Cala went to say something further when a sentry standing to their right shouted a warning. Then a chorus of screams and frightened shouts went up from the masses of people queuing to get into the city. The king and Cala rushed to the battlements and looked towards where the sentry was pointing. Approaching from two different directions were hundreds of mounted soldiers and they were riding full pelt towards the city gates and the people huddled before them.

"The Delarites, they're here," said the king unnecessarily.

Cala's thoughts immediately went to General Tain and his men, presumably laying dead a few leagues up the road. She hoped that he had died well.

"Archers to the battlements. Get ready to close the gates. Time to assume your positions, gentlemen," said the king to the officers standing with him. They all saluted the king before hurrying off to take command of their respective men.

"Father, you can't close the gates yet, there are so many people still out there." The noise from the frightened people below was almost intolerable, as young and old scrambled to get through the gates before they closed. To fall or stumble over was to invite certain death as the frightened masses trampled across their neighbours and friends to save their own lives.

The Delarite cavalry were already among the rear of the crowd now, slicing and hacking at the unarmed civilians with a callous abandon. Cala watched in horror as a woman carrying a baby was knocked to the ground, the baby's cries extinguished by the life crushing force of the horse's hooves. Men, women and children, were being slaughtered regardless of their age and Cala instantly knew that the rumours of the atrocities had to be true.

"Father, we've got to do something, they're committing murder," screamed Cala.

"Archers, target those horsemen and fire at will," shouted the king and instantly dozens of arrows flew towards the enemy. Many Delarite horsemen hit the ground either dead or injured, but as was the risk with such an order, so too did several civilians.

"Sire, look over there," said one of the king's officers after he came rushing up to the king's side.

The king followed the young officer's pointing finger and gasped in shock. Appearing over the ridge from the north-east and marching quickly their way, were what looked like thousands of Delarite infantry, with more appearing all the time.

How did he ever expect to be able to hold up such a force? He glanced to his left and watched the shock creep across his daughter's face. "Close the gates. Close the gates."

"Father, please you can't. Just a few minutes longer," pleaded Cala.

"Cala, I can't, I'm sorry. Those Delarites will soon be here." He glanced back out at the approaching army and was horrified to see how quickly they had crossed the distance to the refugees. Another few minutes and they would be at the city gates. Panic threatened to overwhelm him. "Close the damned gates. Commander, go and find out why they haven't closed the gates."

"Sire," replied the commander saluting smartly before hurrying towards the steps leading down to the gate.

The king looked down in front of the gates and saw that the Delarite cavalry was everywhere. The bodies of dead Lydian people were strewn across the ground; they had murdered hundreds. The king felt his anger rising. "Get those gates shut now!" he bellowed as he turned round, but it was too late. The commander lay slumped halfway down the steps with a Delarite lance protruding from his stomach. The Delarites were inside the city.

Cala heard her father's shout of anger and turned to see what had alarmed him. At the foot of the steps, Lydian soldiers fought sword battles with members of the Gate Guardians. They had been betrayed. Somehow Delarite soldiers had infiltrated the city and taken on the guise of Gate Guardians so that when the attack came, they would take control of the gates and keep them open long enough for the Delarite cavalry to get inside. Cala recognised the soldier who had taken her horse reins as he despatched a Lydian soldier and drew her own sword. No wonder she hadn't recognised him. The Captain of the Gate Guardians wasn't laying indisposed somewhere; he was in all likelihood lying dead with a Delarite dagger between his shoulder blades. With a roar of anger she raced down the steps and engaged the infiltrator, her father's protestations ringing in her ears.

By now the Delarite Army was amongst the civilians, stabbing and murdering like their cavalry comrades, but on a much greater scale. Those who could, fled in whichever direction was open to them, but as the king watched with tears in his eyes, he knew that few would escape. He didn't want to give the next order, but he knew that he had to. The throng of people below now consisted more of Delarite soldiers than it did civilians, live ones anyway, so the time had come to fully unleash the archers and javelins.

The king looked round for an officer to carry out his commands, but there were none. *Very well, then I will give it myself.* "Archers, spearmen, let them have everything you've got." The king was pleased to see that although such an action would result in many civilian deaths as well as Delarite, none of his soldiers appeared to have disobeyed or even hesitated. They were in a desperate position, which called for desperate measures.

A storm of arrows and javelins thudded into the masses below, each missile finding a target whether friendly or foe, but it was only a matter of time. Already Delarite soldiers were climbing the steps to the battlements, whilst hundreds more fanned out through the city. The battle was already lost and it would not be long before the city was in Delarite hands.

The king looked down and saw Cala thrust her sword into one of the Delarites wearing a Gate Guardian uniform before turning and slicing the back of a Delarite horseman. In that moment he was proud, more proud than he'd ever been, something he promised himself to tell her when he got a moment. It was then that the king felt a sharp pain in his side. He looked down, his eyes wide with shock when he saw an arrow protruding from just above his hip. He slowly started to crumble to the ground.

"You men with me, now," said a familiar voice behind the king, though he couldn't immediately recall who it belonged to. "The king is wounded. We need to get him out of here, now. Hang in there, sire, we'll get you to safety."

The king was vaguely aware of being lifted and then slowly moving through the air as three or four members of his personal bodyguard attempted to carry him to safety. All around him as he stared up at the clear blue sky were the sounds of battle and the sounds of men dying. The man carrying the king's legs suddenly grunted and let go of his charge before tumbling over the edge into the courtyard, two arrows embedded in his back.

The king's legs hit the ground jarring the arrow in his side and sending a wave of pain shooting through his body. More screams from behind him as the two men who had been carrying his arms were killed, one by an arrow and the other by a sword thrust. The king heard the captain of the Royal Bodyguard curse as he turned and despatched the Delarite before a sword was thrust right through his body from behind. He looked down at the sword point protruding from his stomach and then at his king. He tried to mouth something which the king never heard before collapsing onto the battlements dead.

Cala had watched helplessly from the courtyard as her father's bodyguard had tried to rescue their king before being killed themselves. Now she watched in horror as half a dozen Delarites converged on her wounded father baying for blood. Tightening her grip on her sword handle she made to charge up the steps to her father's aid, but found her way barred by General Larit and a number of mounted cavalrymen, one of whom was holding a spare horse.

"Time to go, Princess Cala," said the general handing her the reins to the spare horse.

"Get out of my way, General, I've got to save my father," she shouted back.

"It's too late, your highness. I'm sorry. Now you've got to go."

The score of cavalrymen were fighting frantically to keep the Delarites back from the princess, but they wouldn't be able to hold out for very much longer, Larit knew.

Cala glanced over Larit's shoulder at the battlements behind him and a small cry of anguish escaped her lips as a blood-soaked Delarite held her father's severed head high in the air to a great cheer from those around him.

"Go, my princess, please. The men can't hold them back much longer and there's nothing you can do. Go out via the south gate whilst our men still hold it and head south and then west for Remada like your father said. May Sulat protect you," said the general.

"Aren't you coming, General?"

"I've been at your father's side for nigh on thirty years. I'll not leave him now dead or alive. Besides, I'm too old to be running round the countryside. Now please, go, Princess. I will die happier in the knowledge that you are safe and free to avenge us."

Cala mounted her horse and after glancing quickly at her father's stricken body, looked at the general. "I will avenge you, General, you can be sure of it."

"I shall be watching, my Queen," replied the general addressing her by her new title now that her father was dead. Then with a shout he slapped the rump of Cala's horse and it dutifully galloped off, followed closely by the remaining guards.

Larit watched her ride off towards the south gate and offered a quiet prayer to Sulat that she would make it safely out of the city. He was still muttering to himself when a Delarite soldier ran him through with his lance, though Larit still had the strength and resolve to spin round and behead

182

the man before collapsing to the ground dead.

The Delarites were in most of the city by now, but Cala and her escort were able to force their way through to the south gate which was just about still in Lydian hands. Cala couldn't look at the men she was leaving behind to die. These men were buying her freedom with their lives and she wasn't sure she could bear to see the look of resignation in their eyes. No, the best way she could repay and honour these men was to survive and to avenge them she decided.

By the time Cala had escaped the city, her escort had been reduced to just eight men and two of those were wounded. Half a league from the southern gate stood the Forest of Anwin and it was to here Cala and her escort headed. When they were no more than a hundred paces from the entrance to the forest, they saw a long line of horsemen ranged in front of the trees. Cala breathed a sigh of relief when she saw her own standard fluttering in the wind in the middle of the line. These were the Sikari Horse, her own men, who loved her and were fiercely loyal.

Cala gave the signal to stop just in front of the men. "Captain Vylla, I am pleased to see you, all of you."

The captain bowed slightly and smiled warmly. "And I you, my princess."

"I am your queen now, Captain. My father died fighting the enemy with his sword in his hand," said Cala proudly.

"I am truly sorry, my Queen. You know that I held the king in the highest regard."

"Thank you, Captain."

"The city is lost then?" It was a rhetorical question but Cala felt compelled to answer it anyway.

She sat up straight in the saddle and glanced left and right along the line of expectant soldiers. "Soldiers of Lydia. My father, your king is dead." A ripple of noise resonated along the line as the news was digested. "He died fighting like the king he was with a sword in his hand and a pile of dead Delarites at his feet. And how did these barbarians honour him? By cutting off his head and defiling his body." Angry shouts erupted all along the line some even calling for the Sikari Horse to return to the city and rejoin the fight. "Take a good look at our burning city men, and remember what they did to our people and to our king. Remember it well because I solemnly promise you as your queen, that one day I will return to avenge them all. It may take a week, a year or a decade, but I will avenge them."

The men cheered loudly as she rode up and down the line until eventually they started to chant her name. Satisfied that she had them baying for revenge and hungry to fight, Cala gave the order and the Sikari Horse turned south and disappeared into the Forest of Anwin.

Chapter 16

The stranger led them back down the street the way they had come towards the stables. Eryn found himself eagerly searching for Lilly as they passed her house and was strangely disappointed when he didn't see her.

Whilst the other man, who had introduced himself as Arlen on the walk to the stable, watched the street for any sign that they were being followed, Eryn, Tav and Ro, who still hadn't imparted his name, saddled the horses and led them out into the street.

"Anything?" Ro asked Arlen.

"No, I think they've forgotten about us already," he replied.

"That is as well I think. Mount up and let's be away from this place then."

Arlen climbed onto his horse a little awkwardly and it was obvious to Eryn that the man was not used to horses whereas his companion clearly was. But then if he was a priest, what need of a horse had he?

Tav laughed as Arlen finally struggled into the saddle, red-faced and embarrassed. Arlen glared over at Tav in mock anger and then laughed at himself, drawing smiles from everyone else and an almost imperceptible shake of the head from his companion.

They rode out of town as fast as they dared, unsure whether Arlen would be able to remain in the saddle with his horse going full pelt. Ro was glad to see that both of the boys seemed to be able to handle their horses well.

They rode for forty minutes without stopping until eventually Ro signalled for them to halt.

"What is it?" asked Eryn riding up alongside him.

"Nothing, I just think we've ridden far enough to deter any followers. There's a small stream over there by the sound of it, where we can water the horses." He slid from his horse and beckoned for the others to follow suit.

"You think we're safe here?" asked Arlen.

"Safe from anyone in the village stupid enough to try and follow us yes, but safe from enemy soldiers is another thing." He smiled at the young man standing by Eryn, though it was clear to him by the young man's face and the way he spoke, that his mental age did not keep pace with his body. "Tav, isn't it?"

The young man nodded eagerly. "Tav Rhem and this is my friend Eryn."

"Tav, would you do me a really big favour please?" Tav nodded even more eagerly, keen to please the stranger who had come to their aid in the tavern. "Would you mind taking the horses over to the stream and watering them for me? It would be a great help and I need somebody I can trust to do that."

"Tav can do that. He won't let you down," Tav replied as he took the reins from everyone's horse and led them the short distance to the stream.

Ro watched Tav walk away and when he was satisfied that Tav was out of earshot he once again turned to face Eryn.

"My name is Ro Aryk, former captain of the king's bodyguard and my portly friend over there..."

"They already know who I am. I introduced myself on the ride here," interrupted Arlen.

"I see. And you are Tav Rhem and Eryn Martel from the village of Lentor, is that correct?" asked Ro.

"That's right," replied Eryn.

"Then I am pleased to make your acquaintance, Eryn," said Ro offering his hand which Eryn readily shook.

"And I yours, both of you. We owe you thanks for your help earlier and possibly even our lives."

"Again, you are most welcome. You are a long way from home though are you not?"

"We are on a mission," replied Eryn.

"Ah, yes, your quest to rescue the girls the raiders kidnapped."

"That's right, but why do you say it with such a derisory tone to your voice?"

"I meant no insult, Eryn, I'm just not sure that you've thought this thing through."

"We didn't have a lot of time to prepare, but I have a plan," replied Eryn more defensively than he intended.

"Really? Does this plan involve you nearly getting killed in some grubby little tavern in the middle of nowhere?" asked Ro.

"No, but I thought that it might be the sort of place where I could recruit men to our cause."

"The types of men that frequent such places neither fight for a cause nor follow any flag. They are just out for themselves. Your motives were noble just a little misplaced I think," replied Ro trying to smooth out any kinks in their fledgling friendship.

"What did you mean a couple of minutes ago about enemy soldiers?" asked Eryn.

"Have you not heard? The Delarites have invaded. From what we have managed to learn from the odd traveller we have met, the cities of Pirus and Torogora in the north have fallen and Delarite armies are sweeping through our land murdering and pillaging."

"I'd heard about the invasion, yes and we've already stumbled across a field filled with dead Remadan soldiers. How close are the Delarites?"

"Very," replied Ro.

Eryn's thoughts were instantly of Tayla and the others. Bad enough that they were captives of some band of raiders but to now also have to worry about them running into an invading army didn't bear thinking about.

"Which direction did the raiders take the women from your village?" asked Arlen.

"North and that is the direction I must resume tomorrow," replied Eryn.

Ro and Arlen exchanged glances.

"It is from the north that the Delarites come, Eryn. You will run straight into them," said Ro.

"Nevertheless, that is where I must go."

"Where are these raiders from, Eryn, do you know?" asked Arlen.

"Narmidia mostly, but they have others with them."

"Sounds like the men you have been tracking, Ro," said Arlen.

"Yes, it does," replied Ro.

"Sooner or later then they must turn east for home. You could already be heading in the wrong direction," said Arlen thoughtfully.

"I know that," snapped Eryn, "but it's all we've got to go on at the moment."

Arlen nodded.

"Eryn, the people we have spoken to have claimed there are at least three Delarite armies marching through our lands. There are also legions of cavalry rampaging around with the sole purpose of killing, raping and bringing terror to the populace in an effort to subdue us. If they caught you, you could be killed out of hand," said Ro.

A brief flicker of self-doubt crossed Eryn's face, his uncertainty noticed by Arlen.

"Why don't you come with us or better still, head back to Lentor and warn your people to flee?" he suggested.

"No! I vowed that I would only return to Lentor if I was successful."

"Then your path is clear. To return to Lentor would bring you dishonour and to ride north would bring you almost certain death. You must come with us," said Arlen.

"But what about Tayla and the other girls, they are all depending on me?" asked Eryn.

"You're no good to them dead," replied Ro.

"But I can't just abandon them."

"Nobody is asking you to abandon them, Eryn. Once we have figured out a safe route and worked out a plan, you can resume your quest, but for now you should come with us," added Arlen.

"Where is it you go?" asked Eryn.

Arlen looked to Ro for guidance.

"Vangor."

"Why Vangor?" asked Eryn.

"Because it is a garrison city and if I know the city prefect, Kane Devan, he will defend his city until the end."

"I thought the city's defences had fallen into disrepair," said Arlen surprised at his friend's plan of action.

"Neglected perhaps, but not to the extent that they are worthless and not as badly as we've let people believe anyway, as you've just proved. A good commander could lead a determined resistance there," replied Ro.

"And is he a good commander this Kane Devan?" asked Arlen.

"No, he's a civilian, but I am."

"Let me get this straight, Ro. You want the four of us to ride to Vangor, join the small garrison there, which you will take command of and help to fight off the Delarites?" asked Arlen.

Ro smiled broadly. "Yes, that's about it. Once we've beaten them off we can decide how best to help our young friends here."

"You make it sound so simple," moaned Arlen.

"Wait a minute, Ro, Tav and I aren't soldiers. What use will we be?" asked Eryn.

"No, you're not soldiers, yet you go after a band of deadly bandits who are without honour and who would kill you in the blink of an eye. Your courage is not to be doubted and courage is a warrior's best weapon. Besides, the two of you looked like you could handle yourselves back there in the tavern. Come with us to Vangor; it's better than being caught out in the open here. I promise you that when the danger has passed we will talk about what we can do to get your women back. It is for the best I think and your country has need of you."

Eryn nodded slowly in reluctant acceptance. He wasn't happy about it, but what Ro said did make sense. He looked longingly to the north and closed his eyes, offering a silent prayer to Sulat to keep his sister and Tayla safe. *His country needed him,* Ro had said. The words had instilled a new sense of pride into him.

After agreeing a rota for sentry duty between the four of them, Eryn and Tav were soon asleep, the day's exertions finally catching up with them.

"Is it wise to take them with us to Vangor, Ro? They're so young and Tav, whilst he's a great kid, is exactly that, up here." Arlen tapped his head to emphasise the point.

"I know what you're saying, Arlen and I understand your concerns, but with the damned Delarites everywhere, they truly are better off with us. How long do you think they'd survive out here on their own? Look at tonight in the tavern for example."

"All the same they are not soldiers and will be killed in the first assault if the Delarites attack Vangor," said Arlen. "Assuming we get there of course."

"Oh, they'll come, Arlen, you can count on it. The Delarites can't afford to leave a garrisoned city behind their lines for long. As for the boys, we'll just have to make sure that they're somewhere safe when the fighting starts."

Arlen nodded. "Very well, but what about their women?"

"It was foolish and misguided of Lentor to let them go in the first place if you ask me, but to be honest, I don't think they've got a chance of finding them again. They could be almost anywhere by now. They could have escaped, the Delarites could have them or they could be halfway to Narmidia, we just don't know. It's a big continent, not that you should tell the boys any of what I've just said. We don't want them dashing off and getting themselves killed. Now get some sleep. I'll take the first watch and wake you in a couple of hours."

***

In the end, Ro kept watch for just over four hours before fatigue finally demanded that he woke Arlen to take a turn. Neither of the boys had stirred at all and Ro had asked Arlen to let them sleep on and keep watch himself to dawn, which he had willingly done.

After preparing a simple breakfast of bread, cheese and dried biscuits for everybody and seeing to the horses needs, Arlen woke the boys, although Ro was already up and examining a rudimentary map.

They ate quickly and in silence, Arlen noting with amusement that Tav appeared to have an appetite not dissimilar to his own.

It was Eryn who finally broke the silence. "How long will it take us to reach Vangor?"

Ro didn't answer immediately as if considering the question. "Provided we avoid any trouble, we should make it sometime late this afternoon."

"Isn't that pushing it somewhat?" asked Arlen, the thought of his bruised and tender backside taking another hammering in the uncomfortable saddle not pleasing him.

"I'm going to take the direct route straight through Denning Forest. It's risky but it's our quickest way there," replied Ro.

"And if we run into some of our Delarite friends?"asked Arlen.

"Then the journey will become a lot more interesting. Besides, the way things are we could run into them almost anywhere."

"Has anyone ever told you my friend, that you have an unnerving habit of understating every peril?" said Arlen smiling.

"Frequently. Now mount up everyone, the sooner we're on our way, the sooner we'll get there."

It was difficult to tell with the dense canopy of interwoven leaves high above blotting out the sun, but Eryn estimated that they'd been travelling for between three and four hours. They had started out on the horses following a fairly well worn track through the forest, but the track had soon narrowed and become almost impassable for a man on a horse so they had dismounted and led their horses by the reins.

Eryn was wracked with self-doubt and guilt. His heart told him he should bid farewell to his new friends and resume his journey north after the raiders who had abducted his sister and the others, yet what Ro had said made sense. If what he'd been told was true, and he had no reason not to believe so, and Delarite soldiers were everywhere, then his chances of catching up with the raiders were slim. It was far more likely that he and Tav would be taken prisoner or worse. Then where would he be?

Tav, poor Tav. He had taken a beating in the tavern and had barely put up a fight, yet here he was, still cheerful, never questioning Eryn's judgement and happy in the company of their new friends and in particular, Arlen. What right did he have to jeopardise his friend's life like this? Maybe going to Vangor was a good idea after all as he might be able to persuade his friend to remain there if they were successful in their fight against the Delarites. Again it was a lot of ifs.

Ro's right arm suddenly shot in the air, a signal for the

others to stop and be quiet. A few paces ahead of them there was a large clearing in the forest and Eryn watched as Ro scanned the area for any signs of trouble.

Arlen signalled for Eryn to hold his horse and quietly sidled up alongside Ro.

"Trouble?" asked Arlen as his eyes searched the far tree line for any signs of danger.

"None that I can see," replied Ro.

"Then what troubles you?"

"I don't know, just call it a gut instinct."

"A warrior's sixth sense, eh?"

"Maybe, Arlen, maybe."

"Do you want to skirt round it and remain in the cover of the trees?"

"No, we are pressed for time as it is, we'll stay the course. If there are Delarites nearby they'll likely to come down that track," said Ro nodding to a much wider track than the one down which they travelled.

"As you wish," replied Arlen turning to relieve Eryn of his horse.

"Arlen!"

Arlen turned back to face Ro, a questioning look upon his face.

"Remain vigilant my friend."

Arlen smiled and lifted his cloak slightly to reveal the hilt of his sword. "Always."

After taking a last look around, Ro slowly coaxed his horse forward into the clearing, followed by Arlen, Eryn and then Tav who appeared oblivious to the concerns of the others as he slowly chewed his way through a dried biscuit he had saved from breakfast.

It was quiet, Ro realised, too quiet and he couldn't shake the feeling that he was being watched. His eyes constantly scanned the tree line anxiously seeking any sign that they weren't alone. His fingers tightened around his sword hilt as the tension in his shoulders increased. A slight movement just within the trees to his left made him inhale sharply as he braced himself for an imminent attack, but none materialised.

Arlen noticed the change in his companion's body

language and as casually as he could followed his friend's gaze, but couldn't see anything.

Suddenly, from a few paces farther along than where he'd been watching, a wild boar darted out of the tree line making straight for them. Arlen's horse reared up and began to whinny and as Arlen tried to quieten it down, the boar changed direction hurrying back into the tree line down the same track the small party was headed.

Ro watched the creature scuttle out of sight, relieved that the focus of his concern had been nothing more than a wild boar. He turned to help his friend try and calm his horse, fearful that its frightened cries might attract the attention of anybody close by.

Before he could react or warn anyone, something flashed through the air in front of him and it took a second or two for Ro to realise that it had been an arrow. Tav cried out and fell to the ground next to his horse, the arrow deeply embedded in his left shoulder.

Even as the soldiers burst from the tree line to their left, shouting and roaring, Ro and Arlen had drawn their swords and were advancing to meet the threat.

"Eryn! Protect Tav and keep down," shouted Ro as he braced himself for the first clash of swords.

There were about a dozen Delarite soldiers racing towards them and whilst Ro was confident in his own fighting skills and had no doubt that Arlen could look after himself in a fight, it was highly doubtful whether they'd be able to fight off a dozen men. In a straight fight it would have been difficult with such odds, but handicapped as they were in watching out for the boys, it would be nigh on impossible to prevail. Ro quickly glanced over his shoulder and saw that Eryn had notched an arrow in his bow and stood nervously in front of his friend who was sprawled out on the ground wailing in pain. He nodded at the boy in what he hoped was a gesture of encouragement and turned back just in time to parry the first swing of a Delarite sword. The fight had been joined.

Within a few seconds, three Delarites lay on the ground, two dead and one grievously wounded, Ro having despatched two of them, whilst Arlen had cut down the other with a crossbow bolt. Sheer weight of numbers however, made the outcome of the fight a formality, only the duration in doubt. Three men were now hacking and thrusting away at Ro, searching for a weakness and an opportunity whilst others waited patiently behind to take their place.

As he parried another swing before countering with a thrust of his own, Ro caught a glimpse of movement to his right and realised that at least one Delarite had seen the boys sheltering behind him and had decided to attack them. Ro launched a furious attack of his own which pushed his assailants back, wounding one of them. Whilst he now temporarily had the advantage he was not going to be able to disengage and help the boys; Eryn was on his own.

A powerful downward slice from the man directly in front of him was met by a horizontal parry from Ro's sword, but he knew instantly that he'd left his midriff open. Seeing his opportunity, another of his attackers thrust their own sword forward towards Ro's stomach. Ro had anticipated the move and managed to swivel sideways just in time, the sword point merely grazing his side. The man's look of triumph turned to one of pain as Ro sliced his own sword across the man's back as he stumbled forward slightly off balance.

Ro backed off a couple of paces buying himself enough time to survey what was going on around him. Two enemy soldiers lay dead at Arlen's feet with at least another two showing signs of being wounded but Arlen was tiring. Even as he watched, Arlen was knocked to the ground by a powerful blow from a Delarite shield. Before the man could run Arlen through, Ro sprinted over and hurled himself through the air and into the men who were closing in for the kill, sending everyone sprawling to the ground.

Ro was quickest to his feet but the first thing he saw was a Delarite soldier about to run Eryn through with his sword, his comrade having been killed by Eryn's arrow. The man's body suddenly jerked as a small black crossbow bolt buried itself squarely in the middle of his back. Seeing the danger as he hit the ground and regardless of the peril it put his own life in, Arlen had looked to save the boy before protecting himself.

Ro spun round and charged the men closing in on Arlen,

their swords clanging in the still air. Knowing that he couldn't hope to beat them all at the same time, Ro desperately fought on expecting to be cut down at any moment. As Ro held them off Arlen struggled to his feet until the two men stood facing their remaining adversaries of which there were eight. This time it looked like the two friends were going to be charged by all of them at the same time and they would simply be overwhelmed.

"Well it was fun whilst it lasted, friend," said Arlen smiling, his eyes never leaving the line of men before him, watching for the tell-tale signs of an imminent attack.

"That it was," replied Ro as he adjusted the grip on his sword in readiness. "Shall we?"

Arlen smiled in acknowledgment of his friend's suggestion and braced for the order to charge. If they were to die as seemed inevitable, they would die attacking their enemies not cowering. Eryn suddenly appeared at Arlen's side with a sword in his hand. Now it was eight against three though Arlen doubted Eryn would be able to do much against seasoned soldiers.

The first arrow to hit the line went straight through the unsuspecting soldier's throat. The second one hit the man next to him in the arm, his scream of pain barely audible above the shouts of the men who now swarmed out of the forest to their left. The Delarites nervously looked towards the soldiers racing towards them and fled once they saw that they were now heavily outnumbered.

Ro and Arlen seized their opportunity and cut down two of the Delarites who had been slow to react, shocked looks adorning their faces as they collapsed to the ground dying.

Eryn watched as the last remaining Delarites fled towards the trees, hotly pursued by a number of soldiers wearing a different uniform.

"Who are they?" asked Eryn.

"Remadan soldiers, Eryn. Ninth Ligara if I'm not mistaken, though what they're doing here I do not know," replied Ro sheathing his sword.

"Who cares?" said Arlen. "If they hadn't been here we'd all be carrion by now."

The sound of many men marching towards them from the

left drew their attention and they turned to see scores of soldiers marching in column. At their head was an officer Ro didn't recognise and a giant of a man in civilian clothes he never thought to see again.

"It can't be," said Ro smiling.

"What can't be?" asked Arlen.

Ro didn't answer at first and instead watched as the column drew to a halt, the men dropping out for a well-earned rest whilst sentries were assigned to keep watch. The officer and the big man started to make their way over towards where Ro and the others stood.

"Sulat preserve us, it is!" said Ro again to himself.

"Is this a private conversation or are you eventually going to let us in on your big secret?" asked Arlen.

"The man in the civilian clothes," began Ro, his eyes never leaving the figure walking towards them, "that's Teren Rad."

"Teren Rad?" said Eryn excitedly.

"I thought he was dead," said Arlen.

"No, he's not dead; he went into self-imposed exile after a personal tragedy. Lives somewhere high up in the mountains," replied Ro.

"Teren Rad!" said Eryn again a thousand different thoughts racing through his mind. Then suddenly remembering his friend lying injured behind him, Eryn darted off to crouch by Tav's side. He was white and had lost what looked like a great deal of blood to Eryn. He hoped that the soldiers would have a medic or physician with them.

Teren and the officer came to a halt a few paces in front of Ro and Arlen and the four men silently stared at one other for a few seconds.

"Captain Aryk, it is good to see you again," said Captain Baradir earnestly.

"As it is to see you too, Captain. However, I am no longer in the king's employ, so a simple Ro will suffice," replied Ro.

"I was sorry to hear about that Capt... Ro. Our king has made many bad decisions, but none worse than your dismissal."

"That is kind of you to say, Captain." Ro's gaze drifted to Teren. "It has been a long time, Teren."

"That it has, Ro. Looks to me that even though you're no longer in the army, you still can't stay out of trouble," said Teren nodding towards the dead Delarite soldiers littering the ground.

"Indeed. Trouble does seem to have a habit of following me lately." Arlen noisily cleared his throat to attract Ro's attention. "Forgive me. Teren Rad, Captain Baradir, may I introduce Arlen Meric of..."

"Silevia," Teren finished for him. "A priest of the Golden Tree if I'm not mistaken."

"Guilty as charged," replied Arlen extending his hand. For a moment it looked like Teren wasn't going to accept his offer of friendship causing a ripple of tension, but then he smiled and clasped the man's wrist in the traditional warrior's greeting.

There was no such hesitation from Captain Baradir who eagerly accepted Arlen's greeting. "I thought you people were a myth or had perhaps died out. I never in all my days expected to meet a Silevian warrior priest," he said enthusiastically.

"We like to keep ourselves to ourselves, Captain. The fewer people who know about us the better. The less they know the more fearful they are and that greatly increases our chances of being left alone," replied Arlen.

"Yet here you are, priest, in the middle of a war that has nothing to do with you," said Teren. His tone was laced with suspicion a fact that did not escape Arlen.

Ro sensed his friend tense up at the implied accusation. "I suspect that we all have intriguing tales to account for our presence here, but I would respectfully suggest that they can wait for another time. If you have a physician with you, Captain I would be very grateful if he could take a look at the lad lying over there. He's been hit by an arrow and has lost a lot of blood," said Ro nodding towards where Eryn knelt by the stricken Tav.

"Of course, right away," replied Baradir. "Sergeant." Sergeant Renus was at the captain's side immediately.

"Sir?"

"Find the physician and have him see to that wounded lad right away," ordered the captain.

"Yes, sir," replied the sergeant, briefly nodding a greeting to Aryk before walking off and bellowing for the medic.

"Is that...?" began Teren, as if noticing the boys for the first time.

"Eryn and Tav Rhem of Lentor, yes," interrupted Ro. "They were on a quest to rescue some women who were abducted from their village, when Arlen and I ran into them yesterday in Ederik. They were having an open and frank exchange of views with some of the locals at the time. We had just persuaded them to accompany us to Vangor when we ran into these Delarites."

Teren nodded. "You don't have to hide it, Ro, I know that my eldest daughter is amongst the captives."

"I'm sorry, Teren," said Ro.

"Don't be, lad. The only people who are going to be sorry are the people who snatched her if I have anything to do with it. I won't let it happen all over again." Teren's gaze fell on Eryn, who stared back from his position next to Tav. A middle-aged man in a Remadan Army uniform had torn open Tav's tunic and was examining his wound.

"Will he be all right?" Eryn asked the army physician.

"I think so. We've got the arrow out and judging by the colour of the blood it hasn't pierced any arteries, so provided we can staunch the flow of blood, he should be okay. He's going to feel tired and weak for a few days. Why don't you leave him to us, son and go and do something else? He's in good hands."

"Thank you," said Eryn as he clasped his friend's hand. "You're going to be okay, Tav. I'll come back and see you shortly okay?"

Tav feebly squeezed Eryn's hand and nodded at his friend, before two men came and ushered Eryn away.

Eryn stood before slowly walking over to where Ro and the others were still talking. Then when he was no more than a few paces away he suddenly launched himself at Teren landing a solid right hook on Teren's jaw. The big man wobbled but didn't move. Arlen and Ro quickly grabbed hold of Eryn's arms, as he struggled to get at Teren again.

"Eryn, what in the name of Sulat has got into you?" asked Ro, squeezing Eryn's arm in an attempt to draw his gaze away from Teren, but he was not going to be easily distracted.

"Easy, lad," said Arlen.

Teren just stared at Eryn with an amused look.

"Do you wish me to place the boy under arrest, sir?" Captain Baradir asked Teren.

"What? No. Let him go. You're not going to do that again are you, son, because I feel it only fair to warn you that one punch was for free, but the next one will come at a price?"

Eryn still struggled against Ro and Arlen's grip and both felt certain that if they released him, he would once again launch himself at Teren.

"Let him go, lads," urged Teren. He braced himself in case he had misread the lad. *Wouldn't look good in front of the men if I took a tumble.*

Ro and Arlen reluctantly released their grips.

"You and I have much to talk about, lad, but it will have to wait," said Teren smiling at Eryn.

"I have nothing to say to you," spat Eryn.

"Well in that case I'll do the talking and you can just sit and brood or sulk, how's that?" A look of anger flashed across Eryn's face and Ro tensed ready to grab the boy again if he went for Teren, but Eryn seemed to get his temper back under control.

"How about you just stay out of my way and out of my life like you've managed for the last seven years?" and with that Eryn went storming off to where Tav was now standing.

Teren watched him go, slowly shaking his head. This was going to take a lot of work to smooth out, but not now. Now they had to make their way to Vangor, the quicker the better. "Time we were off, gentlemen. Captain Baradir, get the column moving."

"Right away, sir," said the captain hurrying away and barking orders.

"Where are you headed, Teren?" asked Ro.

"Same place as you, lad, Vangor," replied Teren.

"Really?"

Teren briefly filled Ro and Arlen in on how he'd run into the retreating men and persuaded them to join him in going to Vangor and helping with the defence.

"Will we make a difference? Will it be enough?" asked Arlen.

Teren considered the question for a moment before replying. "It will have to be, because aside from a few stragglers we may pick up on the way, this is all there is." Teren nodded at both men before striding off to join Captain Baradir at the head of the column.

Ro went to follow Teren, but Arlen grabbed his arm lightly. "What's the cause of the enmity between Teren and the boy?" asked Arlen.

"Eryn is Teren's son."

"What?" asked Arlen incredulously.

"Come I'll tell you about it on the march if I am able to without others listening," and with that both men strode after the column, which was marching north-east and to battle.

Chapter 17

Kane Devan, the Prefect of Vangor, stared at the maps laid out on the wooden table before him. One was a schematic of the city, the other a map of the countryside immediately surrounding it. If he were a military man he supposed they'd mean something to him in strategic terms and that he'd know how to best deploy the limited military resources at his disposal. Unfortunately he wasn't at all that way inclined and had never served in the military in any capacity.

He had to face facts; he had no idea what he was doing and worse still the men stood around him knew it too. Nevertheless to their credit he noted, they were patiently deferring to his orders. An awkward silence had permeated the draughty room; he was going to have to say something, anything, so long as it was decisive.

Kane cleared his throat and forced his aching back straight, the officers standing around him following suit, expectant looks upon their faces.

"Given the size of the garrison we have at our disposal it's clear to me that we can't hope to defend the whole city bearing in mind the size of the Delartite force apparently heading our way." Kane noticed that most of the officers stood around him agreed with him on that at least. It was a promising start and he drew confidence from that fact. "I therefore propose that we..." A sharp rap on the solid oak door interrupted his new found confidence. "Come."

A young soldier perhaps no older than twenty entered the room and snapped smartly to attention. He looked anxious to Kane, probably unnerved at being the focus of so many officers' scrutiny.

"What is it, trooper?" asked the prefect.

The soldier glanced from the prefect to the officers and back again to the prefect, clearly unsure who he should face when making his report. In the end he decided to focus on a section of wall behind them all.

"Sir, Master of the Guard reports a body of men approaching the city at the march."

"Delarites?" asked Kane alarmed.

"Too far to tell at the moment, sir."

"From what direction?" asked one of the officers.

"From the south-west, sir," replied the trooper, his eyes never leaving the wall.

"The south-west," repeated another one of the officers. "If they are Delarites, that means they've flanked us and that we'll soon be surrounded."

"How many?" asked the first officer.

"Best estimate is three to four hundred, sir."

"It's either the vanguard of their forces or a small skirmish force sent ahead to cause mayhem," replied his colleague.

"Should we send our men out to confront them, Commander?" Kane asked the senior officer of the group.

"That would be unwise, sir. If they're skirmishers they'll just melt away as soon as they see us, but if they are the head of the snake, we could find ourselves stranded out there with the whole Delarite Army bearing down on us. We'd be slaughtered and the city would be defenceless."

The prefect nodded his understanding. "Very well. Might I suggest we go and take a look at this threat ourselves and then decide what action to take?" It was a rhetorical question and as soon as he had finished speaking, the prefect was already heading out of the room and towards the steps which would take him to the summit of the watch tower. The officers and trooper followed after him.

It was mid-afternoon and the sun was high in the sky. By the time the prefect had climbed the seemingly never-ending steps to the viewing platform, he was breathing hard and sweating profusely, neither of which enhanced his mood. The Master of the Guard and his two companions snapped to attention as one by one, the prefect and his party appeared from the stairwell.

"At ease, Master," said the prefect as he accepted the spy glass from his hand. It took the prefect a moment or two to find what he was looking for, but eventually he saw them. Marching in a column four wide with their officers at the head, was a body of men at least three hundred strong as the sentry had said. They were approaching fast. Kane looked down into the city below. Word of the approaching men had obviously filtered down to the populace as everyone was rushing around, gathering their children and provisions and heading towards the city centre.

"May I, Prefect?" asked Commander Baptiste, the senior officer.

"What? Yes, of course, sorry, Commander," replied the prefect distractedly. His mind was racing and deliberating everything that had to be done. He'd been hoping for a bit more lead time before the enemy arrived, but it seemed fate had decreed otherwise.

Commander Baptiste put the spyglass to his eye and studied the column of soldiers who were bearing down on their position. For a moment he said nothing, but then he collapsed the spyglass and began to laugh. The prefect looked at him aghast.

"Commander Baptiste, whilst I admire your cheerfulness in the face of adversity, I hardly think that it's appropriate given our current predicament. Rather than laughing I would prefer it if you were to give me your military assessment of the force approaching us and made some recommendations accordingly."

"Forgive me, Prefect. I recommend that we throw open our gates and prepare to welcome them," replied the commander still laughing.

"Have you gone stark raving mad, man? Those are enemy soldiers and I have no intention of welcoming them or any other aggressive force into the city without a fight, is that understood?"

"Yes, sir it is, but those men are not enemy soldiers. It's torn and seen better days, like many of the men who follow it, but if I'm not mistaken that's the battle standard of the Ninth Ligara down there."

"The Ninth Ligara, but they're..." started the prefect.

"Supposed to be in Torogora, yes I know, but that's in all likelihood fallen and these men are what are left of its garrison," finished the commander.

The prefect snatched the spyglass back from the

commander, hope briefly flirting with his heart. *Could it be true? Were they Remadan soldiers come to aid the defence of Vangor?* "They seem to have civilians walking at the head of the column, Commander. Who do you suppose they are?"

"My eyesight's not as good as it once was, sir, but if I didn't know better I'd say that was Teren Rad and Captain Ro Aryk."

"Teren Rad? Ro Aryk?" The prefect's head was in turmoil.

"May I, sir?" asked one of the junior officers gesturing at the spyglass.

"Be my guest," replied the prefect.

The young officer briefly stared at the approaching men before handing the commander the spyglass. "That's definitely the Ninth Ligara, sir, I recognise Captain Baradir alongside Captain Aryk. I've no idea who the scruffy looking mountain man is or his fat friend."

"You might want to watch your tongue around Teren Rad, Captain Matalis, unless you wish it nailed to the city walls. He doesn't appreciate disrespect," admonished Commander Baptiste. "Now make yourself useful and send the cavalry out to screen their approach."

"We don't have more than two dozen cavalry here, sir."

"I don't care if you have to get the city baker and his family on horses, you get some mounted men out there to protect those men," barked the commander.

"Yes, sir, right away," replied the captain hurrying off down the steps to carry out the commander's orders.

"Will they make a difference, Commander?" asked the prefect.

The commander removed his helmet and wiped the sweat from his brow as he considered the question. "Three to four hundred men won't sway the outcome of the battle, Prefect, they will just delay the inevitable. But every day we buy gives the armies of the south time to prepare and that can only be a good thing."

The prefect nodded his understanding. The fate of everyone within the city was sealed if they remained and remain they must. All he could look forward to was perhaps an extra day or two of life. "So be it, Commander. Let us go down and prepare to greet our guests."

As they prepared to descend the steps the sound of horses galloping out of the courtyard drifted up to the two men. The commander glanced over the parapet at the handful of riders who had just ridden out. If the enemy really were close enough to attack the approaching column and he suspected that they might be, the cavalry would not be able to offer much in the way of protection. It was a token gesture at best and he knew it. With a heavy heart Commander Baptiste started to descend the steps after the prefect.

***

The cheering and clapping as the column arrived in the city's courtyard was almost deafening. Word had spread of the imminent arrival of more soldiers and everyone had wanted to be there to greet what they had hoped would be their saviours. The rumour mill had been working overtime with some estimates describing the approaching soldiers as a relief force of several thousand. When the last of the column struggled in revealing the force's true number, the cheering began to fade.

Captain Baradir gave the order for his men to stand easy, whilst Teren stood observing the crowd nonchalantly, a wry smile on his face.

"That was quite some greeting wasn't it?" said Arlen as he came up and stood by Teren and Ro.

"That it was," smiled Ro. "I think, however, they are somewhat disappointed by our numbers."

"It's not always numbers that count, lad. Sometimes it's about the quality of the men," said Teren.

"Well said, Teren," replied Ro smiling some more.

"Watch out, the local brass is coming," said Arlen taking a step back, as a middle-aged man in civilian clothing approached with an officer wearing the insignia of a commander.

"You're up, Captain Baradir," said Teren.

Captain Baradir tugged his tunic, straightened his back and walked a few paces forward to greet the approaching men. When he was no more than a few paces in front of them, he stopped, snapped to attention and saluted. The commander saluted back.

"Captain Baradir of the Ninth Ligara lately of Torogora."

"Greetings, Captain. I am Prefect Kane Devan. You're a long way from Torogora, Captain if you don't mind me saying."

"I regret to inform you, sir, that Torogora has fallen and my men and I are all that's left of its defenders. However, they are all fine men, sir and I have brought them here to assist with the city's defence if you'll have us?"

The prefect smiled warmly. "You and your men are most welcome, Captain, believe me. This is Commander Baptiste of the City Garrison."

"A pleasure to meet you, sir," said Baradir.

The commander nodded back.

The prefect's gaze travelled to the three men in civilian clothes a few paces behind Captain Baradir. "I think you ought to introduce us to your companions, Captain."

"Yes, of course, forgive me." The captain beckoned for Ro, Teren and Arlen to approach. "Prefect Devan, Commander Baptiste, may I introduce you to Captain Ro Aryk, formerly of the Royal Bodyguard, Teren Rad and Master Arlen Meric, a priest of the Golden Tree from Silevia?"

The men all shook hands and exchanged greetings except for Teren and the commander, a fact noticed by the others leading to an atmosphere of tension. Ro was about to say something and try to break the awkward silence, when Teren saved him the trouble.

"I always thought the city garrisons were soft and ate too much; now I see that it is true," said Teren looking directly at the commander, a steely look in his eyes.

"And I always thought the Ninth Ligara were a bunch of sissy-boys who didn't know how to shave much less fight. You're living proof of the fact," replied the commander with a hard stare of his own.

Arlen shot Ro a worried look and both men tensed ready to step in and quickly break up the ugly fight which was seemingly inevitable.

Teren and the commander stared at each for a few long seconds neither giving ground. Then Teren scratched his unkempt beard before suddenly roaring with laughter. The commander also started to laugh heartily before stepping forward and embracing Teren. Ro and Arlen blew a collective sigh of relief, unsure what had just transpired but nonetheless glad that it had ended amicably.

The two men released their mutual embrace and took a step back as if evaluating each other.

"Time has been good to you, Teren Rad," said the commander.

"Really?" replied Teren, his fractured ego appreciating the boost.

"No, I was lying, you look like Kaden. Make sure that you stand near me whilst you're here; it will make me look good." Both men roared with laughter again.

"I take it that you gentlemen know one another?" said Captain Baradir.

"That we do, Captain. Me and Teren were fighting in the Northern Wars whilst you were still clutching at your mother's skirts," said the commander.

If the captain was offended by the remark, he hid it well.

"Yes, I've pulled his backside from the fire on many occasions. And now it looks like I've got to do it again," added Teren.

Ro and Arlen who had now been joined by Eryn, watched the exchange with amused expressions and were happy to continue doing so, but the prefect had clearly seen enough. He cleared his throat noisily.

"Forgive me for breaking up this happy reunion, gentlemen, but if we could turn to the matter at hand, namely defending this city."

The commander straightened his tunic and took a pace back towards the prefect. "Yes, of course, Prefect."

The prefect was about to say something about his plans when he suddenly noticed Eryn. "And who is this young man might I ask?"

"My name is Eryn, Prefect."

"And what is your role here, Eryn? You're not in the uniform of the army."

"I was on a quest to rescue my sister and fiancée from Narmidian raiders, when I ran into Ro and Arlen. They helped me out of a scrape."

"And now you've come to help us out of one, eh?"

"It seems so, Prefect," replied Eryn.

"Well your father wherever he is, must be very proud of you." The prefect noted the look that passed between the small group of companions, but didn't comprehend what he had said that had been so contentious.

"Eryn is my son, Prefect," said Teren.

"Ah, I see." There was clearly more going on here than he was aware of but now was not the time or place to delve into such matters. It could wait to later if there was indeed to be a later for the men defending Vangor. "Captain, your men must be hungry and thirsty. Commander please arrange for our guests to receive food and water whilst the rest of us retire to my chambers where we can discuss how best to deploy your men." With that the prefect turned and walked off, beckoning for the others to follow.

The commander called one of his sergeants over whom cheerily agreed to show the men of the Ninth to the mess hall and after picking up a couple of his senior officers along the way, the commander hurried after the prefect.

***

"It's not enough is it?" asked the prefect. The question hadn't been directed at any one person in the room.

"It depends on your expectations, Prefect. If you expect a victory here, no it isn't. There can be only one outcome and that's our defeat. However, if you measure victory in the number of days we can hold the Delarites at bay, then yes, we can expect a small victory," replied Ro.

"Seven hundred and ninety-seven men. How can we possibly hope to hold out?"

"You were prepared to try with a little over four hundred, Prefect, so your chances have improved," said Arlen.

"Oh, don't get me wrong, gentlemen, it is my duty to defend Vangor and I would attempt that even if I had but a dozen men. I was merely wondering out loud how much of a difference we will make."

"With the right preparations and it seems to me you've made those, a bit of guts and a large slice of luck, we could tie down a sizeable force of Delarites for several days. Precious time for the men of the south to mobilise and get

208

ready to launch a counterattack," said Teren.

"That's if our king gives the order and doesn't immediately capitulate," said Ro.

"Would he do that? Give up without a fight," asked Arlen.

"He is capable of almost anything. I fear for Remada, I really do," replied Ro.

"Come, come, Captain Aryk, he is not all bad. He has merely been misguided and poorly advised. All the time he's got wise and experienced people like Radek Templar around him there is hope," said the prefect.

"Your loyalty does you credit, Prefect and whilst my own experience confirms your fears about poor advice, I fear your loyalty is misplaced," said Ro.

"That is a debate for another time I fear. Now if we are all agreed on the deployment of our men and the tactics to be employed, I believe there is only one more thing to settle." The small group all looked at the prefect expectantly. "Whilst I consider myself an excellent administrator and prefect in peacetime, I fear I am well out of my depth when confronted by predicaments such as we now face. I therefore propose that I relinquish overall command to you Teren, given your vast experience of such things, with Commander Baptiste as your second-in-command. Does everyone agree?"

Teren was genuinely surprised by the sudden turn of events and was momentarily speechless. "Firstly, Prefect, you may not be a military man, but you've already shown enough guts in your decision to stay and defend the city, for me to feel proud enough to serve you. Secondly, I'm no longer in the army, but Commander Baptiste is and should therefore command the forces."

"I meant no slight to the commander's ability or competence, he knows that. I just felt that if everything I've ever heard about you is true, you should be the one leading us. Commander Baptiste will be there as your second-in-command, as I say."

"Come, Teren, this is no time for false modesty or damaged pride, the prefect is right. I am a garrison commander and have been for some time, but you have led defences like this before; I should know I was with you. It therefore makes perfect sense for you to lead us. Besides, the way Captain Baradir explains it, the only reason the Ninth are here is because the men followed you. Take the command, we need you, old friend," said Baptiste.

"Very well, I will command the forces, but the prefect remains in charge of all things civilian. I'd never be any good at that sort of thing, nor will I have the time," said a reluctant Teren.

"Good, then it is settled. Now if there..." A sharp rap at the door interrupted the prefect mid-flow. "Enter." The same sentry who had disturbed the prefect's meeting earlier, briskly walked in and once again snapped to attention. He appeared even more nervous than the first time the prefect noted. "What is it this time, trooper?"

"The Master of the Guard requests your attendance in the watch tower, Prefect."

"What again? I've only just recovered from climbing those steps last time. What is it this time that he wants me to see?"

The trooper removed his gaze from the rear wall and met the prefect's eyes for the first time. "Delarites, sir. Thousands of them."

The prefect felt the colour drain from his cheeks and forced himself to move towards the steps, but Teren and Ro were already climbing them before him. Within a minute, everybody from the meeting was stood looking over the parapet of the watch tower at the mass of men swarming over the distant ridge like a horde of busy ants. The sentry hadn't been exaggerating, there were thousands of them, far more than was necessary to take the city given its garrison size, the prefect realised.

Unless they don't know that we're below strength.

The prefect wasn't sure whether this was a good or bad thing. He was sure that it should give the defenders some sort of tactical advantage, but not being a military man he didn't know how to exploit it. Teren Rad turning up like that was a blessing in disguise. He'd been able to relinquish responsibility for the city's defence and with it any blame that would be attached should it fall.

When it falls, he corrected himself.

Teren glanced down in front of the city gates and was

pleased to see that the area was clear, with no mass of civilians scrambling to enter the city. "Time to close the gate I think, Commander."

Commander Baptiste didn't hesitate and bellowed down to the guards to shut the gate, which they quickly did.

"To your stations I think, gentlemen," said Teren.

"Where do you want me, Teren?" asked Arlen.

"It is not your war, Master Meric, I don't even know what you are doing here. Nor are you part of the Remadan Army so I cannot order you anywhere."

"Then consider me a willing volunteer."

"In that case, I would be grateful if you would watch out for the boy Eryn. He's my responsibility I know, but I'm likely to be a little busy over the next few hours."

"Consider it done, though I shall have to do it from a discreet distance. He will not react well I think if he learns that I am babysitting him. He is stubborn," said Arlen.

"Hmm. Can't imagine where he'd get that from," said Baptiste laughing.

"You still here, old man?" asked Teren good-naturedly.

"Thought I'd better remain behind to help you down the steps, what with you being so frail and all," replied Baptiste.

"Get to your post, Commander, before I show you just how frail I am," replied Teren raising his fist but laughing at the same time. "Good luck to us all, gentlemen."

The small group nodded to one another and began to descend the steps to assume their various commands and responsibilities.

***

General Malik stared down through his spyglass at the Remadan city of Vangor and smiled. The sense of fear emanating from the city was almost palpable. Soon he would crush this city, plunder its wealth and then move south seeking more glory. Below the ridge upon which he now stood, the might of his army began to fan out and take up their positions. It galled him that he couldn't attack immediately, but such was the size of his army that it was stretched out over several leagues and wouldn't all arrive until the evening. Still, he had enough to launch a small attack if he wanted; he would decide later.

The sound of a horse fast approaching from the rear caught his attention, but he refused to show any sign of excitement or emotion by looking round. He would wait patiently for the messenger to approach and make his report.

The horseman dismounted came round to the front of the general and bent down on one knee with his head bowed waiting for permission to address his commander.

"Speak."

"General, Commander Vantoris sent me to tell you that the Remadan force that was sent out from the city of Vangor earlier has been completely destroyed and that his cavalry will be rejoining you shortly, sir."

"Excellent. Do you hear that, men?" said the general swivelling to look at the small cluster of officers around him. "Their puny cavalry force has been smashed. There can be but a few hundred men in the city defending it. Guards, cooks and men who have seen too many summers. This is going to be easier than I thought."

The officers around him smiled and whispered to each other. The general was right; the city was ripe for the picking.

Another rider approached the small group, but instead of presenting himself to the general as the first one had, he pulled up alongside General Malik's second-in-command and proceeded to whisper something in his ear, before hurrying off again. The soldier's lack of respect and protocol would have to be addressed later as would Avalik's failure to admonish his subordinate. Right now, however, his curiosity was piqued more than his desire to enforce discipline.

"General, the rider reports that before we got here a small force of Remadan soldiers made it into the city," reported Avalik.

"How small?" asked Malik somewhat irritated.

"About four hundred, sir."

The general nodded. A small annoyance, but that's all it would be. "So Commander Vantoris's bold claim of having wiped out the force from Vangor was premature then?"

"No, sir. These men are what remain of the garrison that was defending Torogora."

"What? How did they get here so fast and more to the

point why? They were a completely spent force who broke and ran. Why now do they march to battle and another forlorn one at that?" asked Malik.

"Apparently a man has rallied them and put fire in their bellies once again," replied Avalik.

"And who is this bringer of strength who thinks that by rallying a few hundred men he can withstand the tide which is Delarite?"

"They say that Teren Rad leads them, sir."

General Malik spun round in his saddle to stare at Avalik. "Teren Rad?"

"Yes, sir."

The general turned to look into the faces of the small group of officers gathered around him. The fear and awe the sheer mention of Rad's name had caused was almost tangible. "Why do you quiver like old women? He is just one man and an old one at that. Do you think that one old man can make a difference?"

None of his officers dared look the general in the eye.

The general shook his head and then spat on the ground in disgust. "I am surrounded by children and cowards. Very well. When the battle commences I will seek out this frail old man that terrorises my officers so and I will kill him myself. Then perhaps you will show some backbone in front of your men."

The general returned his gaze to the city a short distance away where even now the men of Remada were making preparations to resist the Delarite attack.

So Teren Rad has crawled out from under his rock after all these years. It is good that he will be here to witness my triumph and glory before I take my revenge and end his life.

The general gently touched the scar on his cheek and smiled.

Chapter 18

Although he would never admit it, the news that Teren Rad was in the city slightly unnerved Malik and in the end he decided to delay his attack for another two days. That would give enough time for his entire army to arrive and deploy. He'd considered charging the city's walls with his cavalry whilst men carrying ladders followed behind, but had decided against it. The city walls were higher than they looked from a distance and although he didn't doubt his men would eventually breach the city, the cost in lives would in all likelihood be steep. He needed to keep his forces intact for greater battles to come. Vangor was no more than a mild irritation, a thorn in his side.

For two days and nights preceding the assault, the Delarite siege weapons had pummelled the city walls, spreading fear and panic within, but doing little to weaken the city's defences. Then early on the third morning, General Malik had ordered his artillery to concentrate their fire on the northern gate and the wall either side. The effect was almost instantaneous. The impact of so many heavy rocks and fireballs concentrated on one spot was devastating. The gate soon began to weaken and cracks started to spread through the adjoining walls, until eventually the wall to the right of the gate collapsed.

General Malik observed the breach through his spyglass and grunted with satisfaction. It was not a clear path into the city by any means as the wall had collapsed into a steep slope of rubble perhaps half the height of the original wall. But it was a start. Many of his men would lose their lives trying to cross the breach, but it was a price he was willing to pay. Time was passing and he yearned for greater glory in the Remadan hinterland, perhaps even its capital if he was quick enough. First though he had to take Vangor.

His generals continued to advise caution, urging him to delay his attack until a larger breach could be exploited or until the gate gave way as it inevitably would, but he was impatient for success. The gate was on fire and would give way soon enough, despite the Remadan's best efforts to protect it by constantly dousing it with their precious supply of water. But his time was now. Glory and a place in history waited.

"General Avalik," Malik called over his shoulder without turning round.

The general's second-in-command inched his horse forward until he was alongside his leader.

"Yes, General."

"Commence the attack, General Avalik."

General Avalik glanced from his leader to the small breach in the city wall and back to his leader. "Surely, General, it would be better to wait until we have enlarged the breach or burned down the gates? The Remadans are going nowhere, sir."

A brief look of anger flickered across Malik's face before he seemed to regain his composure. "And neither are we, General. The longer we stay here the further behind our other armies we fall until eventually all that will be left for us to conquer are a few tiny villages inhabited by filthy peasants. We'll be the laughing stock of the army. Commence the attack."

"But, General, one more day surely..."

General Avalik never got to finish his sentence. He'd known he was on dangerous ground by challenging his leader's orders, but had relied on the fact that the two men had fought side-by-side for over twenty years to keep him safe. He had been wrong. His eyes wide with disbelief, Avalik looked down at the dagger that now protruded from his abdomen, an ever widening pool of blood spreading out from where the blade pierced his body. Avalik looked towards the man who had stabbed him, the man he had considered not only his leader, but also his friend. Malik's gaze, however, was fixed on the city. Without uttering another word, Avalik gently toppled forward off his horse, his dead body hitting the dusty ground with a muffled thud in front of his brother officers.

"General Ilic," Malik suddenly called.

The young officer didn't immediately respond,

recognising his name, but not his rank. One of the other officers nudged his comrade forward. "Seems like you've been promoted, boy."

Startled, the newly promoted General Ilic nervously edged his horse forward until he was alongside Malik, nudging Avalik's redundant mount out of the way. Ilic saluted sharply, trying to stop his gaze wandering to the lifeless body of General Avalik, a man he had considered both competent and wise. "General."

"It seems I have a vacancy for a second-in-command and you are to assume that role with immediate effect. Understood?" asked Malik in a tone that brooked no argument.

Ilic was about to point out that he was one of the youngest men there and that there were far more experienced officers better suited to the role, when his gaze momentarily drifted to Avalik's body.

"Is there a problem, General Ilic?" asked Malik as he slowly turned to face the young officer, his expression cold and hard.

"No, sir, thank you."

"Good. Commence the attack."

"Immediately, General." Ilic turned his horse to face the small cluster of officers behind him. "Commence the attack as we discussed last night. I will lead the first wave as General Avalik would have done. To your positions now!"

The officers moved off to join their troops, some more reluctantly than others. General Avalik had been well-liked and respected by his fellow officers and he had been killed simply for voicing what many of them thought. One more day of bombardment would have seen the breach expanded sufficiently to make the storming of the city that much less costly. Now, to add insult to injury they were being ordered about by a young inexperienced officer with no battle experience whatsoever. Still, if he was leading the first assault, he would in all likelihood be killed soon enough anyway. It was a comforting thought to many of them.

General Malik watched his officers disperse leaving just his personal bodyguard of four men attending him. He had noted the disapproval on some of the officers faces as they left and was already contemplating whom he could and could not trust. Killing Avalik had been distasteful, as the man was practically a friend, but if he were to maintain discipline and with it, the confidence and respect of his officers, then he had to demonstrate that no one was indispensable. From somewhere behind him a horn sounded signalling the start of the attack and Malik sat upright in his saddle to watch the assault begin.

The initial attack was a crude affair. Hundreds of men from the Delarite Datani Regiment, a force made up of foreign mercenaries, criminals and slaves, rushed forward under the cover of archers and made straight for the breach. Those who made it as far as the breach, bunched together as they began to pick their way through the haphazard pile of rubble. They were an easy target for the Remadan archers and javelin throwers. Somebody had to be sacrificed first to test the Remadan defences and who better than foreigners and criminals? Malik would shed no tears at their loss.

***

"Steady men, pick your targets. Make every arrow count." The way the Delarites were bunched together below, desperately scrambling to get up the mound of rubble and through the breach, Ro seriously doubted whether anyone could miss. The carnage below told him he wasn't wrong.

Dozens of men lay dead or dying, the living treading on them in their desperation to escape the hail of missiles. It was a slaughter. Several over enthusiastic Remadans ignored their officer's orders to maintain cover and were picked off by the Delarite archers who had followed the attacking infantry. Nevertheless, the Remadan casualties were but a fraction of what the Delarites were suffering.

"That's the way, lads, make them pay for their lack of respect," bellowed Teren as he stalked along the ramparts behind his men.

"We're committing murder," said the prefect to no one in particular as he gazed down at the men who were dying by the dozen below them.

"Would you prefer it was us, Prefect?" asked Teren.

"What? No, of course not. I just don't know how any man could be so callous towards others, that's all."

"The Delarites don't put any value on the men dying

217

down there. They are the Datani Regiment or the Regiment of the Damned. Prisoners, slaves and foreign mercenaries. There are very few Delarites dying down there, Prefect," said Commander Baptiste.

"But they're still his men, aren't they? They're still fighting for Delarite."

"True, but somebody had to be first to test our defences and those men are expendable to the Delarites. More importantly to their commander, we're using up our arrows and javelins on men he couldn't care less about," added Teren.

The prefect shook his head in disgust.

Somewhere in the distance a horn blew and slowly what remained of the attackers began to withdraw from the breach and pull back towards the ridge where the bulk of the Delarite force was gathered.

"Ro, give them one more volley and then let them go," shouted Teren.

Ro waved his acknowledgment before passing on the order. The sky was suddenly filled with arrows taking another terrible toll on the men withdrawing towards the Delarite camp.

"Cease fire," bellowed Ro an order quickly echoed all along the line.

The prefect looked down at the ground outside the citadel, strewn with bodies. "What a terrible waste."

Teren, Ro and Commander Baptiste had seen it all before, more times than they cared to remember, but for the prefect, a man of peace, this was clearly the first time. "For them it was a waste, Prefect, yes, but not for us," said Teren.

"How so?"

"Because winning battles isn't always about having the most men or the better weapons. Sometimes it's about knowing and understanding your enemy and today I learned two things about ours," replied Teren.

"And what were they, my friend?"

"Firstly, that he's impatient for success. He probably sees this little outpost as a sideshow with the real glory still to come in bigger battles. He wants to crush us as quickly as he can. The smart thing to do would have been to keep bombarding us with those damn siege weapons until the breach was wide enough to pour sufficient men in to overwhelm us. Instead he decided to attack too early and it's cost him."

"If we are so unimportant why didn't he just bypass us and leave us alone?" asked the prefect.

"Small as we are here, we could still be a nuisance to him, harrying his supply and communication lines. No, he had to deal with us before he moved on," replied Teren.

"And the second thing you've learned about our adversary?"

Teren glanced down at the multitude of dead and dying below him. "That he's a ruthless whoreson who is prepared to sacrifice anyone and everyone to achieve his goals. That will make him reckless and unpredictable."

"I see and that's not a good thing I take it?"

"No, Prefect it isn't. Most military men have graduated through an academy or college and have been schooled to fight in a certain way and to respond to situations in a certain manner. This general either didn't pay much attention in class or is just a maverick by nature," explained Teren.

"So how do we counter him then?" asked the prefect intrigued.

"By being unpredictable ourselves."

"I see. How will..."

"Here they come again," shouted a soldier off to Teren's right.

Teren glanced over the parapet and saw thousands of men slowly advancing towards the city. "I'd love to explain everything to you, Prefect, but it's going to have to wait I'm afraid. It looks like their general has decided to try a text book assault this time."

The prefect, Ro and Baptiste edged forward for a better look. Teren watched their faces for a reaction. Baptiste and Ro simply appeared to be appraising the forces arrayed in front of them, but the prefect visibly paled at the sight before him.

"Looks like we're in for a real fight this time, lads," said Teren smiling.

"Good, I had nothing planned for this afternoon anyway,"

said Baptiste making the other men smile, even the prefect.

"Might I suggest you retire to somewhere a bit safer, Prefect?" suggested Ro.

"My place is here with you gentlemen. It's my city after all."

"Your courage is duly noted, Prefect, but if those men with ladders manage to climb up here it's going to get real cosy very quickly and I need to know that the men around me are all fighting men. Please check on the infirmary and make sure they've got everything they need and see how the other gate's holding out," said Teren.

The prefect hesitated clearly caught between the desire to stand and defend his city along with the other men yet understanding that his presence was more likely a hindrance than a help.

"It's okay, Prefect. Let us do what we do best," said Ro putting a reassuring arm round the prefect's shoulders and guiding him towards the steps. Realising that this was indeed no time for false bravado, the prefect acquiesced and descended the steps saying a quiet prayer for the men he left behind.

Ro rejoined the others who were watching the advancing army. The Delarite siege weapons had started up again and rocks and fire balls were peppering the breach and the inner sanctum of the city.

"They mean business this time, Teren," said Baptiste matter-of-factly. "He's sent his skirmishers and archers out first to try and keep our heads down, whilst his light infantry follow up with their ladders. Behind them come the massed ranks of heavy infantry. Cavalry protect their flanks."

"Who are those wild looking men with no tunics on?"

The small group of officers turned to see who had spoken.

"Eryn, what are you doing up here, the battle's about to begin?" asked Teren.

"I'm sorry, Teren, but short of restraining the lad, I couldn't stop him from coming up here. He's chomping at the bit to get involved," said Arlen apologetically. They had joined the small group unnoticed whilst they were observing the enemy formations.

Eryn stared out over the ramparts at the masses of

soldiers below and gasped in surprise. He had never seen so many people in one place at the same time. Knowing that so many men were prepared to die for what they believed in was almost overwhelming. He turned to speak to Tav and only then remembered that his friend was lying in the makeshift infirmary trying to recover from the arrow wound. Perhaps it was better that he was there away from the fighting.

The bombardment of rocks had been terrifying and Tav who was petrified of loud noises would have been scared witless. Most of the missiles had slammed into the walls and gate, but one or two had overshot their mark and landed within the city. Wherever they'd landed there was sure to have been casualties. He would check in on Tav as soon as he could and take him some food; that was sure to cheer him up. It always did.

"It's quite some sight when you see it for the first time, isn't it?" said Arlen as he sidled up alongside Eryn.

"It is," replied Eryn.

"It's not so pretty when half of them are laying dead or dying."

Eryn nodded his agreement. "I wish Tav was well enough to see it."

"The last time I spoke to the medic he told me Tav was doing well, that's the main thing. Now why don't you go down and see him, where it's safer?"

"No, I want to stay up here and help," replied Eryn, his body language suggesting that the matter wasn't up for discussion.

Arlen looked to Ro for help.

"If they get a foothold up here, Teren, we'll never hold and it will be dangerous for the lad," said Ro.

"Then we'll just have to make sure that they don't get up here won't we? Besides, the whole city will become a dangerous place to be pretty soon. The lad can stay, Arlen, but you're to stay close by and watch his back," replied Teren as he hefted his Caliri war axe over his right shoulder.

"What happened to your sword?" asked Ro.

"It's over there," said Teren nodding to where his huge two-handed sword leant against the parapet. "But it's too big for a close quarters fight like this could turn into. The axe is much more versatile. Good for chopping off heads that appear over the parapet."

Ro smiled. He had no doubt that it was going to have a lot of work to do.

"I hate to break up this cosy chat, gentlemen, but we're about to receive company," said Baptiste glancing towards the mass of men below them.

The arrows were pouring over the city walls now although the siege weapons had ceased firing again for fear of hitting their own men.

"Captain Aryk, perhaps you would be good enough to let those lads have their arrows back?" said Teren.

Ro smiled at the man's composure. Any second now he could be struck down by an errant arrow, but he paid them no regard. Instead he stood calm and collected issuing orders and reassuring those around him. No wonder men would follow him to Kaden and back.

"It will be my pleasure, Teren. Archers! Volley fire. Draw. Fire." The city garrison didn't have many archers left, nowhere near enough, but their numbers had been bolstered by civilians and more were coming every minute. "Steady, men. Draw. Fire." A second volley of arrows arched over the city walls and into the massed ranks below.

The arrows took a terrible toll on the attacking force, but it was never going to be enough to halt them or even slow them down. Some of the ladders had already been placed against the city walls and men were climbing up them as quickly as possible.

Ro rushed to the parapet and heaved a ladder away from the wall just as a bearded Delarite was about to climb over. His screams as he fell and those of the other men on the same ladder were lost in the cacophony of noise that surrounded Ro. He looked to his right for any sign of another ladder just as a soldier from the Ninth Ligara took an arrow in the eye. His place was immediately taken by a young lad in civilian clothes, but before he could even string an arrow, he too was hit in the shoulder. They were too few and would soon be overrun at this rate, Ro realised.

Another snarling face suddenly appeared above the

parapet. Ro rushed towards the man and ran him through the throat with his sword, but not before the Delarite had thrown his knife hitting another Remadan archer.

As the Delarite fell, Ro tipped his ladder back sending it crashing to the ground below crushing those who were not quick enough to move out of its way.

The Delarites were getting over the parapet now in greater numbers and unless there was a concerted effort to repulse them, the Remadans would soon be overrun.

Eryn watched from behind Arlen as Teren despatched two Delarites as if he was swatting flies. All along the wall men were desperately engaged in personal battles, with only a few of the archers still free to shoot arrows and assist their beleaguered comrades.

A tall Delarite with a fearsome looking curved sword appeared over the wall and immediately clapped eyes on Arlen and Eryn. Grinning he rushed towards them his sword raised above his head ready to strike. Arlen was on him in an instant, parrying the first two strokes before kicking the man in the groin and then beheading him as he instinctively leant forward. Eryn's eyes were wide with shock and his grip on his sword tightened considerably.

Three more Delarites were charging towards Eryn now and although Arlen had seen them and was already manoeuvring to intercept them, he was never going to be able to shield Eryn from all three. Eryn stood, swallowed hard and took a pace forward holding his sword up in a defensive posture as Kam Martel had taught him many times.

One of the Delarites suddenly dropped to the ground, a small metal object lodged in his eye, but the others were soon upon Eryn. One of them chopped down at Eryn with his sword, but Eryn blocked the strike, the force of the stroke sending vibrations all down Eryn's sword arm and into his shoulder. The Delarite raised his sword again and once more brought it crashing down but Eryn once again managed to deflect the blow. Out of the corner of his eye, Eryn saw that Arlen was embroiled in fighting the third man.

The force of the next blow from his attacker drove Eryn to his knees and he knew that his arm wasn't strong enough to withstand another strike. Eryn stared up at his attacker's face and prepared to die.

***

Teren had watched in horror as three Delarite soldiers had approached his son. He had tried to assess whether he had the time to cover the ground and come to Eryn's aid before the lad was killed, but the answer was a resounding no. Still he had to try. He wasn't about to let some Delarite sword snatch away any final chance of a reconciliation with his son. His hopes had been raised when Ro who had also spotted the danger, had improved the lad's chances by dropping one of the Delarites with a *jemtak.* Arlen too had come to his assistance and was in the process of despatching another of the attackers but it still left a third one for Eryn to deal with. He hoped that his old friend Kam Martel had taught the lad how to defend himself with a sword, at least long enough for Teren to be able to come to his assistance.

Teren began to make his way towards Eryn, but some of the enemy moved to intercept him. The first Delarite who stepped in front of Teren lost the top of his head to his axe, the next finding the blade suddenly buried in his midriff. Seeing the cold look of a man on a mission, the other Delarites began to back off and let him pass, until a bare-chested brute of a man, of similar size and build to Teren, jumped in front of him and swung his axe.

Distracted by Eryn's predicament, Teren had reacted at the last possible moment and the attacker's axe sliced perilously close to his chest, less than a hand's width in front of him. The attacker grinned at Teren before launching a series of powerful swings, their ferocity only matched by the power of Teren's blocks and counter swings. The Delarite was good, but Teren had managed to breach his defences on a couple of occasions, not enough to seriously hurt the man, but enough to bleed and seemingly enrage him, though he displayed no sign of pain. Teren too had been caught by a glancing blow and a wound on his left side was bleeding heavily. It was of no consequence though, as all that mattered to Teren at that moment in time was getting to his son.

After parrying another two powerful blows, Teren surprised his opponent when he swung his axe low, severing the man's right leg just above the knee. The man toppled to the ground howling, not apparently in pain, but in rage. Even as he went down the Delarite had the presence of mind to swing his axe one more time and its blade sliced across Teren's leather greave, but didn't cut him. Ordinarily, Teren might have spared the man's life for his bravery and prowess, but not today. Today was a day for killing and with a massive sideways swing of his own axe and a roar of triumph that startled those around him, Teren removed the man's head in a spray of blood. The head fell over the parapet and down into the courtyard where it bounced off a Delarite's shoulder startling him and making him scream with shock. The brief distraction gave the two civilians who had nervously been facing him, the chance to kill him with their pitchforks.

***

The Delarite soldier fighting Eryn sensed victory and took a step forward before chopping down with his sword in what should have been a killing blow. Anticipating the man's move, however, Eryn had already rolled to his right out of harm's way and the sword sliced through the air missing its target. The momentum of the swing caused the Delarite to stumble forward and lose his balance slightly. Seeing his chance, Eryn kicked out as hard as he could striking his attacker just behind the left knee. With a howl of rage the soldier collapsed to the floor in an unceremonious heap. Eryn was on his feet in an instant and quickly brought his sword point to rest at his enemy's throat.

"What are you waiting for, boy, kill me?" snarled the man defiantly.

Eryn increased the pressure of the sword point on the man's throat, drawing forward the first trickle of bright red blood.

"Well, are you man enough to kill me or not?" Eryn made no attempt to cut the man's throat and the Delarite could see that Eryn was wrestling with his conscience. The pressure on his throat had also eased and he decided to take his chance. "I thought not." Quick as a flash the Delarite kicked Eryn's legs out from under him and Eryn crashed to the floor spilling his sword.

Before he could react, Eryn found himself in the same position as his adversary had just been, flat on his back with a sword point perilously close to his chest ready to be thrust down.

The Delarite grinned down at Eryn. "Let me give you a piece of advice, boy, and the last you're ever going to hear; never hesitate or give your enemy a second chance."

Petrified and unable to move, Eryn watched as the man raised his sword slightly to thrust down into his chest. He wanted to close his eyes and not witness the moment of his own death but his gaze was transfixed on his executioner. Steeling himself for the sudden downward thrust that would end his life, Eryn was surprised when the man's head suddenly snapped back violently before a knife swiftly drew a red line across his throat. The Delarite's body slipped lifelessly to the ground.

"Good advice that," said Teren holding a bloody knife and gazing down at the Delarite's body. "Pity he didn't follow it. Get down those steps quickly, Eryn and join the prefect in the infirmary. This is obviously no place for you."

Caught between the elation of still being alive and the shame of having not been able to finish off his opponent, Eryn didn't move.

"Now!" bellowed Teren as he threw the knife at a Delarite who had charged straight for him. The man dropped his weapon and collapsed to the floor.

Eryn struggled to his feet, his legs wobbly with fear or shock and after bending down to pick up his fallen sword, he hurried down the steps and away from the main theatre of battle, though the odd skirmish was still taking place in the courtyard. As he ran across the square towards where he knew the infirmary had been set up, Eryn realised what it had been that he heard in his father's voice a few moments ago; disappointment. He had clearly been disappointed at Eryn's inability to take a man's life when it had been there for the taking. In truth Eryn had been disappointed with himself. He knew that the Delarite soldier would have taken his life in the blink of an eye if roles had been reversed, which is exactly what had happened only seconds later. Eryn frowned and was still ruing his decision, when from round the back of the makeshift infirmary emerged the prefect leading a large group of men who seemed to have armed themselves with anything they could find.

The prefect clapped eyes on Eryn but didn't slow his pace. "You come to join us, lad?"

"My father, that is Teren Rad, sent me over to help you in the infirmary," replied Eryn feeling slightly ashamed whilst turning to walk with the group.

"Ordinarily I'd be pleased to have your help, but the truth of the matter is that the battle's going badly, very badly. If every able bodied man doesn't pick up arms and help out, there'll be no infirmary or anything else for that matter to defend," said the prefect glancing nervously up at the parapets. "Are you with us, lad?"

Eryn glanced round at the assortment of men with the prefect. The fit and strong civilians had already been conscripted and sent to help in the city's defence and the men with the prefect were what was left; the walking wounded, civil servants and those who had seen too many summers. Eryn drew his sword and nodded.

"Good lad. Fall in with the rest of the fellows will you."

***

Ro pushed as hard as he could but he still needed Arlen's help to send the soldier laden ladder toppling to the ground below. "There's too many of them, Arlen. We'll never hold."

Arlen didn't immediately answer, instead he turned slightly and parried a downward cut from a Delarite officer before smashing his elbow into the man's face and then running him through with his own sword. "I know, Ro. Perhaps it is time to fall back?"

"To where? There is nowhere to run and certainly nowhere as defensible as this." Ro glanced around him. The defenders were thin on the ground now with only the best of the soldiers still remaining, but they were hopelessly outnumbered and more Delarites were arriving all the time. They were going to have to make a last stand right there, Ro realised. "Remadans to me."

Slowly, those who could disengage from their personal

duels did so and made their way to where Ro was trying to rally the men. Not everyone would be able to join him he realised, including Teren who was busily tussling with three petrified looking enemy soldiers.

Seeing that the Remadans were trying to concentrate what remained of their forces, a Delarite officer issued a similar order and dozens of men flocked to his call, including a couple of their berserkers. Although the narrow parapet would mean that the Delarites would not all be able to attack the Remadans at once, their numbers would eventually tell.

The Delarite officer issued an order and the two bare-chested berserkers raced forward and leapt at the small force of Remadans whilst the regular troops advanced in a tight formation behind them.

A soldier to Ro's right was struck in the head with an axe as one of the berserkers came crashing down on the Remadans, but Arlen's upward sword thrust ran him through as he landed. Even with his last few breaths the man continued to punch and kick at the Remadans.

The second berserker had managed to disrupt the Remadan formation on the left, knocking several of them to the ground and one over the edge into the courtyard below where he landed with a sickening thud. Before the Remadans could react the berserker was hacking and slashing at those around him, cutting one man's hamstrings and slicing open another's abdomen. It took several blows from Ro's and Arlen's swords to kill the man. When they looked up, the advancing Delarites were almost upon them.

Ro sensed the anxiety around him as his remaining men tightened their grip on their swords and shields. There would be no winning this fight instead it would be a case of seeing how much damage they could inflict on their attackers before they were eventually overwhelmed. He opened his mouth to issue a few last words of encouragement, but never got to speak, as the Delarites were suddenly attacked in the rear amid a cacophony of roaring voices.

"I don't believe it," said Arlen open mouthed as he watched the prefect and his ragtag group of fighters carve their way into the Delarites.

"Seeing is believing my friend," replied Ro smiling.

The Delarites were just recovering when Teren and another soldier who had managed to finally extricate himself from a fight, slammed into their flank.

"Shall we?" asked Ro turning to Arlen.

"Why not," replied Arlen beaming.

"Remadans, forward," shouted Ro and with a great cheer the remaining Remadans charged at the embattled Delarites.

Faced with an assault on three fronts, the Delarites knew they were doomed and whilst most tried to flee to the wall and climb down the ladders, some fought bravely on including their officer. With nowhere to run though it was a slaughter. Those who did not fall to the avenging Remadan blades either fell to their death in the courtyard below or were pushed over the wall as they tried to climb onto the ladders.

Three short blasts on a distant horn signalled the retreat and those Delarites who had not yet breached the city made an orderly withdrawal whilst those within its walls did their best to escape, though many were cut down by arrows and javelins as they fled.

Ro and the surviving Remadans on the parapet watched as the enemy retreated for the ridge and the rallying points beneath their standards. It was a victory, but a hollow one, Ro knew, for it did no more than delay the inevitable. Still, if they bled the Delarites here and bought enough time, maybe the king would come to his senses and finally muster a meaningful defence. It was an encouraging thought, but Ro wasn't hopeful.

"Is that it? Have we won?" asked the prefect hopefully.

"I'm afraid not," replied Ro.

"Not even after the beating we just gave them?"

"You call that a beating?" asked Teren; he was covered from head to toe in blood and was a terrifying sight. "Look about you, Prefect, what do you see?"

The Prefect glanced around, horrified by the number of bodies lying around the ramparts. Many of them were the men and boys he had persuaded to join him in one last attack. It had been glorious, but ultimately futile it seemed. "I see dead men, Teren, friends and neighbours."

"That's right, Prefect and most of them are ours. This was

no victory, just a stay of execution. They'll be back and soon." Teren looked out across the plain towards the low ridge where already the Delarites were forming up for another attack.

"Sooner than you think," said Arlen who had also seen the Delarites mustering. Still it was a brave thing you and the other men did. If it hadn't been for you we'd all be dead right now and for that I thank you."

"If our friend, Teren is right, it seems that all I have done is prolong the bloodshed. What do we do now – surrender?"

"The Delarites aren't known for their chivalry in victory, Prefect. This is a fight to the death I'm afraid," replied Ro.

"Surely not the women and children?" asked the prefect horrified.

"Best not be around to find out, Prefect," added Arlen.

Ro suddenly noticed Eryn standing at the back of the group led by the prefect. His tunic was covered in blood and he had a shocked expression on his face.

"Eryn, are you wounded?"

Preoccupied with the manoeuvrings of the Delarites, Teren hadn't noticed his son standing in the crowd and at the mention of his name, spun round to face him.

Eryn didn't answer Ro.

"Eryn! Eryn, are you all right?" said Ro making his way towards the boy.

"What? Yes, yes I'm fine," replied Eryn somewhat distractedly.

"But what about the blood?"

"It's not mine," replied Eryn as he gripped his sword handle with both hands and tugged it out from a dead Delarite's chest, before wiping it clean on the man's tunic.

Teren pushed through the group until he was standing just in front of his son. He looked first at Eryn and the familiar sword he was holding, then at the dead enemy soldier and then back at Eryn before nodding slightly.

Was that approval, redemption in the old man's eyes? Eryn wondered.

"I told you to go and help the prefect," said Teren.

"And so I did," replied Eryn.

"In the infirmary."

"He wasn't in the infirmary."

"Well you should have stayed there," said Teren irritated.

"You expected me to cower alone in the dark whilst wounded men, grandfathers and boys younger than me fought and died?"

"I expected you to obey me."

"Well I've news for you. You can't expect to just stomp back into my life after however many years and just expect me to fall in line; it doesn't work like that."

"I don't care how it works, boy, I'm your father," said Teren.

"In name only. The rest you have to earn."

Teren winced at Eryn's last words and it was a few seconds before he went to speak again, but his words were cut off by Arlen.

"Touching as this family reunion is, I think it had better wait. Our friends are on the move again." He nodded towards the Delarites just as their siege weapons renewed their bombardment of the city.

Chapter 19

The small group made their way to the battlements and looked out over the plain towards the distant ridge. The entire horizon seemed to be filled with tight formations of men and more were appearing over the ridge with every passing minute. Arlen let out a low whistle in awe.

"Looks like this is to be the final act, gentlemen. It seems the Delarite general has had enough and this time he's throwing everybody at us. He's even committing his reserves," said Ro.

"Good, that means they'll be plenty to go round," said Teren to nobody in particular.

Ro smiled at the old warrior's bravado.

"What do we do?" asked the prefect, his wide-eyed gaze never leaving the host of men forming up in the distance.

"We stand and hold our ground for as long as possible, Prefect, that's what," replied Teren apparently not in the least bit perturbed. "And we make sure that we hit those lads with everything we've got before we're done. We let them have every arrow, every javelin and every stone. But first we need to make some killing space. Arlen, do you think you can get some lads together and tip these bodies off the parapet? There's no sense us tripping over them during the fight."

"Consider it done," replied Arlen as he walked away pointing to a few men to help him.

"You can't just tip their bodies over the side like that, Teren, it's disrespectful," complained the prefect.

"I don't think they'll care, Prefect. But if you can persuade any of them to put their complaint in writing I'll be glad to consider it when this is all over. They are dead after all."

"Still, it doesn't feel right."

"In little more than an hour or two, we'll all be laying dead somewhere, Prefect, nothing more than worm meat. I don't suppose it'll matter where they're laying then – they'll still be dead," said Teren.

He had a point the prefect conceded and after one last glance at the enemy army he too went to help Arlen clear the ramparts.

"Don't be too hard on him, Teren. This is all new to him," said Ro.

"You think I don't know that? We're going to need every man if we're to hold this little lot off for more than a few minutes, so if I've got to be tough on some who don't deserve it for the greater good, so be it."

"And does that include Eryn?"

Teren glanced towards his blood-soaked son who seemed momentarily lost in a world of his own. "Of course."

"Shouldn't we at least try and get him and some of the others out?"

"Last I heard, Ro, we're completely surrounded, they'd never make it through. Better to remain here and die fighting with us."

Ro nodded his agreement.

"Promise me one thing though, Ro, warrior to warrior," said Teren.

"If I can."

"If I should fall, don't let those heathen animals take Eryn alive. If there's any doubt, I want you to end his life quickly and painlessly. You understand?"

Ro glanced down at the ground for a moment as if considering the implications of what his friend was asking. "If it comes to it, I will."

"Thank you. Now before these lads arrive, I want you to organise a party of men and women to collect up everything we can use as a missile and stack them at regular intervals along the rampart. There won't be many arrows left, but spears and javelins should be lying around even if you've got to pull them out from bodies. Get the women collecting rocks and stones, anything that they can easily throw at the enemy."

"You want the women to fight?" asked Ro incredulously.

"Not fight, no, but they can take a few of the whoresons out for us by throwing rocks and the like. Should be able to do some damage at close quarters I would have thought."

"As you wish," said Ro nodding slightly before heading off to organise the collection of missiles.

Teren went to the ramparts and leant against the cold stone, staring out at the gathering army in the distance.

"Does it always feel like this?" asked Eryn as he sidled up alongside his father. Teren looked at him quizzically. "The first time you kill, does it always feel like this?"

The boy's eyes were wide and pleading and Teren could tell that his son was wrestling with his conscience over what he'd been forced to do.

"What the sick feeling in the pit of your stomach and the desire to vomit?"

"Yes," replied Eryn, unable to meet his father's gaze.

"No, it feels like that every time. It doesn't matter whether it's the first man you've killed or the hundredth, you still feel the same. The trick is not to think about it too much. If you dwell on your actions and try and second guess yourself, you'll end up in knots and most likely dead. You need to always bear in mind that the man you just killed had been trying to kill you. War is a terrible thing and taking a man's life should never be done lightly, but in a battle it's kill or be killed. When those Delarites come yelling and howling over these walls I don't want you to think about what you're doing; I just want you to kill them. The slightest hesitation on your part and you're dead and so too probably is the man next to you. There aren't enough of us to go around in the coming fight, I won't lie to you, and so every man is going to be depending on the man next to him to watch his back. You can't do that if you're wallowing in remorse or self-recrimination. Do you understand?" Eryn nodded. "I certainly hope so." Eryn turned to walk away. "Eryn, if I could get you out I would, you know that?"

Eryn nodded again. "No, this is where I belong, with my friends and my... father. My only regret is that I was unable to keep my promise and rescue Keira and the others."

"Maybe you still will, lad, we're not dead yet," replied Teren.

"I thought you weren't going to lie to me."

"So I did. Still, miracles have happened before, you just have to keep believing. Find something to cling on to mentally and then don't let go."

"Like what?" asked Eryn.

"Like that young girl you've gone and got yourself betrothed to. What was her name again?"

"Tayla. She's Livan's daughter."

"Livan the baker?" asked Teren surprised.

"Yes."

"So what's she like then?"

"She's the most beautiful girl in the world. Long wavy brown hair, hazel eyes, slim body and a smile that lights up every room she enters," replied Eryn smiling, as Tayla's image flashed through his mind.

"There, you have your rock to cling to. Whenever you doubt what you're doing today, you just think of Tayla because the only way you're ever going to see her again is by killing enough of these lads to make them withdraw."

Eryn was going to say something further when a group of old men and women suddenly appeared on the ramparts carrying wickerwork baskets full of stones, rubble and anything else that could be used as a missile. Others carried bundles of spears and javelins. Ro walked along the ramparts organising the distribution of the weapons. He caught Teren's eye as he walked by.

"How is it, Ro?" asked Teren.

"Not good, I'm afraid. We've next to no arrows and even fewer people capable of utilising them effectively. We've a fair few spears and javelins and I'm distributing those so that every man able to fight has at least one to start with. We should be able to hit them with a half decent volley or two. After that all we're going to have to throw at them are a few rocks and some cutting insults."

"Then we'll just have to make them count won't we?"

Mindful that those around them were listening to the exchange, Ro did not respond and instead merely smiled before walking off to continue his distribution of the weapons.

The sound of several horns blowing suddenly filled the air.

"Here they come again," shouted one of the Remadan lookouts.

Teren looked round for his own trumpet blower to call the men back to arms, but remembered that the young lad had been struck in the throat by an arrow. He was going to have to do it the old-fashioned way.

"Every man to his post," he bellowed into the courtyard.

As quick as they were able, the city's remaining defenders, both soldier and civilian, made their way wearily to their allotted post. Most took up positions along the battlements, though the gap between the men was much larger than it had been at the start. Others went to the gate towers, whilst Captain Baradir took command of a group of twenty men armed with spears just inside the gates. Their job was to meet the first group of attackers to breach the weakened gates. He didn't expect to have to wait long.

The old people who could not wield a sword were stationed on the battlements either side of the gates in the hope that their hail of missiles would prevent any earnest attempt at smashing in the gates, at least whilst their missiles lasted.

Teren watched the advancing formations of Delarite soldiers as they steadily made their way across the plain towards the beleaguered city. There were thousands of them and Teren wondered just how long his pitiful number of defenders could hold out.

"There are so many of them," said Eryn as he came and stood by his father's side once again.

"That there is," replied Teren, not really sure what he could say to alleviate his son's fear. "Still, the more we tie up here, the fewer enemy soldiers our lads will have to face when they eventually counterattack. It is a good and honourable thing we do here today." The Delarites were closing on the city fast. "Best go and find somewhere to hole up for a while, Eryn."

"What? You think I'm going to go and hide somewhere, whilst others do the fighting? No, if I'm going to die today and that looks likely, then I wish to die fighting like the other men. Besides, I heard you say to Ro that you would treat me no different to the others my age."

Teren went to protest but the expression on Eryn's face left no room for negotiation.

"Then I shall be proud to have you by my side."

Eryn nodded and took up a position a few paces to his father's left.

"Eryn, I wish things could have been different between us. I wish I could have been there for you," said Teren staring over at the son he had abandoned seven years earlier. He had dramatically come back into his life and was now likely to be cruelly snatched away again. He had so much that he wanted to say to his son.

"It doesn't matter, you're here now and that's what counts," replied Eryn never taking his eyes off the horde of soldiers who now seemed to fill the plain with their tight formations.

Teren nodded proudly at his son. "Fight well my son."

"Archers make ready." The order had come from Ro a few paces to Teren's right.

Teren turned to look down into the courtyard where no more than a couple of dozen men stood with notched arrows ready to fire up and over the walls into the massed ranks of enemy soldiers outside. They would have to do.

Ro glanced at Teren for permission to fire and Teren nodded slightly.

"Fire," shouted Ro and the archers released their arrows.

Teren watched the arrows fly over his head and into the ranks of Delarites below. Ro had gauged their range perfectly, but it was hardly a storm of arrows that could break an attack. Still it was better than nothing.

"Keep them firing, Ro until they run out of ammunition," Teren shouted.

Ro waved his acknowledgment and moments later a second volley of arrows pierced the sky.

"Javelins!" All along the battlements the defenders picked up their weapons and prepared to throw. "Release," shouted Teren as he threw his own weapon. Moments later dozens of javelins and spears slammed into the soldiers below, breaking up formations and taking a dreadful toll on the attackers just below the city's walls.

Arrows were coming in the opposite direction now, a lot of arrows and although the defenders were spread out and behind fortifications, they were so plentiful that it was inevitable that some would find their mark.

"Javelins," Teren again shouted, but this time only two thirds of the men had anything to throw. "Release." Teren threw his second javelin and was gratified to see it hit a fat Delarite sergeant who had been urging his men forward.

Some of the enemy hesitated, but others who had noticed that fewer spears had been thrown at them this time, poured on urging the others to follow.

The arrows too seemed to have dried up and Teren looked enquiringly at Ro who had gone down to the courtyard. Ro merely shook his head and drew his sword before ordering his men to do likewise. He then sent half of his erstwhile archers to join Baradir's men behind the gate and then instructed the other half to follow him to the battlements alongside Teren and the others.

"That's it then, lads, now it's going to get personal," said Teren to the men near him as he hefted his axe in both hands. "The first one to kill ten gets the night off." Some of the men laughed or grinned, but others, mostly the civilians Teren noticed, merely stared ahead ashen faced as if resigned to their fate. Teren glanced left at Eryn and was pleased to see that Arlen had taken up position next to Eryn. Between them perhaps they'd be able to keep him safe. It was a desperate hope and he knew it. "You all right, lad?"

The colour seemed to have drained out of his face, but his voice was steady when he replied. "I'm fine."

"Good. You just stick near me and the monk and you'll be fine." He didn't sound convincing and the look that fled across Eryn's face told Teren that he didn't believe him either. "Remember, Eryn, in the heat of battle things get really confusing. If in doubt – kill." Quick as a flash Teren thrust his axe forward, the butt of the handle smashing into a man's face which had just shown itself at the top of a ladder in front of Teren. The man fell backwards blood streaming down his face from his shattered nose. He was soon replaced by another man and Teren merely repeated his action and this time the falling man took two of his comrades with him.

The man to Teren's right took an arrow in the neck and Teren immediately took a couple of paces to his right to try and close the gap between himself and the next man along. The gaps were constantly getting bigger though and it would only be a matter of time before they were overrun.

Two Delarites suddenly leapt onto the ramparts and took up a position either side of Teren. More were climbing the same ladders they had used. Turning so that his back was to the courtyard below, Teren eyed both men warily trying to judge which man was likely to attack first. Guessing that the man to his left probably posed the greatest danger, Teren rushed forward swinging his axe in a horizontal arc as he went.

His movement had been too quick for the Delarite and Teren's axe had already cut deep into his side before he could even think of moving out of the way or trying to parry the massive blow.

It had been a killing blow Teren knew so without waiting to watch the man drop, he quickly tugged his blade free, dropped to one knee and reverse swung his axe towards the man he knew would be rushing towards him from behind. Teren felt the blade slow as it sliced into bone and muscle before it continued its journey out the other side, such was the power of the blow. The attacker dropped to the ground, his right leg severed just above the knee, not that he had felt it. His body slumped to the ground in front of Teren and as it did, Teren noticed the small metal star protruding from the man's forehead. Teren turned and saw Ro watching from about ten paces away. He nodded his thanks before rushing back to the battlements and heaving a ladder away from the wall.

Below him and to the left, Teren could see dozens of Delarites hammering away at the already weakened gates. When they breached those, it was all over he knew. He looked across to the gate tower desperately trying to spot the prefect. At first he could not see him and Teren feared that he had been killed by an arrow, but then he suddenly appeared next to Baptiste.

Teren shouted over to the prefect, but the prefect failed to hear him above the roar of the surrounding battle. He shouted again and after a few seconds the prefect glanced his way.

"Now, Prefect, now is your time. Target the men below you battering the gate," Teren shouted.

The prefect stared back at Teren before cupping an ear with his hand indicating that he hadn't heard him. Another ladder had appeared to his right and Teren quickly smashed his axe into the face of the man who was just about to climb over onto the ramparts. Then with another heave, Teren sent that ladder crashing to the ground below killing several more of the enemy.

When he looked back towards the prefect he was glad to see the man still watching him. He was about to try shouting his instructions across once again when an arrow bounced off the nearby battlements and sliced his left cheek before dropping to the ground a few paces away. Cursing at the sharp stinging pain, Teren bellowed his instructions over to the prefect before gesticulating excitedly towards the enemy soldiers who were now mere seconds away from beating down the gates. Commander Baptiste who had also now looked over at Teren, understood what was required immediately and was just in the process of telling the prefect when two arrows caught him in the back. Teren watched in horror as yet another of his old friends died before his eyes.

The prefect had understood the instruction though and Teren watched as he looked down as if he was talking to somebody. Suddenly dozens of people, boys, women and old men appeared behind the battlements of the gate house and started to rain missiles down on the men below. The prefect had wisely had the people crouch down out of sight until they were needed to avoid them being targeted by the enemy archers. The ruse had worked perfectly and the attackers seemed genuinely surprised to suddenly be assailed by dozens of people from above.

Deep down Teren knew their actions whilst valiant would be in vain. The rocks and other missiles were taking their toll on the attackers, but the plain truth of it was that there were just too many of them. After the initial shock of the assault from above, the Delarites had replaced their losses at the gate whilst their archers peppered the gate tower, taking a hefty revenge on the exposed civilians.

A loud cracking noise filled the air and Teren knew instantly that the gates had finally given way. The mass of men outside issued a mighty cheer. The battle would soon be over now. Against all likelihood the men on the ramparts next to Teren were holding their own and managing to keep the attackers at bay, but now that more men would be racing up the steps behind them it was only a matter of time.

After quickly despatching a Delarite soldier who had just climbed over the wall, Teren glanced down just as Captain Baradir gave the order for his small reserve force that had been patiently waiting inside the gate, to release their javelins. The first twenty or so Delarites to burst through the gate were cut down instantly, the javelins having been thrown from virtually point-blank range. Then without a second's hesitation, Baradir led his men forward to confront the enemy in the city entrance where the gap was narrower thus reducing the odds.

Someone shouted Teren's name and he spun round just in time to block a downward chop from a Delarite sword. Then as the man raised his sword again, Teren shoulder charged him knocking the Delarite clean off the ramparts and down into the courtyard where his body was smashed on the hard ground. Teren looked round gratefully but had no idea who had warned him. To his right Eryn had just run a Delarite through with his sword whilst Arlen had forced another back over the battlements and on to the men waiting below.

A series of frantic and disjointed horn blows drifted over the battlefield and Teren wondered just who the Delarite general was sending forward now.

"Teren, Ro, quick, come and look at this," called Arlen excitedly as he looked out over the plain in front of the city.

Teren and Ro exchanged a brief worried look before hurrying over to Arlen's side where Eryn too now stood.

"What is it, Arlen?" asked Ro, nervously looking round in case any Delarites were approaching, but the area immediately around them was clear for the moment.

Arlen didn't speak but instead just pointed to the left where hundreds of cavalry had charged into the Delarite flank taking them totally by surprise.

The neat and tight formations of Delarite soldiers were now in total disarray and panic and confusion was spreading like wildfire.

"Are they ours?" asked Eryn excitedly.

"I don't know, but they're sure as Kaden not theirs," replied Teren.

Ro smiled knowingly. "Sikari Horse."

"Sikari Horse? Who are they?" asked Arlen.

"Lydian cavalry, some say the finest horsemen in the known world."

"What in the good name of Sulat are the Lydians doing here?" asked Arlen.

"Saving our backsides by the look of it," replied Teren.

Before their eyes the Lydian cavalry tore through the dense formations of Delarite soldiers, hacking and slicing as they went. Word had reached the men trying to breach the city's walls and unsure of the size of the force attacking them from behind and with no desire to be caught in a two front battle, they had ceased attacking.

The Lydian cavalry finally made it through to the other side of the plain and turned, ready to form up for another attack. Behind them, the Delarite officers ran around barking orders at their terrified and demoralised men.

"Looks like the Lydians are regrouping for another attack. Surely they won't find it so easy this time?" asked Eryn.

"No, they won't, lad, not without help," replied Teren. He glanced down at the courtyard and was pleased to see Captain Baradir's men had repulsed the first attack and were now forming up again, retrieving javelins from any dead bodies lying around.

The prefect came panting up the steps to join Teren and his friends. "Who are those riders?" he asked between huge gulps of air.

"Lydians," replied Ro.

"Lydians! My goodness, I wonder what they're doing here."

"If we don't do something to help them they won't be here much longer that's for sure," said Teren. He turned to face the battlements and glanced down into the courtyard before shouting, "Every man who can bear arms, to the courtyard now."

Mystified by the order and worried about leaving the battlements unprotected, the men who could still walk and

242

carry a sword slowly made their way down to the courtyard, talking in hushed tones as they went.

"Mind telling us what's on your mind, Teren?" asked Arlen.

"He plans on attacking," said Ro smiling.

"Attacking? Have you taken leave of your senses?" asked the prefect.

"Remember what I said to you at the start of this, Prefect? I told you that the only way we'd beat these men today was by being unpredictable. So that's what we're going to be. They weren't expecting the Lydians to show up nor will they be expecting us to come out and attack them. Besides, those horsemen are laying down their lives for us right now. It wouldn't be right to just sit here and watch, now would it?"

"I suppose not," replied the prefect still deliberating the sense in his decision.

"So are you with me, Prefect?" The prefect adjusted his grip of the sword and nodded. "Then let's be about our business," and with that Teren strode down the steps to the courtyard and took up a position in front of the men who had gathered there.

"We have just one chance to survive today, lads and that's by hitting those Delarite dogs whilst they're still shocked and preoccupied with not losing their head to a horseman's sabre. Are you with me?" A muffled yes, went up. "I said are you with me?" bellowed Teren. This time the air rang with the sound of a hundred men shouting their support. Satisfied, Teren turned to face the city's entrance and beyond that, the waiting enemy. Then he charged.

"For Remada," shouted Ro following close behind him and the cheer was taken up by all the men as they charged out of the city and into the unsuspecting enemy.

Some of the Delarites had seen the Remadans amassing just inside the gate and had tried to warn their comrades, but most seemed preoccupied with the host of cavalry that had swept through their ranks decimating their number. By the time enough of them had come to realise the danger they were now in from the defenders of the city, it was too late.

The Remadans poured through the broken city gate and slammed into the confused Delarites milling around just outside. In loose formation and for the most part taken by surprise, they were easy targets for the motivated Remadans.

Instead of attacking the first man he had come across, Teren had charged some way into the Delarite force before stopping and swinging his axe all around him, killing and maiming. Ro and Arlen had soon joined him and between them the three men managed to cause total panic and fear and it was not long before the Delarites around them broke and began to flee towards the ridge. The vengeful Remadans who chased them showed no mercy and cut the panic-stricken Delarites down by the score.

Those who escaped the initial Remadan charge and who were retreating towards the ridge, unwittingly found themselves directly in the path of the oncoming Lydian cavalry who had reformed and were now cutting and scything their way back across the battlefield.

The Delarite officers had now long given up any hope of organising a disciplined defence such was the level of panic and fear amongst their men. Instead they were now desperately ushering their men back towards the ridge where they hoped to reform out of the cavalry's reach. The ferocity of the attack led by Teren was such that many of the Delarites thought they were under attack by a much larger force than they actually were. Only General Malik watching from atop the ridge with his staff officers could see the truth of it, but from that distance he was powerless to do anything other than watch and hope.

"Teren, should we not stop the advance before we over-extend ourselves?" asked Ro as he moved alongside the old warrior.

"Ordinarily I'd say yes, Ro, but we've well and truly got these boys on the run and I think we should press home our advantage before they realise just how few we are. Besides, with the gate down how much longer do you think we'd survive inside the walls anyway?"

Teren was right, Ro realised, they probably should push home their advantage, but still the military officer inside him felt uneasy at their predicament. If the Delarites were to turn now and counterattack, their men would be caught out in the open. They would be easy pickings for an organised force and there would be little the Lydians on their tiring horses could do to help them.

"Forward, lads, kill as many of these whoresons as you can. Don't let them stop or regroup," shouted Teren to those around him as he decapitated the Delarite directly in front of him.

Spurred on by Teren's words and their own bloodlust, the Remadan soldiers and civilians continued to harry the fleeing enemy, though most of the older men were now walking after them as their exertions began to take a toll. Away to their left, what remained of the Lydian cavalry was reforming once again.

"I think this is as far as we should go, Ro," said Arlen as he thrust his sword into the back of a fleeing Delarite soldier. "These men have had enough and our own men are tiring."

"I agree, Arlen, but Teren is for pushing on and totally routing them."

"I don't think these fellows are going to be bothering us again today; look even their officers are withdrawing."

Ro followed Arlen's gaze towards the ridge, where the Delarite general and his officers did indeed seem to be withdrawing. "Stop the advance, stop the advance," Ro shouted, an order quickly echoed by Arlen, Baradir and the few remaining junior officers.

Most heard the order and ceased their headlong charge after the enemy, but some either because they didn't hear the instructions or because their bloodlust was up, briefly continued their pursuit until they looked round and saw that they were practically alone.

Ro looked around him at the panting and exhausted men and was alarmed at just how few they were. He had been right to be fearful. If the Delarites did stop to look back they would surely launch a counterattack as the Remadans had very little left to offer. Ro's eyes suddenly fell on a very disgruntled looking Teren and he was headed his way, blood dripping from his war axe.

"This looks like trouble," said Arlen quietly to his friend.

"Maybe, but it had to be done," replied Ro smiling wryly.

"I thought I told you we were to push on?" snarled Teren as he stomped up to the two men until he was virtually in their faces.

Ro didn't flinch, though Arlen had taken a surreptitious step backwards just in case it was about to turn ugly.

"You did, Teren and I apologise for countermanding your order, but the situation had changed since we spoke," replied Ro, his voice steady and firm. He would not be intimidated by this giant of a man who stood before him, clearly intent on doing just that.

Teren stared at Ro a little longer than was necessary before responding. "How so?"

"The Delarite general and his staff officers turned and withdrew a few minutes ago, thus ending any likelihood of a cohesive counterattack. Coupled with my belief that we risked over extending ourselves and the exhausted state of the men, I believed that it was the right course of action."

The two men locked eyes for what felt like an eternity to Arlen and the handful of men stood around watching the exchange.

"And you were right, lad," said Teren smiling and slapping Ro on the shoulder. "I think I let the excitement of battle get to me and addle my brain. I'm obliged to you."

"Think nothing of it."

Ro was about to say something else when the sound of horses galloping past caught his attention and he looked up just as a small force of Lydian cavalry raced off over the ridge after the Delarites. Another small group of riders were trotting towards Ro, Teren and Arlen. Ro smiled to himself when he recognised Princess Cala at their head.

"Princess Cala, your timing was perfect as always," said Ro bowing slightly.

"So it would seem," said Cala glancing round at the ragtag army that was now congregating around Ro and the others. "Is this all that remains of your command, Captain?"

"It is all that remains, but it is not my command, Princess. That honour falls to Teren," replied Ro. "Teren Rad may I introduce Princess Cala of Lydia?"

"Teren Rad?"

"The same," replied Teren a hint of amusement in his tone.

"I have heard of you. Tales of your bravery are often recounted round Lydian campfires."

"You do me great honour, Princess."

Arlen noisily cleared his throat, drawing a small smile from Ro.

"May I also present, Arlen Meric, Second Priest of the Golden Tree etc. Also, Captain Baradir of the garrison here at Vangor?"

"Gentlemen," smiled Cala.

Both men bowed low. "It is a privilege to meet you, Princess," said Arlen.

"Indeed," added Baradir.

"And I you, gentlemen. Rumours of the existence of your order are rife, Master Meric, but none alive can claim to have met anyone from your Order."

"Ah, well we're very selective about who we meet, Princess," replied Arlen.

"Is that so?"

The sound of a rider fast approaching briefly distracted the princess and she waited patiently for the horseman to rein in his mount before making his report.

"What news, Captain?"

"We pursued the Delarites as far as the river, my Queen, harrying their rearguard. They are attempting to cross the river now. They are in poor order and it will take their commander some days to reorganise their force into anything like a fighting unit."

"Well done, Captain. Have some men patrol the ridge yonder and have the rest withdraw to the city to rest and water their horses, if that's okay with you, Teren?"

"It is," replied Teren.

"Good. See it done, Captain and we will meet to discuss casualties later."

"As you wish, my Queen." The captain bowed and then rode off to carry out his orders.

"Queen?" asked Ro.

An angry look briefly crossed Cala's face, but it had disappeared as quickly as it had arrived. "Yes, with my father's passing I am now Queen of Lydia, or what's left of it."

"Your father passed away?" asked Ro.

"No, he led the defence of our capital so that I and a

handful of others could escape to link up with the Sikari Horse who were waiting for me south of Tahara. He was murdered by the Delarites when the city fell."

"I am truly sad to hear such news. Your father was a great man," said Ro.

"He was and the manner of his passing will not be soon forgotten. I do not care how long it takes or what sacrifices must be made, I will have my revenge on the perpetrators and the Lydian flag will once again fly proudly over Tahara."

"With such determination as yours, I fail to see how it could end other," said Arlen.

"Thank you, Master Meric. But brave words come cheaply. It is our actions which define who we are and how we're remembered."

"That is true," said Ro. "So let us retire to what remains of the city to discuss how Remada and Lydia can right the wrongs visited upon them."

"That is most kind, Ro. Would it be too much trouble to ask for some food for my men? We left in a hurry and are poorly provisioned," said Cala.

"Of course not. Whatever we have we will gladly share. Now come and I will introduce you to Prefect Devan who runs the city. With your leave, Teren?"

"You go right ahead, lad. I'll get this lot back to the city and organise some foraging parties for arrows and javelins just in case the Delarites surprise us and come back for more."

Ro nodded his thanks and together with Arlen, Cala and her closest officers, Ro headed back to the city.

Chapter 20

The Remadan defenders had remained vigilant for the rest of the day, but the scouts Teren sent out all reported that the Delarites had withdrawn some distance and although they were regrouping, there was no sign that they were planning a counterattack any time soon.

"So what is it that you're proposing, Teren?" asked the prefect.

"I'm proposing that we withdraw south and try and link up with the nearest Remadan army."

"You would have us abandon the city after everything we've been through and all the lives sacrificed in its defence?"

A look of anger swept across Teren's face briefly. "I know how many men died out there today, Prefect, I was in the thick of it, but today's fight was never about holding this city forever. It was about bleeding the enemy and delaying their advance. We have done both, but even with Princess, sorry, Queen Cala's cavalry, we are too few to hold on to the city now. To stay would be nothing more than a noble act of suicide."

"Do you agree with this assessment, Captain Aryk?"

"I do, Prefect. Much as it irks me to surrender one foot of Remadan soil to the Delarites, there is nothing but our deaths to be gained by staying any longer. I suggest that we make an orderly withdrawal before the sun comes up, so that if our Delarite friends return in the morning we have put some distance between them and ourselves."

"But what of his threat to kill everyone in the city? If we depart we could be signing the death warrant of every man, woman and child who remains," said the prefect.

"I think that once they realise that the city is undefended, they will not carry out that threat," replied Ro.

"But you do not know that for certain?"

"No, I don't," replied Ro somewhat sheepishly.

"Then the way forward is clear. Either we all remain or

we all evacuate, soldiers and civilians," said the prefect.

"Are you mad? It's dangerous to remain here, but out there is certain death. We'll be the longest and slowest moving target they're ever likely to see. The column of civilians will be too long for us to provide adequate protection. If a troop of Delarite cavalry catch us strung out in the open, they'll cut us to pieces. Forget it, Prefect, it's not going to happen," replied Teren.

"Then I will remain here with the people," said the prefect indignantly.

"Out of the question, Prefect. You must come with us," said Ro.

"I'm sorry, Captain, really I am, but if you are going to force my hand, then here is where I will remain." The prefect's gaze took in the small group sitting around the table until his eyes finally fell on Captain Baradir. "What say you, Captain?"

The captain took another swig of his wine before answering as if buying himself some more time or perhaps collecting his thoughts. When he looked up again his gaze was steady. "My military training tells me that we have done everything we can here, sir and that a tactical withdrawal is the only sensible option. However, I am a Remadan soldier who has sworn to obey orders and to protect its people. If you decide to remain here with the people, sir, then here is where my duty lies and the remaining men of the Ninth Ligara will stay with you."

"Thank you, Captain, spoken like a true Remadan officer."

"You can't do it, lad, you'll be consigning your men to death," said Teren turning to face Baradir. "Besides, there are hardly any of your men left alive."

"Even so, here is where I must remain if the prefect decides to stay."

An awkward silence descended over the room as Teren and the prefect glared at one another.

"What will you do your majesty?" said Ro as he turned to face Cala.

"My men and their horses need to rest, but to remain here would be to invite certain death I think, so we will head south with Teren if he'll have us?"

"You are most welcome, your majesty," replied Teren as he forced himself to break the stare with which he had impaled the prefect.

"What if I was to tell you that a Remadan relief force was on its way?" said the prefect smiling and glancing round the room.

"I'd ask how you'd come by such welcome news?" said Ro.

"And I'd ask why you have not told us before?" said Teren, his irritation at the thought that the prefect had been holding out on them, quite evident.

"A rider arrived from the palace whilst you were chasing the Delarites off, which is why I did not join you until later," explained the prefect. "I had to be certain of your intentions, plus I didn't want anyone else to know in case the Delarites counterattacked and the city fell. The fewer people that knew, the smaller the chance of anyone spilling the news under torture. If we had lost here today I wanted the relief column's arrival to be a total surprise to the Delarites."

His logic made sense, Teren realised, but he was still annoyed that as the commander in charge, he had not been informed.

"What news did this rider bring, Prefect?" asked Arlen. It had been the first time Arlen had spoken in some time.

The prefect sat up straight as if to dignify the important news he had to impart. "There has been a coup at the Royal Palace and the king has been deposed."

"A coup? Led by who and why?" asked Captain Baradir.

"Apparently a group of senior army officers, both current and retired, asked to see the king. They made an impassioned plea for the king to wake up and realise what was happening to his country before it was too late. They asked him to mobilise all the armies including the reserves and to march out and confront the invaders. The king, counselled by that snake, Livic Pendar, refused and accused the generals of warmongering and ordered them to leave. Instead they handed the king a document to sign demanding his immediate abdication to be replaced by a council of generals. The king naturally refused and Pendar ordered the Royal Bodyguard to arrest the generals. The generals, however, had not come alone and a brief battle ensued. The Royal Bodyguard was defeated and those who survived were given the option to swear allegiance to the new government or face execution. The king was taken into custody and is now under close house arrest."

"What of Livic Pendar?" asked Ro.

"He managed to escape during the melee apparently and his current whereabouts are unknown. They'll find him cowering and scheming under a rock sooner or later, but right now he's not that important," said the prefect.

"He is to me," snapped Ro.

"How so?"

"I heard that he had hired some assassins to silence me, my enforced exile not enough for him apparently," replied Ro bitterly.

"I wouldn't go worrying about any assassins if I were you, lad," said Teren.

"And why's that?"

"Because the two Tulans this Pendar fella sent after you ran into a spot of bother in the Lonely Mountains. They won't be bothering you again."

"Then once again I am obliged to you, Teren," said Ro smiling.

"So who is in charge of your country now?" asked Cala getting the conversation back on track.

"A council of generals led by one of this country's greatest heroes, Jeral Tae," replied the prefect.

Teren and Ro shot each other a knowing look.

"Jeral Tae's in charge?" asked Teren smiling.

"So it would seem," replied the prefect. "He has already mobilised all of Remada's armies and deployed those that are battle ready. A column of several thousand men are hurrying here as we speak and according to my calculations, could arrive here by tomorrow lunchtime."

"Well that puts a different slant on things," said Ro looking at Teren.

"Indeed it does. You could have saved us a lot of unnecessary angst had you imparted this information earlier, Prefect," said Teren.

"Apologies, but you have my reasons."

"So what do you reckon, Teren, do we stay or do we go?" asked Ro.

All eyes turned to Teren.

"I guess we'd better stay, but if the Delarites come back in force any determined attempt to take this city is sure to succeed, there just aren't enough of us left."

"Then we'd better hope that the relief column arrives sooner rather than later," said Arlen.

"Well I suggest that we all try and get a couple of hours sleep because tomorrow could be a long day by the sound of it," said Teren.

They all made to get up and take Teren's advice, when Arlen spoke.

"There is just one more thing for you to worry about, Teren."

"And what is that?"

"Eryn. Now that the battle is over and that the danger has passed, at least for the time being, he is going to want to resume his quest."

"Damn, I'd forgotten all about that," said Teren.

"Who is Eryn?" asked Cala.

"He is Teren's son," replied Ro. "A few days ago Narmidian raiders attacked his village and carted off a number of girls to sell as slaves. Eryn's sister and fiancée were amongst those taken. He was on a mission to rescue them with his friend Tav when war broke out and he ended up here. Arlen is right; he will not want to tarry here any longer."

"I am truly sorry to hear about your daughter, Teren," said Cala genuinely.

"Thank you your majesty. I must think on the matter and then speak to the boy."

"Think on the matter?" said Cala incredulously. "Surely there is nothing to think about. You and your son must go after your daughter and her friends. Much as your skills as a warrior and leader are needed here, I would suggest that your daughter's needs are far greater."

Teren glanced round the small group and saw that the others were nodding in agreement.

"I agree with Queen Cala," said the prefect. "Much as I

feel safer when you are swinging your mighty axe nearby, your immediate duty is to your family. I have Captain Baradir and the others around this table to guide me until the relief column arrives. You are remaining I take it?" he added looking at Ro and Arlen anxiously.

"I am," replied Ro.

"And what of you, Arlen? It is not your war."

"No, it isn't, not yet anyway. I suspect that if we don't stop the Delarites and their Cardellan allies here in Remada, their ambition will stretch far from these borders, so for now I remain at Ro's side."

Ro smiled and nodded at his friend.

"Then it is settled. Now let's all get some sleep, because as Teren said, we have a challenging day ahead of us I fear," said the prefect.

***

Teren had found Eryn sitting alone on the battlements staring out across the battlefield which was still littered with hundreds of bodies. As soon as the fighting had ended, Eryn had hurried to the infirmary to see how Tav was doing. When he'd got there, Tav's bed was occupied by a man whose leg had been amputated. Initially Eryn had thought his friend had recovered and was up and about but one glance at the look on the medic's face told Eryn he was wrong. They'd thought that Tav was recovering and had moved him and a few of the others to a small room out the back away from the critical cases, but during the Delarite bombardment a huge rock had come crashing through the roof and crushed everybody in the room. He had died instantly they had told him and didn't feel any pain, but it was scant comfort to Eryn. One lucky shot and one instance of being in the wrong place at the wrong time had been all that it needed to end his friend's life.

Teren stood studying his son for a few moments. The boy had taken his friend's death badly and Teren wished he had greater skill with words so that he could comfort his son.

"I am sorry for your loss, Eryn," said Teren eventually as he sat down beside Eryn and placed a hand on his shoulder. He felt Eryn tense under his touch and removed his hand.

"Which one?" replied Eryn bitterly.

"All of them: Kam, Tav, Keira and Tayla."

"Keira and Tayla aren't dead, unless you've heard something that you're not telling me," replied Eryn eyeing his father suspiciously.

"No, I haven't but it is of them I wish to speak."

"Really? What is it?"

"There is a relief column on its way here, so I'm no longer needed as much as I was. I thought you and I could resume your quest, if you'll have me?" said Teren.

"You mean it?" asked Eryn, his face brightening.

"I do. However, I must caution you that our chances of picking up their trail again are remote. They could be halfway to Narmidia by now."

"We can't just give up though."

"No, we can't and we won't." Teren made to go, but his gaze suddenly fell on Eryn's sword leaning against the battlements. He reached over and picked it up. "A good sword is this. Look after it and it'll look after you. It has seen more battles than I care to remember."

"It has already saved my life once," replied Eryn.

"And long may it continue to do so. Now get some sleep and we'll move out first thing in the morning," said Teren.

Eryn nodded and Teren got to his feet to walk off.

"Father." The word sounded strange to both Eryn and Teren. Some things it seemed were going to be hard to get used to.

"Yes, Eryn?"

"Thank you."

"You're welcome. It is only right that such a blade should be passed down from generation to generation," said Teren.

"No, not for that, though I do appreciate the gift, but for coming with me tomorrow," said Eryn.

"Oh! Think nothing of it. Tav was a really nice lad and I am truly sorry for what happened to him."

Eryn nodded. "When I said I was going after the girls, he was the only one apart from Jeral, to step forward and offer to come with me. People were cruel to him, but he was truer and braver than all of them put together."

"He was a true friend and that is how you must remember him. Now get some sleep and I'll wake you just after dawn, which looking at the sky won't be too long," said Teren.

Teren watched as Eryn threw a blanket over himself and closed his eyes, before he turned and made his way down to the courtyard. Ro was waiting for him at the foot of the steps.

"How is he?"

"Distraught about the loss of his friend, but he'll pull through."

Ro nodded knowingly. "What are your chances of picking up the raiders' trail, Teren?"

"Little, for they have several days' head start and we only have a vague notion of the route they're taking. But if I do not try I will lose Eryn again and this time probably for good. That is not something I am prepared to do. Besides, if I do not go with him, he will go on his own and what chance does he stand out there alone in a world at war with itself? None, that's how much. So whether I think it's a fool's errand or not, I will go with him."

Ro stared at his friend deliberating whether to speak the words that balanced on the tip of his tongue demanding to be aired. He sighed deeply and Teren realised that Ro had something further to add, something he felt uncomfortable about.

"What is it, Ro, what troubles you?"

"You've been down this road before, Teren with your wife. How long did you spend searching the eastern lands for her, a year, two years?"

"Nearly five," replied Teren.

"Five years of your life searching for one woman in a vast land surrounded by enemies. What makes you think you'll have more luck this time?"

"Nothing, but like I said, I have to try if I want to hold on to Eryn."

"But not at the cost of your lives surely?" pleaded Ro.

"Those whoresons stole my wife all those years ago and it nearly broke me. I won't let them steal my daughter and my son."

"Your mind is set then?" asked Ro.

"It is."

"Then as soon as the relief column is here and order restored, Arlen and I will follow you."

"What? Why? This is not your fight," said Teren.

"Then we will make it ours." Ro held out his arm and Teren grasped it in the warrior's embrace.

"Thank you, friend."

"You are welcome. Just one thing though, Teren," said Ro.

"What's that?"

"Don't thank the monk just yet."

"Arlen, why not?"

"Because he doesn't know he's going yet," said Ro smiling broadly.

Teren laughed heartily. "As you wish. It will be our secret."

***

What remained of the garrison defending the city stood to just after dawn. After the officer of the watch gave the all clear, they were allowed to quickly get something to eat and drink whilst a few remained on sentry duty. A couple of hours after dawn, the alert had been signalled and all the defenders had assumed their positions on the walls, as a number of riders galloped towards the city. The few remaining archers notched arrows and stood ready to try and down the riders as they approached the carts that had been hastily put across the city entrance now that the gates were down.

"Hold your fire," Ro shouted across to the archers, "they're Remadan. Move the carts out of the way and let them in."

The men assigned to guard the gate dutifully obeyed and a couple of minutes later about twenty tired and dusty looking Remadan cavalry rode into the courtyard. They reined in just in front of the prefect and Ro who stood waiting to greet them.

The lead horseman, whose tattered uniform bore a sergeant's stripes, saluted the prefect.

"Welcome to Vangor, Sergeant, or what's left of it," said the prefect by way of greeting.

"Thank you, sir. I am Sergeant Pulita of the 3rd Remadan Lancers."

"I see and what are you doing here, Sergeant, not that we're anything but pleased to see you?"

"I am part of a small cavalry force sent ahead by General Tae to scout the area ahead of the relief force, sir. We ran into a large force of Delarites to the east and took a lot of casualties. We weren't meant to engage, but they came out of nowhere and in strength; we were lucky to get out at all."

"That sounds like the men we sent running from here yesterday," said Ro to the prefect.

"Indeed it does. They're reforming to the east, you say, Sergeant?"

"Yes, sir."

"How far away would you say exactly?" asked the prefect.

"About half a day's march I should think."

"Then if they do decide to return it's going to be close as to who gets here first, them or the relief column."

Teren had come down from the battlements and now stood beside the prefect.

"I knew life in the cavalry was soft compared to the foot sloggers, but I didn't realise you were allowed to bring women along with you on patrols now," said Teren looking at the dirty and bedraggled women sitting behind many of the cavalrymen.

The sergeant briefly flushed crimson but quickly composed himself when he realised the scruffy looking man with the huge axe was teasing him. He had no idea who he was but by the way the others deferred to him, he clearly commanded their respect and the sergeant decided that perhaps he should do the same.

"No, sir, these women we rescued from a Narmidian raiding party shortly after we detached from our main force. We were looking for somewhere safe to leave them when we run into the Delarites. We haven't been able to get much out of them as most of them are pretty traumatised, but from what I can gather they were taken from a couple of villages to the south. Those Narmidian dogs and their allies were taking them east to sell as slaves," said the sergeant.

Ro shot Teren a look just as Teren turned to call Eryn, but he was already racing down the steps calling Tayla's and then Keira's names. He walked amongst the riders looking at the grimy faces for his sister and fiancée but couldn't see them. Teren came and stood by his side.

"Are they here, lad?"

"I can't see them." The desperation and disappointment in his voice was clear. "I recognise a few of the faces, but they're not here."

He called out their names once again anyway.

"They're gone, Eryn."

Eryn heard the words but couldn't see who had spoken them.

"Who said that?" he asked.

"I did."

Eryn and Teren turned to see a woman of about twenty slumped against the rider in front of her, her blank almost expressionless eyes staring down at them.

"Bella?" asked Eryn incredulously.

The girl merely nodded.

"What do you mean they're gone? Where are Tayla and Keira?"

"One of the raiders took Tayla. Keira's dead."

The words stabbed at his heart like an icicle. To his right, Teren stiffened at the news that one of his daughters whom he had not spoken to in years was dead.

"What happened?" asked Eryn trying to hold back the tears he so desperately needed to shed for Keira and Tav.

Bella started to speak, but her voice was dry and cracked. Teren offered her a water flask and she drank greedily from it before resuming.

"There was some sort of argument amongst the raiders and a fight. That only left a few guards watching over us and one night Keira tried to run. They caught her a few hours later and slit her throat whilst we watched. I'm so sorry," said Bella.

Teren briefly closed his eyes trying to control the anger he felt inside.

"And what of Tayla, where is she?" asked Eryn.

"One of the raiders who mutinied carried her away on his horse after setting all the other horses free."

"Where was this?"

"I don't know where for certain, somewhere to the

south a couple of nights ago. They could be anywhere by now."

Eryn turned to his father. "Then we need to get after them as soon as possible."

It was indeed good news that they weren't as far ahead as they feared, but tracking one man was going to be far harder than trying to follow the trail of thirty or so men. "We will in good time. Which way were they headed, do you think, Bella?" asked Teren.

"I don't know for certain, but I overheard the leader and one of his men and they seemed to think the tracks headed north, although they expected him to turn east soon for their homelands."

"What did..."

Eryn's question was cut off by the prefect. "I think that's enough questions for now. Sergeant if you would like to stable your horses I think you and your men could do with a meal and a few hours' rest, don't you?"

The sergeant smiled broadly. "We certainly could, sir."

"Very well. Ro could you show the sergeant where to go and perhaps you, Captain Baradir would be as kind as to lead these ladies to the infirmary, such that it is, so the women can check them over?"

"Right away, sir."

The prefect waited for the square to empty of horses and riders before turning to face Teren and Eryn once again. "And now you will be leaving us I take it?"

"We may never get this close to the raider again, Prefect, so yes we must take our leave," replied Teren. "It is going to be hard to follow a lone rider, but with such a recent sighting we must make our move."

"I wish you both good luck and thank you for your help in saving my city," said the prefect earnestly.

"You too, Prefect. I hope that the relief column is here soon," replied Teren.

"We'll be fine, don't worry about us. You concentrate on finding that raider and avoiding the Delarites. And, Eryn, don't worry, we'll see that Tav gets a hero's burial."

Eryn smiled at the thought. "Thank you."

As Teren slung his sack over his shoulder, Ro came

walking back over after seeing to the cavalry patrol. Arlen was now at his side.

"I wish you good fortune, Teren and you too Eryn," said Ro. Arlen nodded his agreement.

"Thanks. Now don't you go killing all those Delarites either; leave some for me," replied Teren.

"Something tells me there'll be plenty to go round," replied Ro. "I'll see you soon."

Teren nodded and he and Eryn quickly mounted the two horses the prefect had ordered brought from the stables for them. Then with a wave of the hand, they turned and galloped off out of the city in pursuit of the one remaining raider and Eryn's fiancée.

"I hope they find her," Arlen said to Ro, as he watched them disappear into the distance.

"As do I," replied Ro.

"By the way, anything you want to tell me?"

"I don't think so," said Ro smiling.

"Really? Nothing along the lines of why or how we're going to see them soon, as you just said to Teren."

"Did I? Must have been a slip of the tongue," replied Ro turning quickly before his friend could see the huge smile on his face.

Arlen was about to try asking the same question in a different way when one of the lookouts on the gate tower shouted down that a large body of men had just appeared over the eastern horizon.

Ro rushed up the steps to the battlements followed by Arlen and the prefect. In the distance to the east, a huge mass of men and horses were slowly appearing over the ridge a couple of miles away, but from that distance it was impossible to see whether they were Delarites or the relief force. After one last glance towards Teren and Eryn who was just disappearing over the horizon to the north, Ro drew his sword and called the men of Vangor to their battle positions.

Lightning Source UK Ltd.
Milton Keynes UK
UKOW04f1107230615

253974UK00001B/9/P